For Penny Cunyghame and Barbara Mortimer

I

Monty expected someone to meet her, but nobody came. She waited at the station for a quarter of an hour, watching the clouds gather, listening for the grumble of thunder. Beside a horse trough of weathered stone, a granite drinking fountain kept up an insistent plopping, a glistening stalactite of calcified drips hanging from its spout. Beyond this, the road meandered through the gorse bushes, into the beech trees. Somewhere at the end of that road, out of sight in the woods, lay her new home. Monty pulled a pamphlet from her pocket. The image – a photograph of a rectangular building looming against a furious sky – was peppered with black specks as though taken from the midst of a whirling tempest. Beneath it were the words 'Bleakly Hydropathic welcomes YOU'. Monty fanned her face with the pamphlet. The air was silent. A gorse pod snapped in the midsummer heat with a sound like impatient fingers. She picked up her suitcase, and began to walk.

Bleakly Hall Hydropathic stood like a workhouse, solid and bulky, among the trees. The road had been steeper than Monty expected and the heat was now infernal. The air seemed as thick as blood, and the further she climbed the more it had become suffused with a stench of brimstone. Here and there among the clustered oaks and beeches, great patches of laburnum flowers hung limply, like beards of crystallised sulphur. Looking across a dishevelled lawn at the building's crooked window frames, Monty noticed that the atmosphere too had become muddy and yellowish. She listened. For a moment she thought she could hear music – the oom-pah oom-pah of a practising tuba – but then it was gone before she could be sure.

It was immediately clear that the black-and-white photograph on the hydropathic's pamphlet had concealed a terrible dilapidation. The walls were blotched with patches of flaking masonry and stains of vivid green oozed beneath the guttering. The lawn was marked out for bowls, though it was no use to anyone as the green was clotted with mole-hills. Looking over this decaying vista, three rows of windows yawned sleepily. At the top, in the centre of the building, projected a square tower, capped by a pitched roof. A beam of sunlight sliced through the clouds, revealing that the damp patches against the lower walls were, in fact, not damp patches at all but people, folded into bath-chairs, moving as slowly as snails along a stone terrace.

All at once, with a 'bang' that reverberated like a gunshot through the trees, a window was thrown open in the tower. A voice cried out, a sharp exclamation of anger, and a small, square object was flung out. It hung for a moment, a dark scrap against the turbulent sky, then it seemed to explode, to come apart into a hundred tiny pieces, each tumbling and twisting, flickering and blinking as it fell towards the ground. Monty felt something flutter against her foot. She bent down and picked up a playing card. It was the Queen of Hearts.

At the sound of her feet crunching over the gravel, pale faces turned to stare. She was close enough to call out a greeting when a motor car hurtled from behind the building. Monty just had time to see a face, eyes wide, mouth open in a yell, staring from behind the windscreen. Then the brakes were screaming, the horn was blaring, the gravel was spraying into the air, and she was lurching sideways and disappearing beneath the undergrowth.

The car swerved to a halt. Monty heard a door open. 'Did I hit you?' cried a voice. 'Are you hurt?'

'No,' gasped Monty from beneath the foliage. She staggered to her feet, waist high in the sea of bracken. 'Hello, Ada,' she said. 'Still driving like the devil, I see.'

The woman beside the car stared at Monty, her expression a mixture of surprise and pleasure. She wiped her fingers on a black-smeared handkerchief. 'Miss Montgomery! They said you was coming but I didn't believe it. They told me to go to the station to fetch the new nurse, but I never dreamed it would really be you. What would *you* be wanting with a place like this?'

Monty stepped out of the undergrowth and threw her arms round the small figure. 'I knew we'd meet again.'

'Steady on, miss,' said Ada, struggling to disengage herself. 'What'll the guests say?'

'I don't care what they say,' said Monty.

'We mustn't upset the guests, miss,' murmured Ada. 'We have to keep the guests happy.'

'And are you happy, Ada?'

Ada blinked at Monty. 'I'm very well, miss,' she said.

Beside them, the car hissed discreetly. Ada flung open the bonnet, releasing an exclamation mark of steam. She wafted a hand back and forth, and peered into the whispering oily darkness. 'I thought she might at least get to the station and back, but it looks like she's done in already. I'll need some help moving her. The garage is round the back.'

'You take the wheel,' said Monty. She tossed her coat and suitcase on to the back seat.

Monty put her shoulder to the car as Ada released the handbrake. They eased the vehicle across the gravel, inching it round the side of the building. The steering wheel refused to turn unless hauled upon by both women, but eventually the car rolled over the threshold of the garage.

'There!' Monty looked about. 'How many motors are in here?'

'Four and a half,' said Ada. 'And two motorcycles. There's only the Audi running at the moment.'

'That doesn't seem to be running either now,' said Monty. She gave the car an appraising glance. It was a sleek four-seater, slim and powerful-looking.

'She will be,' said Ada. 'It's her radiator, that's all. I'll patch her up in no time.' She caressed the car's snout-like bonnet. 'She's an Alpensieger. Strong and fast. But she's an old lady now. There's always something needs fixing.'

'What about the others? Do you have to work on them as well?' Monty squinted into the darkness. The place was as shadowy as a cave and smelled strongly of dark, greasy objects. Against a wall stood a workbench, covered with bits and pieces of engine, cans of oil, rags, spanners and other black, mysterious tools. The walls were hung with ropes and chains, car wheels and tyres, jerry cans and hosepipes.

'I do a bit of everything,' said Ada. 'Serve tea, help the guests, fix the motors. There aren't as many staff here as there used to be. People don't want to be in service. Especially in a place like this.'

'And what about you?'

'Oh, I don't mind, miss.'

'But you could go anywhere. You didn't have to come back here.'

'It's my home,' said Ada. 'Besides, how would Mr Blackwood manage without me? I do the generator too,' she added. 'But Mr Thake, he's been here since before the Hall was built, he does the douches.'

'Mr Blackwood,' said Monty. 'He's the man who hired me. He runs Bleakly Hall, does he? Can't he help you with any of this? The motors, at least?'

'No,' said Ada firmly. 'He can't.'

'Oh.' Monty wiped her forehead with the back of her hand. She felt dirty and begrimed, covered in oil from the car and sweat from her march through the woods. What sort of a person was this Mr Blackwood that he could not even show himself on her arrival; could not even apologise for making her walk so far? She was too tired to care. Besides, there was still the matter of why she had come to Bleakly. Should she wait? She found she could not. 'You said there was a Captain Foxley staying here. In one of your letters. Is he still a guest?'

Even in the dimness of the garage Monty could see that Ada's face had turned red. 'Yes,' she said.

'D'you know him?'

'Know him?' repeated Ada. Her tone suggested that the question was a stupid one. 'Captain Foxley lives here. *Everyone* knows him.' She pulled a spanner from her pocket and tossed it on to the workbench. 'I'll take you inside. Dr Slack'll be waiting.'

Monty followed Ada out of the garage and into the foyer of the hydropathic. Daylight filtered through the open door and through two long windows on either side. Set into the far wall was a shadowy, wood-panelled booth, with sliding mahogany doors atop a dark counter, like a sergeant's desk in a police station. A bell, and a ledger, identified it as the reception desk. On either side a white marble staircase curved gracefully upwards between twin alabaster columns. Here and there great chunks had been smashed from their pale treads, as though something large and heavy had been dragged rudely up (or thrown violently down). These missing chunks had become discoloured and gave the stairs a neglected, slatternly look. Against a wall burbled an ornamental fountain in the shape of Hygeia. Monty could distinguish figures slowly making their way through the shadows, or standing, like insects trapped in amber, in patches of watery sunlight. Was one of them Captain Foxley?

She had never met the man, but she had spent so long thinking about him that she felt as though he would be instantly recognisable. But there was no one nearby who looked remotely likely to be him. At that moment the light outside was swallowed up by rising storm clouds. Monty saw Ada reach up and suddenly the gloom was punctuated by dozens of dismal yellow light bulbs, positioned above paintings that hung about the walls.

'Mr Thake'll take your bag to your room,' said Ada.

Monty jumped as something brushed against her arm. She turned to find a man of great age and thinness stooping at her elbow. He revealed a set of unexpectedly white and youthful-looking teeth, before gathering up her bag in his arms like a thief and disappearing rapidly down the corridor. Monty saw him turn up a distant staircase, then he was gone.

'This way,' said Ada, shouting above the roar of bucketing rainfall. She led Monty through a door and down another, narrower, passage. 'This corridor is for the ladies. The gentlemen have their own hallway to the water treatments. You'll be with Dr Slack, in the consulting rooms, I suppose, though you'll have to be in the treatment rooms too. Some of the douches are quite troublesome, so you might need to get Mr Thake as he's most used to the appliances.'

'I see,' said Monty. She wondered vaguely what might constitute a 'troublesome douche', but was distracted by a resonant juddering sound coming from somewhere beneath her feet. She had already lost any sense of direction, as the corridor seemed endless, with numerous turns and small flights of stairs and ranks of anonymous doors lining the walls on either side. All at once the carpet stopped and instead the floor was made up of squares of black and white linoleum. The doors on either side were surmounted by wooden plaques: *Treatment Baths. Adjustable Douche. Turkish Bath. Russian Steam Bath*. A hissing sound filled the air and a shriek echoed along the corridor. *Swimming Pool*, read Monty, who was quite at home in a world that resonated with the sounds of pain. *Ladies' Recovery Room. Massage Suite. Peat Baths*. The juddering sound gradually faded to a dull throb.

'D'you want to see anything, miss?' Ada spoke over her shoulder. 'While we're passing?'

'*Douche Massage*,' read Monty. 'What about this?'

Ada shrugged. 'As good a place as any, I suppose. At this time of day it'll be the gentlemen what's having the douche massage. We've not actually got many gentlemen with us at the moment. It's probably just as well as there's not many bath men either.' Ada pushed open the door and stood back. Monty peeped inside.

The room was tiled from top to bottom in white and green; the floor covered with sand-coloured stone slabs and bordered by a shallow gutter, slick with a shining ribbon of water, which noisily emptied its contents into a drain in one corner. It was stiflingly hot, but there was an iciness in the air, as though from a miasma of freezing water droplets. In the middle of the stone floor lay a narrow wooden pallet. Monty pointed. 'Is that –'

'A duckboard, yes, miss,' said Ada. 'The army had a hospital at the Hall during the war. All sorts of things was stored here and then left behind. Mr Thake found some duckboards in one of the outhouses last month and we use them instead of the old douche benches. Most of the douche benches were broken.' She lowered her voice. 'It's peculiar, isn't it? Seeing them again. Takes you back.'

On top of the duckboard lay a man. He was shielded from full view by the attendants kneeling on either side. For a moment, a single thrilling second, Monty wondered whether it might be the naked body of Captain Foxley. But almost immediately she realised that the fellow was far too old. She stared at his withered stick-like legs and wrinkled arms quivering beneath the wet, meaty hands of the two burly bath men. Her heart was thumping.

The bath men were dressed in loose gingham shorts and sleeveless shirts of the same fabric. They were barefooted and bareheaded. Both sported moustaches as dark and bristling as broom heads, which hid their mouths and gave them a grave, anonymous air. With their right hands they held the old man down on the board. With their left, they wielded a hosepipe the length and thickness of a python. The hosepipes were black and tumescent, their moist skins glistening with a faint greenish iridescence, as though lightly coated with algae. The tails of the hosepipe pythons were fitted into a cistern in the wall, the quantity and force of the water blast regulated by a sluice wheel and a tap. Their wide brass mouths, gripped tightly between the muscular fingers of the bath men, vomited water over the shaking body, pouring through the slats in the duckboard and across the floor to the gutter.

'It's a hot and cold shower massage,' whispered Ada. 'Nearly everyone gets one sooner or later. It's very technical,

Dr Slack says. Dr Slack's the resident physician. He says that the touch of the bath men on the patient must be precisely prescribed. Depending on the physiology, anatomy and ailment of the patient the massage will be forceful, moderate, or delicate. Dr Slack used to come in himself and shout orders while the treatment was taking place. Well, as Douche Master, why shouldn't he? But the guests said it put them off, having him bellowing like an auctioneer from the sidelines, and they asked him to leave. He's not been down for months now. He stays in his consulting rooms these days and lets us get on with things.'

Beneath the swirling currents of water, the bath men began to pummel their victim, who lay inert, grunting rhythmically as the larger of the two kneaded his chest with one hand and held the hosepipe of freezing water over his abdomen with the other.

'What happens next?' whispered Monty.

'They wrap him in a hot sheet and take him into the recovery rooms next door,' said Ada. They walked a little further. 'Here's the Ladies' Shower Rooms. These are always busy at this time of day. The ladies come in after they've been in the swimming pool, or the peat baths, or sometimes after a massage. D'you want to see inside?' Without waiting for an answer, Ada led Monty into a cavernous chamber, filled with steam and echoing with the sound of water cascading against flesh. The room was semicircular and was divided into stalls, like a tiled stable. The centre of the room was marked by a large circular drain, beside which dribbled a drinking fountain. Ada filled a tarnished metal cup that dangled on a chain beside the fountain and passed it over. Until then,

Monty had not realised how thirsty she was, and she took the cup eagerly and put it to her lips to take a sip. But the water smelt faintly of drains. Surreptitiously, she tipped it out.

From the centre of the room the occupants of each stall could be monitored and their various needs attended to. Through the steam Monty could make out the shapes of gingham-clad orderlies, gathering up wet sheets and towels, and setting out dry linen. Each stall housed a lady – some broad and squat, their bodies made up of great globs of pale fat resting one on top of the other like folds of uncooked pastry; some thin and hollowed, their skin loose over bone and sinew. Each stood unmoving beneath a wide shower head of thundering water.

'Look,' whispered Ada, pointing to the last, and largest, of the tiled stalls. It contained a tall cylindrical cage made up of curved steel ribs. 'That one's *always* popular.' Inside the steel cage, shrouded by clouds of boiling steam, Monty could see the silhouette of an enormous woman. Jets of water hammered out of the ribs on all sides, so that the pale wobbling flesh on her back and shoulders turned pink, then red. The figure in the cage shower shifted her bulk, the descending waters drumming on to her head with a metallic roar. Monty rubbed her eyes. 'Is that woman wearing a steel army helmet?'

'Yes, miss,' said Ada. 'The ladies always wear the helmet in the cage shower. The descending water is very powerful. One of them collapsed, due to the force and temperature of the blast. Mind you, that was a few months ago now. It's been fine since they took to wearing the helmet.'

*

Monty knocked sharply at the doctor's door. She heard an explosive cough from within, followed by a croak, which sounded a little like 'come in', but which may well have been something else. She opened the door and stepped inside. The place was dark and stifling. Was everywhere at Bleakly boiling hot? The glowing coals of an ancient fire revealed that the windows were shuttered and curtained, and that an elderly gentleman was sprawled in an armchair. He rose slowly to his feet, swaying like a strand of kelp tugged by the sea.

'Dr Slack?' asked Monty. She could hear music, a distant dance melody, though there was no gramophone to be seen.

The man nodded gloomily. 'Might you ring the bell for tea before you sit down?' he said. 'Not that anyone'll be likely to come.'

Monty sat opposite the doctor. There was silence between them, the stillness interrupted only by the music of the Jack Hylton orchestra. Monty recognised the tune – the 'Wang Wang Blues'. A probationer in the nurses' home had played it endlessly, but it seemed an odd choice for an elderly doctor. The music appeared to be getting louder, too, though it had no obvious source.

'Confound the fellow,' muttered Dr Slack. 'No wonder my head aches!' He waved a hand in the direction of a sink that stood beside the medicine cabinet. 'Put the plug in, will you? Sometimes I don't mind it, but not today. And why can't he play a bit of Chopin, instead of all those dreadful modern tunes?' Dr Slack fell back into his armchair. 'The water pipes here are like a telephone exchange. My plughole seems to have a direct line to Captain Foxley.'

'Captain Foxley?' said Monty.

Dr Slack did not answer, but rubbed his forehead, as if massaging away a painful recollection. He took a gulp from a glass of water at his elbow. 'A dose of warm chalybeate from the Lady Beaton Well in the pump room to fortify the blood,' he said. 'Does wonders for the system. As for our own famous Bleakly Well, here at the Hall, it's brimming with revitalising minerals – sodium, magnesium and the various therapeutic carbonates. Nature's elixir, you know.' He gave an exhausted sigh. 'You're the new nurse, I presume? What's your name?'

'Roberta Montgomery.'

'Parents hoping for a boy, were they?'

'Yes,' said Monty.

Dr Slack grunted. 'Well, well. You'd no doubt have been killed or maimed over there if they'd got their wish so perhaps there's something to be grateful for after all. You'll be up from London, I imagine? Can't think why you'd want to come here.'

'Mr Blackwood said that I was to act as your assistant.'

'Well, you must be cheap if *he* brought you. I hope you know what you're doing.'

'Of course I do,' said Monty. Yet she *had* offered her services to Mr Blackwood rather cheaply, so desperate had she been to come to Bleakly. *Did* she know what she was doing? Now that she had actually arrived at the place, Monty was not so sure. She had no particular plan and was not certain what she would do when the opportunity arose. Indeed, she wondered now whether she would even manage to recognise the opportunity when it presented itself. A grunting sound started up beneath the sink, as though the stoppered plug-hole was struggling to breathe. Dr Slack sank into his cushions. His eyes disappeared into bottomless eye sockets, his hollow cheeks and bulging forehead glinting like bone in the firelight. Beneath his clothes he seemed as thin as a bundle of twigs, as though he was no more than a skeleton, picked clean by life, the tired flesh having worn away to nothing.

Monty stared at the doctor's cadaverous face. Was he waiting for her to speak? Perhaps she should ask about Captain Foxley. Should she enquire about the doctor's own health (surely a topic with infinite possibilities)? Was he expecting her to question him about her duties? Monty found that her eagerness had evaporated. Instead, oppressed by the warmth and overcome by fatigue, she suddenly felt terribly weary; jaded and lonely, exhausted with misery and thinking and waiting. She sagged in her chair. How sleepy she was. If she allowed her eyes to close she would never be able to open them again.

All at once the overflow drain on the doctor's sink let out a groan. Monty sprang up and looked about in confusion. 'What was that? I heard . . . Who's there?'

Dr Slack gave a gentle wheezing laugh. 'Ghosts,' he whispered. 'They're everywhere at Bleakly. You believe in 'em, I hope?'

'No,' said Monty. 'No,' she said again, this time more firmly as the first 'no' seemed to have stuck in her throat.

'Oh? Then what do you believe in?'

'Science,' said Monty, determined to stay awake and clear-headed. 'Progress.' She stared hopefully at Dr Slack's medicine cabinet, searching for conviction among the familiar bottles and jars. She was not sure that she believed in anything any more. The cabinet glowed with coloured powders and iridescent liquids like the window of a sweet shop. She frowned. Was that a jar of aniseed balls she could see?

Dr Slack gave a cackle. 'Well, I suppose that's something, at least.'

'No doubt there are specific techniques you use here at Bleakly Hall,' said Monty, hoping she sounded efficient. 'I have little experience of this sort of institution, though I'm keen to learn.'

'The only technique you'll need here is patience,' muttered Dr Slack. 'And water. There's not much else to it, whatever anyone else tells you. Did some war work, did you?'

'At a casualty clearing station in 1914 and again later on. And on the troop trains bringing men back from the front,' said Monty. 'I worked in London too. With the wounded.'

'And now you want to work here?' he sounded incredulous.

'Mr Blackwood's letter said that he was expecting a busy season –'

'A busy season!' Dr Slack snorted.

'He has advertised widely and is expecting parties from London.'

'Ha!'

'There will be new treatments. Modern treatments.' Monty began to feel exasperated. 'Mr Blackwood was quite clear –'

'What "new" treatments?' cried the doctor. 'There's nothing new to be found here. We've done everything we possibly can. What new treatments did he mention?'

'Mr Blackwood said –'

'Which Mr Blackwood?'

'Mr Blackwood the proprietor,' said Monty. 'Who else might I be referring to?'

'What does he look like?'

'Who?'

'Mr Blackwood.'

'I don't know,' cried Monty. 'I've never met him. Don't *you* know what he looks like?'

'Of course I do,' shouted Dr Slack.

'Well, then, why are you asking *me*?' Monty stood up. 'I was offered this position by a Mr Blackwood,' she cried. 'A Mr Grier Blackwood. Is there another of that name here?'

There was a knock at the door and Ada entered carrying a tea tray. She set it down on a low table in front of the fire and disappeared.

'Tea?' Dr Slack gazed excitedly at the tray. 'I'm surprised it came at all.' He raised himself from the depths of his armchair. 'No biscuits.' He sounded disappointed. 'I don't know why I keep hoping.'

'*Is* there more than one Mr Blackwood?' insisted Monty, reviving a little at the sight of the tea tray.

'Yes,' replied Dr Slack. 'Certainly Grier Blackwood owns the place. But so does his brother. Grier is the younger brother; Curran is the elder. I didn't think Curran would have hired you. And I'm surprised at Grier.' He gave a snort of laughter. 'Are you expecting to be paid?'

2

M ONTY ROAMED the building in search of Ada. The place seemed to be deserted. More than once, as she walked down a corridor or climbed a flight of stairs, she was sure she could hear voices, a gentle murmuring as though from a crowd assembled somewhere, accompanied by the clatter and scrape of cutlery. But every time she attempted to gauge where these sounds were coming from they seemed to merge with the furious drumming of the rain, so that she was soon hardly sure what she was listening for. The lights flickered anxiously as she walked beneath them; the carpet felt sticky under her feet. Outside, a fine mist hung in the air. The rain thundered down, bursting over gutters and spouting from drainpipes and plunging Bleakly Hall into premature night. From a window on the second-floor landing Monty stared out at a featureless vista. The unkempt bowling green, the trees festooned with their hanks of yellow flowers, the far-off chimneys and rooftops of the village had disappeared into the murk. It was as though the hydropathic had transformed into a ship, vast and unmanned, drifting on a grey and stormy sea miles from anywhere.

Monty was out of bed at six the following morning. After much wandering about the previous afternoon, she had found her suitcase standing beside a table in a bedroom on the third floor. A bunch of marigolds drooped in a vase on the mantelpiece and a basin and pitcher of chipped brown pottery waited on the washstand. Two threadbare towels as rough as cats' tongues lay folded neatly on the chocolate-coloured counterpane. Monty had unpacked her things – a blue cotton nightdress and dressing gown sprigged with embroidered flowers, and a pair of black leather slippers bought in the sale at Whiteley's; an ivory-backed hand mirror and brush that had once belonged to her mother; some well-worn and repeatedly darned underthings; stockings, petticoats and knickers; writing paper and ink. Her uniform, which she hung in the musty wardrobe, had been newly bought from Holdron's of Balham, the nurse's outfitters in London. The suppliers were still suffering from wartime privations and the fabric was a cheap sort of serge, the apron and cap meanly cut. If her work at Bleakly was strenuous, she thought as she buttoned her collar, the material would never last.

Monty washed her face and brushed her hair. She visited the lavatory at the end of the corridor. Once dressed, she threw open the window. The room still possessed the dusty, sulphurous atmosphere she had noticed the night before and the smell seemed to have permeated everything, so that she was sure she reeked horribly of mildew and rotten eggs.

Outside, the sun was up and glinting through the trees; far off, a brass band blared an up-tempo tune into the morning air. Monty listened for a moment. The strains of 'Yes, We Have No Bananas' drifted up from the village.

Downstairs, the foyer was swarming with guests, ladies and gentlemen, none of them under the age of seventy. The gentlemen waited together in an uncertain group beside the reception desk. The wives, widows and spinsters who made up the rest of the crowd strolled about, each tightly buttoned into a coat and hat, as though in preparation for a day at the races. They stared at one another's millinery with covetousness. A jungle of black ostrich feathers and tendrils of ivy in watered silk waved atop a concertina of crimped straw; beside this, a mound of pink velvet roses was loaded about a crown of artfully fashioned felt the width of a bicycle wheel. The cut and drape of coats were displayed with pride by the more agile ladies, who slowly circled the foyer, the patterns of silk-lined appliqué on their hems and shoulders illuminated by the morning sunlight.

At the foot of the stairs, oblivious to this doddering fashion show, stood Dr Slack. Beside the door, a small group of female orderlies and a couple of bath men were gathered, the men with blue serge coats over their clothes, the women in aprons of the same fabric. A man, not very tall but well dressed in a fashionably cut suit, a crisp white shirt and gleaming boots stood uneasily at the edge of the group. His reddish-brown hair was neat, and clipped close at the neck and sides. He was smoking and staring absently through the open doorway into the sunshine. His expression was morose and he had a distracted, disappointed air, as though he had recently received bad news. Perhaps *this* was Captain Foxley? He was the only person she had seen who was young enough. Should she go over and confront him?

All at once, a voice barked out across the foyer: 'Put that cigarette out!'

The man jumped, startled out of his reverie. He took a final puff, and pinched the cigarette between finger and thumb. He was about to stick the half-smoked stub behind his ear – a gesture that surprised Monty, though it was a habit she had seen in a thousand soldiers – but then changed his mind. He tossed the unfinished cigarette out of the door and on to the gravel beyond.

'Glad you could join us, Nurse Montgomery,' added the voice. 'You are three minutes late.' Monty looked about, but had no idea who had spoken. Then, without warning, there came a sharp blast on a whistle. Dr Slack closed the ledger and disappeared, like a conjuror's assistant. The guests began filing out obediently into the sunshine. Soon, there was no one left but Monty and the man, who already had another cigarette between his lips and was striking a reluctant match.

'Don't mind him.' He spoke through a cloud of smoke.

'Who?' said Monty.

'Curran,' replied the man, blowing a lungful of smoke in the direction of the reception desk. 'The voice and the whistle. He likes to make his presence felt in a variety of ways.'

'I didn't see him –'

'Oh, you have to know where to look.' The man's expression was grim. 'I'm sorry.' He held out his hand. 'Glad to see you could make it, Miss Montgomery. I'm Grier

Blackwood.' He shook her hand and smiled with the easy charm of someone who had spent years welcoming strangers. Monty could not help but smile back, partly with relief that the man was not Captain Foxley after all.

'I'm sorry I didn't meet you myself yesterday,' said Grier. 'I had some . . . some business to attend to. Did Ada come for you in the motor?'

'Almost,' said Monty.

Grier nodded. 'Dr Slack said he's told you what's what. Your duties and so on.'

'Yes,' said Monty. There was sure to be a role for her in the treatment rooms, the doctor had said, but he seemed vague as to what this might be.

'Good,' said Grier. He fiddled with his cigarette. 'We're modernising, you know. That's why you're here. We need young people to come to Bleakly Hall.' All at once he laughed. 'Give me a comfortable armchair, a glass of gin and a copy of *Bell's Life* any day.' He looked at Monty sideways, as though realising that as the proprietor of a therapeutic hotel he should not really be extolling the virtues of indolence, hard drink and sporting magazines. All at once his glance darted to the stairs beside the reception desk and his face took on a pinched, vigilant look. Monty glanced round, but there was no one there.

'And is Bleakly Hall busy just now, Mr Blackwood?' she said after a moment.

'No,' said Grier gloomily. 'Not really. Most of our guests have been coming here for years,' he added. 'Which should be something to be grateful for. I think they come to remind themselves how things used to be. It simply can't go on.'

He brightened. 'But I have lots of ideas. I was thinking about a grouse shoot, or a midsummer ball, or an archery contest –'

Monty was not listening. 'Do you have any permanent guests?' she said. She congratulated herself on her craftiness. He would surely be obliged to mention Captain Foxley. 'They can provide a reliable income.'

'We have one,' said Grier. 'But you already know that, don't you, Miss Montgomery?'

Monty coloured and opened her mouth to speak, but at that moment the air erupted with a thunderous booming sound, which echoed around the foyer, resonating upwards so that the light fixtures overhead tinkled nervously. 'What's that noise?' she cried, covering her ears with her hands. 'What's going on?'

But Grier Blackwood had extracted a sporting daily from his jacket pocket. He was examining the back pages and did not appear to have heard her above the din. The noise died away, to be replaced by a determined, angry juddering, a yammering that grew in volume and seemed to be coming from all sides – from below their feet and above their heads; from behind the walls and pictures, as though the entire building was being bombarded by machine-gun fire. And then, just as Monty thought she could stand it no more – just when it felt as though the place must surely be shaken apart – the terrible din stopped.

Monty felt her heart thumping, her ears singing in the stillness that followed.

'The plumbing's lively today,' Grier remarked. 'You'll be heading down to the pump room, now, I imagine?'

'Yes,' stammered Monty. 'Will you?' Her voice seemed loud in the sudden silence.

'Oh, no.' She noticed that his face had turned pale and that his hands were shaking as he folded his newspaper. 'I have something to attend to here.'

'Do you need any help?' said Monty automatically.

'No,' said Grier. 'No, but thank you. It's just –' He glanced up at the stairs, his expression suddenly fearful.

'What is it?' said Monty.

'Nothing,' said Grier. He seemed to be listening. 'Well, you'd best be off then,' he added. 'At least the rain has stopped. The pump room is at the bottom of the hill, across the village square.'

Monty looked up. Was that breathing she could hear? And the creak of shoe leather? 'I think there's someone there,' she said. 'Just out of sight on the stairs. Perhaps one of the guests –'

'Oh, I don't think so –'

'*Coward.*' The voice was the merest whisper, so faint that Monty was not quite sure she had heard it. But there it was again, as faint as the rustle of fallen leaves, but a whispered voice nonetheless. '*Coward.*'

Grier slid Monty an anxious look.

'*Coward!*' screamed the voice. '*Coward! Coward!*'

'A great pleasure to meet you, Miss Montgomery,' said Grier briskly. He seized her hand and pumped it up and down. 'The guests will be waiting so I'll not detain you further. If you'll excuse me?' He bounded across the foyer and disappeared up the stairs.

3

THE BLEAKLY Hall guests made their way unsteadily down the hill. The youngest walked arm in arm for support, the oldest were wedged into bath-chairs wheeled by orderlies. They travelled in silence, preoccupied by their own locomotion, strung out along the road like the remains of a war-torn platoon. Purged of water, the sky was now a flawless arc of blue, though it was soon obscured by the beeches that clustered thickly on either side of the road, their heavy branches forming a vaulted ceiling overhead. The undergrowth, sodden with rain and warmed by the morning, had exhaled a damp yellowish haze, which hung motionless between the trees. Patches of it had encroached on to the road, so that those walking upon it seemed to fade from view, like ghosts.

'Good morning,' said Monty, drawing level with an elderly gentleman who was propelling himself along between two lacquered sticks. Was it the same fellow she had seen enduring the hot and cold douche massage the day before? She had no idea.

The man gave a grunt. 'There's the pump room,' he said. He raised a stick and pointed to a lichen-covered roof just visible through the trees.

'So I believe,' said Monty. 'I've not been before. Do you think you might show me the way?' She held out her hand. 'It's a lovely morning, isn't it? I'm Nurse Montgomery.'

But the man seemed not to hear. He bent to his task with renewed vigour, shuffling forward between his sticks, his gaze fixed anxiously on the path ahead. Monty walked on alone.

The village of Bleakly huddled close to the road, and Monty followed the guests past a number of ponderous villas similar in style to those found in towns such as Buxton and Harrogate. But the villas of Bleakly showed evidence of decay, with peeling window frames overlooking shaggy, unkempt lawns. They stared out silently from among the dark trunks of horse chestnuts, or peeped from behind colossal bushes of untrimmed rhododendron. In the village square a dog sprawled as though dead beneath the window of the post office. The post office had an abandoned air; its sign was faded and dusty, the window speckled with dried-out flies and bedecked with cobwebs. Further on stood a row of shops – a haberdasher's, a bakery, a greengrocer. At the edge of the square, where the road plunged back into the trees, Monty noticed a curious low building of red and orange brick, with small mullioned windows. The sloping roof was emerald with moss, the walls scabrous with patches of yellowish mould. Before it stood a bandstand, inside which, crammed tightly together, a brass band waited – as silent and unmoving as clockwork toys. As the first of the guests appeared from among the trees, the bandleader raised his baton. The cymbals smashed together and the national anthem blared out across the square. The guests came forward, to line up outside the entrance to the orange brick building. From within a fearful eggy odour wafted into the morning. One by one they filed in.

Inside, the walls of the pump room were as dark and green as a pond. The diamonds of glass in the windows admitted only fragments of light, which danced in the gloom like shoals of glittering sticklebacks. The air was cold and damp and thickly malodorous. A marble counter ran the length of the room, behind which six pumps dispensed three different health-giving waters. It was staffed by two women wearing aprons of huckaback and severe expressions who ran the place as efficiently as a bar in a public house. The tiled walls and floor echoed with the sound of murmuring voices and shuffling feet as the crowd jostled for a place at the pumps. Outside, the band began a confident version of 'British Grenadiers'.

Once she had become accustomed to the stench, Monty started assisting the hydropathic's guests up and down the room. ('Perambulation', the doctor had explained, 'aids absorption.')

'Have you been to Bleakly Hall before?' she asked.

'Oh, I've been coming since the place was built,' came the reply.

'Does everyone come down here in the mornings?'

'Yes. Everyone.'

'Apart from Mr Blackwood.'

'Mr Curran usually comes. Mr Grier doesn't always bother.'

26

'And Captain Foxley?'

Monty watched as the smile faded. 'No. Not him. He never comes.'

Dr Slack had been wheeled down to the pump room by one of the bath men and was now standing beside the bar. He downed a tumbler of water in audible gulps and returned the glass for more, sliding it along the marble counter in the manner of a tired gunslinger in a Wild West saloon. 'The Bleakly waters have quite marvellous properties of rejuvenation,' he said.

Monty glanced around at the water-logged guests slowly circling the pump-room floor. In the dim light their clothes appeared uniformly black, their faces as pale as whey. Their hands shook as they raised their glasses to their lips, like mourners making a toast at some sort of macabre funeral. 'They don't look very rejuvenated,' she said. 'Would they not prefer a cup of tea?'

'Tea?' piped a tiny woman standing at Dr Slack's elbow. 'But stimulants are forbidden at Bleakly, aren't they, doctor.'

'Yes,' said Dr Slack.

'But we had tea yesterday,' said Monty.

'You had *tea*?' cried the tiny lady. She stared at the doctor accusingly. 'Dr Slack, is this true?'

Dr Slack blinked. 'It was purely medicinal. Miss Montgomery had had a fatiguing journey.'

'I have spent my life crusading against tea,' cried the lady. 'In its strongest form it is as bad as alcohol or tobacco. I am quite surprised at you, Dr Slack.' She shook a threatening finger beneath Monty's nose. 'Are you not aware what sort of a place this is?'

'No, I don't think I am,' said Monty. 'Perhaps I should try the waters and find out. Do you have a recommendation?'

A pair of small, beady eyes looked Monty up and down. '*Chalybeate*,' said the lady firmly. 'Wouldn't you say, doctor? *Most* reviving.'

Dr Slack nodded. He grinned at Monty as he handed her a glass of stinking water.

'Drink it down, my dear,' cried the lady. 'It's a marvellous tonic for the blood and the digestion. But you'll already be aware of that, I'm sure. Dr Slack tells me that you're the new nurse.'

'Yes, Mr Grier Blackwood hired me.'

'Ah, Mr Grier.' She sipped her water. 'Such a charming fellow. And Mr Curran too, of course. His wife, Mrs Mae Blackwood, was quite a society lady at one time. But that was before they came here. There's none of *that* sort of thing here. Mr Curran likes the old traditions of the place and I can't say I disapprove.'

'Ha!' snorted Dr Slack. 'We're modernising, you know. Those old traditions will disappear, Mrs Forbes, just like everything else.'

'Oh, dear me,' cried tiny Mrs Forbes and began an arthritic rummaging among her mass of silk skirts. She drew out a crumpled leaflet and handed it over. A sketch depicted a woman hesitating outside a public house. Beneath were the words, 'What beauty of womanhood can be found *THERE*?'

'I had a better one,' Mrs Forbes whispered. 'But I can't lay my hands on it right now.'

'Thank you,' said Monty. 'I've not met Mr Curran Blackwood,' she added. 'Is he much like his brother?'

28

'No,' said Dr Slack.

'And what about Captain Foxley?' said Monty. 'I keep hearing his name mentioned. Is he here this morning?'

'No,' said Dr Slack again. He gulped his water and stared at her over the rim of his glass.

Monty sighed. 'Doesn't Captain Foxley take the waters?' she insisted. 'Doesn't he join in anything?'

'He does not.'

'Why's that?'

'I have no idea.'

By now the marble counter and the tiled floor were awash with spilled water. Monty had noticed that the footsteps behind her had stopped and she turned to find that the guests were no longer promenading, but were standing still, staring at her. They looked bloated and uncomfortable, watching her with anxious eyes, their hands pressed over their stomachs, their expressions wary, almost fearful. Then Monty realised they were not looking at her at all, but at Dr Slack.

'Two more minutes, if you please,' cried Dr Slack. He pulled out a pocket watch and a silver whistle, upon which he gave a single sharp blast. The guests released a collective sigh, and began circling the room once more, their heads down like beasts on a treadmill. 'And one glass of warm chalybeate each before we return,' added Dr Slack.

There was a mutinous muttering. But Dr Slack showed no mercy. He gestured to the women dispensing the waters. A bell rang and another woman emerged from a door at the back. Her sleeves were rolled up above pink and muscular arms, and she bore a tray covered with glasses of steaming water.

'It's no more than most of them deserve,' muttered Dr Slack in Monty's ear. 'They live off fruit cakes and claret and haunches of red meat, so it's no wonder that they're all constipated and bilious.' He turned his back on the milling crowds and surreptitiously pulled a hip flask from his pocket. 'They're already dead, the lot of 'em, just like I am.' His face glimmered eerily in the fish-tank light of the pump room. He poured a slug of spirits into two glasses and passed one to Monty. 'For courage!' he said.

4

AFTER BREAKFAST (which turned out to be a bowl of watered-down oatmeal served without sugar or milk) Ada appeared at Monty's side.

'Mr Curran would like to see you,' she said. 'Before you begin consulting. He's in his office.'

Monty followed Ada across the foyer towards a grove of foliage beside the reception. Ada looked miserable. Her eyes were red and puffy, and between her fingers she clutched a moist handkerchief.

'Are you well, Ada?' asked Monty. 'You look upset –'

'I'm very well, thank you, miss,' replied Ada. She stalked forward, as if hoping to leave Monty behind.

'You don't have to call me "miss" all the time,' said Monty. 'I wish you wouldn't.'

'Why?' demanded Ada. 'That's how it is, isn't it?'

'It didn't used to be. Your letters sounded as though you thought me a friend, rather than a . . . superior. In Belgium, things like that didn't matter. Not to me, at least. They still don't.'

'Yes, they do,' said Ada. 'They always did; we just forgot about it for a while. The war made other things seem more important. Other things *were* more important. But now everything's back to how it was before.'

'Not everything,' said Monty.

Ada ignored her. 'No one even notices me,' she muttered. 'No one sees what I do. *That's* just like it used to be before the war. The only difference is that I *knows* it now.'

'I'm sure that's not true,' said Monty. 'I'm sure people do notice you.'

'Oh, only when they wants something,' said Ada. 'Otherwise it *is* true. You know, miss, I sometimes wish the war wasn't over.' She blushed. 'A bit like the Captain, I suppose.'

'Captain Foxley?'

'Yes. We talks a bit about it, him and me. I had such a time out there – oh, I hated the war, make no mistake. But I loved it too. I should have been in the munitions works, but because I could drive . . . I know it's wrong to say it, but in some ways I never felt so happy.' She smiled. 'I drove that ambulance better than anyone, didn't I?'

'Yes,' said Monty. 'You did.'

'A girl gets a taste for things like that.'

'For war?'

'Oh, no, miss, not for *war*.' Ada gave Monty a withering look. 'For *speed*.'

Ada held aside the paddle-shaped leaf of a rubber plant as though operating a turnstile and led Monty towards an open door.

The first thing Monty noticed was the heat. It seemed to pulsate from the walls and strike upwards through the soles of her feet, as if the room were situated over a fissure in the earth's crust. Monty glanced at the grate in consternation (she was not sure how long she would be able to bear such an atmosphere), but in Curran's office no fire burned. Instead, the grate was filled with a collection of plumbing accessories – four brass taps, a large chrome shower head and a coiled length of hosepipe.

The office was illuminated by a small, tightly closed window. It faced on to a cobbled yard at the back of the hydro and afforded a dismal view of rusting downpipes and gutters bearded with green. Within, the walls were lined with shelves laden with ledgers and account books. On one of these, a spiked pickelhaube acted as a bookend. A more conventional coal-scuttle helmet, upturned upon the window ledge, contained a geranium, and a variety of empty brass cartridges were positioned, like a row of dirty yellow teeth, on the mantelpiece. More unusual, however, was the object sitting on a rug in the centre of the room.

'What's that?' asked Monty, staring at the tangle of chrome pipes, nozzles, tubes, dials and wheels.

'That's the adjustable douche,' whispered Ada. 'With its great number of fixtures and settings it can hose a patient in seventeen different ways, using a variety of temperatures and pressures. Mr Thake's fixing it. New pipes are coming up from London. Mr Thake brought it in this morning to show Mr Curran.' Ada nodded to a desk, which stood in front of the window. A man was seated there. Despite the heat he was tightly buttoned into a tweed waistcoat and jacket. He had an account book open before him and a gold-tipped fountain pen in his hand. The pen scratched across the page as he filled in a row of important numbers.

'Miss Montgomery, sir,' said Ada.

'Thank you, Ada,' said the man without looking up. 'And Grier?'

'I don't know where he is,' said Ada. 'He took the motor into the village first thing this morning. I'd just patched her up too. The job's not finished and like as not he'll roast her engine.'

'Could you not stop him?' asked Curran.

'He said he had urgent business to attend to.'

'Damn the fellow.'

'That's sixpence, sir,' whispered Ada.

'Thank you, Ada.' Curran Blackwood pushed a small silver coin across the tabletop and turned his gaze to Monty.

'Welcome to Bleakly Hall Hydropathic, Nurse Montgomery.' He came from behind the desk and held out his hand. 'I hope you'll be happy here.'

Monty had seen dozens of men in wheelchairs and knew that to exhibit any signs of pity, or fear, or revulsion would be a mistake. Curran Blackwood was as handsome as his brother, with the same neatly trimmed reddish-brown hair and the same scrupulous tailoring. Grier's complexion was suntanned and freckled, but Curran's was pale against his high, starched collar, his skin etiolated by a life spent indoors. His trousers sported creases as sharp as knife blades, which were positioned so that they ran exactly down the centre of each of his shattered knees, precisely parallel to one another. A pair of highly polished brown boots sat where his feet should be on the footrest of the wheelchair, but Monty could tell from the drape of his trousers that they were empty, and that the legs that should have led to them were missing.

'I'm sure I'll find it most interesting at Bleakly Hall,' she said. 'Though there are a few things that might be changed.'

'Oh, yes?' Curran looked at her sharply. 'I suggest you wait until you've been here for a while before you begin making changes. Besides, any change must be agreed by myself and Grier. Or by Dr Slack if it's a medical matter.' He examined his watch. 'In fact, Grier is supposed to be here now,' he said. 'He's probably gone down to the Crossed Keys. Grier thinks I know nothing at all about his little habits, but I am well informed about everything that goes on in Bleakly. That's something you may wish to remember.'

'Yes, Mr Blackwood,' said Monty.

'Well,' said Curran. 'We'll just have to start without him. Do take a seat. Ada, would you be so kind as to fetch some camomile tea?'

Monty sank into her chair as Curran proceeded to explain the need to reduce outgoings, which, it appeared, were mounting steadily, in tandem with a decline in the number of guests. This economising was to be achieved, he insisted, by sticking to a regime of diet (which should be frugal), exercise (outside, so as to reduce wear on the fixtures and fittings) and water consumption (guests full of water ate less food). He did not pause, or hesitate as he talked and he neither looked at Monty, nor asked her opinion. For a while, Monty attempted to pay attention. But the room was so warm that she soon found it impossible to concentrate on what he was saying, especially as he illustrated every point with a torrent of economic information. Monty's eyes began to close.

'Where have you been?' cried Curran.

Monty's eyes snapped open.

'Nowhere,' said Grier. He sat down in the chair beside Monty and pulled out a silver cigarette case. He lit one and, stretching out his legs, rested his feet on the principal nozzle of the adjustable douche. 'Hello, Monty. You don't mind if I call you, Monty, do you? So much easier than "Nurse Montgomery" all the time.'

'Get your feet off that douche!' roared Curran. 'And put out that cigarette. This is a hydropathic hotel, not a gentleman's club!'

'There's no one here to see,' said Grier.

'*I'm* here,' said Curran.

'Bloody tyrant,' muttered Grier. He tossed his cigarette into the grate. It lay smoking gently, in the coils of hosepipe.

'And none of that barrack-room language, if you please, sir,' cried Curran. 'There's a fine of sixpence for every foul word uttered on these premises –'

Grier pulled a guinea from his pocket, and waved it at his brother above the tangled limbs of the adjustable douche. 'How many will *this* buy me?' he said. 'I'll bet there's not enough to describe *you* and leave me with change!' He put the coin back into his pocket and turned to Monty. 'You mustn't mind these little scenes.'

'Scenes?' said Curran.

'Differences of opinion. Mainly the fact that I wish to change things here and Curran does not.'

'Mainly the fact that you wish to waste our income and I do all I can to keep us afloat.'

'I'd love to see your hydropathic treatment rooms,' said Monty.

Grier led Monty back into the icy tranquillity of the foyer. 'You mustn't worry about Curran,' he said. 'Did he tell you his plan for watering down the guests' breakfast oatmeal?'

'I ate some of it this morning,' said Monty.

'Ghastly, isn't it? Still, he doesn't mean anything when he speaks harshly like that. He takes a bit of getting used to, that's all. Of course, the war changed so many of us – not that anyone wants to talk about that sort of thing these days.'

'Indeed,' said Monty. And yet how glad, how relieved she would be to have the opportunity to talk about 'that sort of thing'. But no one ever asked her. No one wanted to know, now that it was all officially over.

'Yes, poor old Curran always seems to be angry about something,' continued Grier. 'Usually small things like catching me with a cigarette, or whether someone's used too many pieces of coal to kindle a fire (six small lumps is the maximum number, if you must know). He used to be quite even-tempered. But one can hardly blame him, can one? Stuck in that chair the way he is. And as for Mae, she seems to avoid him these days – certainly she appears to have little to say to the poor fellow since he returned from the front, despite the fact that she was diligent in persuading him to go there in the first place. She spends more time in London than she does in Bleakly.' He sighed and added, 'and then Foxley came shortly after we'd reopened and that just made matters worse. For all of us, I suppose. But we can't get rid of the fellow. We can't ask him to leave. We couldn't do that, could we?' He looked at Monty anxiously, but he was clearly not expecting an answer for he switched immediately to a tone of artificial briskness and remarked, 'But what am I talking about that for? You'll want to know all about our spanking new appliances, won't you?'

'I suppose so,' said Monty. In fact, she was not the slightest bit interested in the appliances. She had seen enough the day before and besides, she had only mentioned the subject so that she might escape from Curran's overheated office. But Grier was looking at her expectantly, as though anticipating a series of probing questions on the nature and performance of the hydropathic's mysterious facilities. 'Did you know Captain Foxley before the war?' she said instead.

'No.'

'During?'

'Yes. Why? D'you know him?'

'No,' said Monty. 'No, I don't. But I knew someone who did.'

'Oh?'

'Sophia,' said Monty. The name echoed flatly off the green wall tiles and black-and-white linoleum. 'She was a friend of mine. Dead now.'

'I see,' said Grier. 'What was she like?'

'Young and very beautiful,' said Monty. It was the first time she had mentioned Sophia by name since the war, the first time she had been asked to describe her. She could see

38

that Grier was not really listening (no doubt he had his own share of dead friends to lament), which gave her the courage to continue. 'She seemed quite innocent, almost childlike, I suppose, but then she *was* little more than a child. Naive, some people might say, but it's not as though she lacked experience of the world. She saw the very worst that men can do to each other every day at St Margaret's. But I . . . I valued her innocence. Especially working in that hospital, with so much sorrow; so much pity and horror. She was funny too, you see. And I can be such a serious person, it made me smile to hear her chattering on about this and that. And despite everything she was always hopeful – a rare quality in anyone, especially back then. She always managed to see the best in everything, in everyone.' Monty wiped her eyes. 'I miss her terribly.'

Grier was now preoccupied by the wall. He stared at it as though at a picture that no one but he could see. 'Look at that,' he said, pointing upwards.

'The cornice,' said Monty, putting her handkerchief away. 'What about it?'

'Dripping,' said Grier. He ran a hand across the wall. 'And she's wet too.'

'Dear me,' said Monty. She cleared her throat. 'Look, Mr Blackwood, I need to see Captain Foxley. I wish to speak to him –'

'Oh, I'm sure you don't really need to do that,' said Grier gently. 'Not right away. Perhaps if you settled in first, got to know us a bit?' He rubbed a hand across the plaster, but did not look at her. 'You'll meet the fellow soon enough. Everyone does. You might like him.'

'I'm sure I shall *not* like him,' cried Monty. 'I am quite determined that I shall hate him.'

At that moment, a man burst out of a doorway at the end of the corridor. He seemed to be wrestling with a hosepipe, which writhed and thrashed in his grasp. A jet of water spurted violently from between his hands.

'Thake!' cried Grier. 'Thake!' He bounded forward as Thake disappeared round a corner. 'Have a look about, Monty,' he cried over his shoulder. 'I'll be upstairs with Thake if you need me.'

Monty opened the door marked *Gentlemen's Steam Cabinets*. Inside, half a dozen wooden boxes were lined up against the wall like miniature wardrobes. Each had a hole cut in the top, designed to allow the head of the beneficiary to poke out while the rest of his body was gently poached. All but one stood with their doors open, as if to lure in the unwary. The cabinet with the closed doors released a seductive wraith of steam from a loose hinge. A towel folded over and again into a thick pad had been placed over the hole in the top. Was someone crouched within? Monty crept forward and knocked on the wooden top.

'Hello?' she said. 'Is anyone in there?' She was answered by a hiss of steam. Monty pressed her ear to the doors – she had no wish to throw them open and find a naked man curled up inside. But she could hear nothing, no breathing, no groan of protest, no moan of pleasure. Monty rapped harder now. 'Hello?' she cried. 'Hello?' She seized the handles and flung open the doors.

Inside was a metal casket. Monty stared at it, sniffing

curiously at the hot wet air. Using the towel she lifted the lid, to reveal a plump pair of trout lying side by side, as neat and brown as shoes. The air filled with a rich fishiness, so that Monty's stomach rumbled excitedly. She stared at the trout, glistening and succulent, reclining on their bed of parsley. And then, as there was nothing else to be done (apart from eating them) she replaced the lid and quietly closed the cabinet doors.

Outside in the corridor the air was unbearably hot. A trickle of sweat ran down her neck and her economically cut uniform cleaved to her body. Far off, she heard what sounded like the roar of a gigantic cistern emptying. The silence that followed was broken by a drip . . . drip . . . drip of water and behind this she could hear a faint hissing. But there was something else too, she was sure of it. There it was again! A groan – muffled and distant, but nonetheless definitely a groan. It had come from behind the door of the Ladies' Steam Room. Perhaps someone had fallen, had lost her balance in the moist and slippery heat, and was lying in pain, unable to speak, awaiting help . . .

As she opened the door, a wall of steam rolled forward to engulf her, so that she could only gasp, opening and closing her mouth, unable even to draw breath. Then, all at once, the steam parted, lifting as silently as a veil in a boudoir to reveal a pair of gleaming white buttocks, clenching and unclenching, rising and falling, moving rhythmically and purposefully and without pause . . . Monty had time only to register this, to see that these eager buttocks were caught between a pair of large, pink, moistly glinting thighs, before the steam descended once again.

5

Monty went upstairs to Dr Slack's rooms. Consultations were to begin at ten o'clock and she did not want to be late. Already a group had gathered in the doctor's hallway, and Monty recognised a number of faces from the pump room and the breakfast tables. A hand seized her arm as she passed and pulled her to a halt. 'Not the Scottish Douche,' whispered a frightened voice at her elbow. 'Tell Dr Slack.'

Inside, Dr Slack was slumped in his chair before the fire, his eyes closed.

'Good morning, Dr Slack,' said Monty briskly. 'The guests are waiting, are we ready to begin?'

The doctor grunted. 'The appliances are not working,' he muttered. 'Grier's just been in. He says the boiler's gone haywire. Thake's working on it, but he's no idea when everything will be back to normal.'

'Whatever "normal" might be,' murmured Monty.

'Ha!' cackled Dr Slack. 'You're fitting in nicely!'

'I suppose we'd better tell the guests. I'm sure there's something else they can do in the meantime –'

'Did you hear that confounded fellow in the night,' interrupted Dr Slack. 'He played his ghastly gramophone for hours. I'll be glad when he goes. I hardly got a wink of sleep, even with the plug in.'

'"When he goes"?' cried Monty. 'Goes where?'

'Oh, only to London. Captain Foxley is never away for long.'

'But I've not even met him,' said Monty urgently. She suddenly felt as though she had been wasting time. She must act, and act at once. 'I need to speak to him.'

'What on earth for?' said Dr Slack. 'I suppose the guests have been complaining about him again, haven't they? They always do. They don't like him a bit. Mind you, there's no point remonstrating with Foxley about it, he just denies everything. Besides, quite frankly they seem to enjoy swapping stories about him. If the fellow actually *did* leave they'd have nothing to talk about. They make half of it up, you know, so that it's hard to tell what's true. Last month, one of them said she had found him crouched in a corner of the Ladies' Recovery Room trying to look up her skirts. She upbraided him about it, but it turned out to be a pile of towels awaiting collection by the laundry maid. She was shouting at a pile of laundry!' Dr Slack rose up from his chair and took a fortifying swig from a glass of yellowish water on the mantelpiece. 'Good heavens, Nurse Montgomery,' he remarked, suddenly catching sight of Monty in the mirror that hung above the fireplace. 'You look dreadful.'

Monty followed the doctor's gaze. She did indeed look dreadful. Her cap was awry on her head, her hair limp and bedraggled. She had a surprised look on her face, as though still stunned by disembodied buttocks, shoving between anonymous thighs like a naked gardener wrestling with a reluctant wheelbarrow. She pulled her cap straight and smoothed her hair. 'And Captain Foxley stays, despite all this? I'm surprised Mr Blackwood doesn't have a word with him.'

'Oh, the guests approached Curran with a petition for the Captain's removal.' Dr Slack opened his medicine cabinet and slung his stethoscope round his neck. 'But Curran won't hear a word against the fellow.'

'Why?' asked Monty.

'The war.'

'Mr Curran knew Captain Foxley too?'

'At the front, yes. They served together, the Blackwoods and Foxley.'

'And now they're all here.'

'They have no one else,' said Dr Slack. 'And nowhere else to go.'

'There's a man in my bed.'

Monty felt a hand tugging at her arm. She looked down into the wrinkled face of a tiny lady of extreme age. Her hair was parted in the middle and looped over her ears in the style of sixty years earlier. Her face was so cobwebbed with lines and wrinkles that she seemed to be peering out from beneath a mask of lace. Monty recognised her from the pump room.

'Hello, Mrs Forbes,' she said.

'A man!' cried Mrs Forbes, her eyes watering between drooping lids. 'In my bed!'

'Who is it?' said Monty.

'Captain Foxley.'

Monty felt no surprise.

Mrs Forbes too seemed more excited than horrified.

'Is he asleep?'

'I have no idea,' said Mrs Forbes. 'I was not inclined to get too close to him.'

'Have you told anyone?' asked Monty.

'I told Dr Slack, but he thinks I'm making it up.'

Grier emerged from the doorway to the treatment rooms. 'Hello, Monty,' he said. 'Hello, Mrs Forbes. That's the adjustable douche fixed, you'll be delighted to hear. Thake and Ada are putting her in position right now –'

At that moment there was a scream, fearful and echoing, as though someone had been pushed from a great height. Silence followed – a brief yawning chasm of quiet – which was shattered by the sound of violently smashing glass.

Grier turned pale. The old lady gasped and squeezed Monty's arm tighter. 'It's him!' she whispered. 'Upstairs in my room. What shall we do?'

'Good Lord,' said Grier. 'In your room? Who?'

'Captain Foxley,' said Monty. 'I was about to go up.'

'I'll come with you,' said Grier. 'Mrs Forbes,' he added brightly. 'Why not join the ladies in the garden for a cup of camomile tea? Ada tells me there's Arrowroot biscuits too!'

Upstairs, on the second floor, the corridor was cold and dark. A draught seemed to be blowing along it, as though from an open window, though it did not remove the smell of damp soil and mushrooms. Here and there electric lights glowed, each one illuminating a dim circle of threadbare carpet. As Monty and Grier hurried along, the bulbs flickered a troubled Morse code of loose connections. Beneath their feet the carpet was worn to a greasy patina, as though a hundred pairs of boots had once marched along it, though there was little to suggest that many people traversed it now. They stopped outside a door.

'The poor fellow probably mistook this room for his own,' said Grier. 'It's easily done, I suppose, as all the doors look the same.'

'Where is Captain Foxley's room?'

'In the tower.'

'How can one mistake upstairs for the tower?' demanded Monty. 'We should remind Captain Foxley where his room is and take him there ourselves.' She knocked smartly on the door and turned the handle. 'It's locked. D'you have a key?'

'No,' said Grier.

Was it Monty's imagination, or did Grier look faintly relieved? 'Well, perhaps you might get one,' she said. 'I assume there's one behind the reception desk?'

Grier disappeared down the stairs. Once he had left she felt alone and wished she had gone with him. The smell of the place seemed horrible and tomb-like, and the flickering lights made the shadows jump alarmingly. Monty tried the door handle again. 'Captain Foxley,' she cried. 'Open the door.' She rattled fiercely and battered on the wooden panels. Where on earth was Grier? Monty pressed her ear to the door. Could she hear breathing within? Perhaps it was just the ever-present draught. Yet she was sure that was the creak of a bed, the shuffle of a footstep. She pressed her eye to the keyhole. A stream of smoky air tickled her eyeball. All at once, on the other side of the keyhole appeared an eye, blue and staring and looking straight into hers. The sight was so brief, so fleeting, that in the blink of her own smarting eye it was gone. Had she really seen it? 'Captain Foxley,' she said, her lips to the keyhole. 'Open up.'

A hand tapped her on the shoulder and Monty could not stifle a cry as she jumped away from the door.

'Is he in there?' hissed Dr Slack. He looked excited.

'Yes,' said Monty. 'I mean, I think he is. The door is locked, but I saw an eye at the keyhole.'

'An eye! Are you sure?'

'Yes,' said Monty, though she was no longer sure of anything. She bent down and peered through the keyhole once more, but it was too dark to see what might be inside. She felt slightly foolish. 'I'm certain he's in there,' she said. And then, in exasperation, 'Where *has* Mr Blackwood got to?'

'Talking to that fellow from the Crossed Keys,' said Dr Slack. 'He owes the chap money.'

'Put your shoulder to the door, Dr Slack,' cried an excited voice. It was Mrs Forbes. Behind her, a group of guests had assembled.

Monty spotted Grier standing at the back. She gave him a cross look. How had this simple undertaking become such a public event? 'Do you have the key?' she asked.

'No,' said Grier. He was fiddling with an envelope. 'I couldn't find it.'

'Use mine.' Mrs Forbes produced a key from her purse, a large pouch of rouched silk that she wore on a chain round her wrist.

Monty fitted the key into the lock and pushed open the door. The crowd surged forward and over the threshold.

'Order!' roared Dr Slack. He followed them inside.

Within, the curtains were drawn close across the windows, so that the chamber was as dark as a glove. The air was thick with the smell of whisky and cigarettes, and Monty could see that the bed was unmade, as though its occupant had recently, and hastily, left it.

'Search the room,' cried Mrs Forbes.

'I'm sure that won't be necessary,' said Grier, though he crouched down and looked beneath the bed. At Mrs Forbes's insistence he flung open the wardrobe doors and wrenched aside the maroon velvet curtains. Behind the curtains, the casement had been thrown wide, as though someone had burst through it only moments before.

'He would surely have plunged directly to his death!' cried a voice.

Everyone rushed forward to the window ledge to look out at the body of Captain Foxley, which was sure to be lying, broken and twisted, on the balustrade of the terrace far below. There was no one there. Had he somehow managed to climb down the wall and run off across the lawn? Had he slithered down the drainpipe like a cat burglar, or swung like a monkey to the ground on a length of ivy? Certainly there was a shattered whisky bottle down there. Perhaps he had followed it on to the flagstones, then risen up, Lazarus-like, and simply walked away?

'The fellow is unstoppable,' cried Mrs Forbes. 'He has nine lives!'

'He's got more than that,' muttered Grier.

Only Monty, standing beside the bed, saw the shadow of a man emerge from behind the dressing mirror and slip into the corridor.

6

Monty found Ada in the yard, rummaging beneath the bonnet of the Audi. Around her feet a great array of spanners and sockets, coils of wire and bits of metal were spread like the bones of a mechanical beast. A large patch of oil had stained the cobbles.

'Hello, Ada.' Monty placed a tray on the edge of a redundant water trough. 'I've brought you a cup of tea.'

Ada's face was smeared with grease, her fingers black with oil. 'It's a long time since anyone made *me* a cup of tea,' she said. 'In fact, I think the last person was you. Out at Furnes. It tasted of petrol, d'you remember? The tea always tasted of petrol.'

'I can't guarantee that this one will taste any different,' said Monty. 'The water here is horrible. Have you fixed the motor?'

'Yes.' Ada patted the car's gleaming brass headlamp. 'She's a beauty, isn't she? Mr Curran bought her before the war. She's fast as lightning.'

'Six cylinder?' guessed Monty.

'No! Four, of course. But she can go at sixty miles an hour when she's flat out. At least, she used to. Two spark plugs per cylinder, you see.'

'Goodness,' said Monty.

'The German army lorries were Audis,' said Ada, sipping her tea. 'Some of them, anyway. Much better than that old Napier we used to drive.' She grinned. 'D'you want to see what she's like?'

'Are you permitted to take the car?' asked Monty, surprised.

'As long as no one wants it for anything,' said Ada. 'And as long as no one wants *me* for anything. Besides, I have to see that she's fixed, don't I? And it'll give us a chance to talk. You could tell me what you're doing here.' She looked at Monty. 'And what you want with Captain Foxley.'

Monty was gazing up at the towering edifice of the Bleakly Hall Hydropathic. An iron ladder ascended the side of the building, affixed there for maintenance purposes when the hydro was built. High above, climbing steadily, Monty recognised the tall and angular figure of Thake. On his back he carried a haversack. Sticking out of it was what looked like (but which surely could not possibly be) a fishing rod.

'Yes, Ada,' she said, suddenly realising how glad she would be to be driving away from this strange place, even for a while. 'Why not? And you can tell me all about Grier Blackwood and his brother.'

Above them, a window opened. 'You there!' cried a voice. 'Down there by the motor. Take me to the station, will you?'

Monty looked up. A woman was leaning out of a first-floor window. She was young and slim, and wore her hair in a fashionable blonde shingle. Even with the sunlight shining in her eyes, Monty could see that the woman's lips were painted with crimson, the brows drawn on to her face in surprised arcs of brown pencil. 'I'll be down in a few minutes,' the woman called. 'Ada, come and get my bags. Tell your friend to collect Captain Foxley's. We're travelling together.'

7

O<small>N HIS</small> return to Bleakly after the war, Curran
Blackwood had installed himself in a suite of rooms
on the ground floor of the hydropathic. Generally, Grier
avoided this domain, preferring instead the open space and
lofty ceiling of the foyer. Now, as he entered Curran's
burrow-like office, he wished he had spent a few extra
minutes out in the comparative brightness of the vestibule.

Curran was seated at his desk. He had an account book
open before him and his gold-tipped fountain pen in his
hand. 'I've received a telegram,' he said without turning
round.

'I see.' Grier sidled into the room and sank into a chair.

'Yes, from London.'

'Oh?'

'A woman,' said Curran.

'What did she want?'

'Can't you guess?'

'A room?' Grier slid a hand into his pocket, reaching for
the cigarette he knew he wouldn't be allowed to smoke.

Why did Curran always have to make such a game of it? Could he not just get to the point straight away?

'Yes,' replied Curran, 'as a matter of fact she did require a room.' His voice had taken on a tight, irritated tone. 'I think you know who she is.'

'Do I?'

Curran emerged from behind his desk. A wet patch from the drippings of the adjustable douche squelched beneath his wheels. 'A Miss Jenkins. From a certain ladies' magazine.'

'Ah, yes,' said Grier. He pulled out a letter from his pocket. He had picked it up from the post office more than a week earlier and had been waiting for an opportune moment to confess to his brother. That moment, somehow, had never arrived. 'She's from *Woman's Weekly*. She wrote to me a few days ago. I didn't expect we'd hear from her so soon. She's writing a piece about –'

'"The modern young lady who deserves to have fun", yes, I know. What on earth possessed you? Do you think this is a place for modern young ladies? Do you think people come here to have *fun*? Half of them are here in the first place because they've had too much fun. They come here to rest and recuperate, not for entertainment and the gratification of their own pleasures –'

'Well, perhaps they should,' interrupted Grier. How he hated these fruitless arguments. He hardly had the energy to bother replying, though, like a geriatric gun dog watching a mallard plummet into a reed bed, he felt a dim, innate obligation to pursue the matter to its inevitable conclusion. 'Perhaps they *should* be coming here for pleasure and entertainment. There's no reason why people can't take the waters *and* enjoy themselves, too. The Pavilion in the village used to hold dances – before the war – have you forgotten? And we could easily hold one here too. In the gymnasium. Besides, there are a lot of young women about these days. It might be just what we need.'

'What we need is for people to pay their bills on time,' said Curran. 'There's nothing here for these so-called *young women*. Young women want to meet *young men*. They want to drink and dance and stay up late. Most of them don't even remember Asquith, you know. Do you want to drive away our existing patrons?'

Grier shrugged. Secretly he thought it wasn't such a bad idea. Before the war all sorts of people had come to Bleakly Hall. Now hardly anyone bothered to make the journey. Apart from Nurse Montgomery, of course. Grier congratulated himself on having engaged such an attractive and assertive young woman to act as resident nurse. She was clearly more experienced than the job required and seemed a little officious at times, but, well, he found he quite liked it when she told him what to do. It reminded him of when he had been wounded and had been obliged to lie still while the nurses flitted about his bed, instructing him when to sit up or lie down, when to eat or drink, when to sleep or wake.

'But you might enjoy meeting some young ladies,' he said, determined, for once, not to be put off.

'I meet young ladies already,' said Curran.

'What young ladies do you meet?' asked Grier, surprised.

'Well . . . there's Ada.'

'Ada?'

'And some of the elderly patrons bring their nieces.'

Grier conceded this fact with a nod of his head, though the nieces had been rather thin on the ground recently and getting noticeably older.

'Besides,' said Curran, 'why are we even talking about this? I don't need to meet young ladies; I've got a wife, remember?'

'So what?' muttered Grier. Not long after their return to Bleakly, just as the army doctors were packing up to leave, Grier had come across Curran's wife in the hydropathic's Ornamental Wilderness. She was on her back, sprawled among the couch grass behind a gorse bush. Her head was thrown back, her blouse undone, her tumbled breasts pointing to the sky. Her skirt had been pushed up so that it was twisted round her waist and the tousled head of a young lieutenant was buried between her thighs.

Some weeks later, Mae had appeared at the door to Grier's room. She told him that Curran was no longer a husband to her; no longer a man in any useful sense; that it pained her to say it, but his physical incompleteness repelled her and she could not bear to be near him. She stood close to Grier and wept. She begged him to understand. She cursed the war and asked him to put his arms round her and comfort her like a brother. He did so cautiously; patting her shoulder in what he hoped was a reassuring way and offering her his handkerchief. After a moment or two of sobbing on to his shirt front and clinging to his chest, Mae took his hand and quickly slid it into her suddenly undone blouse. Grier had a brief, fleeting sensation of something warm and heavily fleshy resting in his hand, before he leaped away from her. She laughed at him then, brazenly stowing her rejected breast back out of sight, and said he was no more of a man than his brother.

Shortly after that, Captain Foxley had arrived.

Grier picked absently at a snagged thread on the arm of the chair. Was the interview over? He was gasping for a cigarette. 'The lady from *Woman's Weekly*, Miss Jenkins –' he began.

'I told her not to bother coming.'

'I see.' Grier stood up. He would reply to her telegram himself. 'Well, it appears that there's little more to be said.'

'Indeed.' Curran moved his wheelchair forward, effectively blocking his brother's exit. He looked up expectantly. His black humour seemed to have evaporated. 'So what do you think of her?'

'What do I think of whom?'

'Nurse Montgomery, of course! Do you think her hair is too short? And she seems a caring sort of person. She must be, to be a nurse, don't you think?'

'What? No. No, I don't think so. About her hair, I mean.' Grier shrugged. 'I don't know what I think of her,' he said, unable to conjure up anything advantageous to say. 'She's only been here a day.'

Curran lowered his voice to a whisper. 'Her eyes are quite marvellous! Did you notice? I didn't notice myself at first, but they are. She looked directly at me, you know. Not at my legs. Mae always looks at my legs. That's when she looks at me at all.' Curran's face brightened again at a new thought. 'Do you think she might have tea with me?

Mae can hardly object, can she? Not to me having tea with a nurse? We might discuss my health problems.'

Grier stepped neatly past his brother and walked out into the dappled shade of the vestibule.

Ada was struggling across the foyer with a large Gladstone bag in each hand.

'Are you leaving us?' said Grier, smiling.

Ada threw him a look of disgust and continued dragging the bags towards the door. Once there, she looked about, then shoved the bags down the steps so that they rolled over and over. 'They're Mrs Blackwood's,' she said over her shoulder. 'She's off to London.'

'Again?'

'Yes.' Ada scowled. 'With Captain Foxley. Miss Montgomery's gone up to get his bag.'

Grier felt a flush of alarm wash over him. He stared at Ada gloomily and abandoned himself to the worst kind of imaginings: Monty foxtrotting down the hallway in Foxley's arms; Monty looking in the envelope he had given to Dr Slack and shaking her head in disapproval . . . All at once he found that he very much wanted her good opinion. After all, he thought, someone had to think well of him.

Grier went outside. Ada was ramming Mae's bags into the back of the Audi.

'Shall I drive, Ada?' he said.

'I can manage, thank you, sir.' She walked round to throw open the bonnet. Grier peeped over her shoulder and stared inside with perplexity. He had no idea how the thing worked, he only knew when it did and when it did not. Of course, he said to himself, there was no need for a man of his class to understand the workings of a motor-car engine. Nonetheless, as Ada vigorously cranked the car into life, he felt strangely redundant.

Behind him, he heard the sound of female footsteps and turned to see Mae standing in the doorway. She was looking puffy-eyed and angry.

'Hello, Mae,' said Grier. He found he didn't want to look at her and turned back to stare at Ada, who had got into the car and was making its engine roar manfully.

'Grier?' Mae folded her arms.

'Can it wait? I'm helping Ada –'

'There's no water coming out of my taps,' said Mae. 'I wanted a bath this morning but the taps don't work. What sort of a place *is* this these days?'

'There's a bathroom further down the hall from you,' said Grier, knowing full well that Mae was quite aware of this fact. 'I'm sure its taps are fine; you could use that one.'

'I want to use my own bath,' snapped Mae. 'Can't you fix it?'

'I'll get Thake.'

'Thake'll take for ever. I want you to do it.' She pushed her pale hair out of her eyes. 'You look like a waxwork,' she added, staring at his shining boots and smartly pressed jacket. She gave a sharp laugh. 'What's the matter, don't you want to get your hands dirty?'

'Not particularly,' murmured Grier. How unkind she could be. He looked down the crease of his trousers to the toes of his boots. He dusted an imaginary nimbus of dust off his sleeve. A waxwork? No doubt it was simply Mae being cross. She only seemed happy when she was complaining about something. She had that in common with Curran, at least.

Mae came to stand beside him. 'There's a damp patch on the ceiling too,' she added temptingly. 'If you come inside I'll show you what I mean. Ada can wait, can't she?'

Grier looked at Mae warily. The damp patches were appearing everywhere, he knew. But he had often been caught out by Mae. She seemed to enjoy asking him into her rooms, claiming a dripping tap or a seeping shower head needed his immediate evaluation. Once they were alone she would allow secret parts of her body to slip into view – a glimpse of thigh, a stocking top, the strap of a brassiere. Once an entire breast had bobbed into sight.

'Come along,' said Mae. She stretched out an arm, long and white against the green silk of her dress, so that Grier was reminded of a snake emerging from a patch of undergrowth.

'I'll get Thake to look at it,' he muttered, turning away from her. 'I'll have it fixed while you're away in town.'

Mae laughed, 'You're such a coward, Grier. Tell Curran I've gone, will you?'

'Tell him yourself,' said Grier. He looked up at the building. The windows of Captain Foxley's rooms looked blankly over the gravel and the lawn. Was Monty still up there? It was impossible to see whether the curtains were open or closed, whether anyone was inside or not. Perhaps he should go up and offer to help with the bags.

All at once, the window he was staring at exploded from within in a hail of glass fragments. Grier cried out, and sprang backwards, kicking Mae's shin with his heel and knocking her clumsily against the car. He heard a woman scream, though realised almost immediately (and with some relief) that it was only Mae. He saw a string of red droplets splatter on to the windscreen; he saw glass tumbling downwards, flashing like knives in the sunlight as it cascaded on to the gravel with a splintering crash. Above, high up in the tower, a face appeared, peering out of a large star-shaped hole in the centre of the windowpane. It was a startled face, with a great welt of red oozing against the temple. And then, just as suddenly as it had appeared, it was gone.

8

CAPTAIN FOXLEY, Monty saw, was handsome but in an unremarkable sort of way. She was surprised and realised that over time, in her imagination, he had assumed unreal, almost mythical good looks. Instead, what she saw was a slim man dressed in ordinary shirtsleeves and tie, with an upright posture that made the most of his average height. His left shoulder seemed slightly lower than his right, as though depressed beneath the weight of an invisible burden. He had blue eyes and blond hair that fell in a thick fringe over his forehead so that he flicked his head, like a man with a muscular tick, over and again to shake it out of the way. He was clean-shaven apart from his top lip, which was decorated with a thin, military-style moustache, the width and colour of a sliver of onion skin. He looked Monty up and down lazily before he held out his hand in greeting.

'Hello,' he said. 'Fancy seeing a nurse up here. Did Curran send you? How thoughtful, though I'm feeling quite well at the moment. Come in, come in. Dr Slack is already here. I must be very sick to find both our medical professionals knocking at my door this afternoon. Have you come to tell me that I've only months to live? I must be sure to make the most of it.'

Captain Foxley pushed his hair out of his eyes once again. He *was* handsome, as Sophia had always said, with symmetrical features and an angular face. Monty looked at him closely. Yet there was something odd about his gaze, some subtle flaw in his apparent good looks ... was one pupil bigger than the other? But then the sun shone through the cupola and he was turning away, so that she could not be sure if she had seen anything amiss at all.

Captain Foxley gave her a dazzling smile. 'Don't you speak?'

'Of course I do,' said Monty. She pulled her hand from his.

'I think we're going to be friends, you and I,' he said easily.

'I see no reason for that,' said Monty. 'You know nothing about me.'

'But I'd like to. And I imagine you know a few things about me.' He opened the door further. 'Won't you come in? I have some tea in the pot. I'm sure I can find another cup.'

Captain Foxley closed the door behind her. His footsteps were as silent as a cat's, muffled by the thick pile of a Turkish carpet. The curtains were thrown back, allowing the sunlight to stream in, and a fire glowed in the grate. Monty noticed a tea plate, a slice of bread and a toasting fork abandoned on the hearth. A jar of strawberry jam stood on the mantelpiece, a single inquisitive bee buzzing noisily back and forth above it. Dr Slack was lowering himself into an armchair. His laboured breathing suggested that he had only just arrived. A white envelope flapped in his hand.

'Come along in,' Captain Foxley was saying. 'Will you have some tea? And you, Dr Slack? Perhaps something a little stronger for you? A brandy?'

Dr Slack's face turned pink with excitement. 'Brandy!' He gave a quick, eager nod.

Monty noticed that Captain Foxley walked with a limp and that beside the fireplace there stood a silver-handled walking stick. The Captain disappeared through another door and Monty heard the sounds of teacups rattling on to saucers.

'What are you doing up here?' whispered Monty.

'Grier asked me to bring this,' replied Dr Slack, waving the envelope. 'He usually sends Ada, but she's off in the motor.' He smiled. 'Foxley always puts a dash of something in my tea. I'd not come up here otherwise, you know!'

Captain Foxley reappeared carrying a tray, upon which there were two cups, a bottle of brandy and a large fruit cake.

'Armagnac, I'm afraid.' He set the tray down on a table beside Dr Slack. 'Might as well put it into your tea, if you can't get the good stuff, eh, doctor? What about you, Miss Montgomery, will you have a splash?'

'I've come to take your bags down to the car,' said Monty. 'I understand you're travelling to London with Mrs Blackwood.'

'Good heavens, can't Thake do that?' said Captain Foxley. 'Don't tell me Grier's got you lugging baggage about the place? Come, have some brandy. There's plenty of time.'

'Just tea, thank you.'

'Cake? It's a Dundee cake, my favourite kind. Ada brought it up from the bakery in the village.'

Monty shook her head. 'No, thank you.'

'Yes, please,' said Dr Slack.

Captain Foxley took neither tea, nor brandy, nor cake, but stood beside the fireplace, watching his guests. Due to a lack of alternatives, Monty was sitting on a low-sprung velvet settee, opposite the doctor. She was glad that Captain Foxley chose to stand, as she could not see that there was anywhere for him to sit, apart from beside her. The fabric of the settee was smooth beneath her fingers, as silky as warm flesh, and she wished she could stand up, to get away from it.

'And so, are you enjoying Bleakly Hall, Miss Montgomery?' He offered her a cigarette (which she refused), before putting one between his own lips.

'I've only been here since yesterday,' said Monty, trying and failing in the bright sunlight to see where his gaze was resting. She didn't bother to ask how it was that he knew her name.

'Of course, of course,' he said. 'Hardly time to get to know the place at all, really, and it takes some getting used to, let me tell you. The plumbing's a law unto itself, though you've probably realised that by now.' As if in response to this criticism, a furious knocking started up behind the wall. Captain Foxley limped over to the sink that stood in a far corner of the room and turned on the taps, filling the basin with a swirl of steaming water. When he turned the taps off the noise was gone. 'Works every time,' he said. 'I've no idea why. Mind you, that bombardment we heard this morning was a different matter altogether ... Ouch!' He stopped, halfway back to his station beside the fireplace, wincing painfully and rubbing his thigh.

Monty rose to her feet and went over to help. Captain Foxley put a hand on her shoulder. Monty could feel the warmth of his touch through the cheap serge of her dress. His thigh brushed against hers as they shuffled across the room together, and she could sense his gaze lingering hungrily on her neck and cheek.

'Thank you,' he said. 'You're very kind.' His voice was as close as a lover's in her ear. 'It's not too bad, most of the time, and then all of a sudden –'

But Monty had assisted many limping men during recent years and she propelled Captain Foxley forward briskly, as though manhandling an awkward mannequin into a shop window. She dropped him like a bag of laundry on to the velvet settee. 'You should stay off your feet when it hurts,' she snapped. 'Never mind who's visiting, or what the plumbing's up to.'

'Do you think you might call me Peter?'

'Why?' said Monty. 'I don't know you at all. Besides, you're one of the guests. It would be inappropriate.'

'One of the guests,' murmured Captain Foxley. 'Yes, I suppose I am.' He smiled. 'Will you sit down again?' He patted the cushion beside him. 'I don't think you finished your tea.'

'No, thank you.'

'Are you always so prim and proper, nurse?' Captain Foxley put his hands behind his head and grinned up at her. 'I do like nurses, you know. They're always so pretty in their starched uniforms and delightful little caps. And so obliging to a chap, too! Are you sure you won't take a seat?'

'I'd rather stand,' said Monty. How hot she was becoming! She looked at Dr Slack. Surely it was time to go? The warmth of the room had made her head ache. But, as she feared, Dr Slack had fallen asleep. His empty plate had slipped down the side of the chair and only a faint constellation of crumbs on his shirt front told of his recent indulgence.

'Oh, there's no use looking at him,' said Captain Foxley. He glanced at the sleeping doctor, his gaze resting on the envelope that lay on the arm of the chair. 'That's for me, I think. From Grier?'

'Yes,' said Monty, though she did not pass the envelope over. She clenched her fists, her resolve momentarily weakening. Should she say something? Should she mention Sophia's name, just to see the look on his face?

'Why don't you put the gramophone on?' said Captain Foxley. 'I've got a marvellous collection. Put on something that you like.'

Monty shrugged. 'I really know very little about music,' she said. 'We should go down. Mrs Blackwood will be waiting.'

'Never mind Mrs Blackwood,' he said. 'She can quite easily go without me. Besides, we can always get a later train. I'm in no hurry. Just put a record on, while I pack a few things.'

'What do you want to listen to?' said Monty, suspecting that the longer they talked about it the longer it would take.

'Anything. Something slow, perhaps; after all, we don't want to disturb the doctor, do we? Perhaps we could dance? I think I'd like that. You might like it too.'

'Certainly not,' cried Monty. 'Why on earth would I want to do such a thing as dance with *you*? What on earth do we have to dance about?'

Captain Foxley looked taken aback. 'Goodness me,' he said. 'You're a hot-tempered little thing, aren't you?'

'I'm not a "little thing",' said Monty.

'But you are hot-tempered. Passionate, one might say. It's nice to meet a woman who presents a challenge. But you do sound a bit cross.' He adopted a look of disappointment. 'What's the matter, don't you like me?'

'No,' said Monty. 'I don't like you at all.'

'But you hardly know me. You might find you like me very much, if you just relaxed a little.'

'I am relaxed,' cried Monty. She had intended to stay calm, to observe and evaluate him, but she seemed unable to keep her feelings hidden. Worse still, he appeared to be laughing at her hostility, as though she were an ingénue who did not know how to govern her emotions in the presence of a man.

'No, you're not,' he said. 'But perhaps a dance might help you to calm down.'

Monty began to wind the gramophone. 'If your leg is still painful you'd be better off resting it,' she said. A tune began mournfully to play. Monty turned to find that Captain Foxley was standing right behind her. And then, before she could say anything, before she could step aside or even shake her head, he had taken hold of her and was marching her across the room in a slow foxtrot.

'There we are,' he cried, guiding her past the mantelpiece with confident steps. 'That feels so much better already.' He lowered his voice. 'Can't you feel it too, Miss Montgomery?' He smiled. For a moment his parted lips were inches from hers, his hand tight against her lower back . . .

'Get away from me!' As Monty pushed him away a fearful anger rose up within her, making her skin prickle, her blood turn scalding hot beneath her skin. She wanted to strike him, to slap his face until his smile of lustful amusement was out of her sight and wiped from her mind. She shoved him across the room, as hard as she could. Captain Foxley stumbled and pitched against the doctor's chair. The doctor grunted. His plate fell to the floor and rolled beneath the table like a wheel, but he did not wake up. 'Don't you dare put your hands on me,' shouted Monty. 'Don't even come near me.'

Captain Foxley stared at her. 'My!' he said. He sounded amused. 'You're a fiery one!'

Monty grabbed a cigarette case from the mantelpiece and flung it at his head.

Captain Foxley ducked, so that the cigarette case landed with a muffled thump among the curtains' crushed-velvet folds. 'Steady on,' he said. 'Umpire!' He began to laugh. How infuriating he was! Monty seized a pack of cards and a candlestick, and threw them at him, one after the other. The music played on; the curtain swayed and danced under its bombardment of missiles. By now the Captain was laughing uproariously. 'You're not much of a shot!'

Monty hurled a box of chess pieces (which opened in midair in a rattling explosion of black and white). She felt the absurdity of her actions, felt tears sting her eyes at her own ridiculous behaviour, but she could not stop. If she could just smack that grin off his face . . . Her fingers, searching along the mantelpiece, curled round a cold heavy object. It fitted comfortably in her hand and she gripped its smooth sides with ease. She drew back her arm as if she were about to throw a grenade, her eyes fixed upon her target, and hurled it at the Captain's laughing face.

9

CAPTAIN FOXLEY staggered to the window, half blinded by the sticky crimson ooze of strawberry jam that had splattered on to his face. It had also spattered the wall and floor, and a great red gobbet of the stuff clung to the curtain. A draught of cold air blasted in through the shattered window, cooling Monty's burning cheeks. She sprang forward. 'Are you hurt?' Her anger drained away immediately to be replaced by embarrassment (though she could not quite bring herself to apologise).

Captain Foxley backed away from her and put a hand up to his face to wipe jam from his eye. 'No,' he said. 'At least, I don't think so. It seems I got through Ypres with hardly a scratch, only to be almost blinded in my own rooms by a woman with a jam jar. Do you always throw preserves at your patients, Miss Montgomery?'

Monty passed him her handkerchief. She could think of nothing to say. She slid a glance in the direction of Dr Slack, who was sitting upright in his chair with his eyes wide, as though jolted awake by a troubling dream. He turned his head slowly to look at Captain Foxley.

'Good God!' he cried. He gripped the arms of his chair. 'Your eye's out!'

'It's nothing,' said Captain Foxley. 'Just jam.'

'And the window?'

'An accident. Nurse Montgomery, there's a towel over by the sink there, if you would be so kind? Thank you.' He wiped his face, peeping at Monty playfully over the edge of the towel. 'I suppose I'd better change my shirt and go to London,' he said. 'To give Thake a chance to mend the window, and Ada time to wash the curtains, and you the opportunity to calm down.'

The door burst open and Grier stormed in. 'What's happened?' he cried. He stared at the scattered chess pieces, the candlestick rolling on the floor against the curtains, the cigarettes strewn across the carpet. 'Monty, are you hurt?' He came towards her, his expression a mixture of alarm and anxiety. 'Did Foxley try to –'

'No,' said Monty. She coloured. 'It was my fault.'

'Not at all. I can be quite provoking and Miss Montgomery simply sought to teach me a lesson.' Captain Foxley gathered up the cigarettes and the silver case from which they had spilled. He lowered himself on to the settee. 'You seem very concerned,' he said, looking up at Grier through a haze of cigarette smoke.

'I know what you're like,' muttered Grier.

'Oh, do you? And does Miss Montgomery know what *you're* like? Has he told you about himself,

Miss Montgomery? He has some very bad habits, you know.'

Monty gave Captain Foxley a blank look. What on earth was he talking about? She glanced at Grier and was surprised to see that his face had turned scarlet.

Captain Foxley smiled at Grier's apparent discomfiture. 'Come, come, old fellow. No need to look so embarrassed. These things are bound to come out sooner or later, aren't they?'

'Really, Captain Foxley,' said Monty, exasperated into speaking. 'I've no idea what you're talking about.'

'Perhaps you should ask your employer. *He* knows what I'm talking about. Why don't you ask him what's inside that envelope he sent up with Dr Slack? Or why he hasn't the courage to give it to me himself?'

Ada was waiting behind the wheel of the car. Mae had gone to her rooms to change. A splash of jam had landed on her green dress, plopping on to the fabric directly over her heart and staining the silk like a bullet wound. She was furious with Grier for kicking her: not only were her new stockings torn but a bruise had risen up in the middle of her shin. By the time she reappeared, they were late for the train.

'You'll have to drive as fast as you can, Ada,' she snapped. 'Come on, Grier, are you getting in or not?' Grier was lingering at the foot of the steps. He seemed unsure whether to remain at the Hall and supervise the boarding up of the Captain's window, or to come down to the station. Monty noticed him staring at Mae's painted mouth, which was irritably telling him that she had forgotten to inform Curran of her departure and that he had better do it. Grier turned away in disgust.

'Come on!' shouted Mae. 'Drive, Ada!'

Monty watched Grier over her shoulder as they pulled away. Engulfed in a swirl of exhaust fumes, he raised a hand in farewell.

'Grier's looking rather hangdog these days,' said Mae. 'What have you two been up to? Why can't you leave him alone?'

'What do you care?' said Foxley. 'Besides, I do leave him alone. It's he who comes to me.' He smiled at Mae and caught Monty's eye. 'Everyone comes to me, for one reason or another.'

'Well, you're welcome to each other. And Curran too, for that matter.' Mae clicked her tongue. 'Can't you go any faster, Ada?'

Monty, who was sitting beside Ada, was jerked forward as Ada stamped on the accelerator. The Audi's engine roared and the car bounded forward. They hit a pothole, and the vehicle seemed to leap into the air. Ada grappled with the steering wheel as the car plunged down the hill towards the village. In the back Mae was thrown across the seat and into Captain Foxley's lap. She cried out, her hands scrabbling to grip on to something. Ada wrenched at the wheel as the car tore round another corner. It skidded in the dirt, careering through the village in a cloud of dust and smoke, swerving to miss the bandsmen who were crossing the square to mount the bandstand. Monty saw the sun glinting off trumpets and tubas, then they were gone.

In the back, Captain Foxley laughed and clapped his hands. 'Bravo, Ada,' he cried. 'Not a man down, not a scratch on 'em!'

In the front, Monty had braced her foot against the dash board. She had driven with Ada many times during the war and she was perturbed neither by the speed, nor the violence of the journey. Only Mae, flung from side to side like a rag doll in a tombola, wailed and cried out.

But Ada, it seemed, was unable to hear over the bellow of the engine. She braked, swerving to avoid another pothole, then accelerated down the hill. They could see the station ahead, see the smoke rising from the funnel of the train and the guard standing on the edge of the platform.

'I tell you what, Ada,' cried Captain Foxley, who had a cigarette between his teeth and had managed to light it even as the car hurtled round the final bend. 'If we miss the train you could probably drive to London and get there before it!' He laughed. 'A few shells going off here and there, and it'd be just like being at the front!'

Monty glanced back at him in surprise. How delighted he looked! His face was radiant, lit from within, so that his habitual expression of cynical boredom was quite dissolved.

Ada, Monty noticed, did not look displeased. Her cheeks had turned red with satisfaction, though whether this was due to Captain Foxley's compliments, to the thrill of the journey, or to the fact that Mae Blackwood was now in tears on the floor of the car she had no idea.

'You were rather cruel to Mrs Blackwood,' said Monty, as they drove steadily back.

'No, I wasn't,' muttered Ada. 'She deserves it.'

'I think she had a black eye.'

'If she did, that's no more than she deserves too. They say she's got a lover in London, that's why she's always going down. I wish she'd stay there and leave us alone. No one likes her at Bleakly. Mr Curran would be better off without her.' Ada blared the horn at a dog that had dared to wander into the road. 'She's a vain and useless creature.'

'She seems to be a friend for Captain Foxley, at least.'

'He don't want her either. He told me so himself.'

'What's he like?' asked Monty.

'Most people don't like him,' said Ada. 'Most of the guests, I mean. But him and me, we get along very well – mostly. It's been a comfort to me, having Captain Foxley at Bleakly. At least' – her lip trembled – 'it *was*.' She clutched the wheel tightly, her eyes staring out blindly at the road ahead. Was she crying? Perhaps it was simply the dust thrown up by the wheels that was making her eyes stream. 'Captain Foxley's a hero,' shouted Ada above the noise of the engine. 'What he did during the war. Not that anyone's interested in *that*.'

'Is something the matter?' said Monty.

'No.'

'Yes, there is,' said Monty. 'Why don't we take this old motor for a proper spin and you can tell me what it is?'

Ada took a deep breath, but said nothing. The houses of Bleakly flashed past, blossom from the cherry trees in the village square whirling into the car like butterflies.

'Come on, old girl.' Monty put her hand on Ada's arm. 'We had some adventures, didn't we? And we looked after

74

each other. Nothing's so bad that we can't sort it out between us.'

'Oh, don't worry about me, miss,' said Ada. 'Anyways, why are you so interested in Captain Foxley?' This time she spat out his name like bile. 'It was almost the first thing you asked me when you arrived.'

'Oh, we had a mutual friend during the war,' said Monty. She glanced at Ada warily. 'I wanted to tell him that she was dead.' Suddenly Monty found that she did not want to share Sophia's story with Ada. She had known Ada in Belgium, but that had been long before she had met Sophia. She had respected and admired Ada, but she had not loved her the way she had loved Sophia. She found she could not possibly explain her situation, not now. 'My friend died quite horribly,' she added instead. 'I wanted to tell him that too.'

◆

Monty had offered her services as a nurse the moment hostilities had broken out.

She was sent to Belgium and spent some time in Ghent, where the trains came in filled with casualties from the German advance. There were nurses everywhere, as though all women thus qualified had poured into Belgium to act as ministering angels to the heroic wounded. An air of excitement mingled with fear hung over the hospital – which had been set up in the grand Hotel Royale – as palpably as the stench of gangrene was to pervade it in the months to come. Incompetence and inactivity prevailed, barely disguised by urgency or experience. Military supplies – food, boxes of uniforms, boots and equipment – piled up haphazardly at the train station and along the roadside; ambulances lined up outside the makeshift hospital. More absurdly, sightseers – guests of various army dignitaries – commandeered these precious vehicles and rode off eastwards to get a closer look at the fighting, hoping to admire the 'plucky little Belgians' as they crouched like gnomes in their hastily dug trenches. When a bomb was dropped in the hotel grounds, a crowd of interested civilians and journalists gathered to marvel at the sight.

Soon, refugees began streaming in from the areas bombarded by the German guns – old men and women, children, dogs, cats, even parakeets. What possessions they had were balanced on carts and barrows, or carried on their own bowed shoulders. Where all these people were supposed to go to no one seemed to know. Every day more and more of them passed through, their expressions dazed and glassy, fixed on the muddy pathway ahead.

Monty was given the task of attending to those refugees who needed medical care, and she spent some days bandaging heads and limbs, and swabbing wounds with iodine. The refugees were too bemused to speak. They demonstrated no gratitude for Monty's hasty attention and expressed no alarm at the destruction of their homes. A dumb stoicism seemed to beset them, as though the events that had swept their lives away were simply a series of misfortunes to be borne, as their existence had been, without complaint.

Monty soon became frustrated by patching up farm workers. There were wounded men at the front who were unable to walk to safety, men who could not be carried back to the regimental aid post or the casualty clearing stations. Could no role be found for so many highly skilled and able-bodied women? The nurses in the hospital scrubbed and cleaned, served tea and made beds. Monty grew agitated.

She left Ghent and travelled west with a Red Cross detachment, to the town of Furnes. It had been evacuated, so that many of the houses were empty – their doors standing open, some with half-eaten meals mouldering on the kitchen table or flowers dried and withered on a mantelpiece. The town, as it had once been, was dead. Yet the place was alive with activity: barely six miles away the fighting was bloody and casualties were coming to Furnes in their thousands. The town's convent had opened its doors as a hospital. Within, the wounded lay everywhere: some still and silent, some noisy and in constant movement beneath their blankets. Monty found them in the library, the refectory, the chapel and the stables. Whichever door she opened, whichever corner she peered into, whichever pew she thought to rest on, a wounded man was there before her. The noise and stench were overwhelming. The surgeons worked frantically, calling out for stretchers so that bodies might be pitched off the operating tables the moment it became apparent that they were dead, or at least beyond saving, so that a less hopeless case might take their place. There were not enough orderlies, not enough ambulance drivers, not enough nurses.

Soldiers came in from Diksmuide, six miles east of Furnes. The fighting there was fierce, as it had been for days, and they reported wounded men lying about on the ground, unable to move or crawl away. The Germans were shelling the area with diligence and precision. Could no one be sent there to help bring back so many unlucky comrades? But there were no doctors able to leave the hospital, and no chauffeurs available to drive the remaining ambulances.

'Can't I take an ambulance?' Monty asked Dr Munro, the youngest of the army doctors. 'We can't just leave those poor men lying there being shelled to pieces.'

'You're talking about driving up to the front,' said Dr Munro. 'It's no place for a woman.'

'It's not much of a place for anyone,' replied Monty. 'Besides, who else is there that might go?'

Dr Munro looked surprised. 'Are you a suffragist?' he asked.

'Of course I am,' said Monty. 'Any intelligent woman should be. May I go?'

Dr Munro had been in the operating theatre for twelve hours without pause. His face was smeared with dried blood. He stared at the mangled foot of a Belgian soldier who lay inert before him. Should he cut it off? It seemed inevitable. 'I suppose you might as well,' he said. He removed a remnant of bloody sock from between the smashed-up toes and gave a sigh. 'Perhaps we wouldn't be in this mess if we let women have more of a say. You are the gentler sex, after all. Besides, we're all in it together now, aren't we? I suggest you ask Miss Bloom to drive. She brought me down from Nieuwpoort and although I'd never say it in front of the men she's one of the best drivers we have.'

Monty found Miss Bloom tinkering with the engine of one of the big Napier ambulances. It was a huge vehicle boasting 40 horsepower and (so she learned later) a six-cylinder engine. It had a covered wagon at the back, inside which a great number of wounded could be accommodated. Bundled into an ill-fitting greatcoat, Miss Bloom was standing on a box to enable her to see into the vast cavity that housed the Napier's engine.

'Miss Bloom?' asked Monty. 'I need to go to Diksmuide. D'you think you can drive me there?'

Ada and Monty drove out of Furnes. Diksmuide could be reached only by traversing roads that had, in parts, completely disappeared into a treacherous shifting mixture of rubble and mud. Monty expected Ada to slow down, perhaps even to stop and claim the journey to be impossible. But Ada did not seem concerned by the periodic disappearance of the road.

'Hold on to the door, miss,' she instructed. 'And put your boot against the dashboard.' Monty did as she was told and the ambulance lurched across the devastated landscape.

Eventually, up ahead they could see a group of shattered houses. Black smoke billowed heavenwards, the firestorm leaping orange into the flat grey skies. Barely a few yards beyond, sharp white flames stabbed again and again, indicating the position of the guns. They passed a burnt-out car, the driver within now incorporated with the steering wheel in a mixture of charred flesh and fabric.

'That's a French car,' remarked Ada. 'Looks like it was hit by a shell.' As if to confirm this alarming possibility, a terrible scream tore overhead and a shell smashed into the beet field beside them. A blizzard of clods and pebbles and mud sprayed against the ambulance, mangled beet raining down upon the two girls in a diabolical red sludge. Ada was suddenly blinded by vegetable matter and the vehicle swerved towards the water-filled ditch on the other side of the road. She scraped at her eyes, wrenched at the steering wheel and stamped on the brake as the front of the ambulance spun out above the putrid water. The engine screamed, and then they were moving forward once again across the shattered Belgian *pavé*.

Monty clung tightly to the door, like a swimmer afraid of being swept out to sea. 'Can't you go any faster?' she shouted, convinced that speed would come to the aid of safety.

'Not here, miss,' cried Ada. 'Or we'll smash the ambulance to bits. The road's badly shelled and there's nothing but rocks . . .'

Before them, a fury of fire and smoke was bursting upwards from the scorched earth, from the smashed dwellings that had once been an uneventful Belgian village. Monty's instinct, the instinct of any rational person, was to urge Ada to turn and drive away. The women exchanged a glance as, with a tremendous roar, the earth before the village heaved apart in an explosion of soil and mud.

'I'm not sure we'll be able to get to Diksmuide, miss,' shouted Ada. 'That's Caeskerke up ahead, we'll make for that instead.'

The noise of the guns grew louder; nearer and nearer came the warning hiss and scream of shells, but at last they were upon Caeskerke. All around came the sharp crack-crack of rifle fire, beneath it the constant noise of terror, the shouts and screams of men. Before them, a French

And yet, were those really moving turnip leaves, or was the ground before her swarming with Germans, crawling forward through the smoke and vegetables to attack Caeskerke from the south? In the darkening light, Monty was not sure *what* she was looking at. She blinked. Here and there she could make out greyish-green humps, some moving slightly, some quite still. Then she realised that these were not soldiers crawling forward after all, but were the dead and wounded, sprawled among the turnips.

Monty ran back to fetch Ada. They crawled down into the sodden vegetables and inched their way forward. Every now and then a shell roared overhead, one such smashing into a farmhouse on the other side of the field so that it exploded deafeningly in a burst of flame. The ground shook, showering them with fragments of masonry and wood, as well as all sorts of other unexpected domestic missiles – a doorknob, a broken pencil, the hands of a clock, a teaspoon.

The first man they reached was dead. It was impossible to say why, as he seemed simply to be sleeping, his face peaceful beneath the smoky sky. The second and third were also dead, one having bled to death of a wound to the neck. He lay as though on a rust-covered carpet, a circle of his own blood sinking into the earth around him. The other had been shot through the head. But there were those among the turnips who were not dead. They moaned and whimpered, some of them struggling feebly to rise, though Monty could see that standing up would attract the attention of snipers and that any rescue work would have to be accomplished crouched down, under cover of twilight, or even darkness. For half an hour Monty and Ada squatted in a ditch at the side of the field. Beneath bursting shells and rattling gunfire they watched the last streaks of pink and crimson twilight bleed out of the eastern skies. Then they gathered up their iodine and their bandages, and crept out into the turnips.

After that, Monty and Ada went up to the front every day. When the fighting was not so heavy they took an urn of soup and another of cocoa. Parked among the ruins of Caeskerke or Oudkarspel, they served the men from the back of their vehicle, or from a dugout constructed beneath the remains of the schoolhouse. There was never enough soup, and never enough cocoa, but it was better than nothing at all. Afterwards, they brought back wounded men to the hospital in Furnes. At times they found themselves barely one hundred yards from the front-line trench. Often they crawled out into the battlefield to drag the worst of the wounded to safety. Sometimes they could only attend to them where they lay, waiting until the stretcher bearers came to haul them back behind the lines. Once a week they stayed up in Caeskerke, camping in the cellar of a tumbled-down house, offering first aid and an ambulance back to Furnes for those lucky enough to find them in the rubble.

It rained often. There was hardly time to think, hardly silence long enough to speak. Monty taught Ada how to stem a spouting artery, how to tie a tourniquet, how to bandage quickly and effectively and how to pack a wound with iodine and lint, though these primitive and simple ministrations were of little use when a man's jaw had been torn off, his abdomen sliced open or his hand smashed to pulp. In turn, Ada showed Monty how to drive the ambulance across the stony, uneven roads that criss-crossed the Belgian countryside without bouncing off into the mud-filled ditch that ran on either side. She demonstrated how to ease a top-heavy ambulance round the rim of a shell hole, how to blast the vehicle through a putrescent cow or swerve past a burnt-out motor, and how to drive through the pitch-dark night without using headlights. Their skills were equally matched: Ada developed little proficiency as a nurse, and Monty never learned to drive with Ada's precision and confidence. Between them, they found a perfect combination of expertise.

'The front is no place for women,' muttered Dr Munro after two weeks of watching them roar off together towards the guns. 'This really can't go on.'

'Indeed,' said Monty, climbing into the ambulance beside Ada. 'But until it stops, there'll always be something for us to do.'

Monty and Ada stayed at Furnes for over eight months. After that, Monty returned to England with pneumonia. Ada moved south to Ypres with the Ambulance Corps.

'We must stay in touch,' Monty croaked, as she was loaded on to a train bound for Calais.

'Yes,' replied Ada. 'Will you write?'

'Of course.'

But by the time Monty was sufficiently recovered to write, Ada had been caught in a gas attack and sent back to Bleakly.

10

'THAT GENTLEMAN had gout,' said Monty as the last patient of the day was wheeled away. Under the instructions of Dr Slack she had been noting down case histories, adjusting regimens and handing out laxatives all morning. She had seen furred tongues, varicose veins, flaking skin, stiff joints, short-sightedness, obesity, and now the characteristic red and swollen toe of the gout sufferer. All had been prescribed copious amounts of pump water. 'Water laced with sulphur will not do him any good at all.'

'Water cleanses,' replied Dr Slack. 'It benefits everyone.'

'It gives no pain relief. There are treatments available –'

'He hasn't come here for physic,' interrupted Dr Slack. 'He can get that at home.'

'Then what has he come here for?'

'For penance. Everyone comes here for that, even our dear Mrs Forbes. She wasn't always a crusading teetotaller, you know. It makes them feel better to be disciplined and I am quite happy to mortify their flesh if that's what they want. But I'm certainly not about to cure anyone.' He chuckled and shook his head at the thought. 'Dear me, no! I'll leave that sort of thing to you. If you can find anyone here worth saving, that is.'

With the departure of Mae and Foxley, Grier's bleak mood evaporated. He put advertisements in *The Times*, the *Manchester Guardian*, the *Scotsman* and *Exchange and Mart*, and congratulated himself on covering 'just about everyone who might want to come'.

'We've ended up between "sport and pastimes" and "Housekeeping",' he said, flourishing Ada's copy of *Exchange and Mart*. 'I gave them an advertisement and wrote a short article on "water treatment". Dr Slack helped me.' He flicked through the pages. 'Look.'

DOGS: weekly bargain list, Monty read. *How to Make Poultry Pay*. Between these articles was a photograph. Monty recognised the square shoulders and staring windows of Bleakly. 'Do people who read this sort of paper want to come here?' she asked.

'Ada reads it,' said Grier, as though this fact were utterly decisive. 'Besides, it was much cheaper than *The Times*. Want to see the bees?' He tossed Ada's paper aside. 'I'm thinking of getting some new hives.'

Monty followed him outside. The beehives were stationed behind the Hall at the end of a derelict kitchen garden.

'The bees of Bleakly Hall used to be famous for their honey,' remarked Grier, leading her through regiments of devastated vegetables. Row upon row of bolted lettuces reared from the earth in defiant green fists. Monty saw caterpillars arching their way across leaves and hordes of greenflies clustered on twisted shoots. The air seemed to vibrate around them, as though filled with the sound of feasting insects.

'The flowers that grow on the hills around here are such hardy species that their pollen is particularly exquisite,' Grier rambled on. 'The honey is very nutritious, so Dr Slack tells me.' He stared at the hives, grouped in a shanty town at the end of the vegetable wilderness. 'Mind you,' he added. 'These hives have seen better days. The army neglected them terribly while they were here and now the bees seem a bit reluctant to stay in such ramshackle accommodation. Thake tells me they're threatening to swarm, but they look quite settled to me.' The bees fizzed about the dark entrance to their home. Monty had no idea what a 'settled' bee might look like, though she had to agree that their hives were looking rather dilapidated.

'Perhaps there might be some hives available in *Exchange and Mart*,' she suggested. They sat down on a rusting iron seat.

'Did you tell Foxley about your friend?' said Grier after a moment. 'Sophia, wasn't it?'

'No, I didn't tell him. I didn't have time before he left.'

Grier sighed. 'Time. That's what we all need, isn't it? Time to remember who we are; time to forget what we did. And if enough time goes by we'll be so far into the future we'll hardly know the past at all. Do you think it would make any difference if you told him?'

'Any difference to whom?'

'To you. Or to him.'

'I don't know,' said Monty. 'I thought it would, but I don't know any more.'

'I see,' murmured Grier. 'You could tell me,' he added. 'That might help.'

'I don't think I can.' Monty picked at a bubble of flaking paint on the arm of the seat. 'I'd like to tell you,' she said, realising that she sounded rather ungrateful. 'But I can't.'

'The thing is that Foxley – Fearless Foxley the men used to call him. We called him Dodger, the officers that is, because he seemed to dodge everything – no matter what Fritz sent over, Foxley always seemed to come through. He's not a bad chap, you know, it's just that these days he's a bit –' Grier closed his eyes. 'What I mean is that it might be better if you sought solace elsewhere.'

'Leave Bleakly? I can't do that!'

'No.' Grier sighed again. 'I don't suppose you can.' From the hives came an urgent buzzing sound. Grier lit a cigarette. 'Is there a future here, d'you think?'

'Oh, yes,' said Monty. It was the same tone of artificial briskness she used when reassuring a moribund patient that his or her return to full health was only a matter of time. 'I'm sure there is.'

'Thanks for your optimism,' said Grier. 'But I don't believe you. I only half believe it myself, though I keep trying.' He shrugged. 'I have to keep trying.' For a moment there was silence between them. Then he said, 'Come along, there's something I want to show you.'

Grier led Monty back towards the Hall. This time, however, his attention was focused on the contents of the kitchen garden.

'D'you know about vegetables, Monty?' he asked.

'I know how to eat them,' said Monty. 'I'm a nurse, not a gardener.'

'Oh.' He sounded disappointed. 'Well, this vegetable garden' – he spread his arms wide – 'was something I was keen to get going. I thought it might be a good idea. I started last year with a little light weeding and so forth. I thought it might cut costs and encourage the guests.'

'Encourage the guests to do what?' asked Monty, looking around at a tangled carpet of bindweed that was encroaching across the ground, climbing up beanpoles and throttling cold frames.

'Well, they could come out here and pick their own peas if they liked. The gents might do some digging. Nature's all the rage these days, you know.'

Monty thought about the hats and fashionable coats, the muffs and stoles she had seen that morning in the foyer. She thought about the pale-faced sickly-looking old men and women she had helped up and down the pump room and the lists of self-absorbed and fictitious ailments she had heard described during her consultations with Dr Slack. She could not imagine a single one of those vain and egotistical individuals wanting to come out into the blast-furnace heat of the walled kitchen garden to pick peas (should they even be able to find them beneath the weeds). Did not such ladies and gentlemen expect others to attend to every human need for them? Had their lives not been devoted to luxury, their world limited to servicing the immediate requirements of their own bodies? It was very likely that not a single one of them had ever seen a pea growing on its mother plant. As for digging . . .

'Or we could sell some of our produce,' continued Grier. 'That might help to raise a bob or two.' He seemed to be talking to himself. 'I need the money, you see, and I'm running out of ideas. The truth of the matter is that I've become something of a regular at the card table since the war. Look at the size of those lettuces!' he murmured. 'What do you think?'

Monty looked at the overblown salad leaves. Those that had not already sprouted and flowered were ragged with the predations of caterpillars and a-crawl with blackflies. '*I* wouldn't eat one,' she said. 'And I don't know anyone who would.'

'It's moments like this when I can really see potential for Bleakly Hall,' said Grier. 'We could be self-sustaining!'

'No, we couldn't,' said Monty. 'Not if you expect us to eat that sort of thing.'

'Look.' Grier lowered his voice, as though the bees that circled their heads might overhear. 'We're friends, aren't we?'

Monty hesitated. 'Yes,' she said.

'Well, then you have to help me.'

'Are you in trouble?'

Grier nodded.

'Is it something to do with the vegetables?'

Grier blinked. 'I beg your pardon?'

'The vegetables.'

'No,' said Grier. He looked at her as though she had gone mad. 'It's about me. And about Bleakly. And of course about Foxley too. Everything is about Foxley in the end, isn't it?'

At that moment they heard a dull thudding sound and

there was a movement in the grass at their feet. They sprang apart as the ground shook, and the earth began to buckle and heave, as though something large and powerful was struggling to emerge. Monty leaped back, trampling unidentifiable leaves beneath her feet as a wide flap of grass slowly opened up before them, like a door into the under-world. A warm breath of rotten eggs wafted out. There was a grunt and the clanking sound of metal striking metal, and Thake's tall thin frame climbed out, in the manner of a newly hatched cranefly emerging from the soil.

Thake stood on the grass, looking down into the open trapdoor. He blinked in the sunlight, his face colourless as though from a lifetime spent crawling through underground tunnels in the dark. In his hand he held a lantern and a large spanner poked from his pocket. His trousers were wet and tiny yellowish crystals adhered to his jacket like a thin layer of frost. His wet clothes gave off a powerful stench of mildew.

'Hello, Thake,' said Grier. He seemed unsurprised to find the man climbing out of the ground before him. 'I had no idea there was a tunnel here. What's inside?'

Monty gazed into the dark hole in the grass. She could see that it had been covered by an iron grating, over which the sod had grown until it was completely camouflaged. From within she could hear the sound of water coursing by.

'There's something wrong,' replied Thake. 'But I don't know what it is.'

The heat continued undiminished. At Bleakly Hall, the coolest place was the foyer. While the boiler was broken its frigidity seemed scarcely to alter, no matter what the temperature outside. Despite Curran's protestations, the guests had dragged chairs through from the drawing room, positioning them against the tiled walls and sitting in silence, as though in a hospital waiting room. Mrs Forbes had placed a thermometer out on the terrace and periodically one or other of them would totter out to take a reading.

'Eighty!' reported a tall thin gentleman with dry and flaking skin. Bits of the stuff clung to the shoulders of his black woollen frock coat like a scattering of oatmeal. He scratched his wrists and exchanged glances of disbelief with his fellow refugees in the foyer.

One morning they got up to find that a great wind had arisen during the night. It was a hot, southerly wind, warmed by the equatorial sun and the searing desert sands of Africa. It snatched Mrs Forbes's purse from her fingers as she stepped out to go down to the pump room, and sent an unoccupied bath-chair careering down the path to the village. The guests retreated back inside, refusing to go down to the village for fear of being blown away. Dr Slack lined them up before the statue of Hygeia and doled out glasses of Bleakly Hall spring water from the hydropathic's fountain.

'It tastes like ordinary water,' murmured someone. 'D'you think it is?'

'Who said that?' barked Dr Slack. He blew a sharp rebuke on his silver whistle and the guests slowly began to circle the foyer.

Monty went out on to the steps to find that Ada had brought the Audi round to the front of the Hall. Grier was busy strapping a wheelchair to the back. One of its wheels revolved gently in the wind like a weathervane. He looked up and waved.

'What's going on?' said a voice at Monty's elbow. Curran had propelled himself out behind her. 'Ada has been working on something in the garage,' he added. 'But she won't tell me what it is. Ada,' he cried, apprehending the chair strapped to the back of the car. 'As your employer I demand to know what you are doing with that wheelchair.'

'You're going for a spin, Curran,' said Grier. He bounded up the steps and seized the handles of his brother's chair. 'It's perfect weather for it.'

'It's perfect weather for airing the rooms,' replied Curran. 'All unoccupied rooms should have their windows opened.'

'I've already done that, Mr Curran,' said Ada.

'The guests might need me,' said Curran. But the wind snatched away his complaints and he did not bother to utter them again. He looked at the gleaming motor and ran a hand over the bottle-green paintwork. 'I drove this car in the Austrian Alps Rally in 1913, you know, Monty. She's a beauty, isn't she? When she's working, that is. She was treated very badly during the war, but whatever anyone might think about Fritz he knows how to build a motor. Ada's done a grand job fixing her up again.'

Ada grinned. 'Thank you, sir.'

Curran allowed himself to be helped into the front of the car, beside Ada, while Monty and Grier climbed into the back.

'Look,' Curran said as they passed the pump room. 'There's a man waving at us. Can you see, Grier? I think its Mr Johnson from the Crossed Keys. I wonder what he's after.' He sounded sarcastic. 'Perhaps he has a "dead cert" he'd like to tell you about. Another one. D'you think we should stop?'

'No,' said Grier. He turned away from the window, avoiding the man's gaze as the car hurtled past. 'I can't think what he wants but I don't wish to speak to him right now.' Grier looked out of the back window at the man now shouting and waving in the dust behind them. 'In fact, perhaps you could drive a little faster Ada?'

Ada pressed her foot down and the car leaped forward. 'D'you remember, Grier,' said Curran shouting over his shoulder above the roar of the engine, 'that time when we were on leave and Dodger and I raced down to the coast on a pair of motorcycles? We were on this very road. Dodger was in front, as usual, and he tore round a corner and almost ran into a flock of sheep. The cycle flew off the road and burst through the hedge, and he ended up upside down in a muddy field. I was right behind him and did exactly the same.' He laughed. 'We thought we'd come home to get away from mud and we ended up covered in the stuff from head to toe. You should have seen us, Monty. Foxley's motorcycle was jammed so deep in the earth we couldn't pull it out. Had to come back with Grier and some shovels and dig the thing out! D'you remember?'

Grier nodded. 'Foxley said he was digging mud out of his ears for a week.'

'Poor old Dodger.' Curran laughed again. 'He said he was tempted to leave the stuff in there, so that he'd not be able to hear what the CO was on about when he got back to the line.'

'I'm not sure he paid much attention to the CO anyway. He had a knack of doing what he wanted to do.'

'And then the CO would pretend it was what he had intended all along.' Curran grinned. 'Remember that cow he found wandering near the lines?'

'Poor thing was mad with fright.'

'We'd not had milk in our tea for days.'

'Dodger sat down on a gun limber and milked the beast!'

'Right there behind the trench.'

'Under enemy fire!'

'Then a whizz-bang came over and the cow kicked him into the mud and disappeared through the smoke. Funniest thing I ever saw! I thought I'd dreamed it until he appeared with a mess tin of milk and showed me where the beast had kicked him on the shin. Fearless Foxley,' murmured Curran. 'The Artful Dodger. When's he due back?'

'Tomorrow,' said Grier.

Monty did not want to think about Captain Foxley. She stared out of the window, watching the larks soaring in the sky and the long grass ebb and swirl in the wind like waves of emerald water. Soon she noticed that the hills had become gentler, and that the beech and horse-chestnut trees of Bleakly had given way to clusters of pine. Barley fields rippled on either side of the road. The car sped along, hedgerows of hawthorn racing by, their fringes of poppies and willowherb whipped into confusion by the wind. More than once Curran urged Ada to go even faster and Ada needed no encouragement.

'There's the sea,' cried Monty as they rocketed out of a grove of pine trees.

They crested a hill and the road wound down towards a long curve of golden sand. A small group of whitewashed houses clustered like mushrooms at the end of the road. Ada slowed the car. 'Here we are,' said Grier. 'Can you drive on to the beach, Ada?'

'Are we going for a walk?' asked Curran.

'Not quite,' replied Grier.

On the beach, Ada sprang out of the car and began untying the wheelchair from the back. 'I've adapted it,' she said, before Monty could ask. 'Can you hold that wheel in place, miss, while I tighten these nuts?' The chair, modified by Ada, now had two front forks, which were joined to a set of handlebars. 'I took some parts from Mr Thake's bicycle and a wheel from one of the bath-chairs,' she said. 'I've attached a sort of harness too. I found some old army belts and webbing, and fixed them to the frame. It should be quite safe.'

'Am I going in that?' said Curran, staring in disbelief at the curious vehicle that was taking shape on the sands.

'So it seems, Mr Blackwood,' said Monty. 'We didn't bring the other chair.' Ada was now unfolding what looked like a silk bed sheet stretched over a slim wire frame. The wind tugged at it sharply. Ada braced herself and hauled on two lengths of twine attached to the tips of the frame. She released the twine slowly, until a huge pair of wings soared overhead. 'Climb on to the back of the chair to hold it still, please, miss,' she cried to Monty.

'Is this a good idea, Ada?' shouted Monty above the wail of the wind. 'To attach a kite to a bath-chair in a gale?'

Ada ignored her. She looped the twine over hooks affixed

to the frame of the chair, and Monty felt the whole structure jerk and strain beneath her. 'Ada!' she screamed. 'Have you tried this thing out?'

'No, miss,' shouted Ada. 'But the chair will be well weighted with Mr Curran in it. I've moved the seat down and back to lower the centre of gravity so it won't topple over, and there are brakes on the handles at the back. I took them off Mr Thake's bicycle.'

'But Mr Curran can't reach the handles!' cried Monty.

'Someone will have to ride on the back,' said Ada.

'Me?' said Grier, looking alarmed.

'Me,' replied Ada.

Leaving Monty struggling to hold the chair still as the wind tore at the kite, Ada went to help Grier lift Curran out of the car.

'This is marvellous, Ada,' said Curran, allowing himself to be lowered into the three-wheeled chariot. Ada handed him a pair of driving goggles, a leather helmet, a scarf and a pair of leather gloves. Above them, the kite strained against its moorings, arching against the wind like the sail of a ship.

'Ada, surely I should go?' said Grier. 'Just in case something happens.'

Ada pulled on a pair of goggles. 'I know exactly what to do, Mr Grier, under any awkward circumstances. I have to go. I'll take over, miss,' she said to Monty.

But as Ada reached out, a savage gust tore at the makeshift parachute. The chair lurched forward and all at once Monty was hurtling across the beach, the wind at her back like a giant invisible hand pushing her onwards. She screamed as her feet scraped across the sand. One of her shoes came off, but the chair did not stop, or even slow down. Should she let go? If she did, Curran would career onwards with no means of stopping – perhaps he would take off into the sky, disappearing towards the sun like Icarus. Should she brake? But her hands had slipped and she could do no more than hang there, trying not to be flung off as the chair raced down the beach. Somehow, Monty managed to swing a leg forward and get her toes on to the footplate Ada had fixed to the back of the chair. In front, Curran gripped the handlebars. Behind, Grier and Ada were far away: Grier was cranking the car into life; Ada was waving her arms and running after them down the beach. Strapped into the wheelchair, Curran was shouting, his voice hoarse with excitement. Monty tried to breathe, she tried to cry out, but the wind forced its way into her mouth and she almost choked. Beneath her feet the ground rushed by, the wheels rattling as they hurtled over ridges of wet sand, so that she was doused in brine and spattered with grit.

'Steady as she goes!' roared Curran. He turned the handlebars and the chair raced towards the sea. The wheels sliced through the shallows, the water spraying upwards like handfuls of sparkling diamonds flung into the air. And then, quite without warning, the chair seemed to stumble. It struck something hard, something unseen beneath the water and all at once it reared and bounced, so that Curran's hands were flung off the handlebars and the frame swerved and jolted. Monty noticed a wheel rising slowly into the sky before them. It hung in the air, disappearing into the sun, before reappearing again, spinning down and down until it plopped out of sight into the sea. Now they were ploughing through the water, listing into the tide, so that Curran was half submerged, only his goggles and the top of his leather helmet visible above the surface of the sea. His left arm waved upwards as he thrashed in his seat, trying to keep the chair erect and his head out of the water. And then, as Monty finally managed to wrench on the brakes, the chair jarred violently and she was catapulted over Curran's head and between the strings of the kite, to disappear with hardly a ripple beneath the waves.

Monty sat in the back of the car wrapped in Grier's jacket.

'You should have braked earlier, miss,' said Ada sullenly. '*I* was supposed to ride on the back. *I* knew she shouldn't have gone into the sea.'

'Sorry, Ada. I did my best.' The chair, minus its third wheel, had been dismembered and strapped on to the car, its wings folded up and stowed away. 'The brakes didn't seem to work properly.'

'Of course they did,' said Ada. 'You just didn't apply them right.'

'Oh?' said Monty. 'Well, apart from that it seemed to perform very well. Can it be fixed?'

'Everything can be fixed,' said Ada. 'If you want it to be.'

'You burst out of the sea like Neptune's sister,' said Grier. 'Seaweed in your hair and everything. I couldn't see Curran at all, just a wheel revolving above the water and the kite tugging at something beneath the waves. Thank God you managed to pull him upright before he drowned.'

'You should have braked gently,' muttered Ada. 'Not on

a bend, not on wet sand. You should have done it when she was going *straight*.'

'I suppose we're learning, Ada, aren't we?' said Curran.

'You don't need to learn by making mistakes if you learned by listening to me, sir,' cried Ada, exasperated. 'You just confuse the wheels when you brake on a wet bend like that.' Ada shook her head. 'Have you forgotten everything I showed you out at Furnes, miss?'

'Not quite everything,' murmured Monty.

'*I* should have gone,' muttered Ada. 'Not *you*.'

'I thought I was finished,' said Curran. He rubbed his hands together gleefully. 'Still, it was a marvellous ride. Well worth being dunked in the sea for. I'd quite forgotten what it felt like to race along in the wind like that.'

'You have Ada to thank for it,' said Monty.

'Dodger would have loved it,' said Curran. 'We could have had a race.' He chuckled. 'Perhaps you could make another, Ada? Next time we'll bring Dodger.'

'We don't need *him*,' snapped Ada. 'I didn't make this chair for *him*.'

Curran looked surprised. He opened his mouth, but seemed unsure what to say.

'Captain Foxley makes his own entertainments,' added Ada before Curran could speak. 'In fact' – she rammed the car into gear and hauled on the wheel – 'you should leave him to his own devices.' Ada looked round at Monty, shivering beneath Grier's jacket. 'Especially you, miss.'

'Me?' said Monty, surprised.

'Yes, you.' The car jerked forward across the sand. 'He's got something planned for you. He told me so himself.'

I I

THE BOILER was fixed. Downstairs, in the hydropathic treatment rooms, it effortlessly created a sweltering vapour for the Russian baths and the steam cabinets. It pulsated hotly through the pipes that lay behind the mock-Byzantine walls of the Turkish baths. It heated the recovery rooms, warmed the indoor swimming pool and ejaculated water from hosepipes and douches.

Grier was delighted. 'You see', he said, 'how well it all works once everything is in place?'

The mechanism for the adjustable douche throbbed urgently. A gleaming tangle of pipes, wheels, taps and dials, it was mounted on a freshly varnished wooden pulpit. A battery of nozzles projected downwards, pointing in the direction of the intended beneficiary. Dressed in his best frock coat, silk tie and starched white collar, from behind the wooden pulpit Dr Slack looked sternly at his victim. Beneath his hands the pent machinery hissed. All at once the doctor swung a lever down, plunged a handle and spun a wheel. A powerful jet of water blasted against a pale, tremulous figure draped over a chromium frame, which stood in the centre of the tiled floor. The figure cried out. Dr Slack spun another wheel and the jet of water split into ten sharp needles. Dr Slack waited for the man's groan to turn into a cry of pain, then he shut the water off.

'Just once more, I think, doctor. You did say only three to begin with.' The patient's voice was a miserable whine.

Dr Slack spread his arms wide. 'That was a mere *taste* of what she can do. I think two more of considerable duration would be quite within the bounds of good health.'

Grier knocked on the door to the ladies' hallway. There was no reply. Cautiously, he opened it and peeped inside. Half way down the corridor a door was just closing. It led to the ladies' recovery room. Was that a man's trousered leg he had glimpsed, silently disappearing within? He waited for a scream, a shout, the emergence of a flustered lady . . . But other than the sound of water splashing against flesh, there was nothing to be heard at all.

Monty appeared carrying a bundle of wet sheets, which she deposited in a basket.

'Monty!' hissed Grier.

'What are you doing here, Mr Blackwood,' whispered Monty. 'Someone might see you.'

'There's an intruder,' he said, suddenly embarrassed. He felt like a naughty schoolboy. 'I need you to come with me.'

The ladies' recovery room was filled with individually curtained booths, each furnished with a sturdy-legged

102

couch. Grier and Monty crept forward, listening for any sounds that might give the intruder away. It seemed more than likely that the fellow had hidden himself behind a curtain, thought Grier. Would they be obliged to throw aside each one in their bid to flush him out? From somewhere up ahead there was a grunt and a sigh, and the sound of laboured breathing.

'There!' whispered Monty, pointing.

Grier tiptoed forward and reached out a hand. What if one of the guests was behind that curtain, reclining on her couch like a walrus on a rock? Perhaps it would be better if Monty did the unveiling. He heard a sigh and a groan, and a voice mumbled something incoherent. Grier dashed the curtain aside.

Captain Foxley was lying on a recovery couch. An empty tumbler was still in his hand and a cigarette had burnt itself out between his fingers.

'Wake up!' hissed Grier. 'Dodger, wake up!'

Captain Foxley noisily exhaled a breath of whisky into Grier's face and frowned in his sleep.

'Perhaps we should leave him to sleep it off,' whispered Monty.

'He's not always like this.' Grier wrung his hands. 'I mean, he's often tight. But he's . . . he's changed recently. D'you think he's sick?'

'Sick?' Monty looked at Captain Foxley's pale, handsome face.

'In the mind!' hissed Grier. 'Some of the lads were . . . you know.'

'From the war? Or from something else?'

103

'I don't know. You're the nurse. Perhaps it's both!'

Monty pulled the curtains closed, shielding Captain Foxley from view. At that moment there came a soft, reproachful juddering from beneath the floor, which was shortly replaced by a single plaintive note, like the mournful sound of a distant bugle. Then, all at once, the silence was broken by a familiar frantic hammering, as though every water pipe in the building were shuddering and vibrating at the same time. Monty covered her ears. An adjacent curtain began to sway and thrash, and one of the guests emerged, her face pale with alarm. She was small and stooped, and walked on arthritic feet in the manner of a burglar creeping along a rooftop. She stole forward, gazing at Grier earnestly.

'Mr Blackwood,' she cried, her voice almost drowned out by the roar of the plumbing. 'Mr Blackwood, such a terrible noise –'

At the same moment Captain Foxley burst into view like a villain in a pantomime. Grier jumped (he had assumed the Captain to be out cold). He opened his mouth to speak, but then all at once he realised that Foxley was brandishing something in his hand; something long and heavy and shaped like a rolling pin, so that for a hopeful second Grier thought that it *was* a rolling pin, but then he saw that the end of it was neatly studded with nine-inch nails. Grier tried to shout out, but no sound emerged. He tried to leap forward himself, but he found that his feet refused to move. Captain Foxley sprang at the creeping figure before him. He grasped her by the throat and swung the spiked club over her head, the cry he uttered obliterated by the rat-tat-tatting of the plumbing. Then, just as suddenly as it had started it stopped. Apart from a steady drip . . . drip . . . drip from a tap somewhere in the room there was silence.

Captain Foxley froze, the club still poised in his hand. 'Is that you, Blackwood?' he hissed. 'Where's Coward?'

Grier swallowed. 'Coward's dead,' he heard himself say. 'You know that.'

'Coward,' repeated Captain Foxley, his voice barely audible. 'Have you seen Coward?'

'Perhaps you should let the lady go,' whispered Monty.

'Who?' Captain Foxley frowned. All at once he seemed to realise what he was doing and he leaped back with a cry. The spiked club clattered to the floor. Beside it, the old lady dissolved into a heap of lace and taffeta, like a handful of offcuts dropped from a haberdasher's table.

Grier did not move.

'I was looking for Coward,' repeated Captain Foxley. He backed away, his expression confused. 'Sergeant Coward.'

'He's dead,' said Grier.

'And Chalmers?'

'Dead too.'

'Just you and I then, Blackwood?'

'Yes.' Grier stared at the rough wood and rusting prongs of the makeshift weapon that lay on the floor between them. 'Where did you get that?' he whispered.

'It was Coward's.'

12

Aparty of young people arrived. They had seen one of Grier's advertisements in *The Times* and had come up from Kensington. Their leader was a young man with curly hair and a booming laugh; his second-in-command a young woman in her early twenties, fashionably dressed and expertly touched up with rouge and lipstick. There were many such confident and pristine young women in Kensington, but none in Bleakly. The glamorous young ladies of the party created quite a stir as they made their way up through the village, chattering and laughing. Their male companions were fewer in number, but they were hearty and vociferous nonetheless. Monty watched them disembark. Judging by their youth, these insubstantial boys (and their effervescent girls) had managed to avoid the war completely.

They arrived accompanied by a mountain of suitcases and hatboxes, in addition to hampers of food and crates of champagne. Thake began the Herculean task of transporting everything into the vestibule and thence up to the various rooms. Monty wondered what Curran would say when he realised what type of modern and energetic individuals had just arrived. She also wondered what sort of a place these people thought they were coming to – and with what sort of exaggerated information about the Bleakly Hall facilities Grier had filled his latest advertisement.

Grier had gone out to meet the guests. Monty watched him shake hands easily, smiling a welcome, exchanging pleasantries about the weather and enquiring cheerily about the comfort of their journey. She saw him look askance at the cases of champagne and the hampers of food, and glance uneasily over towards the building. But Curran was tucked away in his office beneath the stairs.

Despite the warmth of the day, Monty shivered. She turned round to find Captain Foxley standing directly behind her. He was looking out of the window over her shoulder, a cigarette smouldering between his fingers. 'Quite a little party,' he remarked, tilting his head in the direction of the new arrivals. They stood about outside like a gaggle of exotic chickens. 'And there's enough champagne there to give Curran a fit. Does he know what's going on?'

'He's in his office. Mrs Blackwood is with him at the moment.'

Captain Foxley looked surprised. 'Is she? I wondered where she was. She always comes up for elevenses.' He smiled. 'You might like to pop up yourself. Perhaps one afternoon. We might make a bit of a thing of it.'

Monty inched away from him. She had no intention of making a bit of a thing of anything with Captain Foxley. As for Mrs Blackwood . . . Monty had passed her several times in the corridors since her return from London. The woman either ignored her, or bestowed an uninterested smile in Monty's general direction. She did not bother herself to stop and speak. Monty heard from her in other ways, however, as it turned out that Mae Blackwood was a singularly noisy lover. More than once Monty had been obliged to stopper the plughole in Dr Slack's rooms. On one particularly boisterous occasion Dr Slack had gone over to the sink and shouted into the plughole. 'Pipe down, can't you! Pipe down!' But it appeared that the communication network of the Bleakly Hall plumbing was a one-way system and the doctor's pleas had gone unheeded.

Monty was unperturbed by Mae's aloofness. She and Sophia had met dozens like her in the hospital: fashionably dressed women who had spent the war talking about how 'dreadful' it was to have to go without butter; or how 'impossible' it had become to find a decent tradesman. Women who began almost every sentence with that optimistic mantra 'when the war is over . . .' Disappointment had been inevitable, so that now it shone from their perplexed eyes and bowed their disenchanted shoulders; it dripped bitterly from their painted lips and turned their hearts to dust. One could hardly blame them, Monty always said to herself. No one back home had any idea what it had really been like at the front, though the consequences were now theirs to live with, as much as anyone else's.

'I think Mrs Blackwood's going to London again,' said Monty. She pointed to Mae's bags and suitcase, which were standing by the door awaiting Thake's attention.

'So I see.' Captain Foxley was still watching the new guests. 'So soon?'

Grier, Monty saw, was laughing in the company of a young woman. She was wearing a daringly cut skirt that revealed a fashionable high-heeled shoe, the whole of her ankle and good few inches of calf. Monty looked down at her own economical uniform and low shoes, and felt drab by comparison.

'Oh, don't worry about *that*,' said Captain Foxley. He put a comradely arm about her shoulders. 'You don't need to dress like a society dolly to look just the ticket.'

Monty shrugged off his hands, and his sympathy. He pushed his hair aside and she was struck once again by that odd look in his eyes. Not that she wanted to spend any amount of time staring into his face. It would take no more than a single lingering glance to convince Captain Foxley that she was keen to partake in an afternoon version of Mrs Blackwood's 'elevenses'.

'Are you going to London yourself?' asked Monty hopefully.

'Good heavens, no. Not when there's so many new people to meet here.' Captain Foxley gazed at the young men outside. They were as narrow as girls about the shoulders, their trousers hanging like sacks about thighs the width of cricket bats. 'What feeble specimens,' he muttered. 'I suppose all the best ones are dead.'

At dinner time, fuelled by champagne and egged on by Captain Foxley, the hilarity of the newcomers increased. Monty wondered how long it might be before Grier stepped in or Curran objected, but neither man seemed inclined to interfere. In fact, Grier seemed not remotely interested in anything that was going on and had disappeared in the Audi before the meal even started. As for Curran, on hearing the commotion echoing around the vestibule, he emerged from beneath the stairs in a fury. But then he perceived Captain Foxley among the party and retreated, quickly and silently, back the way he had come. He did not appear at dinner and Ada took a tray through for him. She returned for it an hour later. The food upon it was hardly touched: the shepherd's pie congealed and grey, the rhubarb crumble still submerged beneath its wrinkled mantle of custard.

'Is he unwell?' Monty asked.

'No,' said Ada. 'I don't think so. He didn't really say very much.' With a pale face and tearful eyes she watched Captain Foxley cross the foyer in the company of a slim brunette.

Monty noticed that Mrs Blackwood's baggage was still standing beside the hydropathic's main entrance. 'Is Mrs Blackwood with Mr Curran? She'll have missed her train by now.'

'No, he's on his own. I don't know where she is. I don't know anything about Mrs Blackwood,' said Ada stiffly. 'But I wish she *would* go.'

After dinner, the guests gathered into two opposing camps: the new visitors in one and the old regulars in the other. The former group dominated the drawing room, with their bottles of champagne, their cigarettes and Captain Foxley's gramophone. The others were obliged to settle themselves in the chilly billiard room. Monty came across them sipping cups of comforting cocoa – a surprisingly luxurious beverage, which Curran had instructed be sent in to them in an attempt to smooth ruffled feathers.

Mrs Forbes, rendered energetic by an afternoon of cold plungings, had elected herself as spokeswoman. 'And that odious Captain Foxley is encouraging them too,' she said. 'Really, can Mr Blackwood do nothing about it?'

'I'm sure he's doing his best,' replied Monty soothingly. 'But they've already paid in advance, you see. They can't be sent away. But don't worry, I'm sure Mr Blackwood will see to it.'

In fact, Monty had looked in on the new guests a few minutes earlier and had seen no indication that either of the Mr Blackwoods was 'seeing to' anything. The lights were blazing, Captain Foxley's gramophone was playing, and there were bottles and glasses everywhere. Monty saw Captain Foxley standing with a group of young women, a cigarette in one hand and a drink in the other. He was smiling and laughing, his handsome features lit up by the presence of so many attentive females. He tossed his cigarette into the grate and laid his hand on the waist of the girl standing next to him. She did not appear to object.

'Well,' continued Mrs Forbes, 'I might be prepared to let it pass for tonight, but such behaviour really can't continue for the whole week. I can assure you that this kind of . . . of *dissipation* is *not* what I come here for.'

There was a general murmur of agreement. 'Such immodest conduct,' whispered a tall pale lady standing beside Mrs Forbes. Her chin merged seamlessly into her long wrinkled neck giving her a look of constant disapproval. 'Are those young ladies actually *smoking*?'

'I believe so,' said Monty. 'It's quite common these days.'

'And *drinking*,' croaked Mrs Forbes. 'Here, at a *hydropathic*!

And what on earth is Mr Sykes doing in there? He's one of us!'

'Sleeping,' said Monty.

'Perhaps he's had one of his turns,' murmured the tall pale lady. 'It's often hard to tell.'

'I think it best if you all go to your rooms,' said Monty. 'It's ten o'clock already.' At that moment there was a scream, followed by the sound of splintering furniture.

Monty arrived in the drawing room to find that one of the men of the party – the one with the curly hair and booming laugh – was sprawled on the floor beside a smashed side table. Captain Foxley was standing beside the fireplace, nursing the knuckles of his right hand and looking furious.

'What on earth are you doing?' cried Monty.

'Oliver was just saying about the war, when this chap went for him,' cried one of the girls tearfully. 'He wasn't *doing* anything.'

'Is that so?' Monty looked at Captain Foxley. 'If you insist on joining these guests,' she snapped, 'drinking their champagne and smoking their cigarettes, you could at least refrain from assaulting them. What's the matter with you?'

Captain Foxley gave her a sulky look. 'You know what's the matter with me,' he muttered.

'Yes,' said Monty. 'I do.' She looked at the young man with the curly hair. 'Are you hurt?'

'It's nothing.' Oliver held a bloodied handkerchief to his nose.

'It's *not* nothing,' cried the girl. She glared at Captain Foxley. It was the same girl upon whom he had laid a predatory hand not half an hour earlier. 'All Oliver said was "I don't know why you chaps bothered. Rather a –"'

'Yes, yes, "rather a waste of time, if you ask me",' finished Oliver. 'That's what I said. I don't know why he's so upset about it. It's what everyone thinks.'

'No it bloody isn't,' shouted Captain Foxley. 'And nobody did ask you, so you can just keep your mouth shut.'

The girl passed Oliver another handkerchief. Monty knew she should go over and make sure that his nose wasn't broken, but she found that she didn't care. 'Perhaps it's time everyone went to bed,' she said, trying to sound matron-like. Behind her Captain Foxley's gramophone hissed and crackled angrily. The Captain stalked over to it. His face was a furious shade of red, his eyes bloodshot and watery. He seized his gramophone and slammed it closed, hugging it to his chest like a petulant schoolboy taking his toys home.

'Come along,' said Monty. She herded the newcomers towards the door. 'Up to your rooms, please, we have an early start in the morning. You, stay here,' she barked to Captain Foxley, who had been about to slink out of the room. 'I want to talk to you.' He blinked at her and lowered himself into an armchair.

'Are you going to throw something at me?' asked Captain Foxley. He had put his gramophone box on to the floor and was resting his feet on it. His anger seemed to have evaporated, now that the others had gone.

'You can't hit the guests,' said Monty firmly.

'You hit *me*,' replied Captain Foxley. 'Quite violently.

With jam. Don't you remember? Not to mention the near miss with the cigarette case and the candlestick.'

Monty flushed. 'That was different.'

'How?' said Captain Foxley. He was looking pleased with himself now. 'I provoked you, certainly, but then that chap provoked me. That's how it works.' He scowled. 'Little upstart. What does he know about anything? Come on, Monty, you're glad I punched him really, aren't you?'

'No, I'm not.'

'Yes, you are!' He laughed and shook his head. 'D'you think I don't know about you? Of course I do. So it's no use getting all high and mighty about it.'

Monty opened her mouth to speak, but then closed it again. She had said almost nothing about herself, about her past and Sophia, to anyone at Bleakly. How could he possibly know anything? 'What do you know about me,' she stammered at last. 'What are you talking about?'

'We're more alike than you think, you and I,' said Captain Foxley. He struggled to his feet and took a step towards her. 'We should stick together.'

'What do you know about me?' repeated Monty.

'I know that you don't really think badly of me. You'd have done the same thing.'

'No,' said Monty. 'No, I wouldn't.'

Captain Foxley shrugged. 'Have it your own way, but we both know I'm right.'

'You don't know me at all,' cried Monty. 'I'm *not* like you.'

'Aren't you?' Captain Foxley crept closer. 'Why are you here, then? Here at Bleakly Hall? Here, now, in this room?

You asked me to stay for a reason, didn't you? You sent everyone away so that you could be with me. You *are* like me. *Just* like me, lost in the past, looking for someone to help you.' He advanced further. 'I can sense it.' He sniffed the air, like a hungry dog. 'I can smell it. I knew it as soon as I met you. But you can't escape it, any more than I can. The past will consume us both. We might as well make the most of the present until then.'

13

MONTY HAD been working at St Margaret's for three weeks when Sophia arrived.

'This is Miss Barclay,' said Miss Tadworth. 'She's one of our new volunteers. If you could show her the ropes, Nurse Montgomery? You can start by sweeping ward four and changing the beds in ward two. Oh, and Sister tells me that the dressings trolley for ward six needs attention.'

'Welcome to St Margaret's,' said Monty when Miss Tadworth had turned away. She led Sophia down the corridor towards ward four. 'Have you worked with casualties before?'

'No,' said Sophia.

'Have you worked in a hospital before?'

'No.' Sophia looked apologetic. 'I wound bandages for the Ladies' League back home. That's all I've ever done.'

'Oh, you can do some of that here,' said Monty.

'And *un*wind them too, I imagine.'

'Yes, there's plenty of that,' Monty agreed. 'But I think you'd be better off starting with some other duties first. Until you find your feet a little. We don't want you fainting, do we?'

'I won't faint,' cried Sophia indignantly.

Monty smiled. 'How did you end up here?' she asked.

'I went to the Red Cross Recruiting Office. They said VADs were in short supply at St Margaret's, compared to the number of casualties you take in.' Sophia wrung her hands. 'But your Matron, Miss Tadworth, seems to wish I hadn't bothered. I thought volunteers were needed everywhere.'

'Oh, they are,' said Monty. 'But Miss Tadworth fears a decline in standards and she tends to be rather harsh on our young volunteers. I suppose she's told you you're not allowed on to the officers' wards?'

'Yes, it was the first thing she said to me.' Sophia frowned. 'Why's that?'

'Ah, our Miss Tadworth thinks you young girls lack the moral continence of the fully trained nurse. You're bound to fall in love immediately with your heroically wounded charges. All manner of unseemliness could result. Especially when they're wrestling with a barely contained libido due to their endless rations of bully beef.'

Sophia stared at her.

'The moral tenor of the entire hospital is at stake,' whispered Monty.

Sophia covered her mouth with her hand to smother a laugh. 'What about NCOs?'

'You can go into their wards as often as you like.'

'No chance of being enticed down such disgraceful pathways?'

'Miss Tadworth thinks not.'

Both girls laughed.

'Will you look after me?' asked Sophia. She reached out

and squeezed Monty's hand. 'If it's not too much trouble. You're the first person who's made me feel welcome.'

'I'd be delighted,' replied Monty, surprised and quite pleased by this unexpected gesture of affection. Suddenly she realised how much she too would value a friend at St Margaret's. Sophia Barclay, young and smiling, eager and full of good humour, seemed like an antidote to the feelings of gloom and despondency that beset her every day. 'How old are you?' asked Monty.

'I'm eighteen. I'm young, I know, but I can still help. And I learn quickly.' Sophia lowered her voice. 'I bleached my apron to make the red cross look faded. I know I've only just started, but I don't want to look as shiny and clean as a new pin, do I? D'you think I should sprinkle myself with carbolic, so that I don't smell new too?'

'Oh, you'll smell like the rest of us before much longer,' said Monty.

'And the bleaching?' asked Sophia earnestly. 'Is it too much? Only I want to look the part. People might think I don't know what I'm doing otherwise.'

'You look like you've been here for years,' replied Monty. 'And you'll feel like you've been here for years, too, by the end of the day.'

Before she volunteered, Sophia had never touched anything that might be used to clean up dirt or mess. Other than the soft white flannel she had used at home to wipe her own face, she had never squeezed out a wet cloth. She had never laid her fingers on a brush, besides the mother-of-pearl one on her dressing table, and she had only the vaguest idea of what a dustpan, or a mop, actually looked like. Those basic items of food and drink she took for granted every day – cups of hot tea, soft-boiled eggs, even the clean plates on which these items had been carried to her table – had arrived there without her ever having to think about how they might have reached that state of being. Did one actually have to *boil* the kettle before making tea? Was it practical to *sweep* a floor before one washed it? She had been aware of the army of scrubbing, cleaning, cooking women that kept her (and everyone else she knew) clean and warm and fed at all times – but only dimly aware.

After a few weeks at St Margaret's, Sophia could hardly remember a time when she did not know how to disinfect surgical instruments and scrub all manner of stains off floors. She seemed to wash, wipe, scour or sterilise everything she came across over and over again, day after day – bowls, dishes, buckets, floors, operating tables, trolleys, caps, cuffs, aprons . . . She carried trays and stripped beds, ran up and down stairs, folded sheets and towels, trundled vast baskets of laundry around, filled buckets and emptied them, mopped, swept, scoured and scrubbed again. Where once even the suggestion that she might empty her own chamber pot would have caused her nose to wrinkle, she now dealt with bedpan after bedpan of human waste and did not give it a moment's thought. She made up huge vats of Lysol and peroxide every day, and helped to pour this mixture into all shapes and sizes of multicoloured gangrenous wounds, in all manner of male bodily locations she once would have blushed even to think about. The days seemed shorter than ever before, as she hardly had time to look at a clock; yet longer, as she was more tired at the beginning and end of every day than she had been in her life.

'Straighten your cap, Miss Barclay,' Miss Tadworth would shout.

'Take these in to theatre six,' Sister would cry, thrusting bales of gauze and rolls of bandages into her hands.

'We need to change Private Howard's dressings,' Monty would say. 'We'll do it together.'

Months passed. The routine was unvarying. The number of casualties arriving – usually at night so as not to alarm the local residents with their multitude – never diminished. The nature of their wounds remained unspeakable: men without arms or legs; men without jaws or noses; others blinded or with faces burnt horribly. Men came with bits of metal lodged in their heads and bodies – fragments of shell and pieces of shrapnel; with holes and tears in the soft white flesh of their soft white bodies, with organs missing – eyes, tongues, lengths of intestine – the possession of which one might normally assume to have been essential for life to continue. And for many of them life did continue – though it was a darker and less pleasant life. For Sophia, the days and nights passed by in a blur of activity, punctuated by a few hours spent huddled beneath cold bed sheets in a frosty dormitory. At first, she had been surprised to learn that Monty was only twenty-four years old. The black circles beneath her eyes made her look much older. After a month at St Margaret's Sophia had black circles under her own eyes, though she was too tired to think much about it.

Sometimes they were given an afternoon off. Monty and Sophia would go to the zoological gardens or the park, to get some fresh air after so many days trapped inside. Now and again they strolled along the river or took the omnibus into town. Sometimes, they went to the ice-cream parlour near the station, or wandered up and down Oxford Street, arm in arm, looking in shop windows. Occasionally they went to tea with Monty's Aunt Florence. They sat in Aunt Florence's Victorian parlour on hard-backed chairs, encircled by spindly legged ebony tables covered with ornaments and photographs, sipping tea out of fine bone china cups. Surrounded by the unchanged trappings of middle-class gentility – the daintily chiming mantel clock, the embroidered Japanese draught screen, the redundant rosewood piano – the sights and sounds of the hospital's pain-filled world seemed almost unimaginable. Aunt Florence would worry about sugar tongs (the silver ones had gone missing and new ones were impossible to come by), doilies (increasingly costly to repair) and the freshness of the milk (questionable). Her conversation revolved around the wartime privation: the declining quality of bread, the difficulty of finding a competent chimney sweep, the limited selection of dress fabric.

'And what's that terrible smell?' Aunt Florence would say on every occasion.

'Disinfectant,' Monty or Sophia replied (they took it in turns, as the questions were always the same). 'From the hospital. It seeps into our clothes and hair, we can't seem to get rid of it.'

'The hospital!' Aunt Florence looked aghast. 'You're not still working there, are you? What must your poor mothers think?'

'It's for the war,' said Sophia (or Monty).

'You'll never find a husband if you smell like that,' said Aunt Florence, steering the conversation round to her second favourite topic. 'Doing one's bit for the war is all very well, but to sacrifice one's femininity?' She looked askance at the women's sturdy shoes, at Monty's shockingly short haircut. 'Dear me.' She shook her head. 'You'll be wanting the vote next.'

Mostly, however, Monty and Sophia were too tired to do anything but find a tea room and sit with a cup of tea and a plate of cakes. There, they talked about the day's work, their lives before they came to St Margaret's and what they might like to do once the war was over.

'Travel the world,' said Sophia. 'And get married, of course.'

'I don't think I'll ever get married,' said Monty. 'I don't want to trail around after a man. I like men, of course, they can be amusing and some are very brave. But they want things – attention, success, authority – and behave badly when they don't get them. And they would never let you live your own life. "A wife is her husband's best helpmeet," Aunt Florence always says.' She laughed. 'It doesn't sound like a very rewarding arrangement to me. Oh, no, Sophie, I've no intention of attaching myself to a man for the rest of my life.'

'But what about love?' asked Sophia, surprised.

'But I love you. We're friends. We look after each other, we care for each other and we put each other first. That's love, isn't it? The other kind, that's romance. It lasts long enough only to make trouble – usually for the woman.'

Sophia looked disappointed. 'I still think I'd like to be in love,' she said. 'At least for a while. Just to see what it's like.'

14

'AND ONCE you've scrubbed the floor, you can strip Private Steele's bed and take the sheets to the laundry,' shouted Miss Tadworth. Miss Tadworth's uniform was of the old-fashioned kind, as was Miss Tadworth herself, and its straining seams creaked and groaned as rage and indignation swelled like the sea within her. 'And make sure you do it *quickly*.'

'Yes, Matron.' Sophia lowered her eyes. Nothing she did was ever good enough or fast enough for Miss Tadworth.

'What sort of a selfish, useless life were you living before, Barclay?' she would say. 'Really, my expectations are quite of the lowest sort, yet time and again you seem to fall beneath them. If you spent less time bothering Nurse Montgomery and more time following my instructions, you might just about manage to make a useful contribution to this hospital!'

It infuriated Miss Tadworth even more that the men on the wards were oblivious to Sophia's faults.

'When's that pretty nurse coming round, Matron?' they asked.

'Nurse Barclay looks tired, Matron. Why don't you give her the day off?'

'She's *not* a nurse,' Miss Tadworth thundered. 'She's Voluntary Aid Detachment.' She glared at Sophia through tiny round eyes behind small round spectacles resting on a large round face. Unlike Sophia's, Miss Tadworth's face was unremarkable to look at. Her plain features appeared to have been formed with haste and indifference – two eyes, a nose and a mouth – so that she resembled a snowman, with glasses. This comparison Sophia had shared with Monty, as they shivered beneath the bedclothes together on a freezing winter night in the nurses' dormitory. Since then, both of them found it almost impossible to look at Miss Tadworth without wanting to laugh. Still, thought Sophia, it was better than wanting to cry.

Sophia went to the sluice room to get the scrubbing brush, the carbolic and a bucket of water. As she entered the ward, a cheer went up from the men, lying beneath their barely disturbed bedlinen, like ranks of forgotten furniture swathed with dust sheets.

'Here she is!' cried Corporal Foster. 'I've been waiting all night for you, miss. Will you scratch my leg for me? Near the top? I can't get my hands under to do it myself. You'll have to get to it by sliding your hands right down, and *rubbing*.'

'Don't go near him, miss,' said a voice from the next bed. 'His wife was in yesterday and she's given him all the rubbing he needs.' There was a murmur of laughter from up and down the ward.

Sophia waved her scrubbing brush at Corporal Foster. 'I'll shove this down there, shall I, Corporal? That should do the trick. Now, if you need attention I'll have to get Matron. Or Dr Woodruffe.'

'What about Nurse Montgomery?' asked Foster. 'She's nice too.'

'She's on leave,' said Sophia. 'Her brother's been wounded and she's looking after him at home. I don't know when she'll be back.' She walked to the far end of the ward, and got down on her hands and knees.

The rest of the day passed as usual. She scrubbed the floor and emptied bedpans. She stripped Private Steele's bed and made it up with clean sheets for its next inevitable incumbent. She did the same to at least twenty other beds, the names of whose deceased former occupants she could not even remember, so often had they changed in recent weeks. She scrubbed the ward floor again, and fed Sergeant Davies his breakfast, dinner and tea, as he was unable to feed himself. In the next bed his friend Sergeant Owen, also from the valleys, sang Welsh hymns in a rich baritone. His vacant eyes swept the ward anxiously, as though searching a crowd for someone important. By the time the evening came he was hoarse and had to be given a sedative to enable him, as well as the other men in the ward, to get some sleep. Sergeant Owen sang Welsh hymns every day, all day long.

'The Taffs always sing when they're afraid, miss,' whispered Corporal Grayson. 'I've seen it before, in the trenches.' Sergeant Owen's fellow patients had long since given up complaining about him and Sophia had come to dread the day when he stopped (his demise was quite certain, Dr Eldersley said, it was only a question of when), as the silence would fill the ward more eloquently than his singing. Later, as she was about to leave, she heard Dr Eldersley humming 'Guide me, O Thou Great Jehovah' to himself as he strode towards the operating theatres.

When Sophia finished her shift, she found that there were three letters waiting for her. The first contained her mother's usual complaints: *your father is quite unable to get used to the new housemaid. She's not a patch on Lettie, but of course Lettie's in the munitions works now as the pay is so much better. I saw her last week and she's turned quite yellow! . . .*

The second letter came from Monty, explaining that her brother's wounds had now become infected. The doctor (an elderly chap who had taken to wearing the medals he had won the previous century in some long-forgotten Indian campaign) seemed to have no idea about anything and was content to leave Richard in Monty's experienced hands. To reach the point, Monty wrote, she was not sure how long she would have to stay there. She would write again soon and let Sophia know what was happening.

The third letter Sophia had deliberately saved until last. She tore it open. It was little more than a scribbled note, but it told her everything she wanted to know. *Sophie*, she read, *I can hardly think straight without you. Handyside must think I'm a complete idiot, and I don't think I heard two words he said to me all weekend. Meet me at the British Empire Hotel tomorrow. I'll be there at seven. I'll wait all night if I have to.*

Sophia rushed out of the hospital and tore along the

gravel pathway that ran along the front of the building. Running in through another door, she bounded up the stairs and burst into the dormitory she shared with many other nurses and VADs. A fire struggled to burn in the tiny grate at the far end of the room, but whatever heat it gave out was instantly swallowed up by the racks of washing that stood before it. Before the war the room had been a recreation area for junior doctors, and had once contained a billiard table, overstuffed armchairs, crowded bookshelves and racks of medical journals. But that calm and confident world had been violently swept away, along with the men who had inhabited it. The only reminder of the room's former role was a row of dusty and disregarded medical journals stranded on a top shelf above a washing line of greyish-coloured women's underthings.

Sophia took off her uniform. She struggled into her new dress, a fashionably cut garment made of black moiré silk with satin stripes, which she had bought ready-made at Debenham and Freebody's. It fitted perfectly and was just the thing – elegant yet chaste – for pretending she was going out for tea with her maiden aunt. Sister Barnett would never guess where she was *really* going. Sophia pulled on a clean pair of stockings. These, unfortunately, were wool rather than silk, as such ephemeral luxuries as silk stockings could not be justified by anyone who spent twelve hours a day toiling on the hospital wards. She ran a brush through her black shining hair and pinned it back up. Men found her attractive, she knew. But as she had often said to Monty, one could not help how one looked, so there seemed little point in congratulating oneself on it. Besides, men might admire her looks, but did anyone but Monty understand how she felt after an eighteen-hour shift on the post-operative ward? Would any man warm her nightdress, and talk to her all night when she couldn't sleep? But Monty had been obliged to go home to look after Richard. For a while, Sophia had felt lost: alone and adrift in a dark and pain-filled world. Even before Monty had climbed aboard the train Sophia had wanted to burst into tears. 'Why are you leaving me?' she had wanted to say. 'Why don't you take me with you?' But she knew these thoughts were childish and selfish, and she put them to the back of her mind. Instead, 'I hope Richard gets better quickly,' she said. 'He's lucky he's got you to care for him.' She wondered whether she sounded jealous. 'He's lucky to have you for a sister.'

'Will you write to me?' Monty replied. 'I'll try to write. I'm not much good at that sort of thing but I'll do it for you.' She put her arms round Sophia. 'I wish you could come,' she said against her ear. 'I know Richard would love you too. He'd get better much faster if he had you to see every day, rather than boring old me.' She gave Sophia another hug. 'I'll miss you. Don't forget about me, will you?'

Sophia had kissed Monty's cheek. She could hardly bring herself to reply. She, Sophia, would find the separation far worse than Monty would. The days at the hospital were so long and arduous, and the nights so chilly. And who would console her when one of the men died on her shift? Whom would she warm her feet against when the dormitory became so cold it was almost impossible to sleep. Already the weeks without Monty stretched ahead in an unbroken vista of hard work and loneliness. Sophia raised a hand as the train pulled out of the station. 'Hurry back,' she called. 'Hurry back.'

At first, Sophia had gone about her work as usual. Sister Barnett seemed to feel sorry for her now that Monty had gone, and she kept her as busy as possible. Sophia worked extra shifts to keep herself occupied and she wrote to Monty every night. She went to Oxford Street, but the shops looked uninteresting. She went to their favourite tea room, but the cakes seemed dry and tea alone was worse than no tea at all.

And then, one day, she met Peter, and after that everything else faded into insignificance.

Thinking about it (and she often did) Sophia had to conclude that the day she met Peter was the most electrifying day of her life so far. She knew that she might experience other days of equal, or perhaps greater, excitement (the day she would marry him, for example), but until then she could not imagine what could possibly eclipse it.

It had been her first full day off in months. Remembering that the zoo was one of Monty's favourite places (and missing her friend dreadfully), she had gone there for a walk. Sophia felt weary, bored and friendless, and she had been wondering whether she should visit her parents (a definite sign of loneliness). Alternatively, she thought as she wandered by the elephants, she might ask Sister Barnett whether she could work every day until Monty came back, as it was clear that there was nothing worth doing without Monty's companionship. Sophia dawdled past the bears. The day was cold and blustery, but sunny and bright, and her cheeks were pinched pink by the wind. As she passed the bear pit, that same wind tore her new straw hat from her head and flung it over the railings.

Sophia groaned, and peered into the bears' enclosure. One of them could be seen on the far side, standing on a rock, staring with interest at the hat which had dropped from the sky and on to the ground beside its den. With its garlands of artificial pansies and its brim of straw, the hat looked like something a bear might add to its bedding. But Sophia had bought the hat from Oxford Street with Monty on the very day that Monty had left for home. She could not possibly leave such a meaningful piece of millinery to be chewed and sat on by bears! Should she climb in and get it? Should she look for the keeper? But before Sophia could do or say anything, a soldier stepped forward. He passed her his own hat to hold, sprang over the railings and disappeared into the bear pit. Immediately a crowd gathered.

'There 'e is!' cried a man, pointing down into the enclosure.

'Look how fast he runs,' cried another.

'The bear!' screamed a woman. 'It's after him!'

The soldier bounded through the rocks of the bear's artificial environment. He leaped past the beast (later, he was to say he had felt its breath on his neck), snatched up the hat and darted away again. By now the bear was lumbering forward half-heartedly, its chocolatey coat rippling in the spring sunshine. The soldier climbed up the railings like a monkey and dropped down on the other side – still with the hat in his hand. As he landed, the crowd broke into a cheer.

'Well done!'

'*That's* why we're going to win the war!'

The soldier got down on one knee before Sophia and offered up her hat with his head bowed. The crowd, which was now considerable, roared its approval.

'Not a single pansy damaged,' remarked a lady nearby, staring at the flowers round the brim of Sophia's hat. 'Not a mark or smudge on it.'

'What a lucky young lady you are,' commented another.

A man stepped forward and shook the soldier's hand. 'Good luck to both of you,' he said. The crowd began to disperse, smiling at Sophia as they went and giving her companion approving nods and winks.

'They think we're going to get married,' he whispered. 'D'you think we should?'

Sophia met Peter at every opportunity. She no longer thought about visiting her parents (despite their repeated appeals that she do so), and her letters to Monty grew shorter and less frequent. Now, they were filled only with talk of Peter. He had taken her to a music hall (the turns had been both comical and spectacular, she wrote, and she had laughed particularly loudly at the Indian Conjurer and the Singing Dwarves). Afterwards Peter had bought her fried fish and chips, and they had eaten these delicacies sitting on a bench in the park, the two of them wrapped in his greatcoat. He said that he loved her.

Next he had taken her to a boxing match. One of the boxers was a sergeant he knew. As she, Sophia, was now inured to the sight of blood due to her arduous work at the hospital, she told Monty, the spectacle had not alarmed her unduly. (Why Peter should want to witness such brutality while on leave, she added in parenthesis, even if he *did* know the fellow, she had no idea. Perhaps violence was simply in men's blood.) Afterwards he had taken her to the ice-cream parlour and explained in detail about the Marquess of Queensberry. He had taken her dancing on numerous occasions (how good he was at dancing). He had bought her roses (the bunch was almost too large to carry) and taken her to Brighton for the day (she was becoming quite adept at pretending to Sister Barnett that she was visiting relatives). He was so kind and thoughtful, so handsome and exciting, it was quite impossible *not* to be in love with him. *Perhaps*, she wrote more than once, *we will get married after all*.

That evening, as instructed, Sophia met Peter outside the British Empire Hotel. There was a dance band playing and as usual Peter could never resist such entertainments. He swept her on to the floor, waltzing her swiftly through the crowds.

'I'm not going to share you with anyone,' he whispered. 'I can see them all looking at you, but they can find their own girls.' And he pulled her close, so that his lips were almost against hers, and she could feel the belt and buttons on his tunic digging into her flesh. Peter looked about for some of his friends, but there was no one there whom he knew. He seemed disappointed. 'Let's go somewhere else,' he said.

He took her to the Tivoli Tea Rooms. There was more

dancing here and, despite her aching feet (she had been up since five o'clock in the morning), Sophia found herself circling the room over and over again. The Tivoli was a very different sort of place from the British Empire Hotel. There the music had been muted, its dancers sedate and courteous. The Tivoli was crowded and noisy. The air was thick with smoke, the blaring of the band barely audible above the din of shouting voices and laughter. Everyone's face seemed to be red, their gazes lascivious, their mouths wet and hungry-looking. Sometimes Sophia thought she recognised a face in the crowd – was it a soldier she had once nursed, or perhaps one of the other VADs, escaped from the surveillance of Miss Tadworth? But she never stopped for long enough to find out. Peter seemed excited, and tireless. Every now and again he dragged her to the side of the room, drank a glass of whisky, smoked a cigarette and watched the circling dancers. He said very little, but seemed more concerned with scanning the crowd for men he recognised.

All at once his face lit up. 'There they are! Hello, Chalmers,' he said, approaching a tall figure standing against the wall. 'Hello, Lucas.'

'Foxley!' Chalmers pumped Peter's hand enthusiastically. Lucas did the same.

Lucas stared at Sophia. 'Hello,' he said. He licked his lips. Sophia gave a faint smile of greeting and turned away. When she looked back, Lucas's gaze was fixed upon her breasts.

'This is Miss Barclay,' said Peter, ignoring Lucas. 'Sophie, this is Tom Chalmers. Lieutenant Chalmers. DSO now, I believe. Congratulations.'

'Lieutenant Chalmers shook Sophia's hand, then

fumbled for another cigarette, automatically passing one to Peter. They bent their heads together over a match. Sophia sighed. Would Peter not rather spend his time with her than with these men? Men he already knew so well? Did he not see enough of them when he was at the front? 'How long have you got left in Blighty?' she heard Chalmers ask.

'I don't know,' replied Peter. 'Until the doctors say I'm fit. I got a bit of shrapnel in the shoulder. Nothing much. Should be back in a couple of weeks; a month, perhaps.'

'That long? Poor you. I hardly know what I'm doing here. Thought I'd be glad to get home, but –' Chalmers shrugged. 'It's no use. Not that I want to go back, of course.' He nibbled on the edge of his moustache. 'I went to see Handyside in Hastings. He's in a bit of a bad way.' Chalmers pulled on his cigarette. 'You could hear the guns from there. I kept thinking about those poor buggers –' He blew out a cloud of smoke. 'I must say I was glad to get out tonight. My mother keeps inviting her friends round to look at me. I don't know what on earth they expect. Perhaps I should demonstrate a bayonet charge with one of the cushions or something. That might keep them amused.' He fingered his cigarette uneasily. 'Got a nice billet?'

'Handyside's place.'

'Well done.' Chalmers looked at Sophia and gave Peter a knowing wink. '*Very* well done. That'll take your mind off things. D'you want a drink?' he added. 'I'm gasping.'

'Whisky,' said Peter.

'Whisky!' cried Chalmers. 'We can drink to absent friends.'

'We'll need more than a bottle if we're going to do that,' muttered Peter.

Chalmers's smile wavered. 'What about you, Miss Barclay?'

At Peter's instigation, Sophia had already drunk some whisky. It tasted horrible, but she had swallowed it down nonetheless, as this was what Peter seemed to expect. She nodded. Chalmers handed her a glass. Perhaps she would get used to it, she thought. She wondered what Monty would say to see her out like this, smoking and drinking in such a place, surrounded by soldiers, one of whom had his arm round her. For a moment Sophia felt dispirited. When she got back to the dormitory there would be no one to tell. She wished Monty would hurry up and come back.

Sophia drank another glass of whisky. All at once she noticed that Lucas, who had remained silent, was standing beside her. He looked as though he was about to say something, but then he seemed to change his mind. He continued to stare at her, his expression a mixture of dolorousness and desire. Peter put down his empty glass and pulled Sophia on to the dance floor. Lucas's rabbit-like features disappeared behind the crowd.

And now the faces of the dancers swam before her, merging into a blur, until she could make out nothing but the painted lips of women and the hungry, pitiless eyes of men. The thick smoke and raucous music made her head ache. But despite her growing befuddlement, Sophia noticed that one face seemed unmoving in this terrible swirl of people. It was a woman's face, pale and angry. She seemed to be staring at Peter, her expression a mixture of disbelief and recognition. Sophia's legs felt like rubber now and she staggered slightly, hauling on Peter's tunic as though she were trying to drag him down on to the floor.

'Steady on,' he said, laughing.

Sophia felt dizzy. She looked about for the woman, intending to point her out to Peter, but instead she saw only Dr Woodruffe, one of the surgeons from the hospital. 'There's Dr Woodruffe,' she said in surprise. Her words slurred on her lips, so that it sounded to her own ears as though she had said *there's Dr Woof*. 'Dr Woof,' she said with a cackle. 'Oh dear, am I drunk?'

At that moment the crowd parted and Sophia saw the woman once again. She was standing still, while the room full of dancing couples swept back and forth before her. She stared at Sophia and again at Peter. Sophia's smile faded. The woman looked furious. But Peter had noticed nothing. He lurched around the dance floor, his hands gripping Sophia tightly. He squeezed her buttock, as though testing its ripeness. Then all at once Sophia felt him falter in his steps. He ground her toe beneath his boot, his head turning this way and that, as though he was searching anxiously for someone whose face he had glimpsed.

Sophia gasped and staggered against him again. Her hair had come down and she felt clammy all over. Was she about to be sick? She looked about for Dr Woodruffe, surely he was not about to witness her public humiliation? She saw him talking earnestly to the woman. Dr Woodruffe, and the woman, looked over at Sophia and at Peter. Sophia could not read Peter's expression. This was partly because she was suddenly feeling very ill indeed. It was also partly because all at once she seemed to have lost a shoe. And Peter was shouting in her ear. What was the matter with him? Perhaps he felt sick too. It was rather hot in there and the press of people, the smell of smoke and exhaled breath was becoming noisome. Sophia sank to the floor, disappearing from view like a rag doll caught in an undertow. She grabbed her shoe before it was swept away beneath the stampede, yet suddenly she found that she could not get up again. She laughed and grovelled about around Peter's ankles. Peter dragged her to her feet. 'Come along,' he snapped. He glanced at Dr Woodruffe (who now seemed to be consoling the woman) and plunged through the crowd, scything his way through the still-dancing couples, dragging Sophia from the dance floor as he might haul a sack through a hedge. She stumbled after him, her hand caught tightly in his.

Outside, Peter lit a cigarette.

'Did you know that woman?' Sophia managed to ask. She sagged against the wall. The smell of Peter's cigarette made her feel worse than ever. 'She seemed to know you.'

'No,' snapped Peter. He took Sophia's hand and pulled her down the street towards the hospital.

Sophia felt as though she was rising, slowly and with difficulty, from the depths of a deep, dark pond. Her mind seemed still to be sleeping, even as she heard the voices of the others in the dormitory and felt the cold air of the place about her face and neck. Someone pulled the blankets right off her and shook her shoulder vigorously.

'Come on!' called a voice. 'They're here!'

It was almost a quarter to six by the time Sophia appeared

in the hospital. Miss Tadworth was waiting beside the door like a cat outside a mouse hole. When Sophia scuttled in, she pounced: 'Barclay!'

The place was as busy as a train station. A sudden influx of wounded men filled the corridors on stretchers and trolleys, and people were shouting and rushing here and there. 'I'm sorry, Matron,' Sophia said. She glanced in alarm at a man lying mummified in bandages on a trolley beside the door. His entire face and head were obscured, apart from an opening for his lips, so that she could not even begin to imagine what devastation lay beneath. The man began a low moaning and thrashed weakly from side to side beneath his sheet. 'I overslept,' she muttered. 'I didn't mean to. I'm only ten minutes late.' Her head was thumping. 'It won't happen again.' She looked once more at the bandaged figure. The name pinned to his pyjama top was Captain Robert Holmes. Captain Holmes groaned and whimpered something unintelligible from between the folds of his bindings. It sounded like 'mother', thought Sophia, unable to tear her eyes from that masked face and those anxiously moving lips; or perhaps it was 'water'. Whichever it was, could not both things be procured for the man?

All at once Dr Eldersley appeared with a pair of orderlies and trundled Captain Holmes down the corridor. Miss Tadworth was still talking. 'Sister Barnett and Nurse Montgomery speak very highly of your commitment and abilities,' she shouted. 'But quite frankly, I'm tempted to get rid of you once and for all right now. Can you give me one good reason why I shouldn't?'

Sophia opened her mouth, though she was unsure

whether an answer was required – perhaps this was one of Miss Tadworth's rhetorical questions, to which no satisfactory answer could ever be supplied. She was saved from finding out by the sudden appearance of Dr Woodruffe.

'Thank you, Miss Tadworth,' he said briskly. 'I'm sure you've told Miss Barclay how important punctuality is – almost as important as volunteering in the first place, I should say – so if she's ready, I'd like her in theatre two right away. Follow me, Miss Barclay, if you please. Thank you, Matron.' Dr Woodruffe stalked off down the corridor.

'Well, go on, then!' cried Miss Tadworth. She lowered her voice. 'I'll sort you out later.'

'Good heavens, Miss Barclay,' murmured Dr Woodruffe. 'What on earth have you done to annoy Miss Tadworth like that?'

'She doesn't like VADs,' said Sophia. 'She thinks we're frivolous and flighty.' She thought guiltily of her behaviour the previous evening. Should she explain herself? But Dr Woodruffe did not seem to be interested.

'Flighty and frivolous – I had no idea there were such things left in this world,' he said. 'How on earth have you managed to retain such delightful qualities while working here?' Dr Woodruffe gave her a bleak smile. 'No wonder the men like you.'

Sophia said nothing. Dr Woodruffe was always charming to her, in a melancholy sort of way. She hoped he had not noticed how drunk she had been at the Tivoli Tea Rooms. She smiled at him, perceiving as she did so that Dr Woodruffe smiled back, eagerly this time. But she was thinking about Peter now. Peter was in love with her, he had said as much last night. In fact, it was Peter's fault that she hadn't been able to get up that morning. He had pressed her against the wall of the hospital, his hands squeezing warm handfuls of flesh. 'Come on, Sophie,' he had muttered, fumbling beneath her skirt. 'Don't you love me?'

Sophia had somehow managed to wriggle free. 'Not here,' she had said. 'Not like this.' She hiccupped. 'Tomorrow. Wait until tomorrow night.'

Preoccupied by these shameless, but stirring, thoughts of love, Sophia suddenly realised the 'tomorrow' she had promised was now 'today'; 'tomorrow night' now 'this evening' and only a matter of hours away. She felt suddenly electrified and put up a hand to cover her smile. At her side, Dr Woodruffe walked in silence. All at once Sophia realised that his eyes were fixed upon her, so that she almost wondered whether she had moaned out loud, or even murmured something inappropriate. She was obliged to touch his arm, to alert him to the fact that he was about to walk straight into a table, upon which a lady visitor from the Destitute Servicemen's Benevolent Association had left a bunch of cheering (but economical) chrysanthemums.

'Thank you, Miss Barclay.' His cheeks flushed and he cleared his throat. He looked as though he was about to add something else, but a pair of doors burst apart and a trolley bearing a prostrate figure, its head and face wrapped in bandages, thundered between them. Sophia leaped aside. She had time only to see Captain Holmes's still-moving lips, his twitching hands grasping at his coverlet, then he was gone once more and they had arrived at operating theatre number two.

15

A<small>S SHE</small> entered the operating theatre, Sophia knew that the rest of the morning would pass in a whirl of shouted orders, of slamming doors and rattling equipment, of hastily sterilised instruments and even more hastily sliced, stitched and bandaged patients. All the newly arrived men had had their wounds treated already – at the regimental aid post and the casualty clearing station behind the lines. But there had been so many men, so many different and unexpected ways in which the human body could be mangled and splintered, that this initial life-saving activity had been, by necessity, brisk and perfunctory. By the time the wounded reached Blighty, and the hospitals of Southampton and London, the hasty amputations and hurried surgery of the front (and the journey back) had resulted in all manner of misery and ghastliness. Wounds that needed to be attended to several times a day had often been dressed only once every twelve hours; drainage tubes projecting from dried and bloody dressings had become clogged with the very matter they were supposed to be clearing. Gas gangrene had often set in, creeping across flesh in a vivid shining patch-work of green, purple and black. Once, Sophia had been barely able to look at a nosebleed without feeling faint. But time and experience had done their work, so that now she could dress a suppurating stump or stuff a gaping wound with gauze, without thinking twice about it. Only occasion-ally, perhaps as she watched Dr Woodruffe amputate a limb, his crimson fingers knotting arteries as casually as if he had been tying one of his own shoelaces, did she feel queasy.

Afterwards, outside in the coolness of the main corridor, she heard the clock in the hospital tower chime eleven o'clock. Was it not even noon? She felt as though she had been on duty for days.

Dr Woodruffe appeared beside her. 'Dr Paget has taken over. A busy morning, but we're almost done. For now. Well done, Miss Barclay.' He gave her one of his melan-choly smiles. 'Would you like a cup of tea?'

Sophia hesitated. Was he about to rebuke her for being out in a dance hall the night before? She felt ashamed, as she followed Dr Woodruffe meekly along one of the hospital's endless corridors. Despite the hours they had spent in theatre, it seemed to have made little difference to the great mass of occupied trolleys and stretchers whose ranks lined the walls and crowded the floors. Here and there, as though propelled by some invisible tide, an assortment of these now empty conveyances were gathered together, massing against a pillar, or beside a table, like a logjam in a river.

A pair of tea trolleys, each bearing a load of rattling cups and three gargantuan teapots, inched down the corridor towards them. They were steered by three VADs, with two others ferrying trays of cups, brimming with the dark swirling liquid, in and out of the wards.

'Let's take one each of these.' Dr Woodruffe took two full teacups.

'No sitting down on the wards,' said Sophia mechanically.

'Really?' said Dr Woodruffe. 'Well, perhaps we'd better go outside into the quadrangle. Would you mind? It's quite sunny this morning and the fresh air will probably do us both good.'

The quadrangle was a brown square of grass. It was surrounded by a paved walkway and boasted a bronze statue of Queen Victoria at its centre. Sophia and Dr Woodruffe sat down on either end of a wooden bench that stood in a narrow strip of sunshine. They sipped their tea in silence.

'At one point there was talk of taking the Queen away, you know,' said Dr Woodruffe after a moment. 'Of melting her down so that she could be turned into a piece of ordnance to aid the war effort – a few trench mortars, perhaps.'

'I think more hospital beds might have been a better idea,' said Sophia. 'Or some equipment. Bedpans, for instance.'

Dr Woodruffe laughed. 'Goodness me, Miss Barclay. Make sure the hospital's executive committee don't hear you talking like that. I think some of them are under the impression that the Queen is still alive.'

Sophia drained her cup. How pleasant it was to sit down for a moment, she thought dreamily. She and Monty had often sat out there together, between their shifts when the weather was fine, though this was the first time she had been there with Dr Woodruffe.

Dr Woodruffe pulled out his cigarettes. He offered one to Sophia, before taking one himself. 'And when will Miss Montgomery be back?' he asked.

'Oh, not for a month or so,' said Sophia. She blushed, suddenly feeling guilty. She had not written to Monty for a while now. She closed her eyes, feeling the sun warm on her face, as it had been that day beside the bear pit. Sophia allowed the memory of it to linger in her mind.

After a moment she became aware of a movement on the bench beside her. She opened her eyes and realised with some surprise that Dr Woodruffe was closer to her than he had been a minute before. For a moment she thought he might be about to take her hand. The quadrangle was over-looked by more windows than she cared to count, so that she felt like an actor on a stage in front of a full house. If Miss Tadworth was not staring down at her out of one of these numerous windows, then any number of people were bound to be. Was the entire hospital to see her being courted by Dr Woodruffe?

'Miss Barclay,' said Dr Woodruffe. His voice was urgent and close to her ear. Was he about to whisper an endearment? Sophia sat still and silent, hardly even daring to turn her head to look at him, in case he took this movement to be some form of chaste encouragement. Dr Woodruffe threw his cigarette away and cleared his throat. 'May I take this opportunity to ask whether –?'

'Miss Barclay!' The sound reverberated off the walls and

windows, magnifying and multiplying, so that it sounded as though her name had been screeched a hundred times over. But for once, Sophia was almost glad to see Miss Tadworth's enormous figure emerging from a door on the opposite side of the courtyard. She jumped to her feet.

'Miss Barclay,' hissed Dr Woodruffe, springing to attention beside her. 'There's something I feel I really must tell you.'

'Can it not wait?' she asked, watching Miss Tadworth burl her way across the quadrangle. Even from that distance Sophia could see that her face was furious.

'I'm not sure that it can.'

'Please,' whispered Sophia, mortified at the prospect of the handsome and amusing Dr Woodruffe uselessly opening his heart to her. 'Don't –'

'I understand that we have a mutual acquaintance.'

'Do we?'

'Yes.' Dr Woodruffe glanced uneasily in the direction of the Matron's advancing figure. 'Peter Foxley.'

'You know Peter? Really?' Sophia smiled.

Dr Woodruffe did not smile back. 'I'm more of an acquaintance,' he said hastily. 'I knew him at Cambridge. Or rather, I knew *of* him at Cambridge. We had . . . friends in common.' His voice became urgent. 'Miss Barclay, how much do you *know* about Peter Foxley?'

'I beg your pardon?' Sophia frowned. 'What do you mean?'

'Barclay!' cried Miss Tadworth again.

'Are you long acquainted?'

'Almost two weeks.'

'And he's told you everything?'

'I don't understand. Everything about what?'

'There are some things about him that you should be aware of – if you don't know them already, that is.' Dr Woodruffe turned mournful, apologetic eyes in the direction of Miss Tadworth, who was now all but upon them. 'He is . . . not what he pretends to be.'

'I beg your pardon?' insisted Sophia. 'Dr Woodruffe, what are you talking about?'

But it was too late. Miss Tadworth was before them.

'Ah, Miss Tadworth,' said Dr Woodruffe. He sounded almost relieved. 'Miss Barclay and I were just discussing whether it would be possible to move the beds in the wards a few inches closer together in order to accommodate this morning's convoy. Do you think the dressing trolley would still fit between?'

'That's a matter you would be better off discussing with me, I should think, Dr Woodruffe, rather than with a Red Cross volunteer.' Miss Tadworth breathed heavily through her nose. 'I'd like a word with Miss Barclay, if it's not too much trouble.'

'No trouble at all.' Dr Woodruffe turned to Sophia. 'We'll carry on our conversation another time, Miss Barclay.' He stared at her meaningfully. 'Make sure you don't forget what I've said.'

16

CURRAN LOOKED tired and irritable, the cheerfulness and dynamism he had rediscovered on the beach once again overlaid by a grim preoccupation with the domestic economy of the Hall. He was balancing a wooden box on his knee as he came across the foyer.

'Would you like me to come down to the pump room with you?' said Monty. 'There'll be plenty of room down there today.'

'Ada usually takes me after the morning rush is over,' said Curran. 'But she's got the day off today, so yes. Yes, I think I'd like that. We could have a little chat on the way down. I'll just sort this out and then we'll go.' Curran thrust two fingers into a pocket of his waistcoat and produced a key. He opened the box and sifted through its contents. Monty heard the rattle of coins and the rustle of paper. She noticed that there was a slit in the lid of the box with the words '6d, please' painted beneath it.

'This is the swear box,' said Curran. 'It contains a disgraceful amount of money. Our new visitors seemed to find it rather amusing last night to pepper their conversation in the dining room with expletives – just to see how efficient Mrs Forbes's mental arithmetic was. The curly-haired chap was rather inventive, I believe – urged on by Foxley. They made quite a game of it, so Ada tells me. Foxley is usually our main contributor. He pops ten shillings in there at the beginning of each week – to cover his expenses, he says.' Curran slammed the box closed. 'I must admit I was tempted to add a few shillings myself when I saw all that champagne last night but, well, I didn't need to. Self-control, you see.' He glanced over to the stairs, as though expecting the group of 'new visitors' to invade the hydropathic's foyer at any moment, their yawns and 'good mornings' punctuated by profanities.

Outside in the sunshine, Curran's bleak mood lifted. He propelled himself along, waiting for Monty to assist him only when there was a pothole in the road too large for him to negotiate. When they reached the door to the pump room he pulled out his watch. 'Six and a half minutes,' he said. 'Ada and I can do it in five.'

'I had no idea it was a race,' replied Monty.

'Just a little habit of mine,' said Curran. 'Ada says the wind makes a difference. I think that's where she got her idea for the kite. Sometimes she rides on the back of the chair when we're coming down the final stretch.' From the bandstand, the brass band blasted an uncertain version of Beethoven's *Eroica* across the empty village square. Monty opened the pump-room door and Curran peered inside. 'There's no one here at all,' he said. 'The place used to be packed every morning by six o'clock. Before the war, that is.'

On the far side of the room a burly woman stood behind the counter in grim silence. Her sleeves were rolled up, exposing forearms muscular with years of hauling on the Bleakly pumps. Curran asked for a glass of the heavy, sulphurous Lady Beaton. But Monty could not stomach any of the therapeutic waters. 'I'd rather have a cup of tea,' she said, gazing in dislike at the reeking waters that filled Curran's glass.

'Nonsense,' said Curran. He sipped his water, but could not suppress a shudder.

'Is Mrs Blackwood going to London again?' asked Monty. 'I saw her bags by the door last night.'

'Yes.' Curran took a fortifying swig. 'She should be leaving as soon as possible. I told her not to bother coming back.'

'Goodness me!' said Monty. And then, before she could stop herself, 'But she's your wife –'

'Is she?' hissed Curran. 'What does she do for me that a wife should do? Does she take care of me? Does she love me? Does she treat me with respect and honour? Does she speak to me? She can't even bear to look at me.' He looked about. The tiled walls and floor deflected his voice, until it sounded as though an army of whispering ghosts echoed his words. 'Instead, she shames me. She shames me and betrays me. She has a lover in London, I'm sure of it – perhaps even more than one. I sent Thake to follow her last time she was down there and although he was distracted by the ironmonger's on Goodge Street – there were some lengths of copper piping available at very competitive rates – he was quite certain that he saw her entering a hotel with a man on her arm. I assume she only bothers to come back here because the fellow isn't prepared to take her on full time. And who could blame him! I told her that she might as well go to London and stay there for all the difference it made to me. D'you know, she laughed at me; actually *laughed*, and said I had no idea what was going on.' He looked up at her, his expression belligerent. 'Don't tell me you disapprove of my actions?'

Monty shook her head. Some days earlier she had walked into the billiard room to find Mrs Blackwood draped over the table, face down among the balls, with her dress up round her waist. Behind her stood Captain Foxley. Monty had gone straight out again without either of them knowing she had even been there. As she turned from the door she had almost stumbled over Curran himself, who had been silently following her through the ground-floor corridors in order to ask her opinion on the nutritional content of the week's menu. Monty had lured him back down the hallway with a promise to look over the menus there and then, leaving Mrs Blackwood and Captain Foxley to their various pleasures.

'The decision is yours, Mr Blackwood,' she said now. 'And you don't need my approval, or my agreement to make it. But since you ask, I think you're quite justified.'

Curran was looking at her keenly, an expression of doubtful resolve on his face. 'My wife says . . . my wife says she needs more than I can give her,' he said at last. 'But there's nothing wrong with me that some tenderness, some affection, wouldn't restore. You're a nurse, you understand what I'm talking about. I have no *desire* for Mae,' he whispered. '*That's* the problem. Nothing else.'

'I see.' Monty nodded.

'You're shocked. I've said too much. But how else can one explain . . . just because I'm in this chair –' His fingers squeezed at the rims of his wheels. 'I'm sorry –'

'I quite understand,' said Monty. 'And so Mrs Blackwood is leaving Bleakly?'

'I believe so, yes.'

'What about Captain Foxley?'

'What about him?' Curran shifted uneasily in his chair. 'Foxley saved my life,' he said. 'He pulled me out of a shell hole and brought me back to the lines. I'd never have got through the night stuck out in no-man's-land waiting for the stretcher bearers. His behaviour might be not quite what I approve of these days, but he's always welcome in my home. He always will be. It's no more than I owe him.' He tossed back the last of his Lady Beaton as though it was a tot of rum he was drinking, to stiffen his resolve. 'Perhaps it's time we went back up to the Hall,' he said. He did not look at her, but kept his eyes on the ground. 'You might bear in mind what I've said to you. I just didn't want you to think that I'm not . . . that I can't –'

'Of course.' Monty nodded. She was not sure what to say. Had Curran been propositioning her? Was he looking for her endorsement of him as a man? Had he simply been asking for her professional advice on matters of health and morality?

At that moment there was a commotion at the door, a babbling of voices and a clattering of footsteps, and all at once the hydropathic's guests burst into the room. Their expressions were startled. Behind them, like a sheepdog herding a gaggle of geriatric geese, walked Captain Foxley.

'Come along, come along!' he cried. 'What are you all

waiting for? Good heavens, you should all have been down here hours ago. Ah, Mr Blackwood, and the lovely Miss Montgomery, enjoying Bleakly's glorious waters already, I see? Nature's champagne! Especially the Lady Beaton – that slight effervescence makes all the difference, I find. Marvellous, marvellous! Come on, ladies and gentlemen, don't hang back, the pumps are waiting. And let me open the doors, it'll allow in the morning air, as well as the stirring music of our glorious bandsmen. In fact, now I come to think about it, perhaps they can be persuaded to play something a little more rousing and patriotic than that dreadful German stuff they're murdering at the moment. What do you think, Blackwood? What about "Rule Britannia"? Or even "Hearts of Oak"? "Hearts of oak are our ships, jolly tars are our men, we always are ready, steady, boys, steady . . ."' he sang in a clear tenor and seemed pleased with the resonant effects his voice created in the tiled pump room. '"We'll fi-ight and we'll conquer again and again . . ."' He held his arms wide, the silver-topped walking stick clamped in the fingers of his right hand. 'Let's *all* sing,' he cried. 'Bandsmen?' he shouted out of the open door. 'Bandsmen! "Land of Hope and Glory", if you please!'

The men on the bandstand exchanged glances, partly annoyed at being interrupted, partly pleased that someone appeared to be listening for a change. As the first chords blared out, Captain Foxley clambered on to a chair, then on to the pump-room counter. His stick beating time to the music in a pool of spilt water, he began to sing along. '"Land of ho-ope and glor-ry, mother o-of the free" that's it, come along now, Mr Sykes, put your heart into it. "How shall we extol thee", good, ladies, very good. Now breathe ... "Who are bo-orn of thee ..." Miss Montgomery, you too, please.'

Curran and Monty exchanged a glance. 'Is he drunk?' hissed Curran.

'I don't know,' said Monty.

'Bravo,' roared Captain Foxley. 'Bravo everyone! And now, a glass of our marvellous water to wet your whistle. Come along, come along, charge your glasses, please! And I expect to see you all *promenading* too. Chop chop!'

Captain Foxley climbed down and made his way over to Curran and Monty, still humming under his breath. He seized Monty about the waist and swung her round. But the movement seemed to throw him off balance. He staggered and slipped to the floor. Monty bent to help him to his feet. He was panting slightly and when he stood up he seemed unsteady. But he did not smell of alcohol and Monty was certain he was not drunk. She looked into his face. *Was* he unwell? His behaviour, she had noticed, was erratic – punctuated by moments of euphoria and flashes of confusion. Perhaps he suffered from hallucinations too. She had no idea. Was his walk unsteady? It was hard to tell. Monty resolved to pay more attention.

Curran gave Captain Foxley a suspicious smile. 'Are you feeling all right, Dodger?' he asked.

'Marvellous.' Captain Foxley twirled his cane. 'Can a man not enjoy the day?'

'It's just that ... well, you don't usually seem to enjoy it quite so exuberantly. And certainly not at this time in the morning.'

Captain Foxley laughed, his handsome features rendered all the more striking by their expression of elation. But before he could reply he seemed to spot something outside the door and his face took on a look of delighted astonishment. 'Is that Chalmers?' he asked, pointing out into the sunlight. 'What's he doing here?'

'Chalmers?' Curran glanced at Monty. 'There's nobody out there.'

'You remember Chalmers, Blackwood. He and I brought back one of Fritz's officers that time. We gave him his dinner, remember? Portman got some extra supplies – made us some dumplings.'

'Portman's dumplings,' murmured Curran.

'Krause,' said Captain Foxley suddenly. 'That was the chap's name. Nice fellow. Spoke English better than any of us. You and he talked about –'

'Motors,' said Curran. 'The magnificent Blitzen Benz. I'd seen it at Brooklands in 1909 – 200 kilometres an hour and a new land speed record! He said German motor engineering was second to none and I could hardly disagree. We got terribly drunk. Chalmers didn't take him in until the next morning.'

Captain Foxley stared out into the sunshine, smiling. 'That's right,' he said. 'The CO was furious. Chalmers!' he shouted. 'In here!'

Curran looked up at him anxiously. 'Dodger –'

'It *is* Chalmers!' insisted Captain Foxley, starting forward. 'I must go and have a word.' He was using his stick, but Monty noticed now that his gait was more of a shuffle than a walk and he seemed slightly unsure of his own footsteps.

was stealthy and observant; Private Newnes, as he had not been before but had asked to go (he had seemed somewhat awestruck by Coward's swashbuckling behaviour); and Private Jennings, who had been out two nights earlier and (to Grier's private horror) had demonstrated an immediate aptitude for throttling the sentry.

'Stay close to the others, Newnes,' said Grier. 'They know what they're doing and you should learn a trick or two.'

'Yes, sir,' said Newnes. His voice was high-pitched, like a girl's. He sounded breathless – excited and afraid. Back home, Newnes had worked for a baker. The working lives of many of the men had given them calloused fingers, but the skin of Newnes's hands was as smooth and soft as the dough he had kneaded. His fingers, more accustomed to loading the basket on the front of the delivery bicycle than filling sandbags or throwing Mills bombs, had an uncooked look. Newnes's letters home were written in a round script, peppered with spelling mistakes and scabbed with scribbled-out words. Although he had never spoken to Newnes personally, Grier's duties censoring the men's correspond-ence meant that he knew as much about the lad as anyone. He looked into Newnes's face and noticed the bruise, now faded to yellow, that stained his left cheek, and he recalled that Newnes had been struck by a tin of bully beef, which had been knocked off a shelf by a rat – *not much of a war wound, Ma, but I'm not complaining about that*. The rabbit's foot given to him by Little Nellie, Newnes wrote with three exclamation marks, was clearly working its magic. Grier also knew that Newnes hoped Nellie would write soon, and that 'over here' he was unimpressed by the girls, who were

156

nowhere near as pretty as Nellie, and by the bread, which was shamelessly hard. Grier knew that Newnes's mother walked with a stick and that his first name was Percy. He signed his letters, *your very own Perillous Percy*.

Now, Grier saw Newnes move his pale-blue eyes to look at Coward and his hairless cheeks turn pink. Sergeant Coward was sitting on the fire step oiling his bayonet knife. Sergeant Coward was openly dedicated to killing as many Germans as possible. In his leisure moments he had fashioned a terrifying instrument with which he hoped to bash in their heads. It looked rather like a large hairbrush, but where the bristles might be he had inserted row upon row of nine-inch nails. Coward had spent many hours carefully battering these nails into position. He called the resulting item 'The Spiker' (rather unimaginatively, Grier thought) and had practised its efficacy on rats. Coward was not the only soldier to have created for himself a weapon of comforting weight and deadliness to use on patrols. Lieutenant Foxley possessed an item that looked like a cross between a potato masher and a hammer, and Curran had shown Grier a truncheon one of the men had made out of a piece of wood into the tip of which he had embedded a bayonet knife like an American tomahawk. This gruesome medieval instrument had been a gift, presented to Curran as its creator was carried off to the regimental aid post on a stretcher. Curran had used it to great effect – until his legs had been mangled by a German *Minenwerfer* and he too had been sent back to Blighty.

That evening the guns were quiet. To the south the sky was punctuated by bursts of artillery fire, but in Grier's section of the trench there was nothing. Perhaps the

Germans themselves were creeping about between the wire. It seemed likely, as there was no other explanation for the lack of rifle shots or absence of star shells to illuminate the stretch of putrid ground that lay between their opposing trenches. Grier waited while his men checked that their rifles were loaded. And were their bayonets well oiled so that they slipped out quickly and silently when required? Grier peered through a periscope across the shattered earth of no-man's-land. He passed the word along that a patrol was going out.

All at once Lieutenant Foxley appeared beside him. 'I heard you were going over,' he said. 'Handyside's sick. I'll go instead.'

Second Lieutenant Handyside's face twitched. 'I'm quite well, sir,' he muttered. 'Count me in.'

A shell whistled out of the German trenches to smash down twenty yards away. Grier and the others ducked, but Handyside cried out. His arms jerked up to cover his head and he fell to his knees. Grier seized him by the shoulders and dragged him upright. In the light of a star shell that burst overhead he could see that Handyside's face was glazed with sweat. His eyes stared and he had bitten his own lip so that blood stained his teeth.

Grier looked away. 'Foxley's right,' he said. 'Handyside can take the pay books. Newnes, give your pay book and identity disc to Handyside. We don't want to tell Fritz who we are.' He unsheathed his revolver and checked the chamber was full. Foxley did the same. Grier saw that Foxley held a long serrated knife, which he tested for sharpness with his thumb. The potato masher hung from his belt.

Armed with nothing but his revolver, his fear and a deadening sense of gloom, Grier felt underequipped. Should he make more of an effort to cultivate the attributes of manly aggression? Should he fashion a home-made instrument of butchery? Perhaps he should volunteer for a trench raid? He felt sick at the thought. 'Come along then, lads,' he whispered. 'Newnes, keep your head down. You don't want them to see you silhouetted on the top of the parapet.'

Out of the trench, the men lay still, concealed by the lip of a shell hole. Only Newnes seemed unsure what to do. He clawed at his back, wriggling his shoulders against the crawling of the lice beneath his shirt. Grier clicked his tongue with irritation. All the fellow had to do was tumble over the parapet and lie flat. Yet Newnes had reared up above the trench like a cockerel on a dungheap. Grier stared into Newnes's round blue eyes. The lad was panting, his face luminous with fear. Should he send him back? Why had Newnes asked to come if he was so terrified? But Foxley was crawling forward with Harding, and Coward was moving off behind Foxley with Jennings. Grier gestured to Newnes to follow, heading out towards the wire. Newnes now seemed to be having trouble with his bayonet knife, which had snagged on a sandbag. His elbow rose up as he made to disentangle it, waggling this way and that as though he was trying to attract the attention of the German snipers.

Up ahead, Coward turned to see why they weren't following. He saw Newnes scrabbling about, and his expression transformed into one of such fury that for a moment Grier thought he might be about to turn back and club Newnes with The Spiker. At last Newnes extracted his knife from the sandbag and began to creep across the mud.

They inched towards the wire, zigzagging their way to

the German listening post. All was silent, quite the opposite of the cacophony of whistles, booms and rat-tat-tatting that usually filled the night. The only sound came from the hoot of owls and croaking of frogs (though where these creatures actually lived was a mystery). At that moment a star shell was sent up from the trenches opposite and the wilderness through which they were crawling was illuminated by a searing white light. Grier pressed himself into the earth. Up ahead he saw the others do the same, sinking down on to the mud to lie as flat as possible. The night-time world was turned into day. A bemused rat scuttled across the ground in front of his nose, emerging from inside the torn and sodden tunic of a corpse upon whose innards it had been gorging. Grier saw a pale face staring up at him inches from his own. Its features were baggy and flaccid-looking, as though the flesh had stretched in the rain and was now too large for the skull beneath. Empty eye sockets drooped.

Behind him Grier could hear Newnes floundering about, cursing in a strange high-pitched voice. Could the lad not keep quiet? Had he not understood the importance of *creeping*? He was going to get them all killed. Grier squirmed round to see what was wrong. Newnes was on his hands and knees. He was crawling among a sea of rotting uniforms, a look of horror on his face at the open grave he had unluckily stumbled into. He staggered to his feet, illuminated like an actor on a stage.

'Newnes!' hissed Grier. 'Get *down*!' A machine gun began spraying the air with bullets. Grier heard them whizz past his ear and thwack into the ground. He lay still, beside the eyeless corpse, his own eyes fixed upon the terrified figure, floundering among the disembodied legs and arms of his comrades. Private Newnes reeled, as though blown by a strong wind. An arc of blood burst from his cheek and he toppled backwards.

It had not been possible to fetch Newnes until the following evening. Grier came across him lying with a number of other stretcher cases on the fire step of the trench. The bruise on his face had disappeared, ripped away by a machine-gun bullet, and his pale-blue eyes were milky with tears between crusts of blood and dirt. The doctor and chaplain stood beside him, as though waiting to see which might have the more useful job to do. The chaplain eyed a tuft of matted fur that Newnes clutched in his right hand and his face assumed a look of dejection. Many of the men were beset by superstition and Grier knew that all manner of lucky talismans – coins, bits of shrapnel, rabbits' feet – filled their pockets. Newnes clawed at the doctor's tunic with his small soft hands and began making horrible sounds. How thin he looked, thought Grier. The wrists which poked from his sleeves seemed too young and puny to hold anything more substantial than a skipping rope. Grier remembered Newnes's boyish delight at being released from the humdrum job of delivering bread. *'This war will make a man of me, Ma. I'll make you and Nellie proud.'*

Grier went to speak to Sergeant Coward. It turned out that Private Newnes was not nineteen at all, but only seventeen. The fact that his shoulders were as narrow as a washboard and he had not a whisker on his cheek had been overlooked by the recruiting officers, who seemed happy to turn a blind eye to such indications of adolescence. Coward too had said nothing. If the boy wanted to fight, he said, why shouldn't he? Grier was too dispirited to reply.

Foxley was sitting on the bunk when Grier came into the officers' dugout. Handyside was leaning against the wall. Standage and Chalmers sat on either side of the table and Foxley's batman was frying bacon on a dixie. There was another face, too, which Grier had not seen before. The face was young and smooth-skinned. It had slightly bucked teeth and an eager expression. Its owner was younger than Standage or Chalmers and had clearly just come up the line. Grier knew immediately that he had never been to the front before. He looked far too excited.

'Blackwood!' cried Standage. 'There you are. Foxley was just telling us about your patrol last night. He says he and Coward took the sentry and scuppered Fritz's patrol single-handed. You and that other fellow drew their fire with your jumping up and down so that they hardly noticed what was happening right under their noses. Well done. Pity about that young chap . . . what's-his-name.'

'Newnes,' said Grier mechanically. 'His name was Private Newnes.'

'This is Lucas,' said Standage. 'Just got his commission.'

Grier was trying to remember who else had been killed that week, other than Newnes, but was unable to recall any names. At the beginning he had been able to remember the name and rank of every soldier under his command who had been killed or wounded. But the incessant noise seemed to have shaken such useful and sympathetic memories out of his head for ever. Besides, there were far too many names to recall now.

'Whisky?' said Foxley. He poured a slug of the stuff into Grier's tea. Foxley took a mouthful of his own tea and filled the mug up to the brim again with spirits. 'How's that bacon coming along, Portman?' he said. 'Blackwood might want some too.'

'Almost ready, sir,' said Portman.

Grier stared at the crumpled and mud-stained cot which Lieutenant Foxley had recently vacated and upon which he was to spend the next few hours. He was almost too tired to stand, but knew that sleep would prove almost impossible once he lay down. He gulped his tea. The smell of bacon made his stomach turn.

'What adventure d'you think we'll get up to tonight?' said Foxley, rubbing his hands together. 'I think it's time for a raid. The men are bored and need to be kept on their toes. Anyone want to come?'

'I'll come,' said Lucas.

'D'you think you're ready?' said Foxley, without looking up. 'D'you think you've got the guts for it?' Lieutenant Foxley had a reputation for luck. Lieutenant Foxley, it was said, always brought his men back. He chose them carefully and he would never have chosen someone like Newnes. It was Grier's fault that Newnes was dead. 'I'd have taken McAlister,' Foxley had commented. 'He knows how to get to the wire without making a fool of himself.'

'Have you ever killed a man, Lucas?' asked Grier now, hoping to prevent Foxley from describing the specific behaviour required of a man with 'guts'.

'No,' Lucas answered. He grinned. 'But it sounds like an adventure.'

Foxley handed Lucas the potato masher, which was lying beside him on the bunk. 'Think you can use one of these?'

Lucas tested the weight of the thing in his hand. He swung it, as though taking a swipe at a tennis ball. 'It's well-balanced,' he said.

'That's Fritz's blood on the end,' said Foxley. 'Does that bother you?'

'No,' said Lucas. 'I should hope it *has* got Fritz's blood on it,' he added, clearly feeling that a remark of greater force and belligerence was required. 'It's what we're here for, isn't it? Chase 'em back to Berlin.'

Grier watched Lucas dully. Lucas's buttons were shiny, his face vacant and blameless. Lucas's neck was long and angular. An Adam's apple of unusual prominence bulged earnestly above his collar, as though he were permanently searching for something on a high shelf, craning to offer up the most vulnerable part of his body for execution. How easily a piece of shrapnel might gouge out that small lump of masculinity, thought Grier. How neatly a bullet might slice through that young neck, so tall and thin, as pale as butter against the rough khaki of his uniform. Grier could not remember ever holding such naive views about the war. But then he could not remember what sort of a man he had been when he had first come to the front. At the time, he seemed to recall, he had thought himself patriotic, noble and brave. Perhaps he had simply been vainglorious. Now he felt only indecisive and exhausted. And how hard it was becoming to hide the feelings of gloom and pessimism that beset him. The men looked to him for leadership, for courage, but providing these things was sucking the life out of him as surely as if he had offered up the blood of his own veins. No doubt, eventually, that price would be exacted too.

Grier took another gulp of tea and smoothed his moustache with his fingers. He saw Lucas instinctively copy the gesture, running his fingers fondly over his own top lip, upon which he had grown a wispy fringe of blond whiskers. It would be at least three months before Second Lieutenant Lucas was sufficiently experienced to be useful at the front. Six months later, should he live that long, he would be jumping with nerves. For some reason Grier felt certain that Second Lieutenant Lucas's disillusionment would be swift and profound. He would fall apart like a terrified animal, shaken to pieces by sights and sounds against which he would have no resilience. Grier decided to stay away from him.

'Now then, Lucas,' said Chalmers. 'If you want to know how to fight, you could do worse than watch old Dodger here. He's the best.'

'I know,' said Lucas. He grinned again, so that Grier began to feel nauseated by the repeated sight of Lucas's teeth (how long and yellow they were). He looked at Handyside, still standing against the wall. Handyside was unusually quiet. He was sweating and looked nervously over towards the door every time an explosion shook the dugout (an incident which had occurred at least six times since Grier entered). Another roar from above made the walls tremble. A thin line of soil trickled from the ceiling into Grier's tea. Grier affected not to notice. Handyside put his knuckles to his lips.

Lucas was talking loudly now about medals. His father had won the Queen's South Africa Medal and he, young Lucas, was determined to match this achievement.

'Did your father come up against concentrated machine-gun fire?' asked Grier suddenly. 'D'you think he saw a trench mortar, or came across a *Flammenwerfer*?' Standage, Chalmers and Foxley all laughed. 'D'you think he survived a gas attack and lived in a slit in the earth for two years listening to shells exploding and watching his comrades, his men, being killed before his eyes?'

Lucas was looking at Grier warily, as though wondering whether he was suffering from 'funk' or 'windiness', both of which maladies he had heard much about.

'Come along, Blackwood,' said Foxley. 'The lad wants a bit of glory, that's all. Don't we all want some of that? There's not much else we'll get out of this, is there?'

Grier reached out to take the mess tin of bacon and biscuit that Portman was holding out to him. Portman stared at Grier's outstretched hand, then looked away discreetly. Grier followed the batman's gaze. His hand, still extended to take the mess tin, was shaking violently, as though he was scattering an invisible handful of seed to a cluster of imaginary chickens. He was not cold, not frightened, not angry, why was his hand behaving like that? Grier flexed his fingers. He could not feel their gentle oscillation, but could not stop or control it. He stuffed his hand into his pocket and rooted for his cigarettes (would he be able to get one into his mouth without dropping it on to the floor?). 'Put it on the table, please, Portman,' he muttered. 'I'll have it in a minute.'

Second Lieutenant Handyside spent most of the night sitting at the desk in a corner of the dugout, shouting into the field telephone. Every now and again the walls shook, and the air filled with dust and smoke. A hurricane lamp illuminated the corner where he sat with a cheerless yellow light. Beside him Grier was stretched out on the cot, waiting for sleep to come. The telephone jangled urgently. It was GHQ asking for a miner who spoke German. Handyside said he had no idea where they could find one. He woke Grier to ask.

'*You* speak German, Handyside,' said Grier. 'Can you dig too?'

'Only in the garden, sir,' replied Handyside.

Half an hour later GHQ telephoned to say that aerial reconnaissance photographs indicated the presence of a German listening post not fifty yards from their own front-line trench. A patrol was to be despatched that very moment to eliminate it. Grier was woken once more. He replied that this post had already been eliminated.

Shortly afterwards Grier was woken a third time. GHQ was demanding that a sap be dug out into no-man's-land to create their own listening post. The existing sap, which was ten yards further south, was to be filled in. Work must start immediately. Grier sent a runner to inform Lieutenant Foxley of this essential commandment. It transpired that Foxley was out on a trench raid. Grier would have to organise the excavations himself. He waited for the sappers to arrive. As soon as the sappers had received their instructions and left for the front line, Grier lay down. The telephone rang again. GHQ announced that the filled-in sap was to be re-excavated and the one being dug was to be filled in again. Grier sent another runner after the team of sappers.

'Oh, and does anyone there speak German?' added the Adjutant. The line crackled and hissed.

'Yes,' said Grier. 'Handyside does.'

'Is he a miner?' asked the Adjutant.

'No,' shouted Grier. 'He's a teacher in a grammar school.'

'That's no use,' said the Adjutant. 'We need a miner.'

'There are no miners here,' said Grier.

He sat on the edge of the bed, waiting for the next interruption. Overhead, he could hear the whistle and boom of shells. A crash shook the walls and caused the whisky bottles on the table to tinkle. Out of the corner of his eye Grier saw Handyside leap to his feet.

'Want me to take over, Handyside?' asked Grier without looking up. But Handyside had snatched up the field telephone and was babbling into the receiver, something about wire and revetments and duckboards. He slammed the telephone down and scribbled on a notepad. He pored over a map and chewed his lip.

'Handyside?'

Handyside grabbed the telephone again and barked some seemingly unrelated words into it.

'Handyside!' shouted Grier.

'Yes, Captain.' Handyside turned to Grier a face pale and sweating and yellowish.

'Have you seen the medical officer?'

'No, sir.'

'D'you think you should?'

'No, sir. He's got better things to do. I'm on leave the day after tomorrow. I've not got long to go.' The roar of an exploding shell shattered the silence between them. Handyside's face twitched.

At that moment there was a scuffling sound in the doorway. The gas curtain was thrown aside and Foxley and Coward appeared. Between them marched a German soldier.

'Dragged him right out of his trench,' said Foxley. 'No one even noticed!'

The German soldier appeared relieved to have been so rudely plucked from the earth. He looked about, his eyes resting eagerly on the bottle of whisky Foxley was now holding.

'We had a right old time of it, didn't we, Coward? That Spiker of yours came in very handy. We went over and just listened at first. I thought they were asleep. And then one of 'em shouts out, "You chaps, over there. Go away now or we'll have to shoot you." Plain as that! I've never seen Coward move so quickly.' Foxley roared with laughter. 'Both of us scuttled off like rabbits. Curran would have enjoyed it,' he added. 'They'd not have heard *him* creeping up on them. He was always up for a raid or two. Not like you.'

'No,' said Grier, his eyes on the ground. 'Not like me.'

'Anyway, we came straight back after that, but there was nothing going on over here. Besides, Coward was disappointed, weren't you, Coward? So he and I and a couple of others went out again, further down the lines. And we brought back this chap here.' He smiled at the German and squeezed his arm. 'Big chap, ain't he?' He pointed to the

German's insignia. 'Captain too, by the looks of things. D'you think we should call him "sir"?'

'Give him a drink,' said Grier.

'Handyside,' said Foxley, slopping a measure of whisky into a mess tin and handing it to the German. 'Ask this fellow whether he knows there's to be a push tomorrow.'

'*Ja*,' said the German. He drank the whisky down in a single gulp. 'And a mine. We've known for weeks. We're ready for you.'

'There's a surprise,' muttered Foxley.

Grier telephoned GHQ.

'It's too late to change our plans now,' said the Adjutant down the telephone line. 'Besides, the Colonel's gone to bed.'

The following day the word came up that the mine was to be sprung beneath the enemy's defences. The men were to stand to and at 8 a.m., when the mine was detonated, they were to leap out of the trench and dash across to capture the Germans' front line.

Grier tried not to show his despair.

He had been out a number of times and knew that there were lines and lines of barbed wire ahead of them. He also knew that there were machine guns positioned all along the German front line at the very point the mine was supposed to be detonated. Unless the thing was absolutely enormous, it was unlikely that the mine would knock out very many of these deadly obstacles. In addition, for the past two days the German trenches had been unexpectedly silent, so that Grier was sure they had all pulled back, away from the area where the mine was due to explode. No doubt they were waiting, somewhere beyond the range of the predicted devastation, to return as soon as the danger was passed.

At eight o'clock Grier was standing with his men in the trench, waiting for the explosion. It had rained the night before and in the bottom of the trench a rivulet of water had formed. It seemed to be flowing, as though heading somewhere purposeful. The men shifted their feet, strangely concerned with keeping their boots dry despite the prospect of imminent death. Some duckboards would have to be brought up at some point, thought Grier absently. Perhaps tomorrow . . .

All at once a great roar vibrated though the ground and a mass of soil and water, stones, shrapnel, splinters of wood burst up before them in the shape of a monstrous brown conifer. Grier saw the body of a man flung into the sky like a guy being tossed on to a bonfire. More bulky-looking objects were also blasted aloft, though whether these were sandbags or dismembered limbs it was impossible to tell. Beneath the fading roar Grier was almost certain he could hear the sound of screaming, but he could not be sure about that either. His own ears seemed to sing with a high-pitched ringing noise almost constantly, even when the guns fell silent, as though he were continually hearing a very distant but unceasing cry of pain. Grier blew on his whistle and brandished his revolver. He uttered a roar of manly aggression, which he did not in the slightest bit feel (indeed, he was surprised to hear such noises issuing from his own mouth), and clambered up the scaling ladder.

In this instance being first out of the trench was not as hazardous as it usually was, as a great muddy curtain of spray and dust was billowing towards him, shielding him from the sight of the German machine guns. Ahead of him, already out of the trench and over to the left, Grier saw Foxley raise an arm and run forward. Almost immediately he was engulfed by the rolling cloud of powdered earth. Grier uttered another vigorous war cry and leaped across a ditch. He bounded over a shattered gun limber and disappeared, after Foxley, into the dust. On either side his men did the same.

Grier could see nothing at all. A violent wind seemed to have arisen, and all manner of sticks and stones and bits of horrible wet softness were blowing into his face and glancing off his helmet. He lowered his head and stumbled on. He was blind. He could hardly breathe. The air was thick and strangely sulphurous, it was warm and felt coarse against his throat. He coughed and dashed a hand across his smarting eyes. At this rate he might run directly into the German trenches, as he was scarcely able to see his own hand in front of his face. Then the ground seemed to open up beneath his feet and he was sliding down a muddy greasy bank. Grier waved his revolver and tried to grasp at something to stop this frantic slithering descent. Suddenly the brown cloud had blown away and he found he was sitting in the bottom of an enormous shell hole. A number of other men were there, and he recognised Sergeant Coward and Private Broughton among them.

There were at least twenty others, but looking again Grier realised that they were all dead: a mixture of German and British soldiers, tangled together in a pool of brown and crimson water, like refuse blocking a plughole in an abattoir. The smell was fearsome. Private Broughton vomited.

'This way.' Grier waved his revolver, gesturing to the men to move round to the other side of the crater. They clambered up and peeped over the rim. The crater of the mine was visible one hundred yards distant. It had created a void of lunar proportions and thrown up a great mass of wreckage, disturbing a German dugout and spitting out sandbags, duckboards, lumps of concrete, bedding and ammunition on to the surrounding earth. Grier noticed that one or two of these bits of wreckage smoked, like hot coals, as though they had been blasted out of the bowels of hell itself. The barbed wire from both sides was tangled up, knotted and twisted and viciously looped like savage outsized brambles. It seemed not to have been 'swept aside' at all, but had simply been rolled back, towards the German trenches, into impenetrable black hedges. As the air cleared, machine-gun bullets began to spray across the landscape. From somewhere to his far right a voice was screaming out 'Advance! Advance!' A persistent whistle blasted again and again, as though the men were dogs to be commanded forward unquestioningly.

The explosion had wiped out a section of German earthworks completely, like sweeping away a section of railway line. But on either side of the crater the trenches seemed to be intact, and even as the dust from the explosion dispersed Grier could see movement in those trenches, could distinguish the long steel barrels of machine guns nosing into position above the parapet. On either side those men who had not fallen into the shell hole with him were still pushing forward, towards their objective, visible like saplings against that flat and blasted landscape. The machine guns stuttered into life.

*

Foxley bounded into the shell hole and crawled forward to lie beside Grier. 'This is impossible,' he muttered. He squinted above the lip of the crater. A machine-gun bullet thwacked into the earth inches from his eyes.

Grier peeped over the rim of earth, towards the German trenches. He could see bodies scattered all around, some moving, some screaming, some lying still. And the men were still emerging from the trench behind them, picking their way uncertainly forward, looking about for an officer, for someone to tell them what to do. A team of stretcher bearers blundered out of the trench, but then seemed to think better of it and, clambering forward over the uneven terrain, plunged into a shell hole that had opened up a few yards on from the parapet. Then Grier recognised a familiar figure coming towards them, sprinting across no-man's-land, crouching down now and again beside the huddle of a fallen soldier, whispering, making a gesture, leaping up and onwards. It was the chaplain – no longer content to wait in the trenches for the faith-shattered remnants of his Company to be brought back in, but possessed with a terrible urgency to bring spiritual succour to those abandoned beneath the guns. He bounded from one shell hole to another, leaping over dead bodies and lingering over live ones, dancing left and right, bobbing up and down as though such random movements might somehow fox the linear trajectory of approaching bullets. He bent again. Grier saw the pages of the prayer book flapping like a white flag, then he was off once more. With a final heroic leap, the chaplain landed in the shell hole beside Grier.

'God save the King,' he screamed.

Grier noticed that the chaplain's shoulder was pouring

with blood, but the chaplain seemed neither to notice nor to care.

Grier peered over the lip of the shell hole once again. Behind him the stretcher bearers were out in the open once more, floundering about in a mud-filled hollow. In front of him men were still creeping forward, past the crater where the mine had exploded, towards the wire and the German trenches.

'Fall back!' shouted Foxley and Grier together. 'Fall back!'

Directly in front of them a soldier fell to his knees as though in prayer. He remained there for a moment, then tumbled forward. Machine-gun bullets sprayed a shower of bloody earth into Grier's face. He rubbed his eyes with his fists. He had slept for barely an hour the night before and his mind was dazed with terror and fatigue, his senses mercifully numbed, so that he could no longer smell the corpses at the bottom of the shell hole; the sound of the guns had disappeared beneath the faint internal screaming in his ears, and his vision seemed dreamlike and unreal. He felt as though he had been lying there, beneath the bullets, for his entire life. Beside him he could hear the chaplain babbling on about the valley of death, about staffs and rods and fearlessness, and all at once Grier had to get away from this absurd and horrifying place, away from the dead soldiers at the foot of the crater and away from the crazed muttering of the chaplain.

He looked back. The stretcher bearers, miraculously untouched, were still floundering their way hopelessly towards the wire. He looked forward. Their objective lay not fifty yards away. A shell exploded to their left, showering them with mud and shrapnel. Grier found that his hands were shaking so much that he could no longer hold his revolver still. He flung it aside and pulled out his handkerchief. It was surprisingly white, starched and ironed and neatly folded, a tiny square of hygiene in a vast wilderness of ugliness and pollution. He dabbed his streaming eyes with it.

'Grier,' he heard Foxley whisper. 'Grier, are you hit?' He stared into Foxley's face. Apart from Handyside, there was only Foxley left from the original battalion.

'*When the wicked man turneth away from the wickedness that he hath committed and doeth that which is lawful and right, he shall save his soul alive,*' said the chaplain.

'Come on,' whispered Foxley urgently. 'Don't let the men see you like this.'

'What men?' cried Grier. 'There's only you and me left.'

'*The hand of the Lord was upon me,*' shouted the chaplain, '*and carried me out in the spirit of the Lord and set me down in the midst of the valley which was full of bones.*'

'Exactly,' muttered Foxley. 'Only you and me.'

'*Can these bones live?*' screamed the chaplain. He reared up from his bed of earth at the lip of the shell hole and flung his arms wide. '*Prophesy upon these bones and say unto them, "o ye dry bones, hear the word of the Lord!"*'

Grier sprang to his feet. He pulled the chaplain backwards and flung him down into the foot of the crater.

'Blackwood!' cried Foxley.

But Grier was dashing forward, waving his handkerchief in the air above his head. It fluttered pitifully in the murky light, invisible through the smoke, as disregarded as a butterfly. The sound of bullets did not abate and Grier heard them sing about his ears as he sprang forward. He reached a man, wounded in the chest, who was crying out for the help he was certain would never come. Somehow Grier managed to throw off the fellow's webbing and lift him up. How puny he felt beneath the wet fabric of his uniform. Grier turned and stumbled his way back across the mud, all the way towards the trenches from which he and his men had emerged not five minutes earlier. He released the man into the arms of the doctor, who was standing in the trench, his face pale and aghast. Grier ran back, his handkerchief waving once more. He heard Foxley calling out from the shell hole, 'Grier! Grier! Come back!' But he did not stop. He flung another man over his shoulder as though carrying a roll of carpet, and hastened back to the lines. He felt something sting his shoulder, and a sensation of warmth flooded down his arm. He released the man, turned again and went back out into no-man's-land. He could feel his eyes staring in his head, could see the dull shine of the German helmets behind the chattering barrel of the machine gun directly ahead. A bullet ripped his tunic, but this time he felt nothing. Had it missed him? Grier pulled another man up, hands under his armpits. The man's leg was shattered and he had fainted with the pain. Grier managed to hoist the fellow into his arms, the limb dangling like a cut of meat. His legs almost buckling beneath him, Grier carried the soldier back to the lines.

Foxley burst out of the shell hole and ran towards him. 'Grier,' he screamed. Grier was hauling a body into a sitting position.

'This one's a German,' shouted Foxley.

'Does it matter?' cried Grier.

17

THE NEW visitors were becoming restless. Perceiving that neither Grier nor Curran seemed able or willing to do anything to occupy them, Monty encouraged Grier to implement his plan for holding a dance.

'Young people', she said, 'are always keen on dancing.'

'So they are,' said Grier. 'And I had a telephone call this morning. There's a further party arriving at the end of the week. What better opportunity will there be? We can use the old gymnasium. Everyone will return home delighted with their holiday at Bleakly; they'll tell all their friends about the old place, and in no time at all we'll be reinstated as exciting and fashionable.'

'This dance,' Mae said to Monty. 'Should I assume it's in honour of me? A party thrown by my dear husband on my last evening?'

'Your last evening?'

'Oh, didn't you know? Curran and I are to be divorced.' Mae tossed her head. 'Yes, the shame of it, I know. I didn't expect he would be quite so insistently *modern* about things, but you know Curran; he likes to do everything properly.' She sounded more annoyed than upset. Mae took a step closer. 'If I might be plain with you for a moment, Miss Montgomery: I can see that my husband has a soft spot for you. It's a result of his army days, you know, in the hospital . . .'

'Many people find a nurse quite a reassuring figure,' said Monty, perceiving that some sort of reply was expected.

'Quite so,' murmured Mae. 'I'm glad we understand one another. The point is, I was wondering, do you think you might put in a good word for me?'

'About what?'

'Well, I don't want to go back to what I was before, do I? I don't want to have nothing.'

'No,' said Monty. 'I shouldn't think you do.'

Before the war, when Curran had married her, Mae had been a romantic figure – tragically penniless, but with the face of an angel and the figure of a houri. Men had adored her. She had luxuriated in their flattery and admiration, unfurling before them like a sunflower in midsummer. But she had chosen Curran, falling for his good looks and ready fortune. Certainly, Mae had not expected him to invest everything in an isolated and ailing hydropathic miles from London and head off to war to have his legs blown off.

Part of Monty felt sorry for Mae now, but it was a very small part. 'I can't make him change his mind about anything he's decided on,' she said. 'Perhaps you should ask Mr Grier about it.'

'Oh, he's useless,' Mae retorted. 'They're as bad as each other; and worse since the war. I can't imagine why.'

'No, Mrs Blackwood,' said Monty. 'I don't suppose you can.'

Monty stalked off towards the gymnasium. Mae followed.

'But you could say something to him,' she insisted. 'He can't just cast me off without anything. He'll listen to you. You've got that uniform. It gives you authority, you know.'

'I'll see what I can do,' replied Monty, hoping such vague promises would satisfy. She wished Mae would go away.

Monty pulled open the double doors to the gymnasium. Broken and abandoned items were stacked everywhere: screens that had once shielded the beds of the wounded from the horrified gazes of their comrades; a pair of operating tables; four teetering towers of canvas chairs. Here and there, in this sea of wreckage, there was evidence of the gymnasium's more wholesome past – a box of medicine balls, a baggy trampoline and a collection of badminton racquets, their strings snapped and sagging. By the door a personal cache of refuse had been crammed: a suitcase and a huge chest bound with iron bands.

'Goodness,' said Mae. 'Where did all this come from?'

'The army left it. The place was a war hospital.'

'Look,' said Mae, pointing to a set of initials stencilled on to the lid of a large portmanteau. 'P.E.F. It must be Peter's! Shall we take a look inside?'

Monty was about to say 'no', but Mae was already snapping the fastenings open. Monty felt a shiver of excitement. She peered over Mae's shoulder as she raised the lid and was disappointed to see only old magazines. A yellowed and torn fold of paper turned out to be a programme for Speech Day at Oakham School from 1899.

How long ago that century seemed now, thought Monty. She opened the flimsy pages. There, at the end, Peter Foxley was listed as having won the 'Lower School Prize Essay for his lively discourse on the subject of *Bees: Our World and Theirs*, an essay eulogising the humble honey bee and explaining the ways in which this busy creature mirrors our own noble industrial society'.

Beneath this faded memento Monty found a programme for the School Sports Day of 1906. The Peter Foxley of 1906 had been the Captain of the First Fifteen and had led the team to victory in the 1906–7 season. The headmaster had been scheduled to give a speech on 'Manliness and the Heroic Spirit', before the singing of a number of stirring hymns – notably 'Jerusalem' and 'Onward, Christian Soldiers'.

'Curran was a rugby blue, you know,' murmured Mae.

'And Grier?'

'Oh, I don't know about him. I don't think he was much good at that sort of thing.' Mae sounded uninterested. 'Is there anything else in there? It looks like rubbish to me.' She dusted her skirt impatiently.

Monty picked up a familiar-looking square of paper. It was a recruiting chit from 1914. She let it fall from her fingertips on to a dusty stack of old magazines: *The Boy's Own Paper; Union Jack; Pluck (A High Class Weekly Library of Adventure at Home and Abroad)*.

'Look at my stockings, they're filthy with all this grovelling about in the dirt.' Mae's voice grated painfully in Monty's ear. 'Is there nothing else in there? How boring. I might as well go and do something more interesting.'

'No,' said Monty, trying to sound as discouraging as

possible. 'There's nothing else in here.' Her gaze had fallen on a scrap of lilac-coloured paper.

Monty picked it up. The handwriting was not Sophia's. *Dearest Peter, will you reply by return of post to let me know when we might meet?* All at once Monty felt overwhelmed with sorrow and guilt. Why was she examining the paraphernalia of Captain Foxley's past? Had she not had enough of scribbled notes and broken promises? She covered her eyes with her hands. She tried to recall Sophia's face, but she could no longer remember what she looked like. She had promised Sophia that she would never forget. It seemed like another betrayal.

The new guests had gone into town on the train. While they were away the others surged back into the lounge, gleefully reclaiming their familiar sofas and armchairs. Monty noticed Mrs Forbes positioning various moral hygiene pamphlets about the room, in the hope that the young people might read them and apprehend the decadence of their lives.

As Monty crossed the foyer, looking for something to do, Curran trundled out of his office. Rather than his usual flawless white collar, neatly positioned tie and meticulously trimmed hair, he was wearing what looked like a boiler suit. Over this he had a thick jacket. Round his neck was a green woollen scarf, and on his head the same leather helmet and goggles he had worn in the racing wheelchair.

'The place is rather quiet just now,' he said to Monty. 'I'm going out.'

'Where?' asked Monty, gazing with suspicion at this unexpected outfit. 'Not back to the beach?'

'I don't know.' Curran grinned. 'It's another surprise. Ada's fixed the Norton!'

Monty followed the wheelchair out on to the terrace. On the gravel, in front of the Hall, Ada was sitting astride a motorcycle. She was wearing a pair of men's trousers beneath a military greatcoat, which she had cut off at the knee, in order (remembered Monty) to stop it getting caught in the chain. The engine throbbed and burbled between her legs.

'I've done everything I can,' she cried. 'She should reach top speed.' The exhaust pipe coughed a cloud of black smoke. A sidecar, black and shining, was attached to the motorcycle like a monstrous pupa. Ada revved the engine. Beside one of the huge ornamental urns at the entrance to the Hall, Grier and Captain Foxley stood together.

'Well done!' Captain Foxley cried. He laughed out loud and smiled. 'How lucky we are to have one another! Here, at Bleakly. Don't you agree, Monty?'

'Are you sure about this?' asked Grier as Curran propelled himself forward.

'Of course,' Curran answered.

Grier reached into his pocket and pulled out his silver cigarette case. 'Happy Birthday,' he said, placing a cigarette between his brother's lips. He offered the case to Captain Foxley.

'Turkish,' said Foxley in surprise. 'My own brand, too. I'm surprised you can afford such things.'

'I can't,' said Grier. 'I got them for Curran's birthday. If he's only going to have one cigarette a year I can at least get him something better than stinkers.' He touched a match to Curran's cigarette, lit his own and offered the light to Foxley.

Captain Foxley bent his head to the flame. 'Come on, then.' He lodged his cigarette in the corner of his mouth. 'If you're ready, Curran? One, two, three . . .'

Between them, Grier and Foxley hoisted Curran out of his wheelchair and thrust him into the opening in the top of the sidecar. Ada produced a cushion and a blanket, and arranged them about his back and legs. She revved the motorcycle once again. 'Ready, sir?'

Curran pulled the goggles over his eyes, his cigarette still between his lips. He blew out a cloud of smoke. 'Reminds me of those little parcels you used to receive at the front, Dodger. There was always condensed milk, plum pudding and Turkish cigarettes in your parcels from home.' He chuckled. 'The rest of us had to make do with Navy Cut.'

◆

Squeezed into the cellar at Caeskerke were four wounded men, spread on the floor on blankets and straw. A small stove in the corner drew from the cellar's occupants a smell of wet clothing, of mud and dirt, engine oil, coal dust and reeking wounds, so that the atmosphere was as warm and thick as blood. But going outside for a breath of fresh air was impossible, as that evening the German guns had erupted in an ear-splitting cannonade. The crash and roar of shells falling on the village made the cellar's underground walls tremble; and here and there grainy trickles of plaster dribbled from the ceiling like threads.

Ada and Monty had intended to travel back to Furnes with the wounded, but the ambulance had broken down and no other had come up from the hospital that afternoon. Now that such a bombardment had started, it was unlikely that anyone else would be able to bring one that close to the front line. Still, thought Monty, she and Ada had experienced many nights in the cellar at Caeskerke. Ada was crouched beside the hurricane lamp fixing a mysterious part of the ambulance's engine; Monty was ladling soup from a cauldron that sat on top of the smoky and evil-smelling stove. The soup was made from turnips (those which had not been blasted into smithereens by the guns). It also contained a handful of thyme, which Monty had come across growing in the devastated remains of a garden near the road to Oudkarspel. Despite the thyme (or perhaps because of it), the soup tasted as bitter as wormwood and smelt strongly of petrol. As she stirred the lumpy yellowish mixture, Monty could not help but think of all the meals she had picked at or turned away from, all the food she had left on the side of her plate. How hungry she was, standing before that stove in the reeking half-dark cellar. How she wished she had spent more time eating before the war.

Outside, they heard the familiar scream of an approaching shell.

'This'll be close,' muttered Ada.

The scream grew louder. It seemed to fill the air about them as completely as if there had been no cellar, no walls or roof around and above them. Monty and Ada stared at one another, their mouths wide, their eyes fearful, at once comprehending what was about to happen. There was a split second of silence, then the stillness of the cellar blasted apart.

The women were thrown against the stairs. In the opposite corner, where two of the wounded soldiers lay, a haphazard mass of shattered bricks and splintered timbers, soil, roof tiles and fragments of plaster poured down from the obliterated ceiling to form on top of them a terrible sarcophagus.

What was left of the ceiling sagged and groaned, threatening to give way completely. The air had turned cold. It was filled with the smell of wetness and burning, and illuminated by a flashing, dancing light, so that Monty could see that the house above had been torn away and that what she was looking up at was the sky, dark and tumultuous, its blackness broken by the flaring of the guns and the flickering crimson of burning buildings.

Monty and Ada hauled the remaining two soldiers towards the foot of the stairs, which now led upwards to a jagged hole in the splintered floorboards. But one of them had been hit by a lump of masonry and the head wound he had sustained on the battlefield had been torn open once again.

'He's dead,' said Monty, when a star shell lit the sky long enough for her to examine him. 'Leave him here.'

At the top of the stairs Monty and Ada dumped the last man down between them. Monty peeped over the sandbags they had piled up at the entrance weeks before.

Everywhere she looked there were fires blazing. Buildings and landmarks she had once recognised (the schoolhouse, the church, the market cross) were smashed into mounds of rubble. Here and there men zigzagged through the wreckage, in their hands she recognised the sharp, jagged shape of rifles with fixed bayonets.

'There must have been an advance,' she shouted. 'It's not been right on top of us like this before.' The rain was falling steadily and an icy wind tore through the ruins. Miraculously, their ambulance was still there, untouched, beside a tumbled-down barn.

'Have you fixed that ambulance?' cried Monty.

'No,' said Ada. 'We'll have to take the motorcycle.'

Monty looked at Ada in disbelief. 'Three of us?' she said. 'On a motorcycle?'

'You and I on the cycle, him in the sidecar.' Ada looked at the Belgian soldier lolling against her legs. 'He's got an eye out and a smashed arm, hasn't he? He can sit in a sidecar.'

'Yes,' said Monty. 'I suppose he can.'

Before them, far out across the turnip fields the pale outline of a cottage flickered eerily. It was the last house in Caeskerke that was still standing. But even as they watched a shell tore across the sky, bursting the cottage apart in a spray of red and gold. The din of the guns was now so loud that it obliterated all other noise, and the small white building seemed to explode in silence before them. Sparks whirled into the air, mingling with smoke and rain, so that on all sides now the world seemed to be burning: burning trees, burning buildings, burning fields. It was terrifying and yet, thought Monty, oddly electrifying too.

'The world is on fire,' shouted Ada. 'What a sight, miss.'

'Can you drive us back to Furnes?' screamed Monty, surprised though strangely calmed by Ada's undaunted attitude.

'Course I can,' cried Ada. 'I saw a circus once, back home at Bleakly. A man made a dog jump through a hoop of flames over and over again.' She laughed. 'It can't be that difficult!'

Ada clambered over the sandbags and disappeared into the rain. Monty bent to see how their patient was faring. He crouched against the sandbags, unmoving, as the rain poured down upon his bowed head.

When Ada reappeared she was sitting astride a motor-cycle. Between them the two women stuffed the wounded soldier into the sidecar. He was unconscious and as easy to manhandle as a dead body (which, for one moment, Monty suspected him of being). But then he groaned and his head lolled against the rim of the sidecar, so that Monty wondered instead how he would survive the journey along the shat-tered roads. She wound her scarf protectively round his head like a turban.

At first Ada drove slowly. The road through Caeskerke was strewn with debris – rocks and rubble, broken furniture, shredded curtains, shattered roof slates. Everything was washed by the rain, giving it a curiously new and shiny look. And then Monty realised that beneath the roar of the guns she could hear the sharp crack of rifle fire. A bullet struck the ground before them, sending up a splash of dirty water. Ada cried out, finding more danger in a nearby rifleman than in the capriciousness of a falling shell. She crouched low over the handlebars and roared forward through the smoke.

Hanging on to Ada with both arms, Monty was bounced up and down on the motorcycle's baggage rack like a bobbin on a loom. She could not see where they were going, as her head was pressed against Ada's shoulder. She could prepare herself for nothing and every jolt in the road was a shock, every swerve unexpected. More than once the wheels slipped on the muddy ground, the sidecar crashing down into a hole or springing up over a mound of rubble so that Ada had to put out a leg to stop the vehicle from tipping up. Clinging on blindly, at these moments Monty felt as though the entire motorcycle was about to topple over, the sidecar rearing up on the road so that she was sure it would snap off completely, flinging its unconscious occupant into the water-logged fields or mud-filled ditches on either side of the slippery *pavé*.

As they left the village a star shell burst overhead, lighting up a quicksilver path through the craters and debris. Men were swarming towards the ruins of Caeskerke. Ada swerved left round a shell hole and right past a dead cow. She braked, narrowly missing a fallen tree, and lurched to the left once again. Monty bounced painfully and was flung from side to side. Her fingers scrabbled among the folds of Ada's coat to keep hold, but a button burst off and the fabric suddenly yielded. The vehicle slipped. Then all at once Monty was off the motorcycle and in the air . . . She was falling . . . She was smashing against the foul and slippery slope of the road, rolling and tumbling . . . And then she was drowning. Down she sank into the mud. The stuff filled her eyes and ears, and squeezed up her nostrils in a foul paste. Monty opened her mouth to scream and it forced its way into her throat. She thrashed about, suddenly having no idea whether she was facing up or down. At last she emerged, yelling for air and spitting slime, coated from head to foot with freezing black sludge. On either side of her unidentifiable things broke the surface – was that a tree stump or a hand? Was that a fence post or a severed arm? Was that a torso or a sandbag? Monty screamed for Ada. Her clothes dragged at her shoulders, her boots hauled at her feet, so that she felt as though hands had seized her coat, eager fingers had wrapped about her ankles determined to pull her down.

Somehow she managed to shrug off her greatcoat. Her foot found a rock and she levered herself upwards, to where she could make out the edge of the ditch glinting red and black in the light of the burning village. The rain thundered down, drumming with impatient fingers against her skull as she heaved herself out of the water.

'Ada!' She found she could hardly draw breath enough to call out. '*Ada!*'

Ada, it turned out, had not seen the direction in which Monty had been jettisoned from the back of the motorcycle and was frantically searching in the wrong place.

'Get in,' said Ada.

'I think I've cracked a rib,' whispered Monty.

Ada began hauling the wounded man out of the sidecar.

'Leave me,' whispered Monty. 'Get him back to the hospital.'

'No,' said Ada. 'He can wait. He's not moved for a while.'

18

'MAE TELLS me there's to be a dance.'

'Oh, hello, Dodger,' said Grier. He had directed the emptying and cleaning of the gymnasium with a precision and efficiency he had not exhibited since he was an officer. The climbing ropes had been taken down, the wall bars polished and the windows cleaned and left open, so that the place was light and airy, and ready to be filled with music and dancing. A dance band was coming up from town. The kitchens had been ordered to abandon the usual dreary fare and all manner of exotic provisions had been brought in

'Good idea,' said Foxley now. 'I'm sure I've got tails somewhere. I assume it's white tie?'

'Yes,' said Grier.

'I bet our Miss Montgomery looks lovely in evening dress.' Captain Foxley laughed. 'I'll have her off you too, you know, if you don't get on with it yourself.' He patted his pockets. 'Got any cigarettes?'

Grier handed his cigarette case over in silence. Should

he say something? Should he knock Captain Foxley down? But suddenly he felt as though an invisible hand was squeezing his throat, and the thought of violence sickened him. Instead, he said, 'Leave her alone, can't you?' adding rather gloomily, 'And she's hardly "mine". She doesn't *belong* to anyone. She's not a piece of furniture, you know.'

'What?' cried Captain Foxley. 'A lovely girl like that and you haven't even managed to –' He laughed, blowing a cloud of smoke into the air. 'Good heavens, Grier. In France, did you know what the women used to call you? *Le puceau* – the virgin. Ah, those delightful young ladies at that *esta-minet* near Givenchy. D'you remember?' He smiled. 'They said you never so much as lifted their skirts, or tweaked at their corsets. I don't know why you used to come along if all you wanted to do was talk and pipe your eye. They were really most obliging. Especially that pretty young thing . . . what was her name? Marie, or Annette, or Giselle, I really can't remember.'

Grier said nothing.

Captain Foxley pushed the hair out of his eyes and gave Grier a dazzling smile. It was the same smile, wide and open, apparently frank and sincere and delivered with a slightly bashful cant of the head, that Grier recognised as the one he usually reserved for women. 'After all, there's nothing else to do around here, is there?' he added. 'And there's no one else worth having, especially now Mae's leaving.'

The following evening the new party of guests arrived. Grier made sure he went down to the train station to greet them. He was also on hand to help them out of the various conveyances that had brought them up to the Hall. Curran was waiting in the foyer and Grier could see the look of triumph on his brother's face when he realised that the new arrivals were the oldest yet. A number of them had white sticks, and some had to be carried up the steps by order-lies and bath men.

Curran clapped his hands. 'Your advertisement seems to have done the trick this time,' he said to Grier. 'I only hope they can dance!'

The young people were the first to make their way to the gymnasium. Oliver, the young man with the booming laugh, had quietened down since the initial hilarity of their first night. With his friends, he had spent most of the past week picnicking beside Bleakly Tarn, or rowing in a leisurely fashion up and down the water's black and silent surface. Grier had been quietly pleased. Only once (since that first night) had they caused any upset – when one of the men of the party ate one of Mrs Forbes's temperance tracts (seasoning it first with salt and pepper and washing it down with a glass of champagne).

The young people's hampers had been greatly depleted by their excursions and now, on their final day, they had finished off their last bottles of champagne and eaten their final jars of fish roe and anchovy paste on toast before heading up to the gymnasium. Already their faces were flushed and their laughter loud.

Curran had presented Ada with a gown. He had bought it as a present for Mae shortly before the war, but had never given it to her. It was unfashionably long, adorned with ruffles and layered with silk and taffeta. Had women's clothing really been so stiff and elaborate back then? thought Grier. Despite its old-fashioned appearance, it was clearly a very expensive dress and Ada's cheeks were rosy as she wheeled Curran across the dance floor.

'You look like a princess,' said Grier.

Ada smiled. 'Thank you, sir.'

The gown revealed to Grier that Ada was considerably plumper than Mae had been in 1914. Grier was surprised by her thick waist (the dress had clearly been let out at the sides) and by the unexpectedly large bosom that had been squeezed beneath the taut fabric. 'You're the belle of the ball,' he said. 'I do like those glossy spots and the ruffled collar. And the colour suits you marvellously.'

Grier went to look for Monty. As he approached the consulting room, he heard the doctor say 'I quite definitely left it at the front of the cabinet.'

'But you leave it unlocked when you're consulting,' said Monty. 'It's possible that one of the guests took it. And what would I want with any of those things? I don't even like aniseed balls!'

'What's going on?' asked Grier. He stepped into the room. Monty was standing beside the open window looking out at the darkening sky. Despite this ventilation, the place was stifling.

'Someone's been rifling through Dr Slack's medicine cabinet,' said Monty. 'He thinks they've taken some of his medicines.'

'Are you sure?' Grier was surprised that anyone should want to steal Dr Slack's chalk pills or powdered sulphur (and even more surprised that Dr Slack should have noticed). 'What's missing?'

'Mercury. And powdered bismuth. And some aniseed balls.'

'Does it matter?' Grier asked hopefully.

'These compounds are poisonous if not taken in the proper manner,' said Dr Slack. 'Of course it matters!'

'Aniseed balls are poisonous?'

'No, no, not the aniseed balls. Forget about those. But the other things.'

'Well, there's nothing to be done about it at the moment,' said Grier. He clapped his hands. 'There's a dance tonight, upstairs in the gymnasium. Miss Montgomery, you're required to attend. Do you have an evening dress?'

'No,' said Monty.

'Good.' Grier held out his arm. 'Then I don't have to wait a moment longer for you. Dr Slack? Mrs Forbes tells me you used to be the best dancer in Bleakly. And she should know, she's been coming here for almost fifty years. Are you going to show these young people how it's done?'

In the gymnasium, Grier was relieved to see that the evening seemed to be going as planned. The young people were dancing with one another, or standing about sipping champagne. The older guests were executing a stiffer and more sedate version of the same dance. The new visitors had assembled in a shy group beneath the windows and were watching the dancing with bemused expressions. One or two of them, Grier noticed, had balanced pince-nez upon their noses and were struggling to read Mrs Forbes's temperance tracts.

As Grier and Monty entered the room, Captain Foxley appeared in front of them. 'Monty,' he said, smiling and holding out his arms. 'You look beautiful.'

'I look the same as ever,' said Monty. 'I don't have an evening dress.'

'A dance?' Captain Foxley reached for her hand.

'No, thank you,' said Monty.

'Oh, come now. Don't you know Grier has two left feet?' He hesitated. 'Look, I'm sorry about the other night.'

'What "other night"?' cried Grier. What had the fellow been up to now? 'What happened?'

'When our guests from London arrived' Captain Foxley was looking at Monty. 'I'd had a little too much to drink. I was upset. And lonely.' His expression became dolorous. 'I didn't mean anything by it. You ran away before I had a chance to say sorry. I'm saying it now. Can't we be friends?'

In the face of such contrition Monty was looking uncomfortable. It was as though she did not want to say 'yes', but was constrained by politeness from saying 'no'. She was saved from making any reply at all by the appearance of Mrs Forbes, who suddenly burst out of the crowd like a pheasant flushed from a gorse bush. Her eyes were wide, her lips a-tremble with alarm. 'One of the new ladies is feeling faint,' she cried. 'I think she ate a canapé. She may also have had some champagne.' She frowned at Captain Foxley. 'This is all your doing,' she cried. She rooted in her purse and thrust a pamphlet at him. 'Miss Montgomery, you are needed!'

Monty followed Mrs Forbes to the other side of the room. An old lady was slumped on a chair, held erect only by the power of her stays. Dr Slack was standing over her, searching his pockets for salts.

Captain Foxley crumpled Mrs Forbes's pamphlet in his fist and tossed it to the floor. 'Never mind,' he said, watching Monty go. 'There's plenty of time yet.' He looked about, examining the crowd, then made his way towards a long-necked blonde-haired girl. How charming he could be, thought Grier. Despite the fact that less than a week ago Captain Foxley had struck the girl's friend in the mouth, she was soon allowing herself to be swept across the floor in his arms.

'Would you light my cigarette?' said a voice at his side.

'I didn't know you smoked,' said Grier absently.

'Of course you did. I do everything.'

'Curran's over there,' said Grier, watching Ada wheel his brother through the crowd. 'Mind you keep away from him.'

'Don't want me making a scene?' Mae blew out a plume of smoke. 'Ada's looking rather tubby,' she added. 'And what a frightful dress.' She watched Captain Foxley whirl the girl about. 'I thought I was in love with him, you know.'

'With whom? Curran?' asked Grier. He looked at her, at her face powdered and painted in a way that he knew Curran despised. Had she always been so garish, so brassy? He couldn't remember.

'No, no. With Foxley. But Foxley only loves himself. He doesn't care for anyone else.'

'Oh, he hates himself too,' murmured Grier. 'You can be sure of that.'

'Well, I'm going to London in the morning and I won't be back.'

'Where will you stay?' It was only a deeply ingrained sense of courtesy that made him ask.

'With a friend,' said Mae breezily.

'I see.' He wasn't aware that Mae had any friends. Apart from the man he had seen her walking arm in arm with down Regent Street not two months earlier. Perhaps this was the 'friend' she was referring to. He wondered, fleetingly, whether Curran knew about this 'friend', whether Curran knew about Mae and Foxley, or, indeed, whether Foxley knew about the 'friend' . . .

Mae slid her arm into his. 'Do you want to come along and help me pack?' He could feel the soft warmth of her body as she pressed herself against him.

'No, thank you,' he muttered. 'Would you like a glass of champagne?'

The music had stopped, but Grier noticed that Captain Foxley had not let go of the girl. He was whispering something in her ear and holding on to her hand. Mae was speaking again. '. . . I'll be glad to get away from this place, from all of you, stuck out here together in the middle of nowhere.' She downed her champagne and ground out her cigarette beneath the heel of her silk dancing shoe.

Grier noticed that Monty had revived the collapsed lady and had abandoned her to Dr Slack. The doctor had positioned the woman beside an open window and was making her sip a glass of Bleakly water. The music started up again, but Captain Foxley had given up dancing altogether. He was approaching Oliver and dragging his partner behind him. Grier felt his skin prickle with alarm. He looked about for Monty. She would know what to do. Ignoring Mae, he plunged into the crowd.

'Grier!' Curran appeared beside him. 'You've got to stop him –'

At that moment a furious shout echoed across the room. 'Stand up! Stand up and fight, if you're any kind of man at all!'

'Quickly!' cried Curran.

Captain Foxley had pulled out his service revolver and aimed it at Oliver's head.

'On your knees!' cried the Captain. 'On your knees and thank three million dead men for their sacrifice!'

His victim sank immediately on to the floor. A dark stain appeared at the crotch of his trousers.

'Captain Foxley,' said Monty, stepping out of the crowd. 'What on earth are you doing?'

'He's frightened of *this* little thing?' Foxley shouted, waving his revolver. 'Why, I haven't even fired it yet.' And he held up the gun and discharged it into the ceiling.

The guests cried out and covered their ears. The music stopped. The crowd began to jostle and surge.

'Stand still, all of you!' roared Captain Foxley. 'Or I'll shoot the next person who moves!'

'Put it down,' cried Monty. She moved closer.

Captain Foxley climbed on to a chair, and from there on to a table.

'Get back, Monty,' said Grier.

'He stepped in front of her. 'Dodger,' he hissed. 'Will you just calm down? There's no need for all this. Come on, pass the revolver over.'

Foxley laughed. He swung his arm so that the mouth of the gun was pointing between Grier's eyes.

Grier stared into the steel gaze of Captain Foxley's revolver – the same sort of revolver that he had once carried at his own waist – and reflected that no matter how close one was to the barrel of a gun, one would never be able to see the bullet as it came out. In fact, one would be dead before one even realised what had happened.

'What are you doing with that old thing?' he asked mildly. This time the shot went directly over the head of Oliver, so close that a clump of hair was torn from out of the young man's curly locks.

'Dodger!' cried Curran.

Captain Foxley turned. 'Blackwood!' he whispered. 'What –?'

Captain Foxley's leg buckled beneath him, and his arms flailed as he tried to steady himself. The gun waved close to his head. The second shot came at the same instant that he pointed the gun at his own ear.

19

'THERE YOU are,' said Peter. 'I've been waiting for hours. I was beginning to think you'd changed your mind.'

Sophia's feet were aching; her back was sore; her hands were chapped and she could still smell the reek of carbolic in her nostrils. She wished she could sit down with a cup of tea and tell him everything that had happened that day: the ghastly hours spent in surgery; the scolding she had endured from Miss Tadworth; the curious, but truncated, conversation she had had with Dr Woodruffe . . . Not that she could remember very much about that particular exchange. She had been so busy all afternoon that her conversation with Dr Woodruffe had taken on an unreal aspect, as though it had occurred years ago, perhaps even in a dream, or possibly not at all. But generally Peter had no interest in hearing about her work in the hospital, so this hardly seemed to matter. 'Oh, let's not talk about that,' he would say. 'I know all about that sort of thing.'

A cigarette was smouldering between his lips and he threw it away so that he could kiss her. He tasted of tobacco and what he said next made Sophia forget about everything else completely.

'I seem to remember that we had a little arrangement this evening. I'm staying not far from here. Let's go there.'

Peter hurried her through the darkening streets. A cold, heavy rain had started to fall, and Sophia shivered as large icy droplets of water plopped on to her hat and ran down the neck of her coat. As usual, Peter seemed oblivious to the cold and damp, and he stalked through the streets purposefully. He was staying in an apartment that belonged to one of his fellow officers. The man, Lieutenant Handyside, was in hospital in Hastings. Lieutenant Handyside had told Peter that he was welcome to use his flat in London for as long as he wanted.

As they walked, Peter kept up an animated stream of frivolous chit-chat, prattling on as though hoping to distract her from where they were going and why they were going there. 'There's a lady that comes every day to clear the place up and look after me,' he said cheerily. 'Not that there's very much for her to do. I've spent months in the most ghastly billets and cooped up in dugouts, and you get used to taking up as little space as possible. Her name's Mrs Potts, or Mrs Botts, or something like that; I can never quite tell which it is as she hasn't any teeth and it's almost impossible to understand what she's saying. Handyside said she's been looking after him for years. She calls me "Mr Handyside", too, so I don't think she's actually got any idea who's who any more. Still, comes to us all, I suppose. And I must say she makes the most delicious Dundee cake. She said she's making one for me to take back.' He stopped. 'Here we are.'

Sophia looked up at the building before them. It was as black and hulking as a convict ship. Peter pushed open a door and led her up a flight of stairs to the second floor. Sophia shivered and pulled her wet coat round herself tightly.

'You're cold.' Peter opened the door to the flat and ushered Sophia inside. 'Never mind, I'll warm you up.' He put his arms about her. 'Come along in, I've made a fire.' He peeled her coat from her shoulders and hung it beside his own on a hallstand made up of antlers. He took her hand.

The bedroom was so spacious that Sophia could hardly make out the pieces of bulky furniture – a mahogany wardrobe, a chest of drawers with brass handles, possibly a desk – that crouched here and there in the shadows. Peter's kitbag was near the door, propped against a small octagonal table upon which sat the gramophone. Beside it, bits and pieces of khaki clothing were draped across the back of a dining chair. A pair of army boots and spurs, their toes gleaming like chestnuts in the firelight, stood to attention in front of a tall dressing mirror. Sophia saw in it her own face, pale as the moon in the darkness. She looked frightened and doubtful.

Peter stared at her greedily. 'You promised,' he said. 'You can't back out now.'

Sophia had no idea what, exactly, the act of love might entail. She had been under the impression (largely created by Peter's insistent activities on previous evenings) that it would be a panted, hasty, vigorous affair. Was there something she should know about before it began? Her mother had told her nothing about the needs and desires of men, but had merely implied, with a slight shudder, that men required 'relief' on a monthly basis (the implication being that this allocation was more than generous) and that one simply had to submit and endure (in what particular way she had neglected to make clear) until the matter was over.

Peter went over to fiddle with the gramophone. There was a moment's silence (until that hiatus Sophia had not realised how loudly her own heart was beating), then the room filled with the sound of music.

'Whisky?' asked Peter.

'Yes, please,' said Sophia, even though she hated the stuff. But it would give her courage (a much needed commodity these days). Did not all the men drink it for this reason?

Peter handed her a tumbler and watched while she sipped. 'Down the hatch,' he cried.

Sophia did as she was instructed. Was there nothing else she could do to stall him? 'You must come and meet my parents,' she said, noticing as she spoke that her voice sounded strange and squeaky.

Peter gulped his own whisky down.

'My father's in the paper-manufacturing business,' added Sophia. 'His foolscap is shipped worldwide.'

'Is it?' said Peter.

'Yes. Almost everyone has had a piece of my father's paper in their hands at some point or other.'

Peter took her glass away and put his arms round her. The music was slowing now, so that Sophia felt as though time itself were yawning, stretching like elastic, so that every second seemed to be filled with important goings-on she had never noticed before – the ticking of a clock, the crackle of the fire, the faint sound of voices in the street. For some reason she could not get the image of Captain Holmes, the man with the bandaged face, out of her mind. Had he a lover, a wife or a sweetheart before his identity had been blasted away? All at once the music came to an end and the machine hissed and crackled in the darkness. She realised that it was not simply the needle of the gramophone that was making that harsh noise, but Peter's breath, hoarse and eager against her ear. He squeezed her waist. Sophia's attention returned distractedly to the task in hand. Would she be required to remove all her clothes? The nights were chilly and she rarely went anywhere without wearing her most substantial corset, her thickest chemise and heaviest petticoat. One of her stockings had worn at the knee and she had yet to darn it. She was certain she still smelled of carbolic too. What a slattern she must appear! Why had she not changed before coming out? But she had been in such a rush to see him and had not liked to dress up for fear of attracting suspicion about where she was going. She glanced towards the bed, half imagining Miss Tadworth might burst from beneath it.

Peter began to fumble with her dress. She had expected him to be flummoxed by its range of buttons, its secret ties and constraining belt, but in no time at all he had removed the dress completely. The gramophone began a frantic rasping noise, like the sound of an excited old man. Peter seemed not to notice. He steered her towards the bed, tugging at her chemise. He rummaged for her breasts, but they were battened down beneath her corset. Defeated by her upper body, he directed his attentions lower and slid a hand between her thighs. Sophia took a step backwards and toppled on to the bed like a skittle. Peter flung himself down beside her. She shut her eyes. She tried to think about something distracting, something soothing, but all that she could call to mind were the words of the commander-in-chief of the women's Voluntary Aid Detachment, whose stirring message of encouragement had been handed out to all VADs when they enrolled. *Remember that the honour of the VAD organisation depends on your individual conduct. It will be your duty not only to set an example of discipline and perfect steadiness of character, but also to maintain the most courteous relations with those whom you are helping in this Great Struggle* . . . Sophia's eyes snapped open. Could she not forget about the Great Struggle even for an hour? She was in love with the man who now lay almost on top of her, was it not in her power to make love to him, to provide him with solace in the face of what he had to return to in a matter of weeks?

All at once she realised that Peter had managed to loosen the front of her underclothes. Had he cut through them with his penknife while her eyes were closed? He stuffed his hand down the neck of her chemise and hauled out a breast. It lay like a jellyfish among the wreckage of her dishevelled underclothes. Pleased by his prize, though seeming a little wearied by the effort it had taken to get it, Peter laid his head against her naked skin. He squeezed the breast, as though evaluating its weight and quality before going in search of its fellow. Then he burst into life again, wrestling now with his own clothes, wrenching at the buttons of his shirt, tearing at his breeches with noisy impatience, groping desperately for her among the remaining folds of her clothing. He found a naked thigh, a smooth buttock emerging from beneath the thick petticoat, and swung forward on top of her.

Later, they walked back to the hospital. Sophia was so tired now she could scarcely remember where she was going. How many hours would she be able to sleep before she was required back on duty? She could not remember that either.

'I think Lucas and Chalmers are going to the Tivoli tonight,' said Peter. He was walking briskly, almost pulling her down the street behind him. Her feet slipped on the wet pavement but he hardly seemed to notice. 'I might pop along.' Sophia nodded. She hoped he wasn't going to ask her to come. He didn't. Instead, 'Perhaps I should leave you at the corner,' he said. 'I saw that scrawny woman with the red face looking down at us last time and I don't want to get you into trouble.'

'Sister Barnett,' said Sophia. She did not object. She could think only of the pleasure of lying down and sleeping – how welcome her cold bed in the draughty dormitory would be. She worked so hard every day and got so little sleep . . . all at once she felt quite sorry for herself. She did not begrudge either of those things, but she could not help but feel how pleasant it would be if somebody cared about her hardship. In addition, she had spent the last hour or more allowing Peter to slake his desires upon her in any way he chose. Months working with the wounded had given her an intimate familiarity with men's bodies, so that what she saw prior to the act of love was not a surprise. What she felt during it – pain, indignity and (she had to admit) a degree of boredom – were new. Perhaps pleasure, should there be any, would come later. And yet, was it a woman's role to be nothing but the drudge of men? Were they required simply to clean up after the mess men made of the world; the mess they made of each other and of themselves? The bruised flesh between her legs throbbed resentfully. Her feelings were deep and confused. She could scarcely articulate them, or even acknowledge what they meant, and they swirled within her, dark and formless. She looked up at Peter. He smiled and put his arm round her, and at once these turbulent thoughts ebbed and flowed and receded. He loved her. And, of course, she loved him. If she gave him pleasure that was enough. Did he not deserve to have her body when he might be called upon to make the Supreme Sacrifice at any moment?

The following day Sophia received a note from Peter informing her that he had to return to Hastings. Lieutenant Handyside had died 'of wounds' and Peter was heading down, on Saturday morning, with Chalmers and Lucas, to attend the funeral. After bravely badgering Miss Tadworth for weeks, Sophia had finally been given the weekend off and she could not help but feel disappointed, and a little irritated, by this news. How inconvenient of Lieutenant Handyside to die at that particular moment. Would she now have to spend her hard-won and precious weekend all by herself?

Sophia went out into the quadrangle to smoke a cigarette. In those three minutes of leisure, she contemplated her situation and her options within it. She could follow Peter to

Hastings. She would be unlikely to get so much time off again before he went back and surely he would be delighted to see her, whatever the circumstances. And yet, Peter would be with Lucas and Chalmers, who would be well-supplied with whisky, and for reasons she could not quite explain Sophia did not particularly want to see him in their company. She decided instead to do something she had been putting off for months: she would visit her own parents.

She packed a case and went to tell Sister Barnett where she was going. She might even bump into Dr Woodruffe, she thought, recalling that they still had a conversation to finish. She had not seen him since that morning in the quadrangle. How long ago that seemed! She would seek him out now, if he wasn't in surgery or doing his rounds. She would ask Sister Barnett where he was.

Sister Barnett was talking to the chaplain, who had taken to skulking about the wards, his bible at the ready. Her eyes kept darting to the clock above the entrance to ward six. She began to wind a bandage.

'What has happened to their faith?' cried the chaplain. 'Only this morning I was attempting to lend succour to an unfortunate young fellow in ward four and he told me to . . . to go *away* in a most abusive fashion!'

'They don't really mean it.'

'There is something insidious at work here.'

'Is there, Padre?' Sister Barnett spotted Sophia lingering beside the dressing trolley and she beckoned her over.

'God is punishing us for our evil ways, for our descent into unbelief, and He brings against us the champions of Rationalism.'

'Miss Barclay,' said Sister Barnett.

'The Germans!' shouted the chaplain. 'Their whole philosophical canon since Leibnitz has been breeding aggressiveness and violence. It has undermined any sense of mystery in the word of God.'

'Miss Barclay,' repeated Sister Barnett. 'May I speak with you for a moment?'

'Nietzsche!' The chaplain blinked at Sophia accusingly. He lowered his voice to a horrified whisper. 'It is not their bullets we should be in fear of, but their way of *thinking*.'

'For goodness' sake, Padre,' snapped Sister Barnett. 'I don't know what you're talking about. I don't have time for this . . . this nonsense. Go away and leave the men *alone*.'

The padre recoiled. 'You too!' he whispered.

Sister Barnett flapped the bandage in his face. 'Just . . . *go*,' she said. 'I must speak to this VAD. And I have more important things to do than be lectured to by you!'

The chaplain retreated, clutching his bible to his chest. He stood at the door to ward number six and stared bleakly at the rows of beds.

'Are you going somewhere, Barclay?' asked Miss Barnett.

'I was looking for Dr Woodruffe,' said Sophia.

'Haven't you heard? He's been transferred to the Military Hospital at Southampton. We're very sad to lose him, especially as it means there's no one but Dr Eldersley on duty on these lower wards just now. But they needed another experienced surgeon and he had put his name forward a while ago. His replacement comes tonight.'

'Oh,' said Sophia. It seemed as though everyone was deserting her. 'Will he be back?'

'I've no idea. I doubt it. He gave me this, for you.' Sister Barnett delved into the pocket on her apron and produced an envelope.

The handwriting was that same sloping scrawl Sophia recognised from so many of Dr Woodruffe's scribbled reports.

At that moment there was a scream. 'Nurse!' shrieked a voice. 'Nurse!'

Sophia dropped her suitcase and ran with Sister Barnett. Corporal Foster was laying half in and half out of his bed. A patch of blood had appeared in the middle of his bedclothes, in the shape of a huge crimson heart. Sister Barnett leaped forward and whipped the sheets back.

'Haemorrhage!' cried Sophia. 'Haemorrhage! Dr Eldersley, ward six! His wound keeps opening,' she said to Sister Barnett. 'We dressed it this morning, it seemed much better, I didn't think –'.

'Press here,' said Sister Barnett. She seized Sophia's hand and pushed it into Corporal Foster's groin.

The men in the ward were silent, some of them staring at the ceiling, some unable to keep from looking.

Corporal Foster lay as limp as a suit of empty clothes beneath her hands. Her fingers, forced against the artery at the top of his leg, were slathered with crimson, the cuffs of her coat now edged with blood.

'Thank you, miss,' he whispered. 'If I'd known this'd get you to put your hands down there I'd have tried it earlier.'

Sophia forced herself to smile. She heard a footfall behind her and turned to see that the chaplain had reappeared.

'No!' cried Corporal Foster, catching sight of the chaplain's pale face. 'I don't need 'im yet!'

'Padre, can you wait outside, please?' whispered Sophia.

The chaplain crept forward, an ecstatic light in his eyes, '. . . save and deliver us, we humbly beseech thee, from the hands of our enemies; abate their pride; assuage their malice and confound their devices . . .' A groaning sound started up from the men, drowning out the chaplain's voice.

'Shut up.'

'Get him out of here.'

'Piss off.'

'Go on, get out.'

'Please go,' cried Sophia. 'This is not the time for you.' At last she heard the wheels of the dressing trolley squeaking down the ward, and Sister Barnett and Dr Eldersley were there. There was a minute of frantic activity, of tangled fingers slippery with blood, of voices shouting out and gauze flapping. A set of bloody pyjamas and a bundle of bedclothes were tossed to Sophia. 'Clean ones, please,' barked Sister Barnett. Sophia obeyed. And then, almost as suddenly as it had begun, everything was over. Corporal Foster was still and silent, as pale as a sheet of paper folded within the envelope of his bedclothes. His gaze swept restlessly back and forth, scanning the ceiling above as though following a cloud of unseen flies that ceaselessly circled his head.

Sophia had to run to catch her train. It was only as it pulled out of the station that she realised she had left Dr Woodruffe's letter lying unopened on the dressing trolley in the middle of ward six.

20

'Your father's in his study with *The Times*,' said Sophia's mother. 'I've asked Gladys to air your room, but I'm not sure she's done so.' She lowered her voice, as though afraid that Gladys might overhear and seek retribution. 'She's new. She won't do anything, you know.'

'Never mind,' said Sophia. 'I'm sure I can manage.'

'Can you, dear?' Mrs Barclay looked partly relieved that the collapse of her domestic management could be overlooked and partly appalled at her daughter's unconcerned attitude.

'Shall I make some tea?' added Sophia, forgetting she was now back in a world where someone else might attend to those activities.

'Oh, Gladys can at least manage *that*, I'm sure.' She sounded more hopeful than certain. 'Go on through, Sophia, dear. I'll get your father.'

Sophia had forgotten how quiet her parents' house was. As always, a fire crackled in the grate (Gladys, it appeared, had accomplished at least one domestic chore that day), and the clock ticked on the mantel. But there was now a faint air of neglect hanging about the place and Sophia spotted dust on the silver lamp brackets. She sat back, sinking into the needlepoint velvet-backed cushions – a number of whose covers she had embroidered herself – and waited for her mother to return, or for the tea tray to appear, or for her father to come through . . . She closed her eyes, the gentle ticking of the clock sounding in her ears like the clicking of a despairing tongue.

When she opened them again her parents were sitting before her in silence. They each held a cup of tea. She sat up. 'Hello,' said Sophia. 'Have I been asleep for long?'

'Welcome home, my dear,' answered her father. 'Lovely to see you again. How are things in town?'

'As you might expect,' said Sophia automatically. 'Busy, of course, but we're all bearing up.' How she hated these bland, anodyne phrases. Why could she not simply tell them the truth? And what on earth was 'bearing up' anyway? She had no idea and was quite sure her parents had no idea either.

'And how is the hospital?' asked her mother, sipping her tea. She passed Sophia the cup that had been sitting on the tea tray. 'Mrs Wright's son, Walter, was wounded, you know. He might be in your hospital. You should look out for him.'

'I will,' said Sophia.

'Such brave boys,' her mother continued. 'Of course, if I had a son I'd expect him to go too.'

'Indeed,' cried Sophia's father. 'I'd like to go myself, but I'm too old for that sort of thing.'

'What sort of thing?' snapped Sophia. 'Have you any idea what's going on?'

'We'll have to find a nice young chap to take you off our hands,' said her father.

Pleading extreme fatigue, Sophia excused herself and went up to her room.

The following morning some of her mother's friends visited. They were delighted to find Sophia so unexpectedly at home. They all knew that she was working in a hospital in London and, although they secretly lamented the fact that someone as wealthy as Sophia should have to work anywhere at all, at least she hadn't been obliged to turn her hand to one of those dreadful men's jobs that so many women found themselves engaged in these days.

'A bus driver, for example,' said one. 'Or a ticket collector.'

'Or a postwoman,' whispered another. 'D'you know, I saw one of those just this morning.'

'But there's no one else to do these jobs now, is there?' cried the first. 'And where would we be if these girls had not stepped in? Why, there'd be no post arriving at all, no buses running, no cows being milked . . . Still' – she gazed at Sophia with admiration – 'the ministering angel is a woman's role, as much as the urge for war is natural among the male. I'm not sure that some of these other activities come naturally to women. That lady bus driver was most erratic coming down the high street the other day.'

'Oh, it'll all be over soon,' said Sophia's mother. 'And everything will be back to normal.'

'I doubt it,' murmured Sophia, wondering what might constitute 'normal' once the war was over.

But now Mrs Barclay was going on about the past, was

217

speaking about how things used to be, years ago when 'the Queen' had been alive, when everything seemed to have been in its rightful place and she had been young and pretty with 'everything' before her. Back then, she said, England would have flattened someone like that upstart Kaiser before he had even managed to struggle into one of his ridiculous military uniforms. 'I can't think what's happened.' She looked puzzled. 'We have the Empire. Why is it taking them so long to chase the Hun back home?'

'I'm sure they're doing their best,' said Sophia.

'There's a fund-raising bazaar at the vicarage this afternoon,' Sophia's mother told her. 'You must come. The vicarage is home to some convalescent soldiers. The vicar and his wife gave the place over to the military, the bazaar *always* takes place in the vicarage gardens and the soldiers are helping out. I had cook make a cake for the home-baking stall. The Ladies' League will have a stall too, perhaps you should wear your Red Cross uniform, you could –'

'Could what?' asked Sophia.

'Well, I don't know, dear.' Her mother's smile flickered. 'The Ladies' League have a banner. Perhaps you might help to carry it aloft? And your father's to give a reading to the Boy Scouts. You might find it interesting.'

Sophia's father was poring over a hard-backed book, the size and weight of a bible. It was bound in blood-coloured cloth, its cover depicting a battle scene in which slim, square-jawed officers bounded over hulking shadows in spiked helmets. '*Victory Stories of the War*,' he said, tapping the cover. 'I've picked a good one about the cavalry charge – informative and stirring. And then I'll say something about How Boy Scouts Can Help. It's my little bit for the war.' From an inside pocket he produced a sharply folded sheet of his own most expensive foolscap. '"*Scout training sets a boy apart.*"' A teaspoon tinkled against a saucer as his voice boomed. '"*Germany should understand that behind our soldiers there is another, younger line. Eager, like them, to do their duty cheerfully and eventually to join them in bringing about victory.*" I'll be in a tent on the vicarage lawn at two p.m.'

Sophia went with her mother and father to the bazaar. Her father disappeared in the direction of a large bell tent which had been erected beneath an elm tree on the far side of the lawn. Beside it a troupe of twenty or more boys dressed in the 'lemon squeezer' hats and buff-coloured shirts of the Boy Scouts sat crossed-legged on the ground. A large bonfire smoked briskly.

'Oh, Mrs Delaney!' cried Sophia's mother. 'I have a cake for your stall.'

Sophia slipped into the crowd. She watched as a military car laden with young ladies made its way slowly round the perimeter of the garden. Sixpence a Ride in the General's Motor. She wandered past a hoopla stall and a coconut shy. Each was guarded by a dirty-looking boy, who called out as she passed, "Ave a go, miss. Its for the 'ospital funds.' The coconuts were shiny and hairless, like small shaven heads poised on long thin necks.

'Want to see the trench, miss?' said a voice in her ear. 'Want to see what it's like? We dug it ourselves.' The soldier was clearly one of the vicarage's temporary residents, dressed in convalescent blue with a vivid scar running down the side of his face. 'Only a shillin' to see.'

The trench was six feet deep with a high sandbagged parapet facing on to the no-man's-land of the vicarage lawn. Below the sandbags a step had been cut into the earth. This was the fire step, explained Sophia's guide, upon which a man might stand to shoot at his enemy, or for use as a seat. The duckboards exhaled a warm, woody scent in the afternoon sun.

'That there's a traverse,' said the soldier, pointing to a section of the wall that turned in at a right angle. 'Stops Fritz from killing the lot of us if he accidentally gets into the trench.'

'And this?' Sophia pulled aside a heavy curtain of oiled canvas. Behind it, beneath the earth, a large burrow had been excavated. A bunk was set against the wall and a table wedged into a corner. The walls and floor were lined with sturdy wooden boards and it smelled faintly of soil and mushrooms. 'It's a dugout,' said Sophia.

'Yes, miss. This one would be for two officers, but some are much bigger.'

'It's very well made.' As she spoke Sophia felt faintly relieved, as though that brief evaluation of dugout construction gave her one less thing to worry about. She could imagine Peter sitting at the table writing a love letter to her as the artillery fire shook the walls.

'And is this a periscope?' Sophia peered though a slit cut into a rectangular wooden box that was affixed below the sandbags outside the dugout. To the left she could see a group of blue-clad soldiers demonstrating the use of a rifle to a crowd of ladies. Further away, beside the Boy Scouts' bell tent, more convalescents were brewing tea on a dixie. Threepence a cup. In the centre of her view a soldier with reddish brown hair was sitting in a wheelchair, a blanket draped where his legs had once been. He stared ahead, watching the slow progress of the military car and its giggling cargo, his face empty of expression.

Sophia kissed her parents at the station, waved to them until they were out of sight, then sank down into her seat with relief. Perhaps Peter would send her a note that very evening. Perhaps she might persuade him to look for a posting at home. There must be some way he could avoid returning to the front, some way that they could be together. She would ask. Surely he would agree? She stared out of the train window, impatiently watching the countryside go by.

There were two letters waiting for Sophia at the hospital: one was from Peter. He had decided to stay in Hastings for another few days. He would see her when he came back. The note was scribbled in haste, on a scrap of paper that looked as though it had been torn from a rail timetable. Its language was blunt and contained no endearments, no earnestly expressed yearnings and no mention of love. Perhaps he had been with Lucas and Chalmers at the time, thought Sophia, and had felt unable to express himself in anything other than the most brusque and masculine of terms. Still, it was very disappointing. Sophia looked mournfully out of the hospital window at the treetops, their branches still bare of leaves in the cold spring wind.

No doubt there would be plenty of work to keep her hands busy, even if her mind could not be similarly distracted.

The other letter was from Monty. Her brother had died, and once she had sorted out the funeral arrangements and spent a few days consoling her parents, she would return to her duties in London. *I've heard so little from you over these last weeks,*' she wrote, '*I'm beginning to wonder whether this Peter Foxley you've told me about isn't making you rather forgetful of your old friends*. Sophia felt guilty that she had written to Monty so rarely since she had met Peter. But Monty would understand. It was the first time that she, Sophia, had been in love – it had happened so quickly, and so unexpectedly, that it had taken her quite by surprise . . . Sophia thought again of that hour spent with Peter in Lieutenant Handyside's bed, then replaced them with other thoughts – Peter's smile, the way he held her when they danced, the way he pushed his hair out of his eyes.

♦

It was almost a week before she received another note from Peter. He was back in London and would be waiting outside the hospital at two o'clock.

Sophia had felt forgotten and disregarded. She had, by turns, been dejected and tearful, angry and confused. She would have written to him, but she had no idea where he was. Instead, she had written to Monty. She was desperate to talk to her, but unwilling to paint an unappealing picture of self-pity. She told Monty how much she missed her and realised as she wrote the words how true they were.

She had intended to punish Peter by being moody and silent. When she saw him, however, those thoughts vanished from her head.

'You're lucky I could swap my shift,' she said. 'And Sister Barnett is beginning to ask me questions every time I say I need to go out. I'm going to get into trouble. Why did you have to stay in Hastings?' she could not resist adding.

'Oh, don't start on about that,' said Peter. 'I thought you'd be glad to see me.'

'Of course I'm glad to see you.'

Peter put his arm about her waist and kissed her ear. 'How long have you got?'

'Two hours. I'm on duty again at four.'

'Just enough time,' said Peter. 'Handyside left me his flat, you know. What d'you think of that?'

There was evidence to suggest that Peter had been making the most of Lieutenant Handyside's flat; empty whisky bottles, sticky glasses and tumblers, brimming ashtrays, packs of cards, an overturned chair littered the floor. The gramophone sat on a card table, a mass of records spilling untidily from a box at its side.

'Goodness,' said Sophia, surprised. 'What's been happening here?'

'Oh, I had a few chaps round,' said Peter. 'Things got a bit rowdy.' He opened the curtains, then the shutters.

'Is that a stocking?' asked Sophia, pointing to a narrow slip of gossamer, vaguely in the shape of a woman's leg, which was draped over the table like a discarded sausage skin.

'Probably,' said Peter. 'Chalmers brought some girls. He's

gone back now.' He threw open a window, so that a draught of cold air drifted in from the street. 'It's been hard on us all, losing Handyside like that. We had to give him a send-off. I should have cleared this up before you came, I suppose, but I didn't think you'd mind. I couldn't wait to see you.' He smiled, so that the questions Sophia had been about to ask, the anxious thoughts that had been half forming in her mind, vanished like breath on a windowpane.

Sophia was fifteen minutes late for the start of her four o'clock shift.

'Miss Barclay!' thundered Miss Tadworth as she appeared on the ward.

Sophia had a bucket of hot water in one hand and a scrubbing brush in the other.

'A word with you, Miss Barclay.'

'Can it wait a moment, please, Miss Tadworth?' said Sophia. 'Dr Eldersley wants the floor scrubbed down as soon as possible.' She felt her cheeks burn with a mixture of exertion (the bucket was rather heavy) and pain (her finger was going septic again) as well as the almost certain knowledge that such an impudent reply, no matter how practical it might be, would infuriate Miss Tadworth.

'Of course it can *wait*, Barclay.' Miss Tadworth addressed her over the stretcher-bound form of an armless soldier. The soldier groaned and thrashed his head from side to side. Miss Tadworth appeared not to notice. She slid a pudgy hand into the pocket of her apron. Between a thick finger and thumb she produced the letter from Dr Woodruffe, which Sophia had so carelessly left on the dressing trolley.

'I didn't expect you to drop what you were doing right now, but merely to come and see me at *your* earliest convenience. This particular piece of correspondence is clearly of no importance, as you discarded it among the bandages within minutes of Sister Barnett giving it to you and seem to have been too *preoccupied* to think of it again. I was wondering when you would ask for it, but it seems your head is just as empty as I had always suspected it was. I believe it's from Dr Woodruffe, which is the only reason I have not put it straight into the waste.'

'Yes, Matron,' said Sophia. She had completely forgotten about Dr Woodruffe's letter, so absorbed had she been with thinking about Peter, with waiting and wondering whether he would ask her to marry him before he went back. Surely the fact that she had already given herself to him was more than enough to seal their engagement. All that was missing were the words themselves and Peter would be sure to utter them any day now. These thoughts had surfaced particularly powerfully that very afternoon, rising into her mind like bubbles in an opened bottle of champagne as she lay beneath him on the sofa in Lieutenant Handyside's drawing room. She had sighed with contentment (and with the weight of him pressing upon her) and thought to herself: 'Today, Peter will ask me to marry him.' But despite making love to her once again before he escorted her back to the hospital, Peter had done no such thing. Sophia could not help but feel disappointed, though she had to admit to herself that the wreckage-strewn drawing room of Lieutenant Handyside's apartment was perhaps not the most romantic place for a marriage proposal.

'You may have it at the end of your shift.' Miss Tadworth

slipped the envelope, lavishly embossed with the dried blood of Corporal Foster, back into her pocket.

By the time Sophia had a moment to speak to Miss Tadworth it was almost nine o'clock. She found the Matron directing the removal of a patient into another ward, in readiness for an operation the following morning. Even as she drew near, Sophia could smell the familiar stench of gangrene and her stomach clenched like a mollusc within her.

'Hold this stump, Barclay!' cried Miss Tadworth, seeing Sophia approach. Sophia seized the man's truncated thigh, holding it aloft while Miss Tadworth removed the dressing and washed antiseptic solution on to the wound. The man gritted his teeth and trembled beneath her hands, but he did not cry out. Despite almost a year of nursing, Sophia suddenly felt dizzy.

'Heave to, Barclay!' she heard Miss Tadworth cry, as though from a great distance.

At last the job was done. The cleaned stump was packed with gauze and swathed in bandages. Its owner was lifted on to a trolley and borne away down the corridor, the wheels rattling against the floor covering.

Miss Tadworth watched it go. The pallid rice-pudding cheeks of her chubby faced drooped despairingly. She looked at Sophia and gave a grunt of acknowledgement. 'Good work, Barclay,' she muttered. 'I know it's hard but' – she coughed as though the words were lodged in her throat like pieces of bitter fruit – 'you did a good job. Here you are.' She pulled Dr Woodruffe's letter out of her pocket and handed it over. 'Don't lose it this time.'

THE DAY after the dance the journalist from *Woman's Weekly* came to Bleakly Hall. Oliver and his friends were leaving, the girls holding their coats up to their throats as though cold with shock, despite the relative warmth of the day. Oliver's face was as pale as suet and he wore a pad of gauze taped over the graze on his head. The lady journalist stared in surprise at this subdued exodus.

She walked over to Monty, who was standing beside the reception desk, and removed a glove. 'Good afternoon,' she said. 'I'm Bunty Jenkins. I'm looking for Mr Blackwood.' She was dressed in a long woollen coat, expensively cut, with fur at the collar and cuffs. Her legs, a good six inches of which were plainly visible below the hem, were sheathed in fine silk stockings above a pair of patent leather high-heeled shoes. Over her gleaming bobbed hair she wore a cloche hat of watered silk, decorated with a tiny veil. She looked about the foyer with dark, critical eyes and screwed a thin cigarette into a long ebony holder as she waited for Monty to reply.

Monty took the hand that was extended to her. Its grasp was as soft and limp as the empty glove that had covered it. 'Which Mr Blackwood?' she asked, though she already knew the answer to that question. It crossed her mind to fetch Curran. He would tell the woman that she had made a mistake, that she had better get straight back on to the train and return to London.

But at that moment the door behind the reception desk burst open and Grier appeared. He stepped round the reception desk and held out his hand. 'Welcome to Bleakly Hall,' he said. 'I'm Grier Blackwood. And you are?'

'Bunty Jenkins, from *Woman's Weekly*.'

'Of course!' cried Grier. 'I've been looking forward to it.'

Monty said nothing. She knew that Grier had forgotten about the arrangements he had made for the lady journalist to come. He could not take his eyes off her, though his expression seemed to be one of apprehension rather than admiration.

Miss Jenkins smiled and moved her head from side to side (rather like a cobra, Monty thought). 'I'm here to write an article about you,' she said. 'The piece I wrote about the Bellington Hotel in Cheltenham was very successful. They tell me they've never been so busy, every room full this season since I featured them in our magazine. I'm sure you can oblige me?'

'Of course.' Grier smiled. He had perked up at the possibility of filling every room. 'Would you like a glass of Bleakly Well spring water after your journey? It's most refreshing.'

Bunty Jenkins had not let go of his hand. She licked her

crimson lips as she leaned forward. 'Don't you have anything stronger?'

'Aren't you going to plump my pillows, nurse?' asked Captain Foxley after Monty had changed the bandage on his earlobe, part of which he had shot off the night before.

'Do you remember a girl called Sophia Barclay?' Monty said suddenly, adjusting his pillows as violently as she could without dislodging his bandage.

Captain Foxley frowned and rubbed his head. 'Was she one of those pretty young things up from London? The one with the blonde hair and the beauty spot?'

'No.'

'Well, then I don't know who you're talking about. I don't know anyone by that name. Then again, perhaps I do, I just can't remember. I took a fearful bang on the head, you know. Perhaps you might ask me again in a day or two. Mind you . . .' He seized Monty's hand and pulled her down to sit on his bed. 'I remember wanting to dance with you last night. I wanted you to come outside with me, to look at the stars, but then Grier appeared and dragged you off. But it would have been nice to be alone for a while.' His voice had sunk to a whisper. He raised her hand to his lips and kissed her palm, his blue eyes watching her from beneath his blond fringe.

Monty pulled her fingers from his grasp and stood up. 'If you don't need anything else, I'll go.'

Captain Foxley smiled and lay back on his pillows. 'Ah, I almost had you there, Monty,' he said, reaching for his cigarettes. 'I know you try to deny it, but you do rather like me, don't you?' He laughed. 'And I like you *very* much. Will you come up again later?'

'I'll send Ada.'

'Oh, not *her*.' Captain Foxley frowned. 'I don't want Ada any more. Especially not when there's a proper nurse in the place. It's you that I need and only you that I want. Go on, I promise I won't frighten you.'

'I'm not frightened of you,' said Monty (rather too hastily, she thought afterwards).

Captain Foxley laughed again. 'No, but there's something going on between us, isn't there, and I'd like to find out what it is. I'm sure you would too. I shall expect you this afternoon. Say about three o'clock? Good, that's settled, then. Will you put the gramophone on before you leave? I feel quite dizzy when I try to stand. Thanks. And turn it up, will you? Might was well wake old Slack, and I seem to have only one ear working at the moment.'

Monty did not to go up to see Captain Foxley at three o'clock. Instead, she sent two of the bath men to help him downstairs to the treatment rooms. Captain Foxley, Monty decided, should have a wet sheet bath to soothe the bruising on his ribs. Dr Slack was in full agreement and even suggested that a cold sponging, preceded by an alternating hot and cold douche, might also be beneficial, if the Captain could stand it.

'I'm certain he can,' said Monty. 'I'll make sure of it.'

Captain Foxley protested loudly all the way down the stairs, but the bath men were used to escorting reluctant patrons into the treatment rooms and Captain Foxley barely realised where he was going, and why, before he was in the basement. In an instant the bath men had removed his pyjamas and wrapped him in a cool wet sheet. His arms were pinned to his sides, so that only his head poked out, like a human sausage. They covered him in another wet sheet, this time even colder than the first, wrapped him in a mackintosh sheath and abandoned him, prostrated on a wooden bench. Captain Foxley ceased to struggle as soon as it became clear not only that escape was impossible, but also that his ribs hurt when he moved. Once he was fully immobile beneath layers of tightly wrapped linen, Monty appeared.

'The treatment takes up to two hours,' she said, looking down at him. 'You'll feel much better afterwards. And then you can have an alternating douche, followed by a cold sponging.'

'Will you do that?' asked Captain Foxley. Monty saw him wriggle within his cocoon. 'The douche and the cold sponging, I mean. I wouldn't mind it at all, then. I'm sure you'd be very professional about it.'

'The bath men will do a more stimulating job than I,' said Monty.

'Can I smoke a cigarette? You could hold it for me. We could share it!'

Monty moved restlessly. How helpless he looked, wrapped and bandaged. She almost felt sorry for him. 'I'll come and see how you're getting on in an hour or so,' she said.

Upstairs in the foyer Dr Slack and Grier were sitting beside the fountain with Miss Jenkins. Holding a tea tray, and

231

standing as still and silent as an Indian bearer, Ada waited to one side. Miss Jenkins had asked Dr Slack about the various sorts of hydropathy offered at Bleakly Hall and this simple question had unleashed a torrent of information that she was now quite clearly finding wearisome. She had pulled out a notebook and a gold propelling pencil, but her hand had long since stopped moving across the page.

'General baths, as opposed to the dry heat of the Turkish bath or the more therapeutic properties of the wet sheet packings, are comprised of the rain or needle bath, the spray shower, the shallow bath, the plunge bath and the douche,' droned Dr Slack. 'In addition, we have the wave bath, the dripping sheet bath, and hot and cold spongings. These treatments are all most effective for a great variety of ailments, whether they are toxic, idiotic, or deteriorating.'

'I see,' murmured Miss Jenkins.

'Local baths', continued Dr Slack, his eyes turning sleepy now at the monotony of his own voice, 'comprise the sitz, or sitting bath, the douche, or spouting bath, the spinal, foot and head baths – all of which can be of hot or cold water, singly or in combination, successive or alternate.'

'Well,' said Miss Jenkins, putting the cap on to the golden pencil and slipping her notebook into a white kid handbag. 'That's all very well, Mr Blackwood, Dr Slack, but I think my lady readers would expect something a little more . . . modern from their holiday destination. All this sponging and plunging and what-have-you, it sounds more like an ordeal than a pleasure. I'm not sure my ladies want to be douched. They don't have chronic inflammations and lethargy of the nervous system.' She gave a girlish laugh, her red lips parting to reveal square yellow teeth. 'We're not idiotic *or* deteriorating! Goodness me, Mr Blackwood, my ladies and I, we're not *old*, you know.' Though she was quite plainly in her thirties, Miss Jenkins sought to disguise this fact by sheathing her stick-like figure in youthfully fashionable clothing – since Monty had last seen her she had exchanged her long coat and red dress for a black watered silk bias-cut skirt and a sack-like blouse in emerald satin. A fox-fur stole with gleaming beady eyes was draped like a slumbering rodent round her thin shoulders. 'I know it's rather forward of me to say so,' she added, 'but we ladies are *not* what we used to be. We have the vote now. We worked hard in the war and have been justly rewarded. We are independent. We embrace modernity and all that it offers us, and we don't want to go back. And I think I speak for all my readers when I say that we also want a little luxury after such hardships as we endured in the recent conflict, not self-denial.'

Grier attempted a smile. 'Oh, there's plenty of luxury here at Bleakly, Miss Jenkins,' he began.

'*I* don't have the vote,' interrupted Ada suddenly.

Miss Jenkins made an elaborate show of turning to see who had spoken. Ada was still holding the tea tray. She looked as sturdy as a boxer, her bosom ballooning beneath her apron, her stomach plump beneath the fabric of her grey dress. She stood with her feet planted firmly apart, as though expecting Miss Jenkins to try to bolt past her at any moment. 'Neither does Miss Montgomery there.'

'I beg your pardon?' said Miss Jenkins.

'What did *you* do in the war, miss?'

Miss Jenkins began to screw a cigarette into her ebony cigarette holder.

'There's no smoking at Bleakly Hall,' barked Ada.

'Oh.' Miss Jenkins's fingers stopped what they were doing. Her glance darted nervously towards the cigarette held between Grier's fingers.

'Well?' snapped Ada. 'What *did* you do, miss, if you don't mind my asking?'

'As a matter of fact I had a brother at the front.'

'But you didn't *go* there? You didn't go to the front yourself?'

'Certainly not,' replied Miss Jenkins. 'Don't be absurd.'

'I did,' said Ada. 'So did Miss Montgomery.'

'We all endured.'

'What did *you* endure?' persisted Ada. 'You *ladies*.'

'I had mummy to look after.' Miss Jenkins stared at her cigarette. 'It was a very difficult time. And when the telegram came about Alfred . . .'

'I drove an ambulance,' said Ada.

'I applaud you,' said Miss Jenkins.

'But *I* can't vote,' Ada went on. 'No one asks me *my* opinion. No one rewards *me*. No one gives *me* luxury, no matter what I did out there.'

'Goodness, Mr Blackwood,' said Miss Jenkins. 'I think you might be harbouring a revolutionary!'

'I don't want a revolution,' Ada contradicted. 'I just want to be treated properly. And I want someone to see what I do and to value it.'

'*I* value you, Ada,' said Grier, alarmed in case Ada took it upon herself to hurl the tea tray, and all that was on it, at Miss Jenkins's head. He had no idea she held such extreme views. Yet he could not deny the justice of her remarks. 'So does Curran,' he added. 'We know Bleakly wouldn't last five minutes without you.'

'No,' muttered Ada. 'No, you don't. It's only Captain Foxley what understands.'

22

MONTY TOOK Miss Jenkins downstairs to the treatment rooms. The air throbbed about them, a deep and rhythmic pulse. Miss Jenkins pulled her fox-fur stole closer about her narrow shoulders.

'Shall I show you our appliances?' asked Monty.

'No, thank you,' said Miss Jenkins.

'Perhaps you should try one? A Scottish douche or a peat bath? A peat bath is beneficial to the complexion.'

At the mention of complexions Miss Jenkins perked up. 'Oh?'

'Yes,' said Monty. 'And afterwards, the needle douche is *most* stimulating.'

'Oh, very well.' Miss Jenkins sighed. 'And then I might have dinner with that nice Mr Blackwood? I think it appropriate. Is he married?'

'No,' said Monty.

'Good.' Miss Jenkins smiled. 'Then I shall most definitely have dinner with him.'

Monty stalked ahead and threw open a door marked

Ladies' Changing Rooms. Miss Jenkins followed. She glanced at the cracked tiles and dingy curtains, and a look of disgust spread over her face.

Perceiving this, Monty adopted her brisk nurse's voice. 'Now then, Miss Jenkins, to enjoy the peat bath you must remove your clothes and wrap yourself in a sheet.' She pointed to a pile of sheets and towels on a shelf above a radiator. 'One of our lady orderlies will help you undress. I'll go through now and prepare a bath.'

'What happens?' asked Miss Jenkins, her eyes wide in her thin pale face.

'You must lie in the warm peat, up to your chin, for twenty minutes,' said Monty.

'Will I be alone?'

'You are alone in your bath, of course,' said Monty. 'I'll take your temperature and pulse regularly, to make sure your metabolism is not overtaxed. You must stay as warm as possible to allow the sweating to take place.'

'The sweating?'

'It's the body's way of cleansing the system. A natural process.'

Miss Jenkins nodded, subdued by the confidence of her interlocutor and the gloominess of her surroundings. A tap whispered unstoppably. The room was decorated with the dismal Bleakly livery of green wall tiles and black-and-white linoleum. The tiles, Monty noticed, were dull and lustreless, the linoleum worn and buckled. How drab Bleakly was becoming, she thought.

Miss Jenkins and Monty stared at one another in silence.

Miss Jenkins opened her scarlet lips to speak, but Monty turned away. She reached up and pulled a lever. Far off, a bell jangled. 'An orderly will be along at any moment,' said Monty.

Next door, engulfed by a cloud of steam, Ada was filling the peat bath with water. She emptied a sack of dried soily matter into it and mixed the resultant mash with a long-handled ladle. The muddy surface smoked lazily.

'You look rather green, Ada,' said Monty.

'Feel a bit sick, miss,' Ada replied.

'Sit down,' commanded Monty. 'Come along. I'll get you a glass of water.'

'I can manage,' said Ada, though she relinquished her ladle and sat on the chair Monty pulled up. 'I'll be better in a moment.'

Monty swirled the ladle in the peat.

Ada closed her eyes and sipped her water.

'Ada.' Monty leaned on the ladle, like a gondolier resting. 'I'm worried.'

'What about, miss?'

'About you. There's something bothering you.'

'No, miss,' murmured Ada. 'It's nothing. Nothing to trouble yourself about.'

'But there *is* something. And will you stop calling me "miss" all the time.'

'That's how it is,' said Ada. 'And you don't need to worry about me. I can –'

'Look after yourself, yes, I know that. And you can look after everyone else at the same time. It was the same out at Furnes. All those times we went up and down those Belgian roads. Won't you let *me* look after *you* for a change?'

'You drove too, miss,' said Ada.

'Only when the road was clear and there were no shells.'

'Well.' Ada conceded the truth with a shrug. 'I was never any good with the bandages and the iodine.'

'There wasn't much *anyone* could do with bandages and iodine. You did well. No less than I. In those conditions –'

'In those conditions, I think it was enough that we was there,' said Ada. 'The men was always glad to see us. D'you remember that lieutenant who wrote a name for our dugout on a broken plank and nailed it over the door?'

'*Lyons Corner House*.' Monty laughed. 'They said it was our "restaurant" at Caeskerke that kept them going. I think the soup and cocoa were more important than the bandages and iodine.'

'That cocoa was awful,' said Ada.

'Chloride of lime.' Monty smiled.

'When I came back to Bleakly the cocoa tasted like water. Everything tastes of water here.'

'I remember you drying my socks on that old stove we had. You always seemed to have a dry pair in your pocket. How did you manage that?'

Ada shrugged. 'I don't know, miss. You always seemed to get your feet wet. I don't know how you managed *that*.'

'And then I went and cooked one of them.'

'Oh, yes!' Ada laughed. 'That shell went over and one of your socks fell into the soup. The men said it was the best soup they'd ever tasted.'

'They asked how long a sock had to be worn before it was ready to go into the pot.'

'At least three weeks.'

Monty and Ada laughed.

'I was always so glad that you'd asked me, miss,' said Ada. 'That first time that we met. You could have asked any old driver.'

'I didn't want any old driver. You were the best. And I could never have done it, any of it, without you.'

'You'd have managed.'

'No,' said Monty. 'No, I wouldn't. I couldn't have done those things with anyone else. I didn't realise it at the time. I took it for granted that you would always get us out of scrapes and you did. And then, afterwards, when I was out there alone, it wasn't the same. I thought it was because I was . . . heartbroken that it seemed so much worse, but it wasn't just that. It was because we'd shared it. You and I. We shared everything.'

Ada was silent.

'Ada, don't you think you should tell me what's wrong?'

Miss Jenkins's voice echoed off the changing room's tiled walls. 'Hello? Hello!'

'Oh!' said Monty. 'I'd quite forgotten!'

'Best go and see to her,' muttered Ada.

Next door, Miss Jenkins was standing beside a recovery couch. Her clothes had been neatly hung up, and Miss Jenkins herself was wrapped in the Bleakly Hall therapeutic costume of a mackintosh sheet and a threadbare towel. Her black hair was concealed beneath a turban of white towelling. A cigarette dangled between her fingers and she puffed at it anxiously as she spoke.

'That *woman* you left me with,' she said. 'That orderly, she had the deportment of a female prizefighter! She advanced upon me in the most menacing fashion, as though prepared to actually wrestle me to the floor should she have to. She said it would be "easier for everyone" if I just took off my clothes and stopped being "silly".' Miss Jenkins tossed her spent cigarette into the handbasin and looked down at her greyish-coloured coverings with distaste. 'I look a perfect fright.'

'Follow me, please,' said Monty.

The peat baths of Bleakly were long and narrow, the shape of a coffin and wide enough only to hold a body lying prone and motionless.

'I'm to get into *that*?' Miss Jenkins stared at the brown, smoking waters. She looked about, as though for a means of escape, and noticed Ada sitting beside a table mounded with towels. 'Why is she here?' she asked. 'She's the maid.'

'She's everything,' said Monty. 'I'll take your towel and sheet while you get in. Come along now.'

'It feels peculiar.' Miss Jenkins lay back, the dark muddiness leaching about her breasts and shoulders. 'But not unpleasant.' She scrutinised the mildewed curtain that hung beside her bath, and stared up at the cracked and stained ceiling, blinking for a moment at the dusty tulip-shaped light fixture. 'This place is falling apart,' she said. 'I wonder why Mr Blackwood stays here? Why do *you* stay here?' Her face had turned pink and blotchy in the steam. 'Why are you *all* here? I saw the drawing room was full of old people.

They've probably always come here and can't imagine anywhere else. But what about you? You're far too young and pretty to be stuck away in a place like this.'

'I have friends here,' said Monty.

'But what about Mr Blackwood? Why doesn't he just sell the old place and start afresh? Don't tell me he has friends here too? I can't imagine who.'

'He has his brother to think about,' said Ada from her station beside the towels. 'And Captain Foxley. They're more important to Mr Grier than money and redecorating . . . and starting afresh.'

Miss Jenkins snorted. She did not bother to look in Ada's direction. 'The remains of the old regiment, I suppose? Well, I see he has the loyalty of the maid too. I suppose you're also one of his "friends", are you?' She glanced up at Monty with disdain. 'You two with your ambulance driving and what-not? Well, that's hardly a businessman's answer. I'm beginning to wonder whether this Mr Blackwood is in his right mind.'

Grier wandered listlessly from room to room. In the gentlemen's treatment room he found Captain Foxley lying on the wooden bench, rolled in his spool of sheets. 'Hello, Dodger,' said Grier, who had thought Captain Foxley to be still in bed. Captain Foxley's face was pale above his moist wrappings. 'How long have you been here?'

'I don't know,' replied Captain Foxley weakly. 'Have you got any cigarettes?'

'Of course,' Grier pulled one out and stuck it between Captain Foxley's bluish-tinged lips.

'I'm waiting for Monty,' added the Captain. He grinned through the smoke and spoke around his cigarette, like a Tommy. 'She's going to give me a warm sponge bath. It's bloody cold in these sheets and I've been here for ages. Mind you' – he gave a feeble laugh – 'remember that spell we had at Ypres when it rained for weeks? I've been trying to think when it was –'

'1917,' said Grier mechanically. 'November.'

'That's right.' The Captain's teeth chattered. 'Absolutely freezing. And then the place iced over too. Bloody awful. I'm almost as cold and wet as I was then, but not quite.'

Grier looked at Captain Foxley. *Bloody awful*. Was that all Ypres in November had been to Foxley? Grier didn't think the words existed that might effectively describe that place, and the time he had spent there. Perhaps 'awful' would have to do.

'At least the mud was hard. For a few days, anyway.'

'Mm.' Grier took a step backwards towards the door.

'At least everyone assumed I was shaking with cold, rather than with funk.'

'You never seemed windy,' said Grier truthfully.

'Neither did you,' replied Captain Foxley. 'Apart from that one time. And who could blame you for it – I certainly don't. I'm sure Coward doesn't either.'

'Coward's dead,' said Grier automatically.

'Yes,' said Captain Foxley. The silence was broken only by the sound of trickling water.

'But we had some good times, didn't we, Blackwood,' cried Captain Foxley suddenly. 'It wasn't so bad, was it?'

It seemed strange to Grier that when asked to consider

the war and to evaluate his own experiences in it, he found it almost impossible to recall anything coherent. Instead, his recollection of those years seemed to have fragmented into painful shards of memory, like a broken mirror reflecting a shattered and disjointed past. He had only fleeting impressions of it and, at best, nothing more cohesive in his head, or his heart, than an overarching sense of sadness. When were the 'good times' Captain Foxley talked of? Grier could not remember any.

Monty sank into one of the worn brocade armchairs in Grier's sitting room. It was uncomfortably warm and she was sure she could see a thread of steam escaping from between a crack in the floorboards.

'Yes,' said Grier, following her gaze. 'It's been doing that for a while. The whole place is like the tropics.' He pointed to an outsized geranium with waves of tumbling foliage that lolled on the mantelpiece. 'Perhaps I should start growing bananas in here too.' He handed her a tumbler of whisky. 'Would you like some Bleakly spa water in it? It's from the mains really, you know.'

'Is it?' Monty sounded uninterested.

'Yes. You'll be wondering whether anything in this place is as it seems.'

At that moment a shout echoed from the direction of the sink. 'Hello? Is anyone there? Can you help me? Please, help me!'

'It sounds like Dodger!' said Grier. 'Is he still in the treatment room? I'd quite forgotten where he was. I should send someone down. The poor chap'll be freezing in there.'

'He's quite able to stay where he is for a little longer,' muttered Monty, sipping her whisky. 'It's no more than he deserves.'

'You don't like Dodger at all, do you,' said Grier.

'Captain Foxley's not what you think he is.'

'I know precisely what sort of a man Peter Foxley is. There's nothing you can tell me about him that would surprise me. But whatever he is, you can be certain that he's not pretending to be something he isn't.'

'Ha!' cried Monty. 'He's fooled you too, I see.'

'He's . . . he can seem rather bitter, I suppose.'

'And does that excuse him?'

'Excuse him from what? Look, I know Dodger's not all that he seems. He's a hero *and* a villain. He's the bravest man I know, but also the greatest coward. He's in my debt, just as I'm in his. He's my source of comfort, my brother's rescuer, but also' – Grier looked at the papers spread in untidy piles about the desk top – 'my adversary. Don't make him yours too, Monty. You might hate him, but you must forgive him, whatever it is that he's done. You must have pity for him.'

'I can't,' whispered Monty. 'I can't forgive him and I can't pity him.'

'*Why?*'

'Because I can't forgive myself.' Monty put her head back on to the faded cushions and closed her eyes. All at once she felt tired: tired of being alone and tired of holding her secret to herself. Every morning she promised that *this* would be the day she confronted Captain Foxley and every day she found that the opportunity did not present itself, that the time was not right, or the situation inappropriate, so that every evening she went to bed filled with remorse for being so irresolute. Perhaps it would help if she confided in someone. Who else but Grier – intelligent, experienced and sensitive? But even now Monty stalled. Had she suddenly invested Grier with these sterling characteristics simply because he was handsome and affable? Because she was lonely? She knew, in her heart, that he was weak and flawed – distracted by debt and too lost and irresolute to stop the behaviour that led to it. Yet how badly she wanted a friend.

'I've done a terrible thing,' she said. 'Something for which I can never be forgiven. I think I should tell you what it is.'

23

RATHER THAN going up to the dormitory, Sophia rushed straight out into the night. It was cold and dark, though she hardly noticed either of these things. Nor did she notice that she was without a coat, or that the apron of her uniform was stained with viscera from her day's work. The blackout, through which she had walked with Peter on dozens of occasions, now seemed sinister and frightening. Shadows appeared, the shapes of passers-by, their faces pale and curious in the dark. A man materialised before her, stepping out of the gloom like a diver emerging from the ocean. For a moment Sophia thought she had taken a wrong turning, so that all at once she had no idea where she might be, or which way she should turn. Then there, at last, was the street door to Lieutenant Handyside's flat. Sophia pushed it open and ran up the dimly lit stairs. She wasn't even sure whether Peter was in or not. She realised too that she had no idea what she was going to say. She was only convinced that she had to show him Dr Woodruffe's letter. Surely he would have an explanation. She pulled the letter out of her pocket and tore it open once again. But she could hardly bear to look and saw only individual words, phrases or half-sentences: . . . *known Peter Foxley for many years . . . A most sorry story . . . A lady . . . Pregnant . . . Engaged to be married* . . . Sophia closed her eyes, but the words echoed in her brain as though shouted over and over again. *He abandoned her, with no thought for her well-being or for that of her child – his child – which was stillborn. She, and I, saw him with you that night at the Tivoli* . . .

Sophia stuffed the letter back into her pocket. Surely Dr Woodruffe was mistaken? But only Peter could answer that question. She pressed her ear against the door. She was sure she could hear music from within – a familiar tune, one which Peter had played on his gramophone over and over again. *My heart's afire with love's desire* . . . Sophia stood back and hammered on the door with her fist, but when the echoes died away she could hear only silence. Perhaps she had been wrong about the music. She pounded on the door again.

'Peter, it's me. Peter, are you in there?' But there was only the empty stillness of the stairwell. She bent to peer through the letter box. 'Peter,' she shouted. 'Peter, open up, it's important.'

'Oh, it's always important, ain't it? So important you've got to shout about it and wake up everyone else into the bargain.'

Sophia spun round. Behind her the stairs were obstructed by an elderly woman. She was holding a broom before her, as though about to attempt a bayonet charge.

'Oh, excuse me,' said Sophia, surprised at how calm

she sounded. 'I'm looking for Peter Foxley. Have you seen him?'

'Who are you?' asked the old woman. She jabbed her broom towards Sophia's chest in the attitude of a Tommy on sentry duty.

'Sophia Barclay. And you are?'

'Mrs Potts.'

'Of course. Have you seen him?'

'Who, Mr Handyside?' Her accent, rendered all the more impenetrable by her lack of teeth, was pure East End. She pronounced the name 'Endysard'.

'Mr Foxley. Lieutenant Foxley.'

'I don't know any Lieutenant Foxley. I only knows Mr Endysard.' Mrs Potts lowered her weapon, but her expression remained vigilant.

'Mr Handyside's dead.'

'Dead? 'E didn't tell me that.'

'Who didn't tell you?' said Sophia quickly. The mysterious 'he' could only be Peter . . .

'Mr Endysard, o' course.'

'But he's dead.' Sophia's resolve against tears weakened.

'Where?' said Mrs Potts suddenly.

'Hastings.'

''Astings?' Mrs Potts narrowed her eyes. 'Oh, no, miss. Belgium it was.'

'Well, Belgium initially, but he died in Hastings.'

'But I only saw 'im an hour ago.'

'Who?' cried Sophia. Was the woman completely mad?

'Mr Endysard.'

All at once Sophia remembered something Peter had said

about Mrs Potts's inability to distinguish one 'young man' from another. 'Is Mr Handyside of medium build, with blond hair and blue eyes?' she asked.

'That's 'im. Gramophone always playin'; lovely, charmin' young man. Mind you, that place's not been so tidy recently. I said I wasn't clearin' up that kind o' mess. Still, that's young men for you. They needs a young woman to keep 'em neat and tidy, that's what I says.' She smiled, her expression knowing, and revealed a pair of gums as moist and pink as sea anemones. 'That'd be you, miss, would it?'

Sophia blushed. 'Is he in?'

'Why don't you knock an' see?'

'I have, there was no answer.'

'O' course there's an *arn*ser,' said Mrs Potts scornfully. 'The *arn*ser is, 'e's not 'ome.'

'But I heard –'

'Oh, I doubt it, miss. 'E don't stay in of an evenin'.' She began to sweep the stairs, humming under her breath. It was the same tune Sophia thought she had heard coming from behind the closed door of Lieutenant Handyside's flat, but now that it was gusting out of Mrs Potts's lips she was not so sure

'Peter,' cried Sophia again, battering at the door. 'Peter, are you in there?'

'Stop that!' cried Mrs Potts, pausing in her labours. 'Stop that shoutin'. We don't want another disturbance. It's a very respectable neighbour'ood, this.' Mrs Potts stared at Sophia's gore-spattered apron. She lifted her broom back into the offensive position. 'What's wrong with you young ladies these days?' she cried.

'Thank you, Mrs Potts,' muttered Sophia. She stood back from the door, sulkily accepting defeat. 'If you see him, will you tell him I came?'

'Leave a note,' said Mrs Potts. She rummaged in her apron pocket, producing a grubby notepad and a stump of pencil. 'That's what I always tells 'em.'

That evening, Sophia searched for Peter in every place she could think of. As she crossed the street towards the British Empire Hotel, she was sure she saw his face in the crowd, looking up at the searchlights that raked the night sky hunting for the massive ribbed flank of a Zeppelin. And yet he had turned away before she could be certain, had kissed the cheek of a pretty girl hanging on his arm, so that she was sure, almost sure, that it couldn't possibly be him.

She looked about again . . . And yet there! Was that not him, lighting a cigarette on the edge of the crowd? The flare of a match had lit up his face. She was sure she would recognise it anywhere – that aquiline nose, those sharp cheekbones. She pushed her way forward, but when she reached the spot where she thought she had seen him, he was gone. Was that his back, walking away from her? Was that his laugh she could hear over the hubbub of the crowd? She turned again and stumbled straight into a pair of arms.

'Hello, there.'

'Oh, hello,' said Sophia. 'I thought you'd gone back,' she added, unable to think of anything more welcoming to say. But Lieutenant Lucas was blessed with an abundant supply of masculine self-confidence and didn't seem to notice her disappointment.

'That's Chalmers,' said Lucas. 'He's gone back. I've got another three days.' He smiled at her, his expression almost gleeful. 'Forgotten your coat? Here, take mine.' And before she could object he had taken off his greatcoat and draped it round her shoulders.

'No, I'm all right, thank you,' said Sophia, trying to return the coat, but grateful nonetheless for its warmth.

'Nonsense,' said Lucas. 'You're freezing. I can see you shivering and it makes me feel cold just looking at you. In which case I think I'd better stop looking at you. I'll just take your arm instead, how's that?'

Sophia said nothing. She felt Lieutenant Lucas's hand beneath her elbow as he steered her out of the crowd and down the street.

'Now then,' he said after a moment. 'What are you doing out at this time of night on your own? Don't tell me Foxley's actually lost you? How careless of him.'

'Have you seen him?' said Sophia.

'Foxley? No . . . not this evening.'

'Oh.'

'He had to go to see one of the army doctors today, I seem to recall,' added Lucas, his tone more confident all of a sudden. 'Yes, that's it. Perhaps they kept him in for some reason.'

Sophia glanced up at him. How young he seemed, barely older than she was, though she knew he had been in Belgium for over a year. She noticed that his fingers were gripping her arm rather tightly. He was walking rapidly, now, and his smile seemed somewhat fixed and insincere. She realised they were heading up a dark street she did not immediately recognise.

'Thank you, Lieutenant Lucas, I'll make my own way from here,' she said.

'I wouldn't hear of it,' said Lucas. 'I couldn't possibly let you walk home alone. Where would you like to go? I'll take you straight there myself. And if I see Foxley I'll . . . well, I'll tell him he's a fool to leave you like this.'

'To leave me?' Sophia gasped.

'Yes, to leave you wandering the streets on your own. It's not very gentlemanly, is it?'

Sophia said nothing. She wished Lieutenant Lucas would go away. And where on earth was he taking her? He was still walking briskly, but Sophia was sure they were not going in the direction of the hospital. 'I need to go back to the hospital,' she said, in case there had been some sort of misunderstanding. 'It's not far from here.'

'I know where it is,' said Lucas. His fingers squeezed her arm.

'Well, I don't think it's this way,' said Sophia, slowing down.

'This is a short cut,' said Lieutenant Lucas. 'Up here through the trees.'

Sophia shook her head. 'Well, I shan't be taking it.'

'Come on.' His tone was wheedling and his tall lanky body suddenly seemed to be walking too close. 'It won't take a minute.' He put his arm about her shoulders. 'I'll keep you warm.'

Sophia sprang away from him, horrified at his touch, at the insinuating tone of his voice and at her own naivety in allowing him to lead her off into the darkness. She cast aside his coat, like a villain unmasking in a pantomime.

'Oh, don't be like that,' said Lieutenant Lucas. He sounded bored and slothful, but all at once he lunged for her in the darkness. Sophia felt a hand grasp her shoulder. She smelled a breath, heavy with whisky, in her face and (horror!) was that the touch of a pair of lips sliding against her cheek? And then, just as abruptly as he had seized her, Lieutenant Lucas stumbled and crashed down in front of her like a fallen tree. Sophia sprang aside. Was he drunk? Perhaps, but it was not that which had caused his sudden collapse. Instead, his ankles had become fettered by a thick swathe of greatcoat, which lay where Sophia had cast it in the middle of the pavement and among whose generous folds his boots had become ensnared. Lieutenant Lucas struggled to rise. Sophia sprang over him and rushed back the way they had come. Behind her, she heard him stagger to his feet. He began to lumber forward, following her down the street, but then he seemed to think better of it and returned to pick up his coat. Sophia looked over her shoulder, but already he had been swallowed up by the night, and she could only hear his muttering voice, cursing his own blundering stupidity.

24

Sophia scribbled a quick note. *Dear Peter*, she wrote. *I have something I'd like to talk to you about; will you be able to reply by return of post to let me know when we might meet? Or perhaps come to the gates tomorrow evening at 7 p.m. With love, your own Sophia*. Afterwards, she rinsed out some bedpans and replenished the dressing trolley. She scrubbed the floor of theatre two and helped Sister Barnett make up six enormous demijohns of Lysol and peroxide solution.

'Are you feeling sick?' said Sister Barnett. 'You look rather pale.'

'I'm quite well, thank you, Sister,' said Sophia gloomily. She reached for another empty bottle. 'What time does the second post usually come?' she asked, though she already knew the answer to this particular question. There had been nothing for her that morning. Although she could not expect a reply to her own letter until tomorrow, perhaps Peter had sent a note anyway?

'Two o'clock,' said Sister Barnett. 'But you can't pick up any letters until the end of your shift, you know what

Miss Tadworth says about reading correspondence on the wards.'

Sophia hoisted a bottle of the antiseptic solution on to the trolley. She wheeled it out into the corridor, her mood sinking, as it so often did these days, propelled inexorably downwards by a series of dejected, meandering thoughts. Certainly, she had come to dread changing some of the dressings almost as much as the men themselves; and the nearer it came to Peter's return to the front, the more terrifying and awful she found the men's wounds. When set beside the terrible human casualties she saw every day, Peter's conduct, as described by Dr Woofruffe, seemed really quite unimportant. And what if it were Peter's eye socket she were packing with gauze and his face she were bandaging? What if it were Peter's screams she were listening to at night? Would she still love him if he could no longer walk, had no hands to touch her with, or no eyes to see her? It was even more distressing to find that she didn't actually know what her answer might be to these most terrible of questions. If she could not have all of him – strong-limbed and handsome and vigorous as he was now – she wasn't sure that she wanted him at all. She sighed and berated herself for such selfish, small-minded thoughts. Yet she could not stop them from coming, no matter how hard she tried.

There was no correspondence waiting for her when she finished her shift and none the following morning. That night Sophia went out at seven o'clock, but there was no Peter waiting at the gates. Once again it was dark as she walked to Lieutenant Handyside's flat and once again there was no reply when she knocked on the door. She peered through the letter box, but saw only blackness within.

Another consignment of wounded appeared at St Margaret's. Although they had been expected all afternoon, it was almost dark by the time they arrived. A fog had crept up from the river to linger about the hospital buildings. Sophia was on her way down the stairs with a mop and bucket, and she watched from the window as men were unloaded from the numerous ambulances and military vehicles that had been commandeered as makeshift Red Cross conveyances. There was an air of tired inevitability hanging about the place, so that those orderlies, porters, ambulance drivers, doctors and nurses who toiled among the stretchers did so in almost complete silence, attending to their duties with a jaded familiarity that required few words. The only sounds echoing through the darkness (other than the odd muted groan or whispered instruction) were the crunching of gravel underfoot, the slam of doors and the creak of leather and canvas.

Sophia continued down the stairs and trudged along the main corridor towards the sluice room. As was her habit, she looked in on ward six. Corporal Foster had been discharged to a convalescent home and his place had been taken by Captain Holmes, still anonymous beneath his mask of bandages. Captain Holmes's bed was nearest the door – a place generally reserved for those least likely to make it through the night. For days now his only signs of life had been the shudder that passed through him as his dressings were changed, and the plaintive whistling emitted by the tube now fitted where his nostrils should be and which poked out from his bandages like the spout of a teapot projecting from a tea cosy. Sophia noticed a black-clad figure crouched at Captain Holmes's bedside. It was the chaplain. Sophia continued on her way. When she returned five minutes later with Sister Barnett, Captain Holmes was dead and the chaplain, his work completed, was gone.

The next day Monty returned. They decided to go out, to the ice-cream parlour near the station.

'I missed you terribly,' said Sophia, linking her arm though Monty's as they walked along the street. How calm she felt all of a sudden. How relieved she was to have Monty beside her once again. She squeezed Monty's arm and kissed her on the cheek. She thought she had got used to being alone, to having only Peter to think about, but now that Monty was back she realised how badly she wanted to talk to someone. For this purpose only Monty would do. Only Monty would understand. Monty would know exactly what had to be done.

'So,' said Monty once they were settled in a booth. 'Tell me about this Peter Foxley. I believe he's been taking up rather a lot of your time these past weeks.'

Sophia gave a feeble smile. They were sitting in the very booth she had occupied with Peter, weeks ago now, when he was still trying to seduce her. She wondered, not for the first time, whether she had capitulated too quickly, though it was far too late to worry about such things now. Instead, she told Monty everything – where they had met, when they had become lovers, how brave he was and how much admired by his fellow officers (though she omitted to mention how dubious she found the character of some of his friends). Monty seemed to be happy for her, she thought, so that all at once she wished Monty could find someone like Peter to love too. Sophia voiced this sentiment and squeezed Monty's hand warmly. Next, her enthusiasm wilting, she told her how long it had been since she had last seen Peter. He had an appointment with the army doctor, she said, to give him the all-clear before he went back. Perhaps they had found something more serious wrong with him, she really didn't know . . . Finally, almost as an afterthought, she pulled out Dr Woodruffe's letter and showed that to Monty as well.

In fact, Sophia had been feeling so fretful about Peter's mysterious silence that by now she had almost (but not quite) forgotten about the contents of this letter and was increasingly predisposed to ignore it altogether. Now she was disheartened to see Monty's expression change from one of interest to one of concern.

'Of course, Dr Woodruffe might be completely mistaken,' said Sophia.

'I suppose he might,' said Monty, reading the letter over again. 'Though he sounds quite certain. You must ask Peter about it.'

'He might be angry. It'd seem as though I have no faith in him. And even if it *is* true, it was so long ago.'

'It's not *that* long ago.' Monty glanced at the letter again. 'Dr Woodruffe says it was 1915. "*He had returned on leave, having seen some action at the front, and sent her only the most cursory and cold-hearted of notes informing her –*"'

'Oh, I *know*,' said Sophia, snatching the letter. 'But it was two years ago. So much has happened since then.'

'Not much has happened at all,' commented Monty drily. 'The war's the same. Why shouldn't he be the same?'

'Oh, you're so *sensible*,' cried Sophia. 'Can't you look beyond rumours and hearsay and just live for the moment?'

'I don't think I can,' said Monty. 'I'm not like that.'

'No,' said Sophia sulkily. 'I suppose you're not. But I am. I can't just let the chance of love pass me by because it *might* be the wrong thing to do. What if it's the right thing to do? It'd be terrible to look back and think about what you'd missed, all because you were too worried about what others might think, or what might happen, to take a risk.'

Sophia wrote Peter a note and persuaded Monty to come with her to Handyside's flat. It was a long walk, and by the time they reached the place it was almost time to return to the hospital.

'There he is,' cried Sophia suddenly, pointing (so it seemed to Monty) vaguely heavenwards. 'I saw him at the window. Peter! Peter!' She waved an arm and dashed across the street, hardly looking left or right as she went.

Monty looked up at the building. She could just make out the words 'Livingston Mansions' carved on to an unfurling banner of soot-covered stone across the front of the edifice. There was no visible sign of life – no light, no movement, not even the twitch of a curtain or the flicker of a candle to indicate that there might be anyone within. With a sense of apprehension Monty followed Sophia up the stairs to Lieutenant Handyside's apartment. The staircase had once been an example of Victorian opulence, but its wrought-iron railings were now dull and neglected, and the smooth oak banister felt sticky beneath her hands. Ahead of her Sophia stopped and knocked on a door. From within they heard the sound of someone moving about: a throat was cleared and the lock rattled.

'He's here!' cried Sophia. 'I *knew* he was!' The door opened a couple of inches and a watery eye peered out.

'Not you again. I thought I'd told you.'

'Ah, hello, Mrs Potts.' Sophia sounded disappointed. 'I'm looking for . . . the young gentleman who lives here. Is he in?'

'No, miss.'

'I see.' Sophia seemed not to know what to say next.

Monty stepped forward. 'Mrs Potts, I'm Nurse Montgomery, from St Margaret's Hospital,' she said briskly. 'We're looking for the occupier of this flat. Have you seen him? It's really quite important. I'm sure you understand –'

'Yes, oh, yes,' said Mrs Potts. She threw the door wide and gazed at Monty with fearful eyes.

'When was it that you saw him last?' barked Monty. 'If you would be so kind.'

'Oh, this morning, it were. The place were in a terrible mess. 'E told me to come back and see to it while 'e were out this evening. Paid me extra. Not in trouble, is 'e? *Such* a nice young man.'

'Perhaps we might leave this note for him,' said Monty, indicating the letter Sophia was squeezing between her hands. Without waiting for an answer Monty swept into Lieutenant Handyside's flat. 'Perhaps if we left it somewhere that he might see it when he comes back? It won't take a minute and we won't disturb you.' She stalked forward, looking around her.

'Well, if it's important,' mumbled Mrs Potts. She pointed down the hall. ''E's through there mostly. I've got to get on, so if you don't mind –'

'Not at all,' said Monty. 'Thank you.' She strode down the hallway, Sophia trailing miserably behind her. To the left an open door led to a dark and gloomy drawing room. Empty whisky bottles stood on every surface, and the room smelt strongly of cigarettes and stale air. At the end of the hall another open door led into a bedroom. Monty peered in. Upon the bed lay a khaki tunic and shirt, a pair of breeches and a Sam Browne belt. Peter Foxley's uniform, she saw, bore two brass wound stripes on its sleeve and had a used and recently abandoned air to it, as though he had only just that moment cast it aside after a period of sustained wear. Sophia stood behind her, peeping over her shoulder hopefully. Mrs Potts seemed to have disappeared, and she could hear the sound of tuneless humming and the chink of glasses and bottles being gathered together.

It was clear to Monty that Peter had been in the apartment very recently. A packet of cigarettes, a train timetable and a few shillings were grouped together on top of a chest of drawers, as though from a hastily emptied pocket. A half-empty tumbler of whisky stood adjacent, next to a sheaf of opened correspondence – notes and torn-open envelopes, the writing on each of which was quite clearly Sophia's.

Sophia lay down on Peter's bed and stretched herself out luxuriously.

'Well, he's obviously been staying here, and recently too,' said Monty. 'I wonder where he is. Perhaps we should leave your note here, beside the others, and go back.'

'I shall leave it on his pillow,' said Sophia.

Monty turned away. Sophia seemed to be alternating between assertiveness and a dreamy infatuated languor, and Monty was beginning to find this latter incarnation rather unappealing. How disabling love seemed to be. Did one really have to become so distracted, so foolish, so different a person from what one usually was? Not only this, she thought now, but Sophia had not asked her one question about her unhappy weeks at home, had not made a single enquiry about her brother's death. And yet she, Monty, had heard more than enough about Peter Foxley. Indeed, Sophia seemed to be spending an inordinate amount of time thinking about him and talking about him and worrying about where he might be, yet the fellow couldn't even be bothered to let her know where he was.

At that moment there were footsteps in the hall outside. Sophia sat up on the bed and laid a pale hand (rather theatrically in Monty's opinion) against her throat in expectation. Monty put down the letters she had been holding. She felt her cheeks turn pink. What would he say when he found two women in his bedroom, one languishing on his bed like a courtesan, the other (a stranger to him) apparently rooting through his correspondence?

A man appeared in the doorway. Monty opened her mouth to apologise for their intrusion, but the words did not make it to the end of her tongue. This was not what she had been expecting: the man standing before them seemed to be hardly even twenty years old. His hair was thin and yellow, his skin pale, and although he was not unpleasant to look at, he was not quite the dashingly handsome lieutenant she had imagined him to be.

'You!' Sophia leaped off the bed. 'What are you doing here?'

The young officer stared at her in surprise. 'I could ask you the same thing,' he said.

'We should go,' said Sophia to Monty. She stalked towards the door and pushed past the young man who stood in her way. 'I'm going to speak to Mrs Potts and then we'll leave.'

'Who are you?' said the man, now looking at Monty in surprise. 'And what are you doing here?'

'I'm a friend of Sophia's, of Miss Barclay's,' said Monty. 'I gather you're not Peter.'

'I'm Lucas. Second Lieutenant Aubrey Lucas. I was looking for Foxley. I'm leaving in an hour, so I thought I'd come round to say goodbye. The door was open so I assumed he was here.'

'He's not,' said Monty.

'So I see.' They stared at each other in silence. 'Look,' he said at last. 'Your friend, Miss Barclay, she seems like a nice girl. But she's not the first, you know. Not by a long shot. Foxley, well, I can't imagine anyone I'd rather be stuck in a trench with – or any other tight spot for that matter. But when it comes to the ladies . . . that's a different story altogether.' He blushed. 'My own behaviour might not always be perfect, I'm sure Miss Barclay's told you –' He looked at Monty sheepishly. 'I was drunk,' he murmured. 'And lonely. You've no idea what going back does to a chap's head. I just wanted some . . . some company. I didn't mean it. I didn't do anything.'

'I don't know what you're talking about,' said Monty.

'Oh? Well, never mind then.' Lieutenant Lucas cleared his throat. 'The thing is, Foxley's a friend . . . but she's better off without him, if you ask me, and if you're a friend to her you'll tell her so.'

'Oh, I don't think she'll listen to me,' said Monty.

'She thinks she's in love, I suppose.'

'She *is* in love. The trouble is that she thinks he's in love too. Is he?'

Lieutenant Lucas shrugged. 'I don't know.'

'Perhaps he is, then.'

Lieutenant Lucas looked unconvinced. 'He didn't seem to be last week,' he muttered. He lowered his eyes, as though recalling some of Peter Foxley's recent behaviour and finding himself unable to describe it tastefully.

'Thank you, Mr Lucas, for being so candid,' said Monty. 'Good luck,' she added.

25

THEY RETURNED to the dormitory shortly before the nine o'clock curfew. Sophia flung herself on to her bed, her face pressed into the pillow in an attitude of despair.

Monty made her a cup of tea. 'I'm sure there's some explanation,' she said. 'I'm sure you'll hear from him soon.'

'I don't understand,' cried Sophia, her words muffled by the bedding. 'Where can he be? Why has he not come for me?' She sat up, electrified by a sudden spark of hope. 'Perhaps there's a letter waiting for me downstairs! Perhaps he came while we were out. I know it's late but –'

'I'll go and see,' said Monty. She patted Sophia's shoulder. 'Stay here and drink this. I put some sugar in it.'

'Tea with sugar!' said Sophia, distracted for a moment from her pathetic anxieties. 'Where did you get that?' She looked up at Monty fondly. 'You do spoil me. No milk?'

'No,' said Monty, handing her a handkerchief. 'I can't work miracles.'

Monty went downstairs. Convinced of Peter's faithlessness, she wondered how Sophia would react when she learned that there was no letter waiting for her; no message to say that a young officer had called. As she crossed the vestibule to ask for any correspondence, she noticed a boy hanging around in the shadows beneath the clock at the main entrance.

'Are you here to see someone?' she asked.

'I saw that fat ol' matron,' said the boy. 'She told me to get on out, but I've not delivered me message yet.'

'What message is that?' asked Monty. 'Is it a message for your father?'

''E's dead,' said the boy. 'Retreat from Mons. I'll not be sendin' 'im any messages.'

'Then who –'

'I've this note for a Miss Sophia Barclay VAD.' The boy pronounced the name precisely. 'It's from Lieutenant Foxley, at the Cat and Fiddle public house, near Charing Cross.'

'You've come a long way in the dark,' said Monty.

''E paid me a lot o' money,' said the boy. He jingled some coins in his trouser pocket. 'Two shillin'.'

'Goodness me,' said Monty.

'I'm to give the note to the lady 'erself. *Not* to the fat ol' matron. Nor to the skinny one with the red face.'

'Sister Barnett,' said Monty.

'If you say so.'

'Well, I'm Miss Barclay's friend,' said Monty. 'How about I give the note to her for you?'

'I must give it 'er meself,' insisted the boy. 'Lieutenant Foxley said –'

'Two more shillings say you can give it to me,' said Monty. She held up the silver coins and saw the boy's eyes

267

glitter. 'And Lieutenant Foxley need never know anything about it.'

'This came for you,' she said, handing a scrap of paper to Sophia. 'It's from Peter.'

Sophia leaped up from the bed. 'From Peter? When?'

'Just now.'

'Was he here? Is he downstairs?'

'He sent someone,' said Monty. 'He couldn't come himself.' She watched Sophia unfold the note and saw her face bloom with happiness.

'You see,' cried Sophia. 'I knew he'd send me one of his notes sooner or later. Tomorrow night.' She glanced up at the clock above the dormitory door. 'It's nine o'clock already. The sooner I go to sleep the faster it'll come round.' She smiled and hugged the scrap of paper to her chest. 'D'you want to see?'

Monty already knew what the note said. A few incoherent sentences scribbled on the back of some betting slips. *Mrs Potts said you'd been round. You're a persistent little thing, aren't you? Have you been waiting for a note, a billet doux, in which I say 'I love you' over and over again? 'Meet me tomorrow at our usual place, at our usual time'? Forgive me, Sophie dear*

'Is that what he means?' Monty said. 'The usual place at the usual time? Will you go?'

'Of course, I'll go,' said Sophia. 'Wouldn't you?'

Sophia was excessively cheerful for the rest of the evening. As they prepared for bed – sharing a tepid bath in the dilapidated bathroom – she asked Monty about her brother. 'Poor Richard,' she said. 'At least he had you there to look after him. At least he didn't die all alone, in a muddy shell hole or a watery trench.' Her face dissolved into misery at the thought. 'I wish Peter didn't have to go back,' she said, her eyes filling with tears. 'He might be killed if he goes back.'

'Yes,' said Monty. 'He might.'

'But we have to be together. I need him to be with *me*,' Sophia's voice whined in Monty's ear.

'Do you? Are you quite sure? You've only known him for a few weeks –' Monty rubbed herself briskly with a small, crisp towel. How dissatisfied she was by the situation she now found herself in. It had been a relief, at first, to come back to London after nursing her brother and comforting her parents for so long. She had expected to return to St Margaret's to find the same Sophia – cheery, sympathetic and compassionate – that she had left behind all those weeks ago. She had expected to resume her role as comrade and comforter, perhaps she might even have received some comfort and support herself. Certainly, she had not expected to come back to listen to Sophia enthusing about a man who, Monty knew, had no regard for anyone but himself. Yet how could she possibly explain what sort of a fellow Peter Foxley really was? She knew that Sophia would never listen. Sophia was talking now about the 'plans' she had made for their future together. Peter could surely be persuaded to stay at home, one way or another. She had mentioned it to him before. After all, had he not done his duty for King and Country already? Had he not demonstrated his bravery over and over again?

Monty said nothing.

It was clear that Peter loved her, said Sophia. His note and the tryst it promised was evidence of his feelings. He would be sure to take care of her, whatever happened, wouldn't he?

'I don't know,' said Monty stiffly. 'I've never met him.'

Later, when the lights were out, Sophia hopped across to Monty's bed and they huddled together under the covers for warmth. 'It was freezing here without you,' she whispered, sliding a cold foot against one of Monty's warm legs. 'I'm so glad you're back.' And she fell asleep instantly, dreaming, Monty assumed, of Peter Foxley.

The weather had been fine and settled for days. The nights were cold and clear, the days crisp and sunny. The quadrangle of brownish grass occupied by Queen Victoria suddenly became speckled with the coloured heads of tiny crocuses, the base of her pedestal fringed with the slender green pencils of emerging daffodils. Spring was coming and in the hospital, staff and patients alike, seemed to be optimistic. Perhaps the war would be over soon and there would be a new start for everyone.

Monty and Sophia spent the morning attending to the men's dressings. In the afternoon they trundled bales of laundry up and down corridors, and wound bandages. In the evening Sophia prepared to go out to meet Peter. She pulled on her dress and brushed out her hair until it was gleaming. Just before Monty had gone home there had been an outbreak of head lice among the nurses and VADs. Sophia had been tormented by this terrible plague – her hair was long and thick, and the lice had been hard to extract and eradicate. Tired with repeated infestations, and with the great time and effort involved in washing and drying long hair in such difficult conditions (sharing a bathroom and a dormitory was vexing to them all), many of the women in the hospital – Monty included – had cut their hair short. Sophia had not been one of them. Now, as she pinned her hair up again, Monty could see that she was pleased still to have her long, shining tresses, no matter how inconvenient they might be.

'I thought you were going to get that cut off, after the lice,' muttered Monty.

'Oh, I was,' said Sophia. She rubbed a finger over her lips as she gazed at her reflection in her silver hand mirror. 'But Peter likes it long like this.'

'It's a pity he won't be here to comb the nits out of it next time.'

Sophia laughed. 'You grumpy old thing,' she said. 'I think he'll have his own nits to deal with, don't you?'

Monty was sure Peter would have more than nits to worry about, but she kept this sour observation to herself.

'How do I look?' asked Sophia.

'Beautiful,' said Monty truthfully.

'Dear Monty.' Sophia kissed her cheek. 'You're my most precious friend. Now please don't worry about me. I've become quite independent while you've been away, you know.'

Monty watched Sophia pull on her coat and scarf, and

disappear from the dormitory. After a couple of minutes she put on her own shoes and coat, and went out after her into the darkness.

A bank of low cloud had come up, so that the night seemed darker than ever. Sophia moved quickly, eager to get to her destination, so that more than once Monty almost lost sight of her. At length they reached the main road. Sophia stopped outside the British Empire Hotel and looked about. Monty stood in a shop doorway some thirty yards down the street and waited. People wandered up and down the pavement. Monty thrust her hands into her pockets and curled her fingers round the two betting slips she had kept from Sophia. She would show them only if she really had to. She stamped her feet to keep them warm. How long would she stand there? In the distance a clock chimed.

At nine o'clock Monty stepped out from her doorway like a sentry emerging from his box and marched up the street. She walked up to the shivering, dejected figure standing in front of the hotel and put her hand on Sophia's arm. Sophia jumped and turned to face her. For an instant Monty saw Sophia's face register joy – here was Peter at last! – but then she saw that it was only Monty and her smile sagged in disappointment.

'He's not coming,' said Monty gently.

'He is,' cried Sophia. 'He is. He's just late.'

'Come back with me. It's far too cold to wait here.'

'I can't,' said Sophia. 'He might come.'

'It's after nine o'clock. He's not coming.'

'He will!' Sophia insisted. 'Wait with me, he'll be here soon, you'll see. He'd love to meet you.'

Monty shook her head. She felt speechless. In her head, she had mapped out cruel and cutting arguments to get Sophia to see sense – Peter did not love her, Peter had abandoned her, Peter had used her and thrown her away when he had become tired of her – but now Monty found it impossible to say any of these things. She was about to suggest other more positive-sounding incentives – a hot cup of cocoa, perhaps, or a warm nightdress – but somehow these pedestrian alternatives did not seem very enticing when compared to the possibility (no matter how remote) of a lover's embrace. Monty drew her coat about herself and waited beside Sophia in the freezing darkness.

Suddenly, in the distance, they heard the sound of whistles blowing and a fierce rattling noise, as though someone were dragging a broom handle across iron railings. Far off, voices began shouting and there was the distant boom of a muffled explosion. The whistling sound came nearer. A black shadow swerved round a corner and a policeman hurtled past on a bicycle, veering sharply to miss them in the darkness. Monty just had time to see a white face above a dark collar, his eyes wide, his cheeks puffed out round the whistle clamped between his teeth, then he was gone. There was another explosion, closer now, and this was followed at once by more whistling, plaintive and anxious, the sound of a fire engine and the sound of screaming.

'It's the Zeppelins,' cried a man, hurrying past them. 'You'd best get home.'

'They don't usually come this far west,' said Monty, looking up at the sky. Somewhere behind the buildings a searchlight thrust a thin silver finger into the dark sky, but revealed nothing. By now the whistling and clattering was becoming more insistent. Monty detected the faint smell of burning. 'Come on,' she said, seizing Sophia's arm. 'We must go back.'

'No.' Sophia shook her head. 'He'll be here. I can't leave – what if he arrives and finds I'm gone? He'll wonder where I am, he'll be worried.'

An anti-aircraft gun spluttered into life, its exploding shells flickering against the blackness. For a moment Monty was sure she could distinguish the silhouette of something the shape of a huge carp drifting slowly across the sky. But the shell that had illuminated it was as brief as a photographer's flash and the image was gone before she could be certain. The whistling grew louder and another bomb exploded. The air about them seemed to tremble and smoke tickled their throats. The streets, which had been almost deserted, were suddenly full of people running this way and that, shouting and screaming.

'He's not coming. He's not worried about you!' shouted Monty at last. 'Can't you see it? He doesn't love you at all.' She took Sophia by the arms and shook her.

Sophia's face wore a dazed expression. 'You don't know him. He does love me – of course he does!'

Overhead, the beam of a searchlight combed the heavens, shining up into the night sky but illuminating nothing.

'Come on,' insisted Monty. 'I'll look after you. I'll always look after you.'

She managed to pull Sophia across the street, but by now Sophia was crying. Suddenly she sank down on to the pavement like a melting snowman. Then the air was filled with a droning sound, a rhythmic, monotonous, humming noise, and the searchlight's beam fell on a patch of darkness that was not the night sky at all. It was just as black, but it was ridged and curved, and so vast and swollen that it seemed enormous overhead.

'It's here!' cried Monty. 'It's right here. Sophie, come on!' She tried to lift Sophia up, to drag her away, but she was as impossible to move as a bag of wet sand. Behind them, people were pouring out of the hotel, running up and down the street, plunging into basements and scurrying in every direction.

Sophia turned her head to stare dully at the spectacle. She seemed hardly to see the confusion, hardly to register the fear in the air, and oblivious to the running feet and shouting voices. Across the street the door to the British Empire Hotel opened and closed as people ran out into the night: a dim rectangle of light blinking in the darkness. All at once Sophia sat up. 'There!' she cried, springing up from her posture of defeat. 'There he is! Inside the hotel.'

The hotel door swung open and closed, open and closed, flashing its message of false hope and broken promises, but Monty could see nothing that might be the shadow of a man. 'Where?' she shouted above the din. 'I can't see anyone.'

'He's gone!' cried Sophia. 'He must have gone inside to look for me. Peter! Peter!' And then, before Monty could stop her, before Monty could even cry out, Sophia had rushed back across the road, bounded up the steps and disappeared into the hotel.

'It's overhead,' screamed a voice in Monty's ear. 'It's right overhead, come on!' A policeman loomed before her. His eyes were staring, his mouth open wide as though he were about to burst into song. Instead, he stuck a whistle between his lips and blew violently, so that Monty staggered away from him covering her ears with her hands. She saw him speak, but could not hear what he was saying. 'This way,' his lips mouthed. 'Quickly now.' Monty shook her head. She made as though to run past him and follow Sophia across the street and into the hotel, but she found that she couldn't move. Hands had seized her shoulders, were dragging her backwards, pinning her arms to her sides and pulling her down the street. 'It's coming,' bellowed the policeman.

'Let me go!' screamed Monty. 'Let me go!' The air about her seemed to be singing, resonating with a high-pitched whining sound, almost imperceptible over the hubbub. There was a moment's silence, then the British Empire Hotel was illuminated from within by a great flash of light. There came the sound of an explosion, and another, loud but curiously muffled, as though stifled by an excess of bedding and laundry.

Monty wrenched herself away from the policeman's grasp and ran forward. The British Empire Hotel was in flames, smoke billowing from the shattered windows. The glass in the front door had been blown out, though the door still swung to and fro, as though a stream of ghosts were hastily exiting the burning building. Monty burst through. Inside, the air was filled with whirling particles of ash and smoke. The walls were streaked with black, the paper tattered and scorched. Pictures had been torn from the walls and smashed to pieces on the floor; chairs were overturned and thrown about, their cushions scattered across the floor like life jackets floating on a tragic ocean. Flames licked eagerly at the walls, racing along an electrical bell-pull in a burning umbilicus.

'Sophia!' screamed Monty. 'Sophia!' She held a handkerchief to her nose and mouth, and crouched down on to the floor. She crawled forward. The flames were so hot now that she felt as though her face were about to melt against her skull. And was that the charred reek of her own hair she could smell, as it started to catch fire? There was another explosion and suddenly the smoke was sucked upwards, pulled from the foyer by a system of flues created by open doors and smashed windows.

It was then that Monty saw Sophia. She was lying face up, close to the foot of the smouldering stairs. Monty could see that Sophia's hand was moving, twitching up and down as though she was troubled by a fly and sought continually to shake it off. It was a pale hand, white and small. Monty crawled closer. Sophia's legs appeared black in the light from the flames. Her coat had somehow been torn from her shoulders and flung aside.

'Sophia,' Monty whispered. 'Sophia.' And then she saw Sophia's face. It was torn and blistered, her skin mottled red and black; her lips scorched and crusted, her blue eyes milky and unseeing. It was a mask of suppurating rawness, utlerly stripped by the heat and blackened like meat by the flames. Part of her hair was intact, the left half, as neat and glossy as ever it had been. The other side, on her head and about her ear and cheek, was now no more than a mat of blood and skin; charred hair and blistered scalp mingling in a patchwork of horror that neither surgery nor time could ever repair. Monty could see that Sophia was still alive. She did not move, but a moan of agony escaped from between her cracked and fleshless lips. Monty bent her head.

'I knew you'd come,' whispered Sophia. 'I knew you'd come.'

Sophia began to tremble, shaking violently, as though she were suddenly terribly cold. 'I knew you'd come,' she whispered again. 'Look after me. Look after me.' Far off, Monty could hear the bell of a fire engine. The heat was unbearable, her coat and hair smouldering, so that she was in danger of bursting into flames herself. She could not leave Sophia to face the fire alone. Yet even if Sophia were rescued, even if Monty could carry her out of that terrible inferno, it would be utterly impossible to save her. With such sickening burns, she would die, slowly, consumed instead by pain and shock.

'Oh, Sophie,' she cried. 'Sophie.'

'Look after me,' whispered Sophia. Her voice was barely audible. 'Look after me.' Her hand, still twitching among the ashes of her new dress, squeezed Monty's fingers.

Monty picked up one of the cushions. She stared at Sophia's face, at that hideous mask of burnt flesh. She could think of nothing to say. Not a prayer, not an apology, not a goodbye. So she pressed the cushion down hard in silence, her tears burning her cheeks like acid as they fell.

26

CAPTAIN FOXLEY wanted to go to London to attend a regimental dinner at the Overseas Club. 'Of course, given my recent accident on the dance floor I'm not fit to travel alone and was wondering whether Nurse Montgomery might be allowed to accompany me.' Captain Foxley was addressing Curran, was standing in Curran's office, in fact, with Ada and Monty herself.

'Are you sure you should be going anywhere?' said Curran.

'Oh, I feel quite invigorated after my wet sheet bath. As for that hot and cold sponging . . .' He smiled. 'I'll be right as rain – as long as Miss Montgomery comes with me. I'm sure Ada can manage for a day or so without her, can't you, Ada?'

Ada said nothing.

'There you are, then,' cried Captain Foxley, as though silence was a ringing endorsement of any plan.

'I suppose Miss Montgomery hasn't had a day off since she came here,' said Curran, though he was looking at Ada.

'Not that it'd be much of a day off, looking after you,' he added. 'Ada,' he said, 'you look pale. Have you had a glass of the waters this morning? Might I suggest a glass of Lady Beaton? It contains iron and is excellent for the blood.' He reached for a decanter that stood on his desk and filled a tumbler with the murky waters. 'I had Thake bring some up for me this morning. Here you are.'

From the other side of the room Monty could smell the metallic, sulphurous tang of Lady Beaton. Ada looked at the tumbler Curran held out to her. She muttered an excuse and pushed past Monty and Captain Foxley.

Monty helped Captain Foxley on to the train and into their compartment. His ribs were still uncomfortable, he said, and every now and again he raised his fingers gingerly to the cut on his temple, or the plaster on his earlobe, and winced slightly. Monty was surprised by this display of feebleness. She knew he had endured far worse.

'Do you think it's gone septic?' he said, touching his fingers to his mutilated ear. 'It feels quite sore. I think you'd better have another look at it.'

'It's fine,' said Monty briskly. 'Stop fiddling with it. I've already changed the dressing; I'll look at it again later.' Captain Foxley, she noticed, seemed to be having difficulties putting one foot in front of the other, and she took his arm and helped him into his seat.

'*What do you want to make those eyes at me for, if they don't mean what they say,*' sang Captain Foxley. He spread his arms wide. '*You lead me on and then you run away.*'

Monty ignored him.

Captain Foxley watched her from his corner of the compartment. He was wearing his army uniform and he looked very handsome. Monty could see why Sophia, so young and inexperienced, had become infatuated.

'Will you come with me to the regimental dinner tonight?' asked Captain Foxley suddenly. He inched towards her along the creaking leather seats of their compartment. 'Please. You can't leave me alone with all those old military bores.'

'Why are you going, then?' said Monty. 'If that's what you think of them. You could have stayed at home and rested.'

Captain Foxley shrugged. 'I don't quite know why I'm going. Perhaps it's because I'm an "old military bore" too.' He stared out of the window, his expression suddenly despondent. He pulled a hip flask out of his pocket and raised it to his own reflection. 'To good times,' he muttered. 'And old friends.'

Perhaps sensing that Monty would not be persuaded, Captain Foxley did not ask her again to accompany him to his regimental dinner. Instead, he enquired about her accommodation. Was it comfortable? If not –

'I'm staying with my aunt,' said Monty.

'You can stay with me if you like. I have a flat here.'

'No, thank you.'

'But I thought you came to London to help me, seeing as I'm such an invalid these days? And I might be a bit tipsy after an evening with the old military bores.' Captain Foxley put an arm about her shoulders. His voice was a whisper in her ear. 'You should really be with me all the time.'

'You seem perfectly well to me,' said Monty. 'Take a cab so that you don't have to walk, and make sure you don't lie on your sore ear in the night.'

'You're impossible. You're driving me mad.'

'Oh, I don't think that's anything to do with me.' Monty turned her head, as he leaned in close as though expecting a kiss.

'You're not going to change your mind at all, are you?'

'No,' said Monty.

She helped him along the platform. It was just as well he'd brought his stick. For a moment she wondered whether she should stay with him, but then just as quickly she changed her mind.

'Then what about lunch tomorrow?' suggested Captain Foxley. 'There's plenty of time before we go back. And it's not often we get out of Bleakly these days, is it? We might as well make the most of it. What about the British Empire Hotel? We could meet there. They used to have dances there, I seem to recall. I went during the war when I was on leave.'

'Who did you go with?' said Monty quickly.

'Neither of the Blackwoods, if that's what you're thinking. Curran hated dancing and Grier's useless.'

'Who then?' persisted Monty. 'Did you have a fiancée back then?'

'Good Lord, no.' Captain Foxley laughed.

'It took a direct hit from a Zeppelin in 1917,' said Monty.

'So I heard.' Captain Foxley frowned, as though trying to remember something significant. 'So how about it? Twelve o'clock?'

'No,' said Monty.

Captain Foxley groaned. 'You're such hard work. You have to eat, you know.'

'I'll meet you tomorrow at twelve,' said Monty. 'But not at the British Empire Hotel. I'll meet you at the zoo. Beside the bear pit.'

Aunt Florence welcomed her with a watery smile and a dry kiss on the cheek. She ushered Monty into the parlour. The place was jammed with tables, chairs, sofas, mirrors, clocks and pictures. If it had not been for the gently smouldering fire, thought Monty, it would feel as though she had mistakenly stumbled into the back of a removal van. In addition to this excessive lumber of furniture, Monty saw that the room was still populated by a silent audience of gloomy-faced relatives and ancestors. They stared out from a gallery of silver frames positioned on tabletops and shelves, walls and sideboards, the mantelpiece and the piano. Since Monty's last visit these dismal pictures seemed to have multiplied, so that every surface was home to at least half a dozen stiffly posed greyish-looking figures. A number of more recent additions were clad in military uniform. She recognised the face of Richard, her own brother, who looked surprised to find himself suddenly caught among this crowd of dead relations. Monty picked up the picture frame. Poor Richard. She remembered him best as a boy with dirty knees and untidy hair. Seeing him posed and serious in his army uniform made him seem remote, unfamiliar. She closed her eyes. After he had been returned to them, his body broken and mangled, she had done her best to care for him, to make him comfortable. But the task had proved impossible. Monty scrubbed at her eyes with a handkerchief. She sat down in a creaking leather armchair and waited in silence until afternoon tea was brought in.

'So,' said her aunt at last, 'here you are, Roberta.'

'Yes. I'm sorry I've not been to see you for so long, I was in Belgium until the war ended and then –'

'You're not married yet.' It was a statement, not a question. Aunt Florence looked at her pityingly. 'What happened to that pretty girl you used to bring here? I imagine *she's* married, isn't she? What was her name again?'

'Sophia Barclay,' said Monty.

'Yes, that was it,' said Aunt Florence. 'Such a charming, well-spoken girl. You seemed *such* good friends. I saw her once, you know, near St Margaret's, though she didn't see me. She was hanging on a young man's arm. She looked quite in love.'

'She was,' said Monty. 'She was besotted.'

'Besotted?' Aunt Florence's expression betrayed alarm at the possibility of such emotional intoxication. 'Well, I assume she's not nursing any more, then. A husband would never stand for it –'

'She's not doing anything any more. She's dead.'

'Dead? Oh, dear.'

'And she didn't have a husband,' added Monty, unable to stop herself. 'She didn't get married to that man you saw, but died on her own, wondering where he was and thinking he cared for her when he didn't.'

'Oh.' Aunt Florence fingered the beads at her throat.

'And it was all my fault. It was my fault that she was

there and my fault that she waited for so long. I thought I was helping her, but I wasn't. I thought I was protecting her, but instead I ended up killing her.' Monty dashed a hand across her eyes. 'She was burnt, burnt horribly. I couldn't just leave her the way she was, could I? But I miss her, oh, I miss her terribly. I said I would look after her, but in the end I didn't. In the end I let her down.'

Aunt Florence was looking alarmed. 'I have no idea what you mean, Roberta,' she said. Her gaze slid over to the clock on the mantelpiece. 'You're still nursing, I see,' she added, staring at Monty's uniform.

Monty closed her eyes. 'Yes, Aunt Florence.'

'You know you'll have to give it up if you get married.'

'I believe that's what's generally expected.' Monty suddenly felt very tired indeed. Could her aunt think of nothing else to talk about? She took a sip of scalding tea and wondered whether it was too late to follow Captain Foxley to the Overseas Club.

'Not that there's much chance of you getting married to anyone. Not at your age and with so few men about nowadays.' Aunt Florence pressed her lips together and leaned forward. A satisfied look appeared in her eye. 'Surplus,' she whispered. 'That's what they used to say about me, you know; you'll end up *just like me*.' She paused as if to let the significance of this prognostication sink in. 'My poor sister: her boy dead and her daughter working. Let me look at your hands – goodness me, you have calluses like a charwoman!' She held her bony fingers to her face. 'It was all very well during the war, but now? Are you *sure* you can't give it up?'

285

'Quite sure,' said Monty. 'There's no money left, so it's just as well that I can support myself.'

'That's where *I* can help,' cried Aunt Florence. 'When I die, of course.'

During the course of the evening, for Monty's benefit Aunt Florence conducted an inventory of the contents of her house. She listed each item, stating how much it had been worth when she had acquired it, as well as its estimated current value and the sum it might fetch in a few years' time when she (after all, at sixty-eight she was really quite old now) was likely to expire. Occasionally she paused to state regretfully that she might have to leave such-and-such a piece to someone else. Did Monty mind? (No, said Monty, her cheeks burning, she didn't mind at all.) And would Monty please not sell such-and-such an item? It had been brought back from India and simply *had* to be kept in the family. (Of course, said Monty, of course such codicils would be fully honoured.) At dinner Aunt Florence went through the register of the crockery, the linen on the table and the silverware, down to the milk jug and the dessert spoons. At breakfast she added to the account the salt cellar and the napkin rings – items somehow mysteriously absent from the previous evening's table.

'I hope you found everything to be in order,' she cried as Monty prepared to leave later that morning.

'Quite satisfactory, Aunt,' said Monty, unable to think of anything else to say. 'Goodbye.'

Until now, Monty had not thought she was ready to revisit St Margaret's. But all the soldier patients had gone and there were few people still in the hospital who had taken part in those terrible, chaotic times. Only Miss Barnett, once the slim, easygoing and agreeable Sister Barnett, was still there. She was a very different woman from the one Monty had known and seemed to have taken on Miss Tadworth's manner, as well as her uniform size, when she had taken on the matron's job. She greeted Monty with only the faintest of smiles. It was nice of Monty to pop in, but she had a hospital to run and didn't have time for tittle-tattle with old friends. Her eyes roved the corridor, as though in search of nurses who might need a stern rebuke.

'Pity about that pretty young friend of yours,' she said at last, as if bringing up the one subject that might hasten Monty's departure. 'She used to go out at night to meet that young lieutenant. She said she was visiting a sick relative, or an old aunt, but I knew she wasn't. I used to see her with him from the top window, but I didn't say anything. Perhaps I should have; perhaps I should have stopped her. There was supposed to be a curfew and I was supposed to enforce it. But I was so tired, we all were, I didn't bother to check who was in and who wasn't, I just assumed . . . and she worked hard on the ward, I didn't see why she shouldn't have a bit of fun now and again. I wonder whether I was wrong. I think I probably was.' She breathed hard through her nose.

'You can't blame yourself,' said Monty.

'I don't blame myself,' barked ex-Sister Barnett. 'Though I imagine you do.'

'Yes,' said Monty.

'She made her own decisions.' She was gentler now. There was nothing you could do.'

'Yes, there was,' said Monty.

'I'm sure you did what you thought was best at the time.' Ex-Sister Barnett looked over her shoulder, as if checking her means of escape. 'She was lucky to have you as a friend – there wasn't much time for things like friendship back then, was there? Anyway, it's nice to see you, but I have to get on.' She gave Monty's arm a quick squeeze. 'Miss Tadworth lives over the road,' she added. 'She has a room on the third floor of number twenty-six. She watches the gates to see who comes and goes.'

As she walked out of the gates, Monty looked up at the tall Victorian terrace opposite. Sure enough, at a third-floor window she could see a round face, as pale and featureless as a pebble, peering down at her through circular spectacles.

27

MONTY DECIDED to keep Captain Foxley waiting. She could see him beside the bear pit, looking around for her, but she remained where she was, beside the penguin enclosure, watching. He seemed to be holding some sort of dialogue with himself, and every now and again he laughed, and muttered something cheerily to no one in particular. Sometimes he waved his stick in the air, as though saluting an old friend, and called out something in greeting. Passers-by looked at him doubtfully and hurried on.

Monty finished her cup of tea and went out to meet him.

'There you are!' cried Captain Foxley. He seemed pleased to see her and not the slightest bit bothered that she was late. He swung his stick through the air, and whistled tunelessly.

'What on earth did you want to meet me here for?' He was staring into the bear pit. A frown creased his forehead. The bear pit was elliptical in shape and was enclosed by a low wall surmounted by spike-topped railings. A waist-high fence encircled this enormous cage, preventing passers-by from reaching in, or from pushing food through the bars. Within the cage an artificial habitat had been created. A number of tree trunks placed at various angles encouraged the bear's gymnastic skills. Scrub-like bushes grew here and there, beside looming boulders and jutting rocks. The ground between these various topographical features was made up of compacted earth, garnished with patches of struggling grass and pools of muddy rainwater. A scattering of straw about the entrance of an earth-covered dugout indicated the bear's recent industry adjusting his bed within.

'Have you been here before?' asked Monty, noticing Captain Foxley's interest in the place.

'Yes, during the war.' He frowned. 'I rescued a girl's hat from inside.' He pointed to the bear. It was standing in the entrance to its dugout, gazing with gloomy incredulity at the artificial wilderness that surrounded it. 'There he is!'

'What happened to her?' said Monty. 'Do you know? D'you remember her?'

'I beg your pardon?' Captain Foxley seemed hardly to hear what Monty was saying. 'Remember who?'

'The girl. The girl with the hat. What was her name?'

'Oh, I can't recall.'

'Then I'll tell you,' cried Monty. 'Her name was Sophia. You always called her Sophie.'

'Sophie who?'

'Sophie Barclay. She was a VAD at St Margaret's during the war. She met you here. It was her hat. Don't you remember?'

Captain Foxley looked puzzled, but then, almost with

relief, he smiled. 'Of course,' he cried. 'Dark hair, blue eyes. Lucas had a bit of a thing for her also, I seem to recall. Pretty girl. Did you know her too? Can't think what happened to her.' He laughed. 'Perhaps the bear remembers.' He waved his stick, as though trying to attract the attention of the bear. On the other side of its enclosure the creature swung its head from side to side, sniffing the air.

'*I* know what happened to her,' shouted Monty, furious with Captain Foxley's lack of attention. 'I know that you seduced her and then threw her away when you'd had enough. You wrote to her, saying . . . saying the most terrible things. I tried to protect her. I didn't show her your letter. At least, I didn't show her all of it. The worst part I kept in my pocket so that she would never know what you thought of her. I wanted her to know what a brute you were, but I couldn't let her read what you'd written. I let her believe that you'd be waiting for her at the British Empire Hotel. I thought that if she knew you'd left her standing there, alone, then that would be enough. But then the Zeppelins came. It was my fault, but I only did it to protect her. I did it to protect her from *you*.' Monty was crying now, her tears hot on her burning cheeks, her words tumbling out. 'It was *your* fault,' she cried. 'Your fault that I did it and my fault that she waited.'

'I don't understand.'

'Read this.' Monty pulled an envelope out of her pocket and thrust its contents under his nose. 'Read it. It's your last note to Sophia. It would have broken her heart, her spirit, to have read it all. I gave her the first sheet, but kept the other two. I thought that if she waited for you and you didn't come then she'd realise – but then it was too late. She wanted to be your wife, she thought you wanted it too, but I knew you didn't. I only wanted to protect her. I would have looked after her –'

'I don't want a wife,' said Captain Foxley. 'What would I want with a wife?' He seemed distracted, though he took the scraps of paper Monty held out to him. '"*Mrs Potts said you'd been round. You're a persistent little thing, aren't you? Have you been waiting for a note, a billet doux, in which I say 'I love you' over and over again? 'Meet me tomorrow at our usual place, at our usual time'? Forgive me, Sophie dear*" That's not too bad,' remarked Captain Foxley.

'Read the next one,' shouted Monty. 'And the one after that. Read the other two and then tell me that you think that it's "not too bad".'

Captain Foxley blinked down at his own scribbles. '"*Forgive me, Sophie dear, but before you get in any deeper I must tell you that I will never make an honest woman of you. I don't love you and I won't be tied down. I'm not cut out for the tedium of marriage. You're pretty enough and with a bit of encouragement you're as obliging as a French whore. I wanted a bit of fun, another little victory, and you provided me with that, at least. You'll thank me one day for opening your eyes. I know you'll never forget me, though I doubt I'll live long enough to remember much about you.*" Well, it's certainly my handwriting,' said Captain Foxley after a moment. 'It's written on betting slips, I see. What an old romantic I was, even then, eh?' He grinned. 'I suppose I *was* a bit of a brute,' he added, sounding more apologetic. 'But what do you want me to do about it now?'

Monty looked into Captain Foxley's blue eyes. He seemed to be nodding at her, his head bobbing up and down, up and down, as if keeping time to the heartbeat of a song that nobody but he could hear. Every now and again he glanced anxiously into the bear's enclosure.

'I want you to accept responsibility,' whispered Monty. 'She's dead because of *you*. She burnt in that hotel because of you. And in the end I killed her, I smothered her with my own hands, to end her pain, because of you.'

'Look, there was a war on, you know that as well as I do,' replied Captain Foxley. 'I killed lots of people and was congratulated for it too. If I was harsh on your friend I apologise, if it makes you happy. I had no idea she was dead. But if she is, she's in good company. I lost hundreds of men and every one of them deserves to be still alive too.' His face was pale and his gaze now swept the bear pit continually, as though searching for someone, or something, important. 'You can't bring her back,' he whispered. 'If it makes you feel better then tell yourself that Fritz killed her. Not you, not I, but the enemy. The war made ciphers of all of us, you know, one way or another.'

Monty wiped her eyes. 'She was not a cipher. She was never just "nothing" to me.'

'Come on, Monty,' said Captain Foxley. 'Everyone's dead now, apart from us.' He laughed. 'We're supposed to be the lucky ones.'

All at once he tossed his walking stick aside and pulled out his service revolver. 'It *is* Chalmers over there,' he muttered. 'I'm going in.' He threw off his greatcoat and thrust his revolver into his Sam Browne belt. He leaped over the barrier that separated the bear's enclosure from the footpath. In a trice he had climbed up the bars, and was lowering himself into the bear pit.

Monty sprang forward, but Captain Foxley had dropped into the pen and disappeared into the scrub. Alerted by the unexpected movement inside his territory, the bear lumbered into view and clambered on to the rocks in the middle of the enclosure.

Monty climbed over the first barrier and rushed to the bars. Captain Foxley had completely disappeared, though whether he was in the bushes, or behind the rocks, or whether he had gone into the bear's dugout she had no idea. The bear gazed down at her with interest. Was that hunger she could see in its eyes? She wondered whether to bang on the railings with a stick, reasoning that if the bear's attention was directed towards her *outside* the enclosure, at least it was not directed at Captain Foxley *inside*. She looked about – Captain Foxley had dropped his silver-topped cane on the footpath. Then Monty noticed something lying in the grass on the other side of the railings. It was the service revolver. Monty stuck her arm into the enclosure (hoping as she did so that the bear would not leap down from his rocky pedestal and tear her hand off). She forced her shoulder between the bars and scrabbled about in the dirt with her fingers. But the revolver was too far away and she could not reach it. She retrieved Captain Foxley's walking stick and thrust it through the railings. For a moment, as she hooked its curved silver handle on to the barrel of the gun, she had to take her eyes off the bear. When she looked back it had gone.

'Captain Foxley!' shouted Monty. The revolver was heavy. It was unexpectedly warm from its time spent nestling against Captain Foxley's person, so that it felt as though she were holding a piece of him in her hands. She rattled the walking stick against the railings. 'Captain Foxley!' she cried. 'You can't stay in here. Chalmers is dead. They're all dead, you said so yourself.'

Monty heard a rustling sound in the foliage. Between the leaves she glimpsed a ripple of brown fur. She climbed on to the wall at the base of the railings and peered into the bear pit.

And then she spotted him. He was crawling forward, towards the fallen trunk of a dead tree. Its broken branches pointed upwards like bayonet knives. The bear's dugout was his objective and he crept forward stealthily, his body parallel to the ground, his movements measured and furtive.

All at once Monty saw the bear emerge from the bushes to the left of Captain Foxley's creeping figure. At first the Captain did not seem to notice. 'Chalmers!' Monty heard him whisper. 'Chalmers!'

At that moment the bear reared up on its back legs. In an instant it became enormous, casting a dark hulking shadow over Captain Foxley, who was now crouched on the ground beside the dead tree.

Captain Foxley looked up and let out a scream. The bear roared in reply and staggered forward. Yet it moved sluggishly and without conviction, as though not entirely certain whether humans were its friends or not.

Monty watched as the Captain grovelled in the mud at

the feet of the bear. Would it not be a fitting outcome if he were mauled to death on the very spot where he and Sophia had met? Besides, it would save Monty the trouble of having to exact revenge herself (especially as she was no longer certain she was up for the job).

Captain Foxley was on his knees in the dust. The bear seemed to have made up its mind about the violence of its character and was lumbering forward, its legs akimbo, its jaws snarling. Monty looked at the revolver in her hands.

28

MONTY PRETENDED to be asleep for much of the train journey home. In her mind the scene in the zoo played over and over again – Captain Foxley crouched at the feet of the bear; the roar of the bear as it prepared to attack; her own hesitation. In the event, unwilling to watch any man being torn apart by an animal, she had fired a shot into the air, frightening the beast back into its dugout. Captain Foxley had sprung back over the railings. Now, not half an hour later, he seemed to have forgotten the whole event and the conversation about Sophia that had preceded it. He sat in the corner of the carriage, smoking and reading the late edition of *The Times* and humming military tunes under his breath. At length, he stretched out his legs and arranged himself for a doze. Monty opened her eyes and watched him. What had she expected from him? Remorse? Sorrow? Regret? With hindsight those expectations seemed ridiculous and she wondered how she had entertained the possibility that he might demonstrate any of those emotions. At least, at last, she had confronted him about Sophia. But in doing so she had also confronted the paltriness of her own desire for revenge. It wasn't Peter's fault that Sophia had fallen in love with him. In trying to blame him Monty had been trying to shift the responsibility. Sophia's death had caused her such anguish that she could not bear to contemplate it; she had cast around instead for a scapegoat. And she had chosen Peter because he was her rival for Sophia's affections and because Sophia had chosen Peter over her.

'Remembrance is a strange thing,' murmured Captain Foxley drowsily from his corner of the carriage. 'With love its pain is bearable. With bitterness it simply destroys.'

Monty stared at him. His eyes were closed. His face, in repose, looked deathly, his skin as pale as bone, his cheeks and eye sockets shadowed with darkness. His hand rested on his half-empty whisky bottle. He seemed to have fallen asleep.

'There's been a development,' cried Mrs Forbes, as Monty assisted her towards Lady Beaton's pump. 'There is to be a séance. We're all *most* excited. One of the new people, Mrs Thornycroft, is a medium, you know – a private medium, of course. She's very highly regarded. She's been a member of the Society for Psychical Research for many years and she's staying here for the whole of this month. It seemed like the perfect opportunity. It's going to be tonight, in the drawing room. Mr Curran was rather against it at first, but Miss Jenkins, from that ladies' magazine, was *most* persuasive. She lost a brother in the war, I believe, and is hoping for some sort of message from him. Will you come? I think you should. There might be a spirit message for you, Miss Montgomery; wouldn't you like to hear what it might be?'

Monty handed Mrs Forbes a glass of Lady Beaton. After a while she saw Grier push Curran's wheelchair into the pump room.

'Hello,' said Grier. 'How was London?'

'Never mind that,' interrupted Curran. 'Look, Monty, I wonder whether you'd go up and speak to Mae when you've finished down here. She's still in her room and no one's seen her for days. She refuses to open the door, even to Dr Slack. Would you let go of me, please, Grier,' he added impatiently, fidgeting in his chair. 'Has either of you seen Ada? I'm wondering whether we should try out her little invention with the wheelchair and the kite again, only this time we might make it with two seats, with the brakes operated by the navigator, as it were.' He looked about the room. 'There she is! Ada? Ada!' And he propelled himself through the scanty crowd of people towards Ada, who was handing a glass of Chalybeate to one of the guests.

Grier leaned towards Monty. 'Did you tell Foxley?' he whispered.

'Yes,' said Monty. 'You were right. He didn't remember. At least, I don't think he did. He sees the dead. Chalmers. Handyside. Why doesn't he see Sophia?'

Grier closed his eyes. For a moment he was silent. Then, 'Foxley loved the men, Monty. And his brother officers. What bound us together, all of us, is something no one back home can understand.'

'*I* understand,' said Monty. 'I was out there too.'

'But *she* wasn't. Look, Monty, no matter how beautiful

or innocent or loving your friend was, she was always just another part of Blighty. Blighty's boring – to Dodger, at least. She was always competing with others – Handyside, Chalmers, Lucas, Curran and I, even Coward – and she didn't stand a chance. He was always wholly ours. Back then it was his strength. It doesn't seem to have much purpose now. Now there's nothing. Nothing but boredom.'

Monty helped Thake arrange the drawing room in a manner suitable for Mrs Thornycroft's séance. Mrs Thornycroft herself was to sit at the front, on a hard chair, positioned between two candles. Everyone else was to be arranged before her in a semicircle. The Bleakly Well fountain – the statue of Hygeia which stood in the foyer and which emptied a continual stream of water into an alabaster bowl – was to be turned off, in order to achieve the quietude needed for the spirits to make themselves felt. (Mrs Forbes had also pointed out the disruptive effect that might be created by the sound of running water acting on so many elderly bladders.) Once Mrs Thornycroft was in position and was ready to begin, the lights would be extinguished and the room plunged into candlelit darkness.

Curran watched these arrangements from the doorway, an angry look on his face.

'Did you see Mae?' he asked Monty.

'No,' said Monty. 'Not yet –'

'Why don't you go now,' said Curran. 'See what she's doing up there and get her out.'

Monty climbed the stairs to Mae's room. She was not sure what to say once she got there. If Mae was refusing to see anyone, it was unlikely that she would even open the door. Outside Mae's room Monty listened. From within there was silence. 'Mrs Blackwood,' she called, knocking briskly. 'Mrs Blackwood, it's Miss Montgomery. Is anything the matter?'

Inside the room she heard the creak of bedsprings. No one answered.

'Mrs Blackwood?' Monty knocked again. 'Are you sick?'

Footsteps shuffled across the floor. 'Leave me be.' Mae's voice spoke through the closed door. 'I'm not feeling well, that's all.'

'Can I help?'

'No.'

'Shall I fetch Dr Slack?'

'No.' Monty heard the key turn in the lock. The door opened, but only wide enough for one of Mae's eyes to peep out at her. 'The only thing *he* knows about is water,' said Mae. 'He's not a proper doctor.'

'Yes, he is,' said Monty.

'Then why doesn't he have any proper medicine?'

The light in the corridor was dim, but bright enough to illuminate Mae as she peered out of the partly open door. Her eyes without make-up looked old and faded, and she smelled strongly of stale cigarettes. She looked frightened and Monty saw that the skin on her cheeks was covered with a dark, brownish-coloured rash. Mae put up a hand to pull her robe close at her neck. The same circular lesions covered her palm.

'I suppose it depends what sort of medicine you want,' Monty said. 'He can't cure everything. You may need to see a specialist.'

'It's only a rash from those ghastly canapés I ate at the dance. And a touch of the flu. I don't need a doctor. I'll feel better soon. I'll leave this wretched place when I'm ready. And you can tell *that* to Curran too!'

Miss Jenkins had made a great effort with her costume for the séance. She was dressed in a loose-fitting, smock-like dress in canary yellow, which revealed an extensive amount of her bony décolletage and a good six inches of ankle and calf. Monty, who was sitting beside Mrs Forbes, watched the lady journalist enter and look around. Miss Jenkins seemed disappointed to see only wrinkled, elderly faces gathered before her. Dr Slack produced a box of Abernethy biscuits and began handing out the contraband. A corpulent gentleman in the front row waved to Miss Jenkins and patted the empty chair beside him with a liver-spotted hand. Miss Jenkins affected not to notice this encouraging gesture and headed towards a seat at the back.

Mrs Thornycroft appeared. The excited hubbub of voices died away, so that, apart from the distant sound of Captain Foxley's gramophone, there was silence. The tune, Monty knew, was one of Captain Foxley's favourites, though where it was coming from nobody knew. It seemed to Monty to be echoing out of Hygeia's urn on the Bleakly Well fountain.

Dr Slack turned the lights out, leaving only the candles on either side of Mrs Thornycroft's chair. Mrs Thornycroft closed her eyes. She raised her chin until her head rested against the back of her chair. Her lips and eye sockets sank into blackness. She began to breathe deeply.

There was a gurgling sound, like a large stomach

rumbling, or a pipe belching out a pocket of air, then a curious, disembodied voice spoke into the gloom. 'Come on, Blackwood, it's your only chance.' The voice had a deeply resonant, echoing quality, as though it had come from a long way off.

There was a gasp from the audience. 'It's for Mr Blackwood!' cried Mrs Forbes. 'It's a message for Mr Blackwood!'

There was a hollow, booming laugh. 'And what about that handsome nurse.'

'Oh, my dear,' cried Mrs Forbes. 'It's a message for *you*!' Everyone turned to look at Monty.

'I'll play for her,' said the voice.

The fountain gave a moist belch. '*Play for her, play for her,*' echoed the urn. From deep within the building the pipes began an urgent knocking sound, as though someone was battering at a locked door. Were the spirits trying to break through from the other side?

Mrs Thornycroft opened her eyes and looked about in bewilderment. 'What in the name of heaven is going on?' she cried.

Monty slipped out into the vestibule and turned the fountain on. Captain Foxley's music, and his words, were washed away down the plughole.

Mrs Thornycroft was persuaded to begin once more. This time Monty stood at the back. Not five minutes later she was joined by Grier.

'Hello,' he whispered. 'Has it started?'

After a moment or two the door opened and Monty saw the glow of a cigarette. Mrs Thornycroft was calling out names in a high-pitched, childish voice. 'William is here. He says he is quite happy.'

'William,' sobbed Mrs Forbes. 'William. He was killed at Loos. He was so young –'

Mrs Thornycroft threw back her head. 'I have a message from . . . from . . . Alfred.'

'Alfred,' shouted Miss Jenkins, leaping to her feet. 'Yes, that's my brother. He was a Captain in the Royal Welsh Fusiliers. He was killed –'

'The Somme!' croaked Mrs Thornycroft.

'Third Ypres,' stammered Miss Jenkins. '1917.'

'He says you're not to worry.'

'I'm not worried,' said Miss Jenkins. She sounded perplexed. No doubt numerous Alfreds had been killed at the Somme and a great many more at Ypres. There was bound to be some confusion among this crowd of identically named men who were gathered at the heavenly gates. 'Is there something I should be worried about?' cried Miss Jenkins. 'Ask him what it is.'

Monty saw Captain Foxley weave his way through the room until he was standing right behind Miss Jenkins.

'What about Coward?' he roared all of a sudden. 'Have you got a message from him?' Captain Foxley pulled a bottle of whisky from his pocket and took a swig from it. 'Coward,' he shouted. 'Lucas, Handyside, Chalmers, Standage, where are you? Come out and speak to me, you rascals!' He sank into the chair beside Miss Jenkins. 'Want a drink?' And he poured a splash of his whisky into Miss Jenkins's empty teacup.

'Come on, Foxley, leave the lady alone,' said Grier, stepping forward in the darkness.

'Coward?' cried Captain Foxley. He looked about expectantly. 'Coward!'

'Coward's dead,' said Monty.

'Exactly,' said Captain Foxley. 'Doesn't he have a message for me? Or for Blackwood? Surely he's got something he'd like to say to *you*, Blackwood, even if he doesn't want to speak to me. Coward!' roared Captain Foxley again. 'Blackwood's here. Grier Blackwood. You remember him, don't you?' All at once, Mrs Forbes switched on the electric lights. Everyone blinked, apart from Captain Foxley, who seemed unconcerned by the brightness.

'He's drunk,' cried Mrs Forbes in disgust.

'Of course I'm bloody well *drunk*.' Captain Foxley's hair was awry and a slapdash effort with his razor had left a great smear of red on his collar, as though he had sought to cut his own throat, but had given up the attempt halfway through. 'You're dressed like a whore,' he said to Miss Jenkins and he leaned forwards to thrust a hand down the front of her dress.

Miss Jenkins parted her crimson lips and screamed. Hands pulled at Captain Foxley, dragging him this way and that, hauling him off Miss Jenkins and into the crowd of black-clad, white-faced old people, so that for a moment he resembled a suit of clothes swirling in a washtub. His whisky bottle fell from his hand and rolled beneath a table, glugging out its contents. Miss Jenkins seemed about to swoon, but then she righted herself and tottered backwards, collapsing stiffly on to the chairs. Captain Foxley sank to the floor, felled by a blow to his head from Dr Slack's biscuit tin.

29

THE FOLLOWING morning, at Curran's insistence, Grier went up to see Mae. He walked slowly, going first to make sure that there was an adequate supply of clean towels in the gentlemen's steam room, then outside to examine the stability of the beehive and the fecundity of the vegetables, and finally into the garage to speak to Ada about the health of the motors.

Mae's bedroom door was standing open. Grier peeped inside. Within, a jumble of tangled bedding and discarded clothes was piled on the bed; a broken suitcase and a crushed hatbox projected from a mound of tumbled blankets.

Dr Slack appeared in the bathroom doorway. 'Curran sent me up when he saw you sneaking off into the garden, but it looks as though she's gone.'

'Oh,' said Grier, relieved.

'Did you see her before she left?'

'No,' said Grier. He stepped into Mae's room and looked about. It was littered with brimming ashtrays and tumblers with lipstick smeared stickily about their rims. The air was musty and unwholesome. Grier opened a window. 'Did you?'

'Yes,' said Dr Slack. 'She was rather heavily powdered, but I could see what the problem was. She probably thinks she's cured it, but she won't have.' He pointed to the dressing table, upon which stood, among the jars and brushes Mae had left behind, a white, opaque medicine bottle labelled 'mercury' and a glass jar. Both were empty.

'Good heavens,' said Grier. 'Are those the medicines you were looking for? It looks as though she finished them both.'

'She took them from my medicine cabinet,' said Dr Slack. 'Mercury and bismuth. But you can't cure syphilis with them. You never could. That's why I can't help Foxley. And besides, that's not bismuth, its bicarbonate of soda. I use it for indigestion. I should have said so before but, well, I could hardly tell Miss Montgomery that my medicine cabinet was no more potent than the average larder, could I?' He shrugged. 'There's not much cause for bismuth or mercury at Bleakly Hall, especially not these days. There's not much cause for anything, really. Most of the bottles on my shelves contain bakery ingredients: ground nutmeg, vanilla essence, molasses. I've not used proper medicines for years, but it'd never do to let the guests know. Of course, you could make a nice little Madeira cake or some peppermint creams.' He licked his lips. 'I have got iron tonic though, and powdered senna. D'you want some? You're looking rather pale this morning. A good purging and a dose of iron might be just what you need.'

'No, thank you,' said Grier. He was thinking about the conversation he had had with Captain Foxley the night before while everyone was preparing for the séance and he suddenly felt quite faint. 'I need a little air, that's all.' Grier went to the window and leaned out. Below, on the gravel in front of the building, he could see a slim woman wearing an aquamarine-coloured wool coat climbing into the back of the Audi. He saw Thake get into the driver's seat. Curran appeared at the top of the steps, waving and calling out 'Goodbye, Miss Jenkins.'

Grier went downstairs.

He met Curran in the foyer. 'Mae's gone,' he said. 'I don't think she'll be back.'

'Good. That's one problem out of the way for now, at least,' said Curran briskly. 'Have you been up to Foxley? He should see a bloody doctor and sort himself out.' He dropped a coin into the swear box. 'Heaven knows what Miss Jenkins will say about us. And some of the guests have threatened to leave, you know.'

'I'm sure they have. Has Monty gone down to the pump room? I need to speak to her.'

'I wanted to speak to her too,' said Curran. 'I was thinking of asking her to marry me; d'you think she'll say yes?'

'Marry Monty?' Grier could not keep the surprise out of his voice. 'You?'

'Yes, me,' snapped Curran.

'Really?'

'Why ever not? You needn't look so surprised. Miss Montgomery and I understand one another perfectly well. And now that Mae's gone and I've contacted my solicitor, there's no reason why I can't make my intentions towards her perfectly plain.'

'Do you love her?'

'I think she's very nice indeed. And she understands my needs as well as my . . . my capabilities. I explained them to her some time ago. She was very understanding.'

'But what about love? Never mind your capabilities.'

'Oh, don't be so romantic,' Curran replied. 'It's practicalities that count in a marriage.'

'What about Ada?' said Grier.

'What do you mean?'

'What do you think I mean?' cried Grier. 'What do you think I mean about Ada?'

At that moment, Grier detected a movement from among the potted ferns. He looked up to see Ada herself peering out through the greenery and he knew that she had heard everything.

'Ada,' cried Grier, leaping forward. 'Ada, wait –' But it was too late. With a rustle of leaves Ada disappeared back the way she had come. Grier heard the sound of a muffled sob and a door slamming, then all was quiet. He knew he would never find her in the warren of passages and store-rooms.

'You idiot, Curran,' he cried. 'It's Ada who loves you and you love Ada, if you might just open your eyes and see it.'

'Ada?' said Curran. He sounded astonished. He stared in disbelief at the foliage into which Ada had disappeared and his face turned crimson.

'Yes, Ada,' shouted Grier. 'She does everything for you, willingly and without complaint, but you hardly even notice.

Since you got out of the hospital and came back here you've forgotten who you are. You're searching for the past in a dead place, in Bleakly, and you're blinded by your loyalty to a dead man. To Foxley.'

'Dodger?' whispered Curran.

'Yes,' cried Grier. 'Can't you see it? He's sick. He has no future, not if he keeps on the way he's going. But you do. And Ada does.'

Curran opened his mouth, then closed it again. He stared at Grier, his expression filled with remorse. He blinked unhappily at the spot where Ada had stood only moments before.

'You complete bloody idiot.'

'That's sixpence, if I'm not mistaken,' whispered Curran. He indicated the swear box, but his eyes were now fixed upon the tips of his boots – boots that Ada had buffed to a mirrored shine and positioned on the footrests of his chair that very morning. 'Sixpence, please, Grier.'

30

MONTY WAS struggling to push one of the guests back to the Hall from the pump room when she noticed someone moving along the top of the building. As she watched the figure stumbled, a leg dangling precariously above one of the drooping gutters. It was Ada.

'Wait here,' said Monty. She rammed the bath-chair into the soft earth of an untended flower bed. 'Ada,' she shouted. 'Ada!' But her voice sounded flat and dead. Trapped by the surrounding beech trees it travelled no distance at all. Monty sprinted round to the back of the building. The Audi was parked on the cobbles, bits of its engine spread about on all sides. Monty grasped the rungs of the maintenance ladder that led to the roof and began to climb. She did not look down.

At last, with shaking hands, she clambered on to the roof of the hydropathic. She had expected to see a flat expanse. Instead, the roof space was dominated by a huge rectangular pond, the size and shape of a swimming pool. But there were no tiles lining its sides, no steps leading into cool inviting waters. Instead, she realised she was looking at a cistern, vast and deep, a rooftop reservoir sunk into the very fabric of the building – no doubt designed to gather and hold the endless volumes of water needed to fill the throbbing arteries of Bleakly Hall. But the pipes and douches through which the waters had once coursed were now old and ill-used, they were broken and blocked, so that this hidden rooftop reservoir had backed up, filling its lead-lined tank permanently to the brim. The neglect of many years was evident everywhere – in the greenish slime that coated the rim of the tank, the clumps of grass and moss that had colonised its banks, the clusters of lily pads that punctuated its surface in floating emerald discs. The silent meniscus was rumpled in places by the passing of water boatmen, and the air vibrated with the sound of frogs. On the far side of the reservoir loomed Captain Foxley's tower. Up ahead, a chimney stack projected from the waters like a ruined castle. A narrow iron walkway crossed from the side of the cistern to the chimney, and from the chimney back out to the other side of the roof.

Ada was standing beside Captain Foxley's tower.

'Ada,' shouted Monty.

Ada turned away. 'Leave me alone,' she cried. She lumbered off. Monty followed. Ada walked rapidly round the edge of the reservoir, with Monty in pursuit. She mounted the metal walkway that spanned the waters, as though hoping to lead Monty on, then double back towards the ladder. The iron fretwork, rusted and crumbling, groaned in dismay at the burden it was suddenly required to support.

'Ada,' cried Monty. 'Come back –'

She heard the snap of breaking metal, the screech of twisting ironwork, and then the black and silent waters closed over Ada's head.

◆

After Sophia, Monty requested to be sent back out to the front. The need for nurses was greater than ever and she was despatched without hesitation to Armentières, south of Ypres, where she worked at a field hospital. The letters she wrote to Ada, now convalescing at Bleakly, were short. What could she write about apart from her own feelings of misery and loneliness? Monty told Ada the size and specifications of the new ambulances she had seen, though in all likelihood the censors would not permit such captivating information to be sent home, and Ada would receive a letter that said nothing at all.

Out in France, alone now and sick with grief, Monty grew reckless. She gave her rations to hungry soldiers, and stayed up working in the wards and the operating theatres for days and nights at a time. There was hardly any water (despite the fact that they seemed to be surrounded by canals and water-filled shell holes), and the supplies of bandages, antiseptic solution, surgical instruments, food and clothing were always late coming up the lines and always in short supply. The nights were colder than she had ever known, so that frostbite soon sank its teeth into the soldiers' already tortured feet. The nurses camped in bell tents beside the hospital, sleeping in their clothes, coats and boots.

Monty thought of those chilly nights in the nurses' dormitory, when she and Sophia had shared a bed for warmth, whispering together in the darkness.

The field hospital was packed with soldiers, their faces filled with fear and incomprehension. Every one of them hoped for the ticket from the doctor that might send him home, away from this terrible place. Part of a team of anxious but uncomplaining nurses, Monty scrubbed, bandaged and swabbed. She carried out the dead and carried in the living. She brewed tea and dished out rations. She cleared pus from wounds, washed instruments and cut off flaps of blackened skin. She hummed as she went about her work, a cheery expression set on her face like a mask. Monty made no friends. Now that Sophia was gone, she wanted none. She spoke when she had to and worked as hard as she could.

Volunteers were requested to work at an advance dressing station nearer the front. Indifferent to her own safety, Monty rode there in the back of an ambulance. At the dressing station, the wounded poured in from the battle-fields and poured out again to the field hospital. It was never-ending, unvarying in its horror, so that Monty felt as though she had become part of a vast factory, a huge and pointless machine whose sole purpose was to mangle bodies and try to patch them back up again for repeated suffering. There was no time to think, no time to reflect, and limbs were lopped off as unceremoniously as slicing up a loaf of bread. Piles of bodily offcuts mounded up beside the operating tables, to be loaded into sacks and taken away. The place swarmed with people, many of whom were caked in the mud that was churned up everywhere, so that at times it looked as though the earth itself had come alive. Less than half a mile away the British guns pounded the skies relentlessly. The German artillery did the same, time and again sending over shells that occasionally landed close enough to shower the station with mud and stones. One night a shell ripped away the roof of the hospital, exposing the men and women seething within, like an ants' nest discovered beneath an overturned stone.

Monty was given a day off. The sun was shining and she noticed flowers dancing in the wind on either side of the road. They were the same flowers – tiny crocuses – that she had seen growing about the feet of Queen Victoria, when she sat with Sophia in the quadrangle at St Margaret's. She joined a team of stretcher bearers who were climbing into an ambulance bound for the front. There was a village nearby whose buildings had been pounded into rubble. Monty had heard that there was a wounded man there, stuck at the top of a bell tower. She had stuffed some bandages and iodine into her pack, and requested to be set down there as they passed through.

The bell tower had belonged to a convent long since smashed apart, though here and there ragged sections of wall remained. The area was still being bombarded, and every now and again a shell screamed overhead, crashing into the ground and sending out showers of flying stones and bits of metal. Monty was informed that the soldier had been at the top of the bell tower for three days and, despite an injured leg, seemed still to be alive. The Germans had been firing at him, but had at length given up, assuming him to be if not dead, then almost so. It was, she was told, impossible to reach him.

Monty arrived at the rubble-strewn foot of the tower. Halfway up, the steps and part of the external wall had been blasted away. Monty climbed the first part of the stone staircase easily enough. But when she came to the missing section, at first glance further ascent looked impossible. Monty took off her greatcoat. She seized the edge of a broken stair and pulled herself upwards, wedging the toe of her boot into a crack in the masonry. She found another handhold between two bricks and a toehold against a chunk of shattered stair. A lump of fallen masonry, which had lodged against the wall, and a shred of banister provided further opportunity to scramble higher. She looked down. Here and there she could see the bodies of men, lying about in the rubble, shrouded in dust. It had been impossible to see them from the ground, but from up high their pale, ashy figures were visible among the ruins like ghosts. She felt suddenly sick and dizzy. Her foot slipped and for a moment she dangled precariously over the abyss. She became aware of the approaching scream and whistle of another incoming shell. Monty climbed on. The shell exploded, blasting the rubble of a tumbled-down cottage into powder, which fell like icing sugar on to the dead.

At last she was at the top. The sniper in the bell tower was not dead. When Monty emerged on to the ledge upon which he was trapped he said, 'I don't suppose you thought to bring any sandwiches?'

Monty removed the remains of his tattered puttees and blood-soaked boot. His left foot had been shattered by the same shell that had knocked away a section of the tower. She bandaged him as best she could.

'Now we're both stuck,' he said.

Monty stared down at the steps, wondering what to do.

'It's impossible,' muttered the soldier. 'Even if I 'ad two good feet, it's impossible. Why don't you just climb back down yourself and leave me 'ere. Besides,' he added gloomily, 'all the lads are dead. It's not like there's any point in coming down, is there?'

'Of course there's a point.'

'What's that, then?'

His face, Monty noticed, was as grey as porridge. He looked exhausted, crouched on a mound of rubble in his torn and bloody uniform. Monty adopted her loud and firm nurse's voice. 'Your friends are all those men who're in this war with you,' she announced. '*That's* the point. They'll always be there for you and you must be there for them. Even more so once it's all over. If it's ever all over.' They looked at one another bleakly. 'Who else would believe us?' she muttered. 'We only have each other now.' She patted his hand. 'Come along, Corporal, I'm sure we'll manage.'

Monty helped him down the steps as far as they could go. The bits of stone she had clung on to in order to climb up now looked impossibly precarious, so that she wondered how on earth she had negotiated her way up at all. A shell tore over from the German lines and smashed into the ground not twenty feet away. Monty felt the tower shudder. 'They can see you,' said the soldier. 'You're flapping about like a seagull!'

Monty dragged him on to the ledge beside the missing

317

steps. Below a canal glimmered like pewter. There was evidence that a shell had fallen there recently, as a huge pool of water, greyish and tranquil, had formed, though it was impossible to say how deep it was. No sandbags or barbed wire protruded from its surface. Mind you, thought Monty, what choice did they have? They could not stay up there for ever. A bullet smacked into the crumbling masonry beside her hand. She seized the soldier by the collar and bundled him forwards.

'What –?' He clung to the stonework and stared into her face wildly. 'Are you mad?'

'I don't know,' said Monty. 'We'll soon find out.'

Monty's leap from the bell tower was soon news around the dressing station. The tower itself had taken a direct hit only moments after the two of them had landed in the canal. The water was mercifully deep and the man she had saved soon added his mangled left foot to the mountain of offcuts on the floor of the operating theatre.

◆

Beneath the icy waters of Bleakly, the spring sunlight painted everything a shimmering silver. It illuminated a silent, muffled world of gently wafting weed and small darting hydra. It splashed the lead walls with light, revealing a velvet coat of emerald slime, adorned with weedy filaments, through which snails and water beetles moved. Monty felt something long and sinuous drag against her leg and she almost cried out. She looked about, searching for Ada in the watery gloom. A stream of silver bubbles, glittering like sixpences, provided an eloquent trail. And there was Ada, her apron billowing in the waters, her face a pale, perplexed moon surrounded by a crown of swirling weeds. Monty grabbed at the weeds, seizing what she hoped was actually a handful of Ada's hair, and hauled her towards the surface.

Monty and Ada sprawled side by side on the lead flashings at the side of the cistern. 'Are you mad?' gasped Monty, once Ada had stopped coughing.

Ada did not speak, but stared miserably at the sky.

'What are you doing?' said Monty. 'Why are you up here?'

Ada looked at her from a pink and puffy face. 'What's it to you?' she mumbled. 'What do you care?'

'Of course I care,' said Monty. 'Don't be silly. What are you doing up here? And going across the walkway, too. You can't swim, can you?'

'I wish I was dead,' mumbled Ada. She sat up clumsily.

'Who's the father?' said Monty.

Ada melted back down again, lying in an Ada-shaped pool of water. 'Where can I go, what can I do?' she cried.

Monty had been watching Ada's gently ballooning body with interest over the past couple of months. She wondered whether Ada would confide in her, whether she would seek her out for help and advice, but Ada had said nothing at all. 'Why didn't you tell me?' Monty asked now. And, not waiting for an answer to this question, added, 'Is it Captain Foxley?'

'Of course it's *him*.' Ada drew a ragged breath and blew

her nose lavishly on her sodden scrap of handkerchief. 'He said he loved me. Then when I told him about my . . . condition he just *laughed*. He said it was nothing to do with him. And now . . . now Mr Curran wants to marry *you*!'

'I'm not marrying Mr Curran,' said Monty.

'Yes, you are, you just don't know it yet,' cried Ada.

'But I don't want to,' Monty protested. 'And he doesn't want to marry me; you're quite mistaken.'

'He does, I heard him.'

'Oh, he's just . . . confused,' said Monty, though she was beginning to feel rather confused herself. 'Why on earth would I want to marry anyone? I'd end up stuck at home mending and ironing and always having to ask before I did anything.' She sighed. Could not fulfilment be found without relying on a man to provide it? Many women, she knew, would now be obliged to try. 'Anyway, never mind that,' she went on. 'You can't stay up here. We must get you out of those wet clothes.'

'Give me one good reason why I should come back down?'

'You'll catch cold.'

'I don't care.'

'It's lunchtime soon,' said Monty (even though it was hardly past breakfast). 'You don't want to miss lunch, do you?'

Monty went up to see Captain Foxley. At the top of the stairs, against the cupola, a pair of bees battered themselves lazily against the glass. She knocked. Within she could hear the sound of someone humming and the rustle of a newspaper.

'Come in,' cried the Captain. His voice sounded muffled. No doubt he was still in bed, thought Monty crossly.

Monty opened the door. The glazier had repaired the window and the sunlight poured in, illuminating the velvet settee (unpleasantly stained with blotches), the armchair (scrofulous with cigarette burns) and the blood-coloured carpet with its scattering of toast crumbs, tobacco fragments and ash. The table, which had previously stood to one side, had been pulled into the middle of the room. A sunbeam sliced through the dusty air like a searchlight, illuminating a dozen jars of different sizes – jam jars, pickling jars, potted meat jars, marmalade jars – which littered the surface of the table. Each jar contained a single furiously buzzing bee.

Captain Foxley was sitting at the table. He was dressed in his pyjamas and dressing gown, which was not unusual for that time in the morning. What was unusual, however, was the fact that he was also wearing a gas mask, a scarf and a pair of felt oven mitts. He gave her a cheery wave with one of his oven-mitted hands. 'I wouldn't want to get stung, would I?' he said by way of explanation.

'Certainly not,' said Monty.

Captain Foxley screwed the lid on to another jar and held it up. Its buzzing occupant hovered uncertainly in the centre of this gleaming glass prison. 'Eighteen,' he said. He looked about the room, his head turning quizzically this way and that. His eyes appeared small and close-set behind the wide glassy gaze of the gas mask, so that he resembled a huge pyjama-clad locust. Another half a dozen bees droned clumsily backwards and forward overhead, or tapped optimistically at the windows, trying to get out. Captain Foxley rose slowly to his feet. Monty saw that he held a rolled-up copy of *The Times*.

'These bees are from Thake's hive in the grounds,' he said. 'Thake's been neglecting them – their hive's a disgrace, you know – due to the plumbing taking up so much of his time. I went down to see how they were getting on and they followed me back here!' He flexed his rolled-up newspaper. 'They're here for a purpose,' he cried. 'Can you guess what it is?'

'No,' said Monty.

'I try to stun them first.' Captain Foxley crept forward into the middle of the room and watched a hovering bee intently. 'It's taken a while to master it. If one doesn't get the force of the blow just right they're dead and that's no use, is it?' He pointed to a row of dead bees lined up on the mantelpiece.

'What's wrong with just opening the window and letting them out?'

'I can't let them out!' cried Captain Foxley. 'Each one of these bees carries on its back a single thought; a single one of *my* thoughts. I can't let them go or I'll never remember anything. They're here to help me *remember*. I remembered that I used to know about bees, for instance. "The hive, with its society of bees, is an inspiration to us all, a model of our own industrial civilisation." You see?'

'What about those ones?' Monty pointed to the mantelpiece.

'Oh, it's too late for those.' Captain Foxley's voice was brusque. 'I have to accept the loss and just hope that those thoughts were not too important.'

Monty looked about. No doubt the bees had come up from the garden. Perhaps they were creating a new nest in the roof or under the eaves. 'I wanted to speak to you about something,' she said.

'What is it?' Captain Foxley swiped at the air. The bees buzzed around his head in rage and confusion, and increased their speed droning up and down the room. 'I must catch these first. Perhaps you could help? Make sure you stand behind me, some of these blighters are quick and quite vicious too – I think those particular ones must be carrying the angriest thoughts. One of them actually went for my face, you know; that's why I decided I'd put the old gas mask on. Bloody uncomfortable, but better than a bee sting in the eye, wouldn't you say? I'm gasping for a cigarette too, but I don't want to take the thing off until I've caught the last of them. There's something about a girl I once knew that I'm trying to remember, but I don't know what it is. I'm hoping that particular thought is on the back of one of these little chaps here. Unless it's over there.' He looked at the mantelpiece. 'There's no hope of remembering it if it's over there.'

Monty picked up an empty pickling jar from the tabletop. The Captain advanced, holding his rolled-up newspaper before him. At length, after dancing forward and backward through the room, his newspaper flashing and jabbing left and right up and down about his head, all the remaining bees were captured. Each was imprisoned in a separate jar.

There were no more casualties and Captain Foxley seemed pleased that he had perfected his technique. He pulled off his gas mask and gauntlets, and stuck a cigarette between his lips.

'Have you remembered your thought about the girl?' Monty could not help but ask.

'I beg your pardon?' Captain Foxley frowned at her through the smoke. 'What girl?'

'Look,' said Monty despairingly, 'I need to speak to you about Ada.'

'Pretty girl,' said Captain Foxley. 'Rather tubby these days, but I think it quite suits her.'

'She's tubby because she's pregnant,' said Monty.

'Is she?' He shrugged. 'How careless of her. And something of a cliché, too, don't you think, the maid getting herself pregnant? Perhaps she's been reading too many novels.'

'You don't get pregnant by reading novels,' shouted Monty. 'Can't you do the honourable thing, just for once?'

'And what might that be?'

'Marry her, of course.' Monty hesitated. Did Ada really deserve such a fate? And yet, how else would she manage with a child to take care of? In a place as small as Bleakly people could be unforgiving. 'Or at least look after her,' she added. 'And in the meantime get yourself to a doctor.'

'Marry Ada? Good Lord, why on earth should I do such a thing?' Captain Foxley was staring at his collection of humming jam jars. A look of satisfaction appeared on his face. 'I think I've remembered what it was I'd forgotten,' he said. 'That's the chap. That big one there in the middle, the one with the fuzzy legs. He's carrying all my memories of Handyside. I wondered why I hadn't been able to remember the fellow. There was one time that Handyside and I were –'

'Handyside's dead,' snapped Monty.

'I know,' replied Captain Foxley, 'but it doesn't mean I have to forget him, does it?'

'What about Ada?'

'Well, I haven't forgotten Ada, have I? I can remember her quite clearly, though I can't understand why you want me to think about her. Look, so I might have comforted her now and again – she's in love with Curran, you know – and things got a little out of hand. But that's no reason to make me set up house with the girl. She knew what she was doing as much as I.'

'You told her that you loved her.'

'Did I? I don't remember that.'

'Well, perhaps you should ask one of these bees,' cried Monty. 'For goodness' sake, what's the matter with you?'

Captain Foxley hummed a tune and fingered his gas mask. 'This thing saved my life,' he said after a moment. 'Pity some of the other chaps couldn't say the same.' He sighed and polished one of the glass lenses with the sleeve of his dressing gown. 'Why can't someone have a *nice* war, just a friendly little war somewhere out of the way? I'd be up for that. Wouldn't you?'

'No,' said Monty. 'No, I wouldn't.'

31

THAT AFTERNOON a brown envelope arrived in the post for Curran. Grier saw it sitting on the reception desk, beneath a pile of credit notes and unpaid bills. Having seen Miss Jenkins sign her name in the hydropathic's ledger, Grier recognised her handwriting instantly. He wondered whether he might be able to sneak the thing away before Curran saw it, but even as he pulled it out from among the pile of correspondence his brother appeared. Grier handed it over and waited.

'I suppose you know what this is,' whispered Curran after a moment.

'No,' said Grier. 'But it looks like a letter from Miss Jenkins.'

'A letter from Miss Jenkins? If only it were nothing more than that. She might have said anything at all in it if it were no more than a *letter*.' Curran's voice became louder. His words echoed around the foyer and along the ground-floor corridors. 'She's sent a draft of her article for that *Woman's Weekly*.'

'Look,' muttered Grier, 'it wasn't my fault. About Foxley, I mean. I tried to explain; I thought she understood.'

'Apparently not.' Curran scanned the typewritten page. *'Bleakly Hall is a place of ghosts . . . lost and drunken inmates . . . living in the past . . . the war is not quite over at Bleakly.'* He crumpled the page. 'We'll have to sell the Audi.'

Ada crept forward. 'Mr Grier,' she muttered. 'Mr Thake said to fetch you.' She stole a glance at Curran, whose face had turned scarlet, and her eyes filled with tears.

'Ada,' stammered Curran. 'Ada, don't cry.' For once his voice was almost inaudible. 'I need to talk to you.'

At that moment Captain Foxley also appeared. Grier was relieved to see that he was not wearing his gas mask and his dressing gown, but was dressed quite normally. What was not normal, however, was the fact that the Captain was almost running (as far as he could manage to do so with his limp and his curious shuffling gait). In his hands he carried a large pickling jar, which he held out before him like a bowl of hot coals. In addition, his face wore an expression of such horror that Grier almost wished that he *were* wearing the gas mask. Captain Foxley bounded across the foyer and disappeared through the doors. Once outside, he ran across the flower bed and on to the gravel driveway beyond. He flung open the jar and held it aloft, his eyes averted in terror. Grier watched as an enormous bee emerged, rising slowly from the jar as though pulled by an invisible wire. Captain Foxley sagged against a neglected bird bath in an attitude of relief. He watched the bee become a dot against the sky, then disappear completely. 'Thank God,' he whispered, as Grier came up. 'Thank God.'

'What was that?' said Grier.

Captain Foxley looked confused. Then he smiled. 'I don't know,' he said. 'I can't remember.'

Thake was standing in the middle of the vestibule beside the statue of Hygeia. The fountain was ominously silent. 'Mr Grier,' he shouted, brandishing his spanner like a mace. 'The furnace needs regulating.'

'Oh.' Grier had no idea what the man was talking about, though the look on Thake's face suggested that he should. 'Look,' he said, 'I have something else to attend to at the moment; can't you see to it for now?'

'But –'

'And what's happened to the fountain here?' added Grier. 'Has someone switched it off?'

'That's another problem,' said Thake. 'There's a blockage. Someone'll have to crawl in.'

'Crawl in?' repeated Grier. 'Crawl in where?'

'Into the system.'

'Well, can't you do it?' said Grier. Crawling suggested entering somewhere narrow and pipe-like, somewhere confined and cramped and claustrophobic. He turned pale at the thought. Surely Thake did not expect him to enter such a place? 'Perhaps we could talk about this later,' he said. Without waiting for a reply Grier stalked off across the foyer and disappeared up the stairs to look for Monty.

Monty was not in her room. She was not in the drawing room or the library or the billiard room either. In fact, the hydropathic seemed all at once to be quite deserted and Grier's footsteps echoed eerily along the corridor as he headed back towards the reception desk. Even Curran seemed to have disappeared, as he was not in his office beneath the stairs, nor anywhere else that Grier looked.

Grier went downstairs to the treatment rooms, but these too were empty. The atmosphere was more humid than ever and a thin layer of water vapour covered the walls like sweat. He poked his head into the adjustable douche, the gentlemen's treatment rooms and the various recovery rooms. These too were still and silent. There was nobody in the swimming pool and Grier gazed at the smooth surface of the water despairingly. The swimming pool, with its steam-heated water supply, had once been Bleakly Hall's most exciting attraction. Ladies and gentlemen, their bodies swathed in voluminous swimming costumes, had bobbed there like jellyfish, or swum up and down in its health-giving water. Now, no one had been in it for months.

On impulse, Grier began taking his clothes off. He folded them neatly and placed them on the bench that ran round the wall. The water, at first sight so alarmingly green, now seemed quite pond-like and inviting. He did not notice the wraiths of steam drifting lazily from it surface, so that it was only as he dived in that it became clear that the water was not delightfully chilled at all, but was, in fact, un-expectedly hot. Grier surfaced rapidly and swam to the side. He hauled himself out and lay on the bench beside his discarded clothes, a towel wrapped round his torso. Could one not even take a swim without some dreadful mishap? He was lucky he had not been parboiled, like a potato.

He was still prostrate at the side of the pool when Monty

found him. Grier sat up and pulled his shirt on. 'Where is everyone?'

'Thake said the "system" was dangerous and he made us all go outside. He said he was "going in." He seemed quite upset. He gave me this to look after.' Monty held out a box. 'He said I was to pass them on to his son if anything happened.'

Grier opened the box. Within, reclining on a bed of wood shavings, was a gleaming set of false teeth.

In the boiler room Thake's jacket hung over the heating pipes, beside his favourite spanner and a length of coiled hosepipe. Next to these a panel had been removed from the wall, revealing a wide brick-lined drain, dank and cavernous and echoing. In the distance Grier could hear the sound of water – water dripping slowly and steadily; water hissing and bubbling; and, far off, water rushing, as though somewhere deep beneath the building a great torrent was passing by. The sound of Thake clearing his throat echoed from the hole, borne forward on a whiff of rotten eggs.

Grier took a deep breath and climbed into the drain after Thake. He began to crawl forward. Before long the light from the boiler room was far behind. He lit a match and held it up. The walls gleamed with iridescent greens and pinks, like the flank of a trout. The drain was large enough for a man to make his way along quite comfortably, if he remained in a crouched, simian position. The match burnt out. Grier dropped it, sucking his fingers as the flame was snuffed out in the inch of water that lapped around the sides of his boots. The warm darkness closed about him like a cloak and for a moment Grier felt a terrible fear wash over him. What if he could not find his way out again? Would he be lost for ever in the underground plumbing? A draught of stale air sighed out of the darkness, borne forward on the swirling waters. It smelled heavily of dark wet earth and sulphur. Beneath this came a whiff of putrescence and rotting matter. And for an instant – for a hideous, fleeting moment – Grier was somewhere else entirely, somewhere dark and terrible, the air hot and putrid, his fear and horror choking him like a scarf tightly wound round his throat so that he could not hear anything but the sound of his own heart beating in his ears, and a muffled thumping and scraping, as though from hands scrabbling and feet kicking some-where close to his own. The moment passed. He searched for his cigarettes. Ignoring the shaking of his hands, he drew in a comforting breath of smoke.

Somewhere up ahead Grier was sure he could hear the sound of Thake muttering in the blackness. It seemed to be coming from deep within the brick oesophagus and as his eyes became accustomed to the dark once more he could just make out a faint gleam of light reflected off the brick-work like a pale moon glimpsed through a thick bank of cloud. He groped his way forward.

After a few yards, Grier found that he was forced to crawl on his hands and knees. This might not have been too bad, but he was now moving through six inches of water and in no time at all his clothes were soaking. Moreover (and more alarmingly), he was becoming increasingly certain that the water was rising: whereas it had initially covered no more than his wrists, it was now swirling about his elbows and thighs. His cigarette dangled forlornly from his lips, extinguished by an accurate drip. The air seemed to have become unbearably hot.

Grier came upon Thake at a bend in the pipe. 'Hello, Thake,' he said. His voice sounded flat and dead in the confined space, and seemed unnaturally loud in his ears. 'You should have waited for me. Is everything in order?'

Thake's lantern was set on a ledge in the brickwork, its light glinting on the black and swirling waters. It threw his features into diabolical relief, so that for a moment he looked like Satan, or Phlegyas, perhaps, crouched in a tributary to the Styx. In addition, Grier was startled to see that the lower half of Thake's face appeared to have collapsed in on itself, like a folded slipper. Thake mumbled something urgently, but Grier was unable to make out what the man was saying. *I had no idea one's teeth were so essential to intelligible communication*, Grier thought. He smiled grimly and nodded, and said, 'I see' (though in fact he didn't see at all), then added (more cheerily than the situation warranted, he thought afterwards), 'Well, is there anything I can do to help, now that I'm here?'

Thake pulled out a long stick-like object. It was this which he had been fiddling with beneath the water. He produced another and indicated to Grier that he should screw the two sticks together, thereby making an even longer stick.

'Right-oh,' said Grier. 'And Thake, is it me, or is the water rising?'

Thake nodded.

'And is it getting hotter down here?'

Thake nodded again and thrust another stick into Grier's hands.

Once the extending stick was of a sufficient length, Thake began ramming it up and down beneath the water that flowed between them. Grier waited. The stream that now filled the drain where they worked lapped about his waist and made him shiver.

All at once a great belch of air erupted from beneath the water. Immediately, the hot, reeking atmosphere was filled with a stench of drains and rotting matter, of faeces and latrines and earth, so that Grier felt his stomach heave and his fear returned tenfold. He cried out and lurched back-wards as a great mass of sludge bubbled up into the black and churning waters. In the lamplight Grier glimpsed a plug of hair, as thick and tangled as a human scalp, a scrap of khaki, a filthy bandage and an army boot, dark and slimy, swirling in the boiling torrent; he saw mud and leaves and what looked like a bird's nest (but which might have been more hair) and some scraps of newspaper. He screamed and floundered about in the water. His feet slipped on the wet bricks and he disappeared beneath the very flotsam he had been trying to avoid, so that the tainted water poured into his ears and up his nose, he could taste it in his mouth and it was as bad as he remembered it.

Grier was again trapped beneath the shattered earth of Flanders with the guns pounding above them. It had been there, in that terrible noise-filled darkness, that putrid suffo-cating hole, that Peter Foxley had slit Sergeant Coward's throat. And Grier had ordered him to do it, Grier had screamed at him to silence that horrible gasping, gurgling sound that Coward made as his lungs filled with blood and he gasped for air and life, for help, for his mother and for God, in the cramped and awful blackness of their impromptu tomb. How was he to know that the next shell Fritz sent over would unearth them all again? How was he to know that within minutes of being buried, he and Foxley, along with the corpses of Coward and two others whose names he could not even remember, would be disinterred? Was there even the slightest chance that a party of stretcher bearers might have found them? Should they have let Coward die in his own ghastly, pain-filled time? Were they wrong to have finished him off: Grier the summary judge and jury, Foxley the unrepentant executioner?

Grier had done his best to forget those moments of unspeakable terror as he lay buried alive beneath the mud of Ypres. He had blotted out all thought of the endless minutes spent on his back in that tiny pocket of air, crushed by the earth, entombed in the remains of that dugout with Foxley, two corpses and a noisily dying man. He had allowed other memories to overlay those moments, burying them beneath alternative visions of horror, of which there had been so many to choose from. But now, in the turbulent waters of Bleakly Hall that misplaced memory returned. Grier cried out once again and thrashed about in the receding flood. 'Dodger!' he shouted. 'Dodger!' He floundered forward and struggled to stand upright. But this posture was impossible to execute in the drains beneath the hydro and he cracked his head on the brickwork, so that in the end there was, as he had always suspected, nothing but blackness.

32

M RS FORBES told Monty that her help was required at the end of the lawn beyond the rose garden. Not that there were any roses in the rose garden, said Mrs Forbes disapprovingly, as it was actually filled with rhubarb. Oceans of the stuff, so that it was no wonder it was served up for dessert every night.

'Oh, and Thake said would you bring his teeth and a blanket,' she added almost as an afterthought. 'It seems that Mr Blackwood has had a bit of an accident. Thake had to float him down the storm drain, like a log, until they reached the place where it comes out at the foot of the garden.'

By the time Monty arrived with the teeth and the blanket (she also took it upon herself to bring an old bath-chair from the ground-floor storeroom), Grier was surrounded by a ring of concerned faces. He was swathed in shawls and scarves, so that he resembled the pupa of some monstrous caterpillar: his unconscious head sticking out from one end and his stockinged feet (Mrs Forbes had thoughtfully taken off his squelching boots) from the other. With Thake's help Monty removed this swaddling of miscellaneous coverings, wrapped him tightly in the blanket and wedged him into the bath-chair.

It was late in the afternoon before Grier regained consciousness. Dr Slack dressed the wound on his head and proclaimed him to be concussed, but otherwise fit and well. Monty was adjusting his pillows as he opened his eyes. He groaned. 'My head feels like a football that's been kicked against a wall.'

'You should rest,' said Monty. 'Or Dr Slack will give you a glass of chalybeate.'

Grier peered at her anxiously from beneath the bandage Dr Slack had wrapped round his head. 'Where's Curran?'

'I don't know. I've not seen him all day. Does it matter?'

'Yes.' Grier struggled to sit upright. 'Look, Monty, I wonder whether you might bring me the accounts from the office. There should be a ledger on the desk and I think he keeps receipts in a tin in the drawer. Only if he's not there, of course. Don't mention it if he's in there.'

Monty looked at Grier's flushed face and urgent expression. 'I'll get Dr Slack,' she said.

'No,' cried Grier. 'Just the accounts. Curran guards that office like a dragon watching over a pot of gold. It's my only chance. It's got to be now. Please!'

Curran was not in his office. He was not in the foyer or the drawing room, or anywhere else that Monty looked for him. She rummaged in his desk and returned to Grier with the accounts ledger and the receipts tin from the desk.

'Did you bring the swear box?' said Grier.

'No,' said Monty. 'I didn't see it. I didn't know you wanted it.'

'He's probably locked it in the safe anyway,' muttered Grier.

He propped the ledger on his knees and squinted at the pages. They were crowded with Curran's neat, sloping hand. Grier leafed through the pages, his expression troubled.

'You're still concussed,' said Monty. 'Perhaps I can help. Is there something in particular you're looking for?'

'What's the figure in the last column?'

'Six pounds, three shillings and fourpence.'

'Oh, dear,' said Grier. He pulled opened the receipts tin and spread handful after handful of bills and credit notes on the bedcovers. 'There's a coal scuttle in my sitting room, next to the book case. It's full of papers; would you bring it here, please?'

The coal scuttle was indeed filled with papers; so many, in fact, that they would have tumbled all over the floor had they not been weighted down with a large lump of coal. Now, Grier tossed the coal on to the floor and rooted through the contents beneath. After a few minutes he put his bandaged head in his hands and groaned.

'What is it?' asked Monty.

'You're the only friend I have,' muttered Grier. At least, that was what Monty thought he said, as his voice was muffled by the bedclothes. 'I meant to tell you before, but I just couldn't. Even when you told me your own secret. I was too ashamed.'

'Tell me what?' insisted Monty.

'Because of me, there's no money at all left in the hotel's account.' Grier put his head back, resting it against the bedhead. His eyes were firmly closed, as though he hoped to remain oblivious to this terrible confession even as he uttered it. 'Bleakly Hall Hydropathic is almost – but not quite – insolvent. A few nights ago I lost every penny the place has left.'

'Lost?' said Monty.

'Gone,' said Grier. 'John Johnson has it. He's the fellow who owns the Crossed Keys, down in the village. He's a sporting man, a decent chap, on the whole. I've already lost a fortune to him. I just thought I could recoup some of it and then some extra to pay Dodger. I owe him rather a lot too.' He gave a theatrical sigh. 'Yes, Monty, it is a truth almost too terrible to acknowledge, but I now own nothing but the clothes you see me in. Even the motor is Foxley's. I lost it in a card game one evening last month.'

'I see,' said Monty. 'What about the money from the party of young people –'

'Oh, that's gone too.'

'Does Curran know about any of this?'

'Of course not!' cried Grier. 'And you mustn't breathe a word of it either. He knows I like a flutter, but he doesn't really know anything, least of all the fact that I'm up to my ears in debt to Dodger. I have no idea how I'm going to get out of it. John Johnson seems happy enough to take what money I have, whenever I have it. He's a bookmaker mostly, but he doesn't mind a game of pontoon. He's got a drawer full of my IOUs, but now he's asking for his money. He refuses to play with me since I owe him so much. But Dodger's a different matter. He'll play until he's cleaned you out and keep going as long as you want. He'll play for cars, watches, cigarettes, whisky, anything.'

'But Curran owns half of the Hall, doesn't he? It's not as though you'll both be homeless.'

'I've run up debts against the value of the place,' whispered Grier. 'Dodger practically owns it!'

'What on earth does he want with somewhere like this?'

'Oh, I know. The place is quite hopeless. I think Dodger's worried that Curran might want to sell it if things don't pick up. He's afraid he might lose his home, his friends. I suppose he's got nowhere else.'

'Why didn't you just stop once you realised?' said Monty. 'Why did you carry on when for every win there might be two, three, even four losses?'

'I'd count four losses as a very minor setback indeed,' muttered Grier. He closed his eyes, thinking about all the nights he had spent sitting in Captain Foxley's rooms, allowing his fortune to pour into the other man's pockets. How glad he had been to play cards with an old friend, one who never said 'no' or 'go away', or 'pull yourself together'. Captain Foxley had understood Grier's fear of the dark. Peter Foxley's fear was of a different kind; a fear of the future – long and tedious and without comradeship.

'I suppose I thought I could make everything all right if I just did it one more time,' he said. 'And when that didn't happen, perhaps the next time would be the one. It's no excuse, but I only played at night, usually when I couldn't bear to sleep.' He swallowed. 'I knew it was a mistake, but playing cards stopped me thinking. Dodger knew. He understood. He didn't want to talk, only to play, and play, and play, for as long as I was prepared to go on. In some ways he was doing it to help me.' Grier looked confused. 'But he had to take my money. He said there'd be no point otherwise – there has to be a stake, doesn't there, or it doesn't mean anything? How else would it be exciting? It *is* exciting. There's not much one can say *that* about these days.' He shrugged. 'Dodger understood that too. But now it's gone too far. Will you help me?'

Monty wondered what sort of help she would be required to give. Was Captain Foxley to be disciplined? She sighed. She was becoming rather tired of contemplating revenge. 'Help you to do what?' she asked.

Grier turned his attention back to the scattered paper on the bed. 'I'm looking through these, they're mostly bills and promissory notes, but I wanted to see whether there was any hope . . . any chance that I might have something . . . Apart from this coal scuttle.' He found his cigarettes beneath a sheaf of unpaid bills and pulled one out. 'Mind you, I probably don't own the coal scuttle either.'

'Perhaps we might go through these things together,' said Monty. 'It might not be as bad as you think.' Monty looked at the drifts of paper that covered Grier's counterpane like a thick snowfall. 'Or perhaps Captain Foxley can be persuaded to let the matter drop. He seems quite absentminded these days. Perhaps he might simply . . . forget.'

'Oh, there are some things he'll never forget,' muttered Grier. 'Besides, Foxley has offered me the chance to win it all back again. One last game, and if I win he returns everything he's taken, the promissory notes, the money, the car, everything. Curran need never know and we can just carry on as usual.' He sank back on to his pillows and closed his eyes. 'The thing is, he's not really interested in the money, or the Hall. It's you he wants, for a chance to be with you, alone and without interruption, and I won't play for stakes like that.'

*

340

Shortly afterwards Grier fell asleep. Monty removed the smouldering cigarette from between his fingers and pulled the curtains closed. She cleared everything off the bed and into three neat piles – bills and invoices, money due from guests and debts owed to Captain Foxley. It was obvious from her brief examination of these muddled papers that Grier's situation was irredeemable. In fact, from what Monty could make out, he actually owed Captain Foxley far more than he realised. She wondered whether Captain Foxley had any idea how well off he now was.

Monty left Grier sleeping and went upstairs. Captain Foxley was in his rooms, reading *The Times*. The curtains were closed once again and the air was warm, and filled with the sound of gently humming bees.

'I believe Grier owes you some money,' she said.

Captain Foxley lowered his newspaper. 'Yes, as a matter of fact he does.' He smiled. 'Poor fellow. He never seems to concentrate, that's his problem.'

'He's had an accident –'

'So I heard.' Captain Foxley sounded bored. 'You don't expect me to feel sorry for him, do you? It's just a bang on the head, apparently. You're not here to persuade me to forget how much he owes me, are you? You know, I don't actually know how much it is. Quite a lot, I seem to recall. Perhaps it's everything. I don't care, you know; I don't care about anything. Was there something else? Only I fancied a nap.' He stood up. 'I don't suppose you'd help me over to the bed, would you, nurse?'

'I'm here to play cards with you,' said Monty. 'Pontoon.'

'Pontoon?' Captain Foxley laughed. 'What hidden depths you have! I suppose Grier sent you?'

'He doesn't know I'm up here.'

Captain Foxley smiled again. 'And what are the stakes in this exciting and unexpected card game?'

'If I win, Grier gets everything back. If you win, you take everything – Grier's share of the Hall, the motor, everything.'

Captain Foxley shook his head. 'That's hardly fair, since I already own everything he has, one way or another. I'm afraid you'll have to do better than that. Have you nothing else to offer in exchange for Grier's freedom? I'm sure you can think of *something*.'

'I can't,' said Monty.

'Well, I can.' Captain Foxley stood up and took a step towards her. 'I can think of something very enticing indeed. Something *quite* worth playing for. We'll play for *you*. If I win, I get to spend a night – just one night is all I ask – with you. You can keep the Hall, I'm not the slightest bit interested in it. And if I lose, I shall leave Bleakly and all Grier's debts behind me. You have my word as a gentleman.'

Monty snorted.

'Is that a "yes"?'

She picked up the deck of cards that lay on the table beside a buzzing jam jar. 'Shall we shake hands on it?'

In France, in the field hospitals and on the troop trains, the men had played pontoon all the time. The rules had seemed simple enough and, although Monty never played, it hadn't looked too hard. Besides, she thought, the game was more about luck than skill and surely it was time that Captain

Foxley's luck ran out. She shuffled the cards. Captain Foxley watched her with an amused expression on his face, though he didn't say anything. A card fell to the floor. 'Butterfingers,' he murmured as he bent to pick it up.

Monty dealt two cards each.

'Would you like to practise first?' asked the Captain in his most charming and courteous voice.

How patronising he was, thought Monty, though she had to admit that this suggestion was a good one. 'No, thank you,' she answered stiffly. 'I think we should just play the game.'

'So brisk, Miss Montgomery! And so serious.' He pulled a face. 'So terribly serious!'

Despite Captain Foxley's remarks, at that moment Monty felt a bubble of hysterical laughter welling up within her. How on earth had she found herself in this unenviable position, risking her own virtue in a card game she was playing for someone else? Did she really know how to gamble? Perhaps it was easy – and besides, Captain Foxley was not always in his right mind (though she had to admit that he seemed perfectly sensible at that particular moment). Although it might not be exactly sporting to take advantage of his illness, would it not improve her chances?

'Right-oh,' said Captain Foxley breezily. 'And are you quite sure you want to bet everything on this one game? Would you not rather play for the Audi first? The stakes might be as follows – you win, you get the car; you lose, I keep the car and you give me a kiss. And so on, until we agree to stop. That sounds more than fair to me. What d'you say?'

'We play for everything,' said Monty. For a moment (but only a very brief one) she wondered whether kissing Captain

Foxley would really be so terrible. Besides, it might allow her more than a single chance to recoup Grier's fortunes. But no, she said to herself, she would win. It was right and fair that she should, and there was no need to compromise. She looked at her cards.

Thirteen: the six and the seven of hearts. On the other side of the card table Captain Foxley was humming an unidentifiable tune under his breath, but he gave nothing away. A bee buzzed in the air beside his ear, but he did not seem to notice it. Monty watched uneasily as it alighted on his shirtsleeve.

'Shall I put the gramophone on?' He extended a finger and allowed the bee to crawl over his hand. 'It might lighten the mood a little.'

'I don't think so,' said Monty.

'We used to play pontoon all the time in the trenches, you know.' Captain Foxley sat back in his armchair and lit a cigarette. 'There were lots of times when there was nothing else to do – if you were back in billets or waiting to go up the line. There was a lot of waiting about for things to happen, most civilians didn't realise that. I remember playing pontoon with Blackwood, Grier I mean, behind the lines near Armentières. The sun was shining and there were wild flowers all around us in the long grass. Poppies, I think they were, and these little blue and white ones, all bobbing and dancing in the warm breeze. There were bees and butterflies every-where. You could even hear the birds singing and, behind that, in the distance, the sound of the guns. We'd lost a lot of men and rations were still coming up the line for twice as many, so we ate like kings for at least three days and had double rum rations too.' He smiled. Another bee settled on the back of his hand and he gazed at it fondly. 'Grier won on that particular occasion, I seem to recall. Perhaps he should have stopped while his luck was in. Cigarette?'

Monty took the cigarette but did not smoke it. She needed a clear head.

'You still look terribly glum,' added the Captain. 'Perhaps another card might cheer you up?'

Monty took another card. She now had twenty-one! She almost laughed out loud. How simple it had been. She would stop and ask to see Captain Foxley's hand. If he could not better her then she had won! He would need to have twenty-one with his two cards (unlikely, she thought) or take another and reach twenty-one that way (and even then he would have to beat her six, seven and eight of hearts).

'Your turn!' she cried. 'Will you take another?'

But Captain Foxley didn't seem to want another card.

'Ha!' cried Monty. She laid her hand on the table with a flourish. 'There!'

'Not bad,' said Captain Foxley. 'Not bad at all. Of course, I hardly care whether you win or not. I still think you should give me a kiss.'

'No!' cried Monty.

'Oh, well.' Captain Foxley tossed his cigarette end into the fire. He smiled at her lazily as he laid his cards – the ace of hearts and the jack of hearts – on the tabletop. 'How about this instead – you come to bed with me right now and I'll forget about Grier's debts altogether.'

Immediately, Captain Foxley shrugged off his braces and begun unbuttoning his trousers. Monty leaped to her feet.

He must have cheated somehow. No doubt he had exchanged his cards for the winning combination while distracting her with his talk about poppies and rum rations.

'Don't you *dare* unbutton yourself,' she cried, stepping back. 'I have no intention of coming anywhere near you.'

'But you promised,' Captain Foxley said. 'You gave me your word.'

'What would you know about keeping your word?' said Monty, and she snatched up the pack of cards from the tabletop and flung them at his head. Captain Foxley laughed as the cards fluttered about his shoulders. He sprang out from behind the table like a cat. What had happened to his bad leg and shuffling gait, thought Monty as she dashed towards the door. But somehow Captain Foxley was there before her.

'You can't leave yet,' he said. His trousers were partially undone and, with the effort of rushing across the room to bar her exit, they had tumbled down around his knees. The braces swung about his ankles. He bent to haul them up and Monty seized the moment. She leaped at him, her hands outstretched to shove him aside, but he dropped his trousers and snatched at her wrists, catching them both in his hands. Half crouched, Captain Foxley began to drag her towards the sofa. His face was furious. 'Come along now,' he panted. 'You can't run away from this. You can't run away from *me*. You promised and a promise made over cards is binding. Every soldier knows that.'

'You cheated,' shouted Monty, twisting her hands in his grasp. She pulled sharply, but his grip was fierce.

'I never cheat at cards,' replied Captain Foxley. He dragged her across the room.

Monty struggled. She leant forward and tried to bite his hand. 'That's no use,' he said, laughing. She tried to kick him, to stamp on one of his slippered feet with her heel, but somehow he always managed to move away. 'I'm an excellent dancer,' he remarked, laughing again at her efforts. 'I never allow a lady to stand on my toes.'

By now they were only a foot away from the sofa. All at once Captain Foxley seized her about the waist and began to wrestle with her clothing, pulling up her skirt with one hand as he pinned her wrists behind her back with the other. His face, with his floppy blond fringe and curving lips, was bent over hers in such a way that his features seemed to fill her entire field of vision. She looked into his eyes, but they were so close to hers that she could focus only on one at a time. How blue it was, she thought, and how cold and lifeless it looked.

'Let me go,' screamed Monty into his ear. 'Let me go. Let me go!'

Captain Foxley winced. 'Goodness me,' he said. And he released her hands so that he could cover his ears. Monty staggered back, away from him to the other side of the room. 'What a mandrake you are!' said Captain Foxley. 'The nurses in the field hospital were always so polite and quietly spoken. I suppose you metropolitan nurses are a coarser breed altogether. I like a bit of a challenge but I'm not sure I want you if you're going to be so loud and aggressive.'

Monty stood against the wall. 'Did you think you could force me to –'

'Oh, I've never forced a woman to do anything.' Captain Foxley sighed. 'I thought I might frighten you a little, that's all. If you'd have accepted defeat and got into bed quietly as you were supposed to, as you promised, I'd have told you to put your clothes back on and go away. I've got other things to be getting on with at the moment and don't want a woman getting in the way.' He looked at his bee-filled jam jars affectionately. 'Ho-there, Standage!' he cried, smiling at a small jar containing a single large drone.

Monty rubbed her wrists. 'I don't believe you.'

'No?' Captain Foxley shrugged. 'Well, it's too late now to find out. I suppose you'll just have to carry on thinking the worst of me.' He stepped forward to pick up his cigarette case from the tabletop. But as he did so his foot became snared by one of his dangling braces and he was thrown off balance. He toppled backwards, making no effort at all to save himself.

Captain Foxley lay sprawled where he fell, which fortunately for him was on his sofa. His head rested on a cushion, its damson brocade scarred with cigarette burns. His clothes were awry, his hair dishevelled, and he stared up at the ceiling with a look of joy and pleasure on his face. He seemed no longer to be aware of Monty's presence. High above, a bee droned about the light shade, its movements leisurely and explorative, its buzz warm and resonant. Captain Foxley watched it in silence. The sun came out from behind a cloud and its light fell across his face in a bright square of gold. He did not appear to notice. He did not blink, or raise a hand to shield his eyes, but continued to stare at the bee, which was soon joined in its orbit around the lampshade by two more. He smiled fondly and gave a gentle laugh. 'There they are,' he murmured, gazing upwards. 'I knew they'd come for me.'

*

When Monty came back downstairs, the vestibule was teeming with guests. 'There's a flood in the drawing room,' cried Mrs Forbes.

Across the foyer Monty noticed a dressing-gown-clad figure carrying a bundle of papers in his arms. She pushed through the crowd and followed Grier down the steps to the treatment rooms. The air was suffocating and filled with a loud hissing sound. She opened her mouth to call Grier, but at that moment Thake bounded out of a doorway, blocking her path.

'Listen,' he whispered. 'You can hear her.' Monty listened. She could hear a faint tick-tick-tick, though she had no idea what it signified (she learned later that this was the sound of metal expanding under great and sudden heat). Thake's nostrils flared, as though he was sniffing the air for something significant, then he vanished back into the building's mysterious intestines. Grier was nowhere to be seen.

Back in the foyer Mrs Forbes was pointing to a pool of water creeping across the parquet flooring of the vestibule. 'The waters are rising,' she cried. 'Are we to be flushed out? Rinsed away like spiders down a plughole?'

'Mr Curran has gone down to the village with Ada,' cried Mrs Forbes. 'Miss Montgomery, we look to you to save us now!'

Monty tiptoed into the flood. In the drawing room the furniture was sitting in two inches of water. Monty could see the rugs below the surface, like patches of weed or algae at the bottom of a lagoon. The chairs and tables looked like ancient trees or strange swamp-dwelling plants, their reflections eerie in the afternoon light. It was as though nothing was amiss at all, and the lake of water had always been there.

As Monty rejoined the crowd, Grier burst into the foyer. She noticed that the papers he had been carrying were now nowhere to be seen. His face was smeared with soot and his dressing gown smouldered.

'FIRE!' he cried. 'FIRE!'

From behind the doors that led down to the treatment room there came a tremendous roar, like the sound of a mine detonating beneath the building. The faded pictures that hung about the walls rattled in their frames and a fine mist of plaster dust descended on the guests' startled heads. The statue of Hygeia which, since Grier's foray into the plumbing, had been gushing lavishly, stopped. There was a moment's silence, then a groaning, splintering sound.

'I stuffed the accounts, the bills and everything into the furnace,' whispered Grier. 'Then I popped in the petrol can for good measure. There was only a bit left in it. D'you think that was a mistake? The petrol can, I mean? I thought if I destroyed the evidence . . .'

'What about Captain Foxley?' repeated Monty. 'Curran and Ada have gone out, but Captain Foxley's upstairs.'

'Dodger!' cried Grier. He lurched towards the stairs, as though preparing to leap to the Captain's rescue, but his legs buckled. 'Try the fountain.' He staggered over to an armchair. 'Use the urn as a receiver. It connects to Foxley's sink. I've no idea how.'

'Captain Foxley!' Monty shouted into the statue's marble pitcher. 'Captain Foxley, can you hear me?'

There was a moment's pause, and then: 'Yes,' echoed a voice. 'What is it?'

'There's been an explosion,' shouted Monty. 'Can you come down, please?'

'An explosion!' The Captain's voice had a hollow, funereal ring to it. 'How exciting!'

With Thake's help, Monty dragged Grier out of the building, across the flower bed and over the grass to where the others were assembled beneath the beech trees. Was everyone safe? Monty started to count heads.

Behind her, from somewhere deep within the bowels of the Hall, came a throaty rumble, like the sound of coal trucks being shunted in a goods yard. She looked back to see a slim, dressing-gown-clad figure struggling to emerge from the hydropathic's doors. The late afternoon sunlight glinted off the lenses of his gas mask. Captain Foxley seemed to be holding something cumbersome in his outstretched hands. At first, Monty assumed he was carrying a jam jar, but the object he struggled with was much bigger. It was dark and shapeless, rather like a bundle of washing. The object heaved and swelled in his hands. Captain Foxley walked gingerly over the flower bed, past the broken bird bath and across the lawn. Behind him, the windows of the hydropathic's upper storeys had been transformed into gleaming rectangles of gold. But this tranquil vista was suddenly shattered by a thunderous roar, followed by a great creaking sound, the splintering of timbers and the crash of masonry, plaster, fixtures and fittings tumbling to the ground.

Bleakly Hall now had a lopsided, slightly drunken air.

One of its golden windows was gone and there was in its place a black square. An uneasy murmuring broke out from among the guests. But at the sight of Captain Foxley, clad in his bee-husbandry outfit of gas mask, dressing gown and oven mitts, they fell silent. It also became clear what Captain Foxley was carrying in his hands. It fizzed and bubbled over his mitts, pulsating against the protective material of his dressing gown. Parts of it dripped on to the ground, where it effervesced for a moment, before rising up and alighting on his hands once more.

'They were making a nest,' cried Captain Foxley. His voice was muffled behind his bug-eyed breathing apparatus, like the sound of a wireless in a distant room. 'I couldn't just leave them, could I? Can't you see how important they are?' The bees fizzed warmly and surged over one another, creating a large pendulous mass. 'These are my thoughts, Blackwood. All of them. Can you see them?' He raised his hands and held the swarm aloft. 'How black they look when they're all together. No wonder my head's been buzzing recently!'

As Captain Foxley raised his hands the bees began to throb. For a moment it seemed as though they might settle, but then all of a sudden they rose up, fragmenting into a great tornado of buzzing, whirling bodies. The guests screamed, and began running hither and thither, up and down the grass, white handkerchiefs flapping in the air against the storm of insects.

Captain Foxley stood with his arms outstretched, surrounded by the spiralling swarm. 'No!' he screamed. 'No, come back!' The bees reeled and hummed, streaming back and forth in the sky above the beech trees. Then all at once they unified into a cloud and made off, past the bird bath and over the flower bed. They seemed to drift, like a shadow, up the flank of the Hall, towards the tower, before gathering darkly outside Captain Foxley's window.

'Come back!'

Even through the leather helmet and glass eye sockets of the gas mask Monty could hear his voice break in a sob.

'Peter!' she cried. 'Wait!' But already Captain Foxley was sprinting across the wet grass. He sprang across the flower bed and disappeared back into the Hall.

The building now had a silent, tragic air, and a strange sort of stillness, as though it was holding its breath. Its single shattered window stared down at her reproachfully. A bank of dark cloud had gathered overhead and evening shadows now stained the walls like a tidemark. Another dull rumble echoed from within. Then, suddenly, the building burst apart.

The explosion flung Monty on to her back. A ball of flame appeared, red and orange and burning like the sun, but this was extinguished almost instantly and followed by a curious hissing sound, as though a vast bucket of water had been flung on top of it. A great cloud of steam, smoke and dust rolled out across the flower bed, the lawn and the bowling green. It brought with it a fine mist of water, which pattered on to the scattered debris.

33

WHEN CURRAN and Ada reappeared, and were told about the explosion, Curran insisted on being taken up to the devastated hydropathic immediately.

'There's nothing left to see,' said Grier. 'Not much, anyway.' He was still wearing his charred dressing gown, but seemed now to be almost elated by the destruction of the building. 'The place looks as though it was hit by a twelve-inch shell. Perhaps it was. Or something similar.' He looked at Curran closely. 'Those Mills bombs you had in your office. Are you sure they were duds?'

'We can't possibly begin again,' said Curran.

'Thank goodness,' Grier muttered. He hummed a snatch of a song under his breath. It was the 'Wang Wang Blues'. 'I think we should try something different,' he said briskly. 'D'you have any ideas?' He began to wheel his brother up the hill.

Ada and Monty went to sit on a bench opposite the band-stand. The sun had come out and it felt warm and pleasant on their faces. Dr Slack had shepherded the now-homeless guests into the pump room for a fortifying glass of Lady Beaton and Monty could see their shadows moving about within. The shuffle of footsteps and the murmur of voices drifted across the square on a breath of familiar brimstone.

'Mr Curran has asked me to marry him,' said Ada. 'He don't seem to mind about me being pregnant.' She looked at Monty. 'In fact,' she added, 'he seemed pleased. He said he would treat the baby as his own. Especially seeing as it's Captain Foxley's.'

'And did you say yes?'

'I did,' replied Ada.

'Good,' said Monty. She kissed Ada's cheek. 'Congratulations.'

'Well, miss,' said Ada. 'I've always managed on my own before, you know that, and I'm not saying now that I needs his help. But maybe he needs mine. *And* Mr Grier. They'll never manage with only each other.' She ran a hand over her belly. 'If I've got one to look after I might as well take on two more.'

'How will you manage?' said Monty. 'Grier's quite hopeless, and Curran's –'

'I know.' Ada smiled. 'But don't worry about me, miss. I'll sort them out. Besides, I've got this.' Ada patted the courier's bag she was wearing across her chest. She pulled it open, revealing a thick sheaf of white notes. 'Money!'

'I thought there *was* no money?' said Monty.

'There weren't,' said Ada. 'This is new money, made from the very last of the old.'

'How –'

'This morning Mr Curran asked me to take him to Mr Johnson, Mr Grier's friend from the Crossed Keys. It was about Mr Grier's debts. I takes care of Mr Curran and Mr Curran takes care of Mr Grier. It's only right.'

'And . . .'

'Mr Curran took the swear box with him. There was lots in it and more from it he'd put into the safe over the past months. But it turned out that there wasn't enough to honour Mr Grier's debts. So I says to Mr Curran, "Why not put it on the horses?" So I chose the runners and Mr Curran worked out the odds.' Ada rubbed her chin thoughtfully. 'It was what's called an accumulator.' She turned her face to the sun and closed her eyes. 'We paid off Mr Johnson and brought the rest back with us.'

Monty laughed aloud and Ada said, 'You know, miss, I used to think that being a wife was something to look forward to, something that a woman needed to do, that would make things better. But what you said to me on that roof that day got me thinking a bit. I wondered whether I really *do* want to look after a man for the rest of my life. If I got married it'd be "fetch this, Ada" and "bring me that, Ada".' She shrugged. 'But then what else do I know about? I've always looked after people. I can't stop doing it now, can I?'

'I suppose we all want to look after the people we love,' said Monty.

'Besides,' said Ada, who was not really listening. 'There's no reason why I can't be married *and* do what I like. Mr Curran, he likes a fast motor as much as I do. I thought about racing.'

'Horses?'

'Motors,' said Ada. 'After the baby's born, of course.'

Monty prepared to leave. She possessed nothing more than the clothes she wore – her grey nurse's dress with its white cotton apron, both blotched with grass stains and smoke smuts – and this made her feel liberated. She told Grier she didn't want any of the money Curran and Ada had won with the swear box.

'I'll take the wages you owe me,' she said. 'I can find work quite easily in London. I don't need anyone else's money.'

'You can't leave us now!' said Grier. 'Just when everything's changing.'

'Nothing changes at Bleakly,' said Monty. She could see the pink corner of the *Sporting Times* projecting from the pocket of his jacket. 'Isn't it time for you to leave too?'

'Leave Bleakly!' Grier sounded aghast. 'I can't leave Bleakly, I can't leave Curran, not now.'

'He has Ada. And the baby.'

'Yes, but he still needs me. Ada needs me too. We need each other.' The bandage round his head gave him a forlorn, vulnerable appearance. 'Don't you want to stay? You were out there too, Monty. You and Ada, just like Curran and me. And poor old Dodger. You're one of us. *Quis separabit* and all that.'

'Is that some sort of military motto?'

'*Who shall separate us*. It belongs to the Irish Rifles. Dodger said it was our motto too.'

'Well, it isn't mine,' cried Monty. 'I'm *not* like "poor old

Dodger" and I'm not "one of you". I want to go away and *not* look back. I want to see distant lands and beautiful places; I want to speak to people who don't know who I am or what I did; I want new memories and . . . and *joy* – d'you remember what that is? Bleakly saved me from the past, but now all I want is to . . . to *fly* –'

'When will you fly away?' asked Grier gently. 'Tomorrow? Perhaps in a week or two. You'll wait a bit longer, at least. I'll drive you to London. The old Audi might just make it.'

'I'll go as soon as possible. And quickly too. I have to, or I might not leave at all.'

'Well,' said Grier. He hugged her clumsily. 'If speed is what you're after, why don't you take the Norton?'

The road through the beech trees seemed unusually quiet and still. Monty realised that this was because she could not hear the blaring of the brass band and that there was no one coming up the hill from the pump room, no voices echoing through the trees. The signs of life she had once hardly noticed had vanished, leaving an awkward yawning silence, which she knew would soon become commonplace there.

Monty emerged from the trees on to the edge of the bowling green. Bleakly Hall had not burnt down. Instead, its heart had been blasted out, so that it resembled a cavity in a rotten tooth. Within, the ground floor had disappeared and the treatment rooms obliterated, so that nothing was left but a dark and dripping hole, filled with water and tumbled masonry. A single remaining window glittered angrily from beneath a torn and drooping ribbon of guttering.

Over the past few days the men from the village had trawled through the rubble, looking for Captain Foxley. But other than a single blackened oven mitt he was nowhere to be found. His clothes, his possessions – the card table and gramophone, the box of records, the gas mask and silver-topped walking stick – had also vanished. It was as though he had never existed at all.

'At least it was quick,' Curran had said when he heard. 'We all hoped it would be quick when it came. Poor old Dodger.' He sounded relieved. 'Only you and I left then, Grier,' he added.

'And Dodger's baby.'

'Ada's baby,' said Curran. 'And Dodger's. And ours now too.'

In their search for Captain Foxley the men had unearthed all manner of mysterious objects from the wreckage. These they had lined up on the gravel at the front of the building, like an exhibition of unusual sculptures. As Monty approached, she recognised the familiar silhouette of the adjustable douche. It had been grotesquely twisted by the force of the blast, its nozzles blackened and warped and pointing this way and that. There was also a collection of pipes of varying sizes, a couch from the ladies' recovery room and a charred bath-chair. Some of the other objects standing on the gravel she could not recognise at all.

Monty went to sit on the bench that looked over the trampled flower bed towards the building. A large bee emerged from somewhere within the rubble and buzzed speculatively back and forth, before zigzagging away towards the trees. Had it known Captain Foxley? Which one of his memories might it have carried on its back? She sat in the gathering darkness, her thoughts turning, as they so often did, to Sophia. She found that her friend came into her mind less urgently, less unbearably now, and that these thoughts, when they did arise, were no longer accompanied by a terrible aching sense of sorrow and guilt. It seemed, at last, that she could choose how to remember and her choice was always a memory that brought her pleasure rather than pain. And so, thinking of Sophia as she remembered her best, hurrying down a ward with a trolley of teacups, her face smiling in greeting, Monty took from her pocket Captain Foxley's last letter to Sophia, written in haste on three tattered betting slips. She took out the cigarette he had given her as they played pontoon and struck a match. In an instant the paper, and all that was written on it, was gone, the black fragments of ash spiralling away on the breeze.

ACKNOWLEDGEMENTS

With thanks to Sarah Bryant and Marc di Rollo for reading, commenting and generally encouraging. To Jane Conway-Gordon and Penny Hoare, thank you for standing by me through difficult times, and for your patience and fortitude with the various drafts of this book. Thanks also to John Burnett for lengthy conversations about writing; to David Marsden, who has no interest in reading or writing fiction but always asks, and listens to me going on about it; and to Helen Wilson, my most vocal supporter – I write this acknowledgement with love and gratitude.

BIBLIOGRAPHICAL NOTE

During the writing of this novel I consulted a large number of books, a few of which are noted here.

For the experiences of VADs in the hospitals of Britain and Belgium I drew on Vera Brittain's *Testament of Youth* (London: Virago, 1978) and Irene Rathbone's semi-autobiographical *We That Were Young* (London: Virago, 1988). More specifically, for nursing conditions and experiences on the western front see *A War Nurse's Diary: Sketches from a Belgian Field Hospital* (New York: Macmillan 1918) and Yvonne McEwen, *It's a Long Way to Tipperary: British and Irish Nurses in the Great War* (Dunfermline: Cualann, 2006). Lyn Macdonald's *The Roses of No Man's Land* (London: Penguin, 1993) proved particularly useful. The experiences of Monty and Ada, and their exploits amongst the ruins of Caeskerke, were inspired by the extraordinary work of Mairi Chisholm and Elsie Knocker, as recounted in *The Cellar House of Pervyse* (London: A&C Black, 1916).

There are many useful sources about the soldiers' experience on the western front. Robert Graves, *Goodbye to All That* (London: Penguin, 1929); Max Arthur, *Forgotten Voices of the Great War* (London: Ebury, 2003); Richard Holmes, *Tommy: The British Soldier on the Western Front 1914–1918* (London: Harper, 2005); and Lyn Macdonald, *Voices and Images of the Great War* (London: Penguin 1991) are some excellent examples.

For detail about the post-war period in Britain see Robert Graves, *The Long Weekend* (London: Sphere, 1991) and Martin Pugh, *We Danced All Night* (London: Vintage, 2009).

Douglas Mackaman, *Leisure Settings* (Chicago: University of Chicago Press, 1994); E.S. Turner, *Taking the Cure* (London: Michael Joseph, 1967); Guy Christie, *Crieff Hydro 1868–1968* (Crieff: Crieff Hydro Ltd, 1986); and C. Finlayson, *The Strath: A Biography of Strathpeffer* (Edinburgh: St Andrew's Press, 1979) provided information about health spas and hydropathic treatments before and after 1918.

Elaine di Rollo, Edinburgh, 2011